Trail Magic:

Lost in Crawford Notch

by

M. H. Sullivan

Romagnoli Publications

Third Edition

To order additional copies of this book,
contact: www.romagnoli-publications.com

ISBN-13: 978-1-891486-06-7 (paperback)
ISBN-13: 978-1-891486-19-7 (hardback)
ISBN-13: 978-1-891486-07-4 (eBook)

Romagnoli Publications
Manchester, NH, USA

email: romagnoli.publications@gmail.com
website: www.romagnoli-publications.com

Library of Congress Control Number: 2026913974

We are all lost ...

... and found.

"Not till we are lost, in other words not till we have lost the world, do we begin to find ourselves, and realize where we are and the infinite extent of our relations." (Thoreau)

Table of Contents

ONE

Treasure Hunt in the Woodshed

August 2006
Sawyer River Wilderness Campground, Crawford Notch, NH

*** *Angie* ***

It was the end of August 2006. I know that's not the Ides of March on the foreboding scale, but maybe it should've been. Who knew that within the next couple of days four-year old Melanie Jacobs would wander away and get lost in the wilderness, my fifteen-year-old sister, Kay, would fall in love with an eighteen-year-old thru-hiker, my dad would fall for a psychic, and I would nearly be killed? I mean, come on! Who would believe it? Still, the story needs to be told and since I was apparently the one at fault (because I was supposed to be babysitting Melanie at the time) I guess I'm the best one to begin it.

Melanie was a cute little girl. I know that probably all four-year-old girls are cute, but she was especially sweet looking. She had long brown hair a shade lighter in color than mine and pulled back in a small ponytail with bangs that were cut straight across her forehead just above her eyebrows. Her eyes were blue, but not just regular blue, more like the dark blue that makes you think of the really deep part of the ocean. I thought they were a really cool color and they made me wish my eyes weren't such a plain old brown.

I'll tell you something else about Melanie. She was bear crazy! She had this little stuffed teddy bear she named Brownie that she carried around with her everywhere; sometimes hugged up against her chest, sometimes dangling at her side by his fat little arm. Brownie was a pretty sorry looking bear. It's no wonder. I saw Melanie put his little plastic bump of a nose in her mouth and suck on it. I'm sure it wasn't the first time, either. That can't be a good thing, can it? Yuck.

Now before I continue, I should say that I have other things to do around the campground besides babysitting small campers. For one thing, there are lots of chores to do. It sucks, but there it is. Every day there's something that has to be done and usually my dad, his partner, Jeb, or Aunt Tessie will assign me or Kay to do it. When I grow up, I don't think I want to run a campground. People think that it's all lying around and enjoying Nature, but it's a lot of work, really.

For instance, we trade off manning the front desk to deal with arriving or departing campers – you'd expect that, I guess. But there's also sweeping the campsites, picking up trash, making sure there's toilet paper in the bathrooms, cleaning the campers' bathhouse, or hosing out the two hikers' shower stalls located behind the lodge. Kay is the world's worst at chores. Not only does she do a lousy job, but she's always trying to get out of doing them, or she doesn't do them and then says she forgot or that it wasn't her turn. She has more excuses than a politician. Let's just say that if there was a responsible kid and an irresponsible one in this family, there's no question which of us is which. So, it was kind of weird that I was the one babysitting when Melanie disappeared. I think it was just cosmic bad luck.

Anyway, on that Wednesday, the day before Melanie got lost, I was assigned kitchen duty for breakfast and lunch, but I finished early and then got really, really bored. Most people have no idea how boring a campground can be!

Dad says that teenagers are the only ones who ever get bored. He says we have too much energy and are in too big of a hurry. I don't know about that, but it was August and except for getting ahead on some reading, I had nothing to do, and I was bored,

bored, bored. I moped around and eventually found my dad fishing in the stream that runs behind the lodge. When you're bored, bugging your parents is one way to pass the time, at least, although it can occasionally backfire into them thinking up new things for you to do.

It was a beautiful late summer afternoon in New Hampshire's White Mountains and the sun was streaming down between the tall pines and flecking the water with sparkles that jostled and melded into each other as the current created eddies around the rocks under the surface. If I hadn't been so bored, I might have appreciated the scenery. Usually, I love how peaceful it all is.

"You said the campground would be booked out for the weekend, but we still have a couple of sites open," I said to my dad as I plopped down next to him and dipped my toes into the cold stream.

"Don't scare the fish," he said eyeing my feet. "Besides, it's only Wednesday. I'm not worried," Dad replied, laying his fishing pole across his lap as he fingered the loose dirt in the plastic container next to his thigh. He smiled as he held up the wriggling clump of dirt for me to inspect.

My ponytail had come loose, and I pushed a few stray strands of hair from my face and eyed the worm critically. "That one is kind of big for the little trout in this stream, don't you think?"

"Maybe I'm not trying to catch the *little* trout," Dad answered with a shrug that said he didn't really care about my opinion, and he proceeded to wind the worm onto the hook.

"This place is so boring," I said getting right to the point.

"You're just a spoiled American kid. Three-quarters of the people in the world would give their right arms to be where you are at this moment."

I rolled my eyes. It's not like I hadn't heard that one before – that and the one about the starving children who want my uneaten dinners. "Well, I'd trade places with them, too, if they'd just step forward and send me an air ticket."

He groaned because he'd heard that one before, too. "You'd last about three seconds in their shoes – if they even have shoes. Heck, you're so soft from all this easy living, you wouldn't be able to make it as the Peace Corps volunteer sent to HELP the poor shoeless kid!"

"Oh, puleeze! I could do it. After all, you did and look at you!" I laughed.

"What do you mean? I happen to be in great shape." He looked slightly offended as he patted his stomach, which actually didn't look that bad for an old guy in his forties.

I saw his gesture and figured I'd let him off the hook. "Yeah, Dad, but I'm not talking about how fit you are. I'm saying you'd have to leave this place. That's the part I bet you couldn't do."

He smiled as he glanced around taking in the trees and the stream before him. "You might be right about that, Angie. When you've got a good thing..."

"Good and boring," I interrupted.

A glimmer came into his eye as he turned to me and casually said, "The guys that used to live here didn't find it all that boring, I bet."

I looked up at him, slightly interested. "Oh, yeah? What guys?"

"The CCC guys." I saw him look away, sort of nonchalantly, so I knew something was up.

"CCC?" I repeated. "Are you making this up? Is that like the CIA?" I honestly had never heard of it.

"No, I'm not making it up. And no, it's nothing like the CIA! CCC stands for the 'Civilian Conservation Corps'. Haven't you learned anything from Tessie about American history and the Depression yet?"

I shrugged and waited for him to continue, because, of course, I knew he would continue if there was a history lesson in it. He felt like it was his duty to impart whatever little jewels of the past he could remember. I swear sometimes he could pull out the craziest little details that I often wondered if he was relating them from first-hand knowledge. You know how some people just seem like they could've lived at another time? That's the way my dad is.

"The CCC was an army of guys that built the road in from the highway and cleared these grounds. In fact, this campground used to be a CCC camp during the Great Depression."

"Really?" I said looking around. "So why isn't it still their camp? What happened to them?" I snapped a twig in my hands and tossed a piece of it into the water and watched it twirl around in the current.

"World War II happened. That's what. All those young men were put to work being soldiers instead of trail and park builders."

"Trails and parks? Is that what they did up here?"

"Uh huh. It gave them work, three square meals a day, and a roof over their heads." He eyed his pole and then fingered the line a bit and stood up.

I smiled. "And yet they chose to go to war instead of staying in this so-called paradise?" I shrugged. "Maybe they got bored with all this, too."

He scoffed. "No, they left because they didn't have a choice. America was attacked when the Japanese bombed Pearl Harbor. All the young men went to war. The ones who didn't join up right away were drafted."

"Is this my history lesson for the day, Dad?" I asked, realizing that he had drawn me in to an interesting story that was turning out to be educational. I threw the rest of the twig into the water and wiped my hands on the legs of my jeans.

"Sure, it's a history lesson. But it's more interesting when it's personal, don't you think?" OK, he had a point.

We were quiet for a few minutes as Dad prepared his pole and line for the cast. He swung the line out once and then again in practiced motions before flicking his wrist and sending the hook and worm to the middle of the stream. He smiled as it landed pretty much where he wanted it to be. Slowly he reeled the excess line back in.

"So did they leave anything behind?" I asked, an idea starting to gel in the back of my mind.

For a second I think he had forgotten I was still there. He glanced at me with a blank sort of look, and then nodded. "Sure. They left roads, they left blazed trails, they left fire towers on the tops of mountains..."

"No, not that kind of stuff. I mean did they leave anything around here, in our campground?"

He frowned. "Like what?"

"I don't know. Like treasure, maybe..."

He laughed and it lit up his face. "Honey, these were poor, godforsaken unemployed guys from the small towns around New England. I don't think they had what you might call 'treasures.'"

"How do you know? They might've found some gold or maybe some precious stones and hid them around here." In my mind, I could see it clearly enough – the dark of the moon, an old guy looking like a shabby prospector scratching out a hole in the ground and burying a jewel-encrusted treasure chest. It could've happened.

"Not likely," he snorted. He tugged lightly on the fishing line. When he felt my eyes on him, he looked up. "Well, anyway, there's not much left from those times." He glanced around then squinted. "Except for maybe that old woodshed there. That might've been left over from their camp."

I sat up straighter and turned around to stare at the old shed. "Why do you think that?"

"Because I remember asking about it when we bought the place. Let's see...Jeb and I first came here something like 20 years ago when we were hiking the Trail, right? The old guy we bought it from had owned it for about 35 or 40 years, I think. And he said that the woodshed had been here for as long as he could remember."

I studied the woodshed. "What'd they keep in the shed back then, do you think?"

"Wood. Same as now. Some things don't change much." He smiled.

I swatted him on the arm, "Dad! Come on. I'm serious. Do you remember if there was anything in the shed when we moved up here?"

"Dead bugs and maybe some kindling." He reeled the line in.

This was a waste of time. I stood up, brushing off the seat of my pants. "Well, if you won't tell me. I'll just have to find out for myself, won't I?"

He looked amused. "Find out what, honey?"

"I don't know. I guess whatever mystery there's left about it."

"Mystery?" He made a hooting sound that kind of grated on my nerves. "Angel, there's no mystery. The CCC was here for a few years back in the 1930's. They worked real hard blazing trails and building roads through these mountains — for which I have mixed feelings — and then ten years later World War II started, and they all left to become soldiers. End of story. There's no mystery."

"Aw, come on. There's always a mystery when a bunch of people are thrown together and then 100 years later there's no trace of them. Why, I'll bet there were a million juicy stories in this camp!"

"Maybe, but first of all, it wasn't 100 years ago, it was only maybe 60 or 70 years. And juicy stories aren't the same thing as mysteries." He studied me for a second, and continued, "Angie, you must be pretty bored if you're getting curious about a shed and a bunch of unemployed guys living in a conservation camp!"

"I AM bored, Dad! That's what I've been trying to tell you. We live in the middle of nowhere and there's nothing to do!"

"Some things never change. You know, I used to say the same thing to my parents...and I spent all my time on Jeb's ranch in Montana – what could be cooler than that?"

"Well, it sounds like a lot more fun than a campground hidden away in the mountains of New Hampshire!" I said defiantly.

Dad just shook his head.

"So do you think I'll find anything?"

He had that blank look on his face again and it was obvious he was off in another world. When I nudged him, he just said, "Huh?"

"Da-ad, I asked if you think I'll find anything?"

"Find anything? You mean in the old shed?" He shook his head. "Nope. And you know why? Because people who don't have much, don't have much to lose, which means there's nothing for you to find." He flicked his wrist and his fishing line sailed out to the middle of the stream again. We both watched it as it swirled in the current and slowly made its way downstream.

"Can I look anyway?" I asked.

He glanced up at me and sighed. "OK. Go ahead. But don't mess up the shed, all right? And remember, whatever dirt you dig up has to be put back in the hole when you're done!" He raised his voice and said the last words to my back as I headed across camp to the old shed. I waved a hand over my shoulder, sort of like swatting a black fly.

And that was how everything started: With me looking for treasures left over from the old Sawyer River CCC camp. I know; how cool is that? And it would've been; that is, if Melanie hadn't ended up lost.

TWO

Living in Africa

June 1998
Lake Langano, Rift Valley, Ethiopia

*** *Alex* ***

Long before owning the Wilderness Campground in New Hampshire, Alex had worked for the U.S. government overseas in Africa. That was before Kathy had died and his life had come to a crashing halt. Now when he thought about it, there was his life before Kathy had died and there was his life after Kathy had died. They were two separate lifetimes and the only link between the two were his daughters, Kay and Angie. The girls were an ever-present reminder because they were so much like their mother – Kay in her graceful and lithe body, and Angie, in her smile and humor.

Alex vividly remembered the summer Kathy died, the summer of 1998. Sometimes scenes of that time sprang up whole, all of a piece, in his dreams at night. That summer in Addis Ababa, Ethiopia, was one of the few truly carefree times he remembered they had ever had as a family.

Before being sent to Ethiopia, he and Kathy had each done TDY's (temporary duty assignments) in various embassies in the Middle East and Africa. He'd spent six months in Botswana and another six months jetting between Syria and Jordan; Kathy had spent nearly a year in Sudan. His job had been designing security systems for the embassies; hers was in Consular Affairs, arranging for visas mostly. But Ethiopia was the first time they had managed to get a two-year overseas assignment together.

They arrived in Addis Ababa, Ethiopia in January of that year. It was a beautiful time of year in the Horn of Africa, where although situated close to the equator the weather was near-perfection – a temperate 70 degrees year-round. This was due to the location of the capital, perched as it was on the Ethiopian plateau, 9000 feet above Africa's Great Rift Valley.

Alex was doing security work for the U.S. Agency for International Development (USAID) and Kathy, was moving up the ranks in the Consular Office at the American Embassy. Kay had been a sassy six-year-old then, and Angie, a more soulful five-year-old.

Ethiopia was a country in turmoil, even though it had been seven years since Mengistu and his reign of Red Terror had finally passed into dark history. Part of the continuing unrest was a by-product of the recurrent droughts and famines due to the country's total reliance on the rains. If the rains came and were plentiful – but not too plentiful – then famine was held at bay. If not, then there was drought, hungry people, and all the disease, death and upheaval that result when whole villages flee to the cities for food and relief.

Ethiopia normally had two rainy seasons each year – one from October to December – referred to as the "Little Rains" because although it rained a lot, it wasn't an everyday deluge as it was during the "Big Rains" that came in June and usually lasted through August.

The rains hadn't been as dependable as they once were. There had been a drought every few years since the 1970's. The worst had been in 1984-85 when 200,000 people died. That was the one that made 'Ethiopian famine' a household term in the West with its horrible images of starving women and rail-thin children. The last big drought had been 1993-1994, four years before Alex and his family had arrived in Ethiopia.

Life was peaceful for the Jackson family, though, and the future seemed bright and full of adventure and novelty. They loved being overseas together again. Alex and Kathy had joined the Peace Corps after college but after a decade of paying their dues as lowly government workers in Washington DC with the occasional – and always solo – temporary duty assignments, this was their chance to try out overseas living as a family. They were confident this would be the beginning of a new and amazing chapter in their lives.

In Alex's memory, everything had been perfect until the camping trip. They had settled into their new home and new jobs with ease. The American community had been welcoming and six-year-old Kay adapted to the mid-year change in schools without any problem. She was a gregarious confident child, the type that would never suffer from "new kid" nerves. They found a French kindergarten program for Angie, and they were pleased when she started picking up the foreign language as if born to it.

That was their life before the June camping trip to Lake Langano, a lake resort just south of Addis. Alex didn't think it was ever the same afterwards. It was as if somehow, they had displeased the gods on that trip. They had nearly lost the children at the lake and less than two months later, Kathy would be dead.

They'd known she would be leaving at the end of July for the regional meetings at the embassy in Nairobi, Kenya and would be gone for several weeks. They'd wanted to take a short vacation and spend some quality time together as a family before she left. After asking around, they decided on a family camping trip to Lake Langano, a tourist spot 200 kilometers south of the capital. Everyone assured them it was a good place to camp and the water was safe to swim in. They were advised to go before the 'big rains' started, which, if they were on time, would begin sometime in late June.

Lake Langano was a three and a half hour drive down from Addis' high perch on the escarpment of the Ethiopia Highlands. The lake is one of a string of deep lakes that dot the Great Rift Valley, from Ethiopia to Kenya. And more importantly, it is one of the few lakes that isn't infested with bilharzia, so they could swim in it without fear of being infected with the debilitating parasitic worms that take up residence in a person's veins and like little vampires, feed on their blood.

Alex borrowed a tent, and they joined up with two other Embassy families who also were planning a camping trip. Safety in numbers, Alex had figured. And for their first time camping, he heartily approved the plan, even though he and Kathy were both comfortable in the outdoors and in Africa. They had been in the Peace Corps in Tanzania, after all, back in 1982. This little camping trip couldn't compare to the hardships they'd experienced back then.

Kathy had joined the Peace Corps because she thought it a good way to see if she was suited to a life of travel and overseas living. Her brother, Tim, had been in the Peace Corps in Thailand and the life he described of close friendships and doing good works appealed to her. Alex's motives were far simpler and more straightforward. He joined for the adventure and to be with Kathy.

Alex, Kathy, and the girls arrived at Lake Langano mid-afternoon after a long, dusty ride from Addis. The three families set up their tents next to each other surrounding a central fire pit where they would cook the food and sit around the campfire in the evenings.

Kay and Angie had loved the camping trip, their first ever, from the moment they arrived at the lake. It was a novelty and even the mundane task of putting up the tent and finding kindling was exhilarating to them. They loved the small gravelly beach shaded by the thorny acacia trees that umbrellaed above them. They were so hyper by early afternoon that Alex wondered if they'd ever be able to wind down their high-pitch giggles when it was time to put them in their sleeping bags to sleep.

Kathy took it all in stride. She smiled at them as they chattered and chased each other around the campsite, splashing in the shallow alkaline waters of the lake, and in and out of the tent, zipping and unzipping the tent flap with a flourish that drove Alex nuts.

The other two families had children slightly older than Kay and Angie. Joseph and Keri Oliver had a son, Peter, who was nine and turned out to be a bit of a loner. The other family, Stan and Joanne Daniels, had two girls; Lauren aged eight and Tina who was eleven. Tina, being slightly older, was used to serving as babysitter for her younger sister, and soon she was keeping an eye out for Kay and Angie, as well. It wasn't until too late that Alex and Kathy understood how much false faith they had put on Tina's small shoulders, but initially they were impressed with the little girl's quiet self-assurance.

Each family had brought along a servant to cut wood and help with chores and to serve as night zabanya (guard) for the campsite. The servants were Oromo men, for the most part, from the southern part of the country.

Alex and Kathy had brought Arage, a young man who had appeared at their gate the third day they had been in the country, offering himself for work. He spoke no English and it quickly became clear that he had never been inside a Western home either. It was the first time in his life that he had come face to face with indoor plumbing, electricity, and hot water – three particular marvels that apparently confirmed his belief in magic and miracles.

Arage had come to Addis from the Oromo areas in the distant south along the Kenya and Somali border. He was not a Coptic Christian, the dominant religion in Ethiopia, nor was he Muslim as many of the Oromo were. He had apparently been baptized by an American Protestant group who had come proselytizing in the region. He often spoke of "Jesus" coming to his village, but Alex and Kathy were never able to decipher exactly which Protestant sect he belonged to.

He began working as their zabanya (guard) and occasional gardener until he showed interest in becoming an "inside" servant. They agreed to teach him the intricacies of cleaning, vacuuming, making beds and so on, but only on the condition that he promise to take a bath at least once a week. He hesitated, but finally accepted the terms. As a matter of fact, Kathy had never met a more agreeable person, but she soon learned that just because he agreed cheerfully to any task, it didn't necessarily mean he had the foggiest notion of how to do it. It didn't matter. He was honest and hardworking and as long as they took the time to show him what needed to be done, he was an ever willing student.

One of the luxuries of traveling, particularly camping, with servants is not having to lift a finger to do all the mundane cooking and clean-up tasks that camping usually entails. So, after dinner on that first evening, Kathy grabbed Alex's hand and said, "Let's go for a walk, Alex."

It was the perfect opportunity since the girls were immersed in playing a game with the other children in the Daniels' tent and the sun wouldn't set for another hour or so.

"You two go ahead," Joanne Daniels said when she overheard Kathy. "My Tina will keep an eye on the girls for you."

Kathy smiled warmly at her. "Thanks, Joanne. We won't be long."

Alex knew that Kathy had wanted some time alone with him. It seemed even overseas, they didn't spend nearly enough time together and they never seemed to get the chance to really talk – not about the important things, anyway, like about the girls. Kathy always wanted to talk about them, he remembered. She was concerned about whether Kay had missed anything in the transition to the American Community School. It was a good school, but the curriculum was different from the one she had had in Virginia. And what of Angie in the French kindergarten? Was that confusing to a five-year-old? Would it prepare her for first grade?

Kathy had wanted to share her concerns with him. She didn't like the idea that she might be carrying the entire burden of parenting. He knew that. He wished he had been better at it all back then. They had agreed, in principle anyway, that they would share the raising of their daughters. How had they gotten so off-course? Was it just their busy schedules during the years in Washington?

Sure, they both had demanding jobs and they both wanted to do well in their careers, but the girls were their priority, weren't they? Maybe he had expected her to pick up the slack simply because she was "the mother." It wasn't fair. But when she wasn't in a feminist huff about it, he wondered if she didn't feel that way, too. She always seemed to feel far guiltier than he did if she couldn't be home with them when they were sick. How did she end up so conflicted? he wondered now.

Alex had taken her hand as they picked their way across the pebbly sand heading towards the cliffs that bordered the end of the lake, just beyond the small hotel. The beach, such as it was, was blanketed with acacia thorn trees with their spindly branches that provided some relief from the equatorial sunshine. It was still warm out, but it was already cooling off as the sun began to dip behind the hills.

They were quiet as they walked. They knew the sun would go down soon, but they thought they'd be able to walk to the bend in the lake and back before full dark. African twilights were short once the sun set. Alex had tucked a flashlight in his back pocket just in case.

There was tinny Ethiopian music drifting on the air from the outdoor restaurant attached to the hotel. There seemed to be few patrons that evening, though. It was off-season, what with the rains due to start any day. There was a German family camping a little ways down the beach from them, but that was all.

"What do you think of the Daniels girls?" Alex asked. "That Tina seems to keep all the other kids in line, don't you think?"

Kathy nodded and smiled, "She's a nice little girl, isn't she? Do you think Kay or Angie will turn out like her?"

Alex thought about it, "Bossy, you mean?" he grinned. "Well, Kay has all the makings, I'd say. She is quite a little social bee, huh?"

"Yeah, did you see the way she was checking out Peter Oliver?" Kathy laughed, a sound that always reminded Alex of tinkling bells.

"She's going to be a heart-breaker, that's for sure," Alex agreed.

"Hey, what's that up ahead?" Kathy asked pointing as she pushed her bangs back from her forehead.

Alex squinted. "Hmmm, must be the old Peace Corps boat Stan Daniels mentioned. He said it's been there for something like 30 years, just rotting away. Sort of a landmark, I guess."

"Did the Peace Corps own it?" Kathy asked as they drew closer to it. "Or did one of the volunteers buy it, I wonder?" She could see the rotted wood and peeling paint. Gray? It was impossible to say what color it might've once been.

Alex shook his head, "I don't know. But when did the Peace Corps ever have extra funds for recreational equipment? Don't you remember how it was in Dar es Salaam? We couldn't even get them to spring for a cab to the Embassy. 'You can take the chicken bus,' they'd say!" he mimicked and laughed.

"It was fun, though, wasn't it?" Kathy said softly, pulling Alex to a stop. "And gratifying to be involved the way we were – helping people to learn to read and setting up small family farm plots and irrigating that bit of land across from the stream behind our little house."

"Shack, you mean." Alex nodded. "Seems like a long time ago, doesn't it?"

"And here we are fourteen years later together in Africa again," Kathy said, looking around.

Alex pulled her into his arms, "Yeah, back in Africa and posted together, for a change. Maybe it's just what we needed, huh?"

Kathy looked at him and nodded more seriously, "We were really drifting apart in DC, weren't we?"

Alex shrugged, "Well when you have kids, things change. People were always telling us that, but we didn't believe them."

She smiled sardonically, "I guess we do now, huh?"

He tilted her chin up and kissed her gently. "Hmmm, this gives me an idea..." he said, a wicked grin spreading across his face.

"Alex! We can't! Not in a tent with Kay and Angie, and with the Daniels and Olivers right next door. God, they can hear every little whisper, as it is!"

"Not in the tent, honey," Alex said, pulling her down. "I meant right here, right now."

"Alex, someone will see us," Kathy said and then giggled.

"We'll be behind the boat, and it will be dark soon so no one will be able to see us. Besides who'll be coming down to this end of the beach anyway? Come on, what happened to that free spirit I married in Dar." He caressed her waist.

She breathed out, "Alex..." But then she shrugged and put her arms around him, and they lay back on the gritty sand.

Alex remembered thinking at that moment that being a responsible adult was highly over-rated.

* * *

But that was a long time ago, Alex sighed as he pulled gently on the fishing line. The afternoon light gleamed on the gurgling water of the stream, but the shadows were growing longer. He turned around and looked at the lodge building, the garage, and the woodshed. He felt pride in how the buildings seemed to blend in and belong to the woods and the mountains.

He could just make out the camp road beyond the lodge that wound through the campground, lined with small campsite numbers nailed to trees. The road was worn smooth from the tires of campers, cars, and people.

They were lucky to have this place, he thought for the millionth time. He had been fortunate to find such a peaceful place to bring his family where he could keep them safe.

THREE

Back to the Woodshed

August 2006
Wilderness Campground, Crawford Notch, NH

*** *Angie* ***

I reached the shed and slowly walked around it. I could see the spaces between the boards, the tilt of the walls of the old building. It wasn't much, standing there blackened by wood fires that had been built too close, and streaked with pine pitch that dripped from the trees overhead. I could see the shed was old, ancient even, but I'd never really thought about how old it might be, or who built it, or why.

I slowly walked around to the front of the shed, running my fingers lightly over the old boards. The surface was rough, and I lightened my touch so I wouldn't get a sliver. I imagined that I was an archeologist discovering an old civilization. I stopped in front of the door and tugged on it. It was held closed by a rusty old latch, but no lock. When I pulled, it swung open with a loud creaking sound. My dad never locked anything at the campground. He said the day he started locking things up, he might as well go back to Washington to live. And the thought of Washington would start a tirade about what's wrong with big cities and the idiots who lived in them. Well, even if there were idiots, I, for one, wouldn't mind moving back.

I don't remember a lot about living in Washington, but I do remember a little of living in Africa before that. We've always moved a lot because both of my parents worked for the State Department and were stationed at embassies overseas. I don't usually bring it up in conversation, at least, not with kids I meet here in the States. I only mention it to explain a little about me.

When we lived overseas and I was around other kids who were used to living overseas just like me, I'd talk openly about where I was born, what countries we'd lived in and what my early childhood was like, but I don't bring it up around kids here in the States. They look at me funny, like I'm bragging or being stuck up or something. I'm not, but I know how it must sound to them. The thing with not talking about it, though, is that no one ever really knows me, the real me, I mean.

The other reason I don't like talking about it is because people always ask questions about my mom and what happened to her. It's bad enough that she's dead, but I really, really don't like talking about the bombing at the embassy in Nairobi. Heck, we didn't even LIVE in Nairobi. It's all so complicated – explaining why she happened to be there at all, for instance – and, I don't know, it feels sort of embarrassing, I guess, like it was all a big mistake that my family had made somehow.

It was warm and dark in the shed, and it smelled pungently of decaying wood. I waited until my eyes adjusted to the dimness. Neatly stacked logs surrounded me. That was all. I was glad that the shed wasn't full at this time of year, although in another month or two my father and Jeb would start chopping up the trunks of the downed trees that were drying near the clearing on the other side of the stream, to get ready for the coming winter.

Suddenly I heard a sort of scratching sound behind me, and I jumped. OK, the truth is, I leapt completely back out through the open door. My skin crawled at the thought of a nest of little field mice bustling around near me, or worse, one big fat rat jumping out at me and maybe running across my feet. I shivered and paced back and forth in front of the door and talked myself through it. I knew I was being dumb. What am I like twenty times their size? I took a deep breath and squared my shoulders. I couldn't let some little critter stop me now, could I? I took another deep breath, which I guess might've been a stalling technique. Oh. All right, I was stalling.

I pushed on the door ever so gently with the tip of my shoe. I'm sure my eyes were bugging out as I scanned the ground just inside the shed. After a tense second or two, I saw what was making the scratching sounds and all the air whooshed out of my lungs in relief. There was a small chipmunk frozen like a tiny statue sitting on top of a log. He could've been starring in a Disney flick, for God's sake.

"Ohhhhh, hey, you little cutey," I murmured. "Come here, little guy." I made a clicking sound with my tongue, but in a lightning flash he shot between the logs and was gone. A chipmunk! It's funny how I'm not afraid of chipmunks, but mice give me the creeps. They are both small furry animals that scurry around underfoot, so why is one cute and the other repulsive? That's the sort of thing that always stumps me.

I stepped back into the dark shed and squinted. There was a shorter stack of logs right near the door and taller stacks filling the back wall from floor to ceiling. I decided to start by moving the stacks so I could see the ground along the back wall. This would let me see the oldest and least disturbed section of the shed, and might even help my father, when it came time to fill the shed with the newly cut logs. He'd want the green stuff in the back, anyway, with the older seasoned logs up closer to the door.

Once I had decided on a course of action, I quickly set to work. I'm good like that – I know how to make a plan and then execute it. My dad says those skills will help me when I grow up. I believe him, too. Look at all he's done in his life, after all. He was the son of a political science professor in Montana, he finished college, he went to Africa with the Peace Corps, worked for the State Department, and has been everywhere. He knows a lot of stuff; like foreign languages and interesting things about other countries and the people who live there. I think I'm a lot like him.

I propped the door open with a log to catch whatever breeze there might be on this humid afternoon, and also to give me some light. Back and forth, I hauled the logs and stacked them neatly outside, one on top of the other. When the wood was out of the way, I walked slowly along the newly exposed length of the back wall. I squinted, trying to see along the ground where the wall met the dirt floor. But it was dark, and I couldn't see a thing. "Darn!" I said out loud. I knew I'd have to go over to the lodge and find a flashlight.

As I said before, the lodge is the heart of the campground. All camp roads led to it, and it was where all the business of the campground was conducted. It's a large building that's both our home and our business. The main floor has the camp's kitchen and a large high-ceilinged main room with a massive river stone fireplace that rises with its huge flues and chimney through the center of the roof. In front of the fireplace are a couch and some chairs. At the other end of the main room is a family-style dining room area with three long wooden bench tables to feed hikers who passed through, as well as the occasional camper who didn't feel like cooking. The stairway and upstairs hallway overlook the main room. Upstairs, there are four bedrooms – one that I shared with Kay, one for Tessie, one for Jeb and one for my dad. There is also a tiny office where we keep the computer with the Internet satellite link.

At the back of the lodge upstairs is a loft area that can be reached by way of a set of stairs from the kitchen. The loft is filled with bunks that we rent out by the night to long distance hikers who might be passing through. Out back, beyond the kitchen, there is a clean-up area for the hikers, with a couple of individual shower rooms sporting hot and cold running water, mirrors, sinks and nearby there's a small laundry room with a commercial size washer and dryer.

I went into the lodge the back way, past the clean-up area and into the kitchen. The lodge was quiet during the daytime. There wouldn't be much activity until dinner, unless some campers suddenly arrived. It was midweek, though, and we weren't expecting a crowd until Friday. We'd be full for the weekend unless it rained. Summers in New Hampshire were short, and the weather was unpredictable. That's why they make so many jokes about New England's weather, I guess. The people – the locals, I mean – are considered to be as contrary as the weather. Maybe they are, but most of the ones I've met here have been pretty decent, friendly even.

I rummaged around in the junk drawer at the kitchen desk, closed it and looked around. I knew there were flashlights in the kitchen somewhere because we had enough power outages in the winter that they needed to be handy. I raised my sights a little and then I saw them – four flashlights lined up neatly on the top of the refrigerator. I grabbed the smallest one, flicked it on and off to test it, and hurried back outside. I jogged back to the shed.

"What're you looking for?" a voice asked as I came to a stop in front of the door.

Surprised, I turned to find a nice looking guy sitting on the ground with his back against the large oak tree just to the left of the shed. There was a huge backpack resting next to him and his hiking boots were off and lying one next to each foot. He was young, although older than me. I figured he was probably eighteen or nineteen, and I'm usually spot on with my guesses about people's ages, at least, when it came to kids.

"Looking for?" I repeated.

"Yeah, you've got a flashlight in your hand and you're going into a dark shed, so...you know...what are you looking for?" He smiled. It was a nice friendly smile and I relaxed.

I shrugged. "Nothing much. Just looking." I didn't know if he'd think it was dumb – my looking for treasure, I mean. I stood shifting from one foot to another, anxious to get back inside the shed, but at the same time curious about the hiker. Did I mention he was good looking?

"I like looking for nothing, too." He nodded. "I almost always find it."

I grinned and shrugged. "No harm in looking, though, right?" I turned and opened the shed door. I leaned down and propped it open with the log again.

"I hope you don't need any help," he said, moving slightly, as if to get up, but it was obviously a half-hearted attempt.

"No thanks," I said, letting him off the hook. "But I'll let you know if I find anything interesting,"

He nodded and smiled back, leaning his head against the tree. "Good, it's a deal. I'll be right out here." He closed his eyes with a sigh.

I clicked on the flashlight. I liked the hikers who stopped at the campground. The day hikers were all right, but the ones with the best stories were the ones who were hiking the Appalachian Trail from Georgia to Maine.

I planned to do the AT someday myself, just like my dad and Jeb did when they were young. It's one of my goals.

Goals are important. I've already started a list of all the things I want to do in my life. Right now, hiking the AT is near the top of the list. Eating a whole warm apple pie all by myself is also on the list, but further down. You may think that eating a pie is too easy to go on a lifetime goals list, but I believe you should always include things on your list that you know you'll be able to cross off sort of easily. That way if you die early, you will, at least, have accomplished something you wanted to do during your lifetime.

My mom wanted to hike the Trail, but never got a chance to. I hope I live long enough to do it; if I do, I'll hike it for both of us.

I tried to be methodical in my search of the shed, scanning one part of the floor and then the next. I was shining the light right along the bottom edge of the back wall when I thought I saw a lump wedged between the floor and the base of the wall. I moved the light back to it. A stone, maybe? I kicked at it with the toe of my sneaker. Small clots of dirt jumped and then I could see the light catch something shiny. A coin.

"Yes!" I said under my breath, my heart was thumping like crazy. I knelt down and brushed the dirt away and dug the coin out with my fingers, the thick dirt caking under my nails. I scraped the dirt off the coin with my thumbnail and I shined the flashlight on it. I squinted. It looked like a buffalo head nickel. "Cool!" I said aloud. I rubbed the coin gently between my thumb and index finger and put it right under the flashlight beam. "It looks like 1937. Wow! 1937!"

"1937?" The hiker's voice came from outside. I must've said it louder than I thought.

I hurried outside. It was great having someone to share it with. "Look! I found a coin from 1937!"

"Wow!" He grinned. "Let's see it." He took the coin from me and tipped it towards the sunlight to read it more easily. "Yep, it definitely looks like 1937!" He glanced towards the shed. "Is this what you were looking for in there?"

"Well, actually I didn't know what I'd find. I was just looking. I thought I might find something, though. My dad said this used to be a CCC camp during the Depression. I was looking to see if I could find something from that time."

"Well, looks like you did. Congratulations!"

I clicked off the flashlight and pushed it into my back pocket. The sunlight was streaming through the branches of the tall pine and birch trees that arched above us.

"So, this used to be a CCC camp?" the hiker asked looking around with interest. "No kidding. My grandfather was in one of the camps up here somewhere. He used to tell everyone that he helped build the Appalachian Trail, but it's hard to know if he was making that part up."

"He could've. My dad says the CCC did all kinds of forest work around here. Building parks, blazing trails, all that kind of stuff."

"Are you camping here?"

"Oh. No. I'm Angie Jackson. My dad owns the campground."

"No kidding! Hi, Angie. My name's Joe Carlton, but on the Trail, I'm just called 'Crunch'."

"Crunch? That's a cool trail name."

"Yeah. So, you know about trail names, huh? I didn't exactly choose 'Crunch' for myself. It's mainly what everyone's called me since junior high."

"Really? How come?"

"Well, it's the name of my favorite junk food, and also, I like to think I'm good in one..."

"Good in a...Oh, I get it! That's an awesome name." I loved it when things had double meanings.

"So, your dad owns the campground? Then, I guess, I should talk to him. I heard he rents out showers to hikers. Is that true?"

"Sure. The showers are behind the lodge. Come on. I'll show you where everything is." I shut the shed door and pushed the latch onto the metal hook so the door would stay closed. I slipped the coin deep into my pocket. "You need a place to sleep, too?"

"A campsite, you mean?"

"No, I'm talking about a real bed. We have a bunkroom in the lodge for hikers. It's cheap. Only $5 a night, and that includes a hot shower and dinner."

"For $5? Seriously?"

I nodded and grinned. "Of course, that price is only for thru-hikers. My dad has a soft spot for them. But I should warn you, if you go for his deal, you better be ready to tell some stories at dinner."

"What do you mean?"

"You've heard the expression 'sing for your supper'?"

He nodded.

"Well, my dad likes to hear hikers talk about their trips. He and Jeb can't get enough of the trail talk."

"Jeb?"

"My dad's partner. They own this campground together."

"So, they like a good story, huh? Well, we've had a few close calls that might satisfy them," he said as he picked up his pack and heaved it over his shoulder with a groan. He reached down and scooped up his boots with his other hand.

"You said 'We'?" I looked around expectantly.

"Oh, yeah, me and my hiking partner, 'Pacman.' That's his trail name. His real name is Kevin. He'll be back here later this afternoon. He hitched a ride into the Bartlett post office. He's expecting a package from his folks with some warm gear in it. He's been freezing his butt off these past two nights, if you'll excuse my French."

"Yeah, it's like that up here this time of year. We go from hot and humid in the daytime down sometimes to 40 or 50 degrees at night."

We reached the lodge just as Kay came storming out from the kitchen, slamming the screen door extra hard behind her.

"Whoa!" Joe jumped back, but it was too late. Kay came crashing into him. He fell back onto his backpack and Kay fell right on top of him. She couldn't have planned it more perfectly. God, she's so obvious.

"Kay!" I yelled. "Watch where you're going!"

Kay scrambled to her feet, but Joe just lay there looking up at Kay with a silly smile on his face. "It's OK. It's been a pleasure... uh, meeting you."

She grinned down at him and blushed prettily. "Sorry, uh..."

"Joe Carlton."

She held out her hand for him to shake it, but he thought she was offering to help him up, and he nearly pulled her back on top of him again. She caught herself in time and they both laughed, like they'd known each other for years. Then she reached down again and helped heave him to his feet.

"Hi, Joe. I'm Kay Jackson."

"God, Kay! That was graceful!" I said with a roll of my eyes.

Kay gave me a withering look. "You could've given me some warning that you were coming in, Squirt." She turned back to Joe. "So, are you staying with us, Joe?"

"I hope to. But it's just for a night or two if your dad's got room."

"The bunkroom's empty at the moment," she said with a wide smile. "Come on, I'll get you squared away."

"Hey! I was going to show him around," I said.

"Angie, Dad said I'm supposed to check in the campers today."

"That's for the campground, not the bunkroom!" I said and, yes, I probably sounded a little whiny. She brings out the worst in me, as I may have mentioned earlier.

"Dad's looking for you anyway," Kay said over her shoulder as she held the door open for Joe to go through.

"No, he's not. He's fishing. I just talked to him not even an hour ago!"

"Then maybe it was Jeb. Yeah, Jeb needs your help cleaning up the double site, number 22."

I frowned. "The double site is number 21," I corrected.

"Whatever," Kay answered as she turned away.

"See you later, Angie," Joe said with a wave, but even he barely glanced at me. Talk about becoming invisible.

"Yeah," I replied, turning away. Like I always said, who needs a sister?

FOUR

Cleaning Tentsite with Jeb

August 2006
Wilderness Campground, Crawford Notch, NH

**** Angie ****

I turned and headed down the dirt road towards the tent sites in the woods to the west. I knew Kay was pulling a fast one, but I figured I'd better go and check to be sure. A three-family group had been renting the double site for the past two weeks and they had just packed up and left early that morning. The campsite needed to be raked out, the picnic tables returned to where they belonged, and the fireplace checked for trash and then the excess ash shoveled out and buried.

Number 21 was a popular site because of its unusual size and location, right up against the forest with a pretty brook cutting across one corner of it. We charged more for it, but that didn't seem to matter. It was nearly always filled.

I saw Jeb's tall, angular body through the trees. He was intent on the job, sweeping the rake over the ground with long even motions. He stopped and squatted, digging at something.

"What did you find?" I asked as I came up behind him.

He glanced up at me, his light blue eyes looking paler than usual. "Hey, Angel. Come here and see this." He sometimes called me "Angel" instead of "Angie"; it was a pet name, I guess. I sort of liked it.

I walked over and bent down to look where he pointed. "What?"

"Look." He pointed, his index finger moving in a large rectangular shape in the air over the ground.

"Huh? Oh!" I said and then laughed as I saw the tent stakes still in the ground. "What a bunch of...." I said, shaking my head. The campers, who had left the site that morning, had left six stakes in the ground where their dining tent had been.

"Looks like they just untied the tie-downs for that screened-in dining tent of theirs and never bothered to pull up the stakes!" Jeb said. He walked around and yanked each stake up in a smooth even motion, tossing them into a pile near the rusty old golf cart that he used to get around the campground and to carry his equipment and tools. "I imagine they'll be in for a surprise when they go to set it up the next time, huh?"

I had to grin, just thinking of it. "So, you need some help here, Jeb?" I asked.

Jeb eyed me suspiciously. "Are you volunteering, or did someone send you?"

"Well, Kay said you might need some help, but I think she was just trying to get rid of me."

"Really? Why was she trying to get rid of you?"

"A cute hiker just arrived. Suddenly, she's the 'hostess with the mostest'. You know how she acts." I fluttered my eyelashes to give him a demonstration.

Jeb chuckled. "That's our Kay, all right." He handed the rake to me, and he took the big, blue-handled shovel. "Here, you rake, and I'll bury the ashes."

We worked for several minutes in silence.

"So, who is this cute hiker then?" Jeb asked over his shoulder.

"A guy named Joe Carlton. I think maybe he just graduated from high school. He looks sort of young. He's doing the AT and says he's hiking with a friend, but I didn't see the other guy. Apparently, the friend went into the Bartlett post office to get his mail."

Jeb nodded. "So, we ought to have some good stories at dinner tonight, eh?"

"Maybe. If Kay doesn't try to keep him all to herself."

Jeb hooted. "Maybe she'll get tired of him before then."

"I doubt it," I said. "She is such a flirt. It makes me nauseous."

"I'm going to remind you of this when you start flirting with the hikers in another year or two, my girl."

"You have a long wait then. I'll never do that. Not after seeing what an ass it's made of Kay!"

Jeb grinned at me. "We'll see, Angel. But it could be you'll be different. You certainly have been up to now."

I smiled back at him. "I've got better things to do with my time," I said primly. Then I remembered and smacked my forehead lightly. "That reminds me!" I pulled the nickel out of my pocket. "Jeb, look what I found in the old shed!" I handed him the nickel. "Look at the year on it!"

Jeb squinted and held the coin to the light. "19...37, is it?"

"Yeah! 1937! Isn't that something? Dad told me that this camp used to be a CCC camp and that the woodshed might be from that time period. So, I started investigating. I moved the wood around and found this coin along the back wall of the shed."

"Huh." Jeb turned the coin over and rubbed at the back of it. "Hey, look at this, Angel."

I came over closer. "What?"

"Look at the buffalo on the back of the coin. It looks like he only has three legs. You'll need to compare it to another nickel from that same year, of course, but this coin could be valuable."

"Really? How valuable?"

"I don't know. Probably not thousands, but I'm sure it's worth more than a nickel!"

"Thousands of DOLLARS?"

"No, probably not, but who knows? Could be a hundred or so."

"DOLLARS?" I repeated.

"Yeah," Jeb said with a smile. "But get those dollar signs out of your eyeballs. I could be wrong."

I took the nickel back and turned it over several times in my fingers. "Maybe, but you might be right, too. I wonder if there are any more?"

"Uh Oh," Jeb said. "What have I started here?"

I looked at him and handed him the rake. "I want to go see if there are more of these in the shed. Can you finish up here without me?"

He shrugged and picked up the rake. I was gone before he could answer.

FIVE

A Marine in Beirut

October 1983
Marine Barracks, Beirut, Lebanon

**** Jeb ****

Jeb whistled as he raked the leaves at the campsite. It was a nearly soundless and probably a nearly tuneless tune. That's what he loved about working at the campground – he could spend hours alone, working up a sweat and just thinking.

But when he spent more than a few minutes in reverie he always ended up back in Beirut. It was like a puzzle that he hadn't quite figured out yet and his mind seemed to toy with it, turning it this way and that, as if another perspective would suddenly make it all come clear and it would somehow all make sense.

Although he had vivid memories of Beirut, he was never quite sure which were actual memories, and which were just fractured images from the nightmares he had about it later on.

He had arrived in Beirut on September 29, 1982, a 22-year-old Marine lieutenant on a "peacekeeping" mission, or so he thought. His unit, the First Battalion 8th Marines, was deployed in Beirut as part of a multinational force to help keep the peace after the 1982 Israeli invasion of Lebanon. When he'd first heard about the deployment, he'd been happy and excited to be going. It was exactly what he thought he should be doing with his life – saving the world and keeping the peace. It was like all the gears of the universe were meshing perfectly and he was precisely where he ought to be and going where he could do the most good.

He and Alex and Kathy had graduated from the University of Montana the previous June and Alex and Kathy had decided to join the Peace Corps while Jeb had opted for the Marines. He couldn't say exactly why. Perhaps it was because his father had been a Marine during the Korean War. Or perhaps he joined because he hadn't done as well as Alex on the Peace Corps' language aptitude test. Or maybe he just needed some time to be on his own for a while.

Alex and Kathy were getting to be a pretty tight twosome and he sometimes felt like a third wheel when he was with them. Perhaps. But now some twenty years later, he believed that it was simply fate that led him to the Marines and ultimately, to Beirut.

Arriving in Beirut, he discovered that the Marines had set up their base in a section of the Beirut International Airport, bounded on one side by the tarmac runways and on the other by the slums at the outskirts of Beirut. They were so close to the runways that the Air Traffic tower was visible just on the other side of the Headquarters' building.

Jeb worked next door in the Command Operations Center but was billeted in the HQ building. He had been assigned to the communications group and he found the movement of classified material between Beirut and Washington fascinating, filled as they were with the detail that coordinated their activities with those of the Italian and French peacekeeping troops.

Back when the Marines had first arrived, the Lebanese had welcomed the multinational peacekeeping forces with open arms. It was thought that, finally, Beirut could return to normal: the cosmopolitan, peaceful, and confident city it had once been. However, as time went by and the foreign armies didn't leave - worse, when they appeared to be settling in – and Beirut wasn't any safer than when they had first arrived, the sniper action against the peacekeeping forces began and quickly intensified.

Jeb had liked the Lebanese people, but he was appalled at the destruction and chaos in the capital city. He'd had drinks one evening with a pilot who had attended the American University in Beirut back in the late 1960s. Jeb was fascinated to hear how wonderful the city had been back then. It had apparently been a sophisticated place, the Middle East banking center, a regional mecca for shopping with lively discos at night, and the streets and cafes were once filled with beautiful stylish women. Jeb wished he could've seen it back in its glory days. He'd met Lebanese emigrants in the U.S. and had heard how harsh the civil war had been, destroying not only the infrastructure of the city but also the banking system that was the economic backbone of the country.

There was one Lebanese family who had settled in Missoula and had opened up a Lebanese bakery not far from the University of Montana campus. It was one of Jeb's favorite memories: the morning ritual of stopping by the bakery to grab something warm and buttery straight out of the oven.

But Jeb never knew Beirut other than as a bombed-out has-been city with scared people who scattered like mice to their bombed-out hovels when the sun went down. It saddened him and the longer he was there, the more discouraged he became that there was anything he or any of them could do.

Early on in his deployment, he had met a kindred soul, Sal Solvino from Brooklyn, New York. Sal worked in the radio room deep in the cement basement under the Command Operations Center. Sal dealt with all the top-secret communiqués from the Pentagon in Washington, from the U.N. Headquarters in New York, from NATO headquarters in Belgium, and from his counterparts with the French and the Italian forces in Beirut. Sal was a short squat guy - maybe 5'8". With his special boots on he might possibly pass for 5'9". Jeb, at over 6 foot, towered over him. Sal had olive skin and dark eyes and he seemed even shorter and darker when he was next to Jeb who had a pale complexion, sandy brown hair, freckles, and a lanky physique. They were the proverbial Mutt and Jeff.

Jeb knew the exact moment they had become friends. They had been lined up one early dawn in front of the coffee machine of the first floor snack bar. A major was at the front of the line, then Sal, and then Jeb, with several more men behind him. No one had spoken. It was too early for anything but a friendly nod of the head, too early even for a smile. Suddenly, there was a pinging sound and then the thick glass of the window – the one facing the parking lot – began to crack in slow motion. Jeb remembered staring at it as the cracks zigzagged out from the small starburst hole. It was several moments before the group connected the pinging sound of the sniper's bullet to the breaking pane of glass, and in an instant they all dropped to a crouch, with their arms covering their heads.

The problem with reacting to a sniper's bullet when there is only the single bullet is this: how do you know when it's safe to stand up again?

"Jesus!" the major in front of Sal had exclaimed.

That's when Sal piped up with, "Nope, I'm thinking it wasn't Him, Sir."

The room broke into guffaws and the tension of the moment was broken. That was when Jeb knew he and Sal would become friends. In the next fifteen or twenty minutes, they all slowly got warily to their feet, and someone left to report the broken window and to bring back some duct tape. Eventually, the others resumed getting their morning java. There was a lot more chatter than there had been before. The adrenalin shooting through their bodies had woken them up as no cup of coffee ever could.

Later, someone dug the high caliber bullet from the wall above the coffee machine. It was just about at Jeb's eye level. Lucky for him, he thought ruefully, that he was third in line and not first or he'd have gotten it in the back of the head.

Jeb and Sal hit it off from that first morning. It was as if they'd known each other for years, or in another lifetime, perhaps.

"So, what do you do for fun up there in Montana, Cowboy?" Sal asked one evening when he was on duty in the radio room and Jeb had come down to keep him company.

"Fun? Oh, you know, we wrestle with bulls, that sort of thing," Jeb answered, keeping a straight face.

Sal looked up at him and blinked. "You're shittin' me, right?"

Jeb shrugged. "Out west, we don't shit people. Is that an Eastern Yankee thing?"

Sal grinned, "No, come on. Really. What's it like out there? I'm picturing you living in a log cabin, grassy hillsides, horses, herds of cattle..."

"You just described "Little House on The Prairie", Sal. And that took place like 100 years ago." Jeb shook his head in mock disgust. "Don't you New Yorkers ever travel west?"

"Sure, we travel west, straight from JFK to LAX, skip right over all that mess in the middle of the country," he said laughing.

"So, what about you? What's fun in Brooklyn?" Jeb had asked. He'd actually spent some time in New York City, but razzing Sal was too much fun.

"Eat, man! We E-A-T! My uncle owns an Italian bakery on 86th Street in Brooklyn. You wouldn't believe the bread, the cannolis, the amaretto cakes, the pignoli cookies. Oh, man! It makes my mouth water just thinking about that place. The aroma when you walk in the door. Bam! It hits you and you start salivating." Sal's eyes took on a distant look and Jeb knew he was back in Brooklyn. Sal came back with a shake of his head, "When I get back, Cowboy, I'm going to take over that bakery when my uncle retires. We've already talked about it."

"Doesn't he have any kids to leave it to?"

"Hey! I'm his nephew, man! His *favorite* nephew, I might add; the one who was named after him, too," Sal said with obvious pride. He shrugged, "Besides, Uncle Salvatore got stuck with four daughters. He figures they'll all get married, and he doesn't want to leave the place to a friggin' son-in-law."

Jeb laughed. "That's not really fair to your cousins, is it?"

"Sure, it is. We're family. I'll always take care of them. They know that." Sal thought about it and looked up at Jeb. "You don't understand about Italian families, Cowboy. We're tight," he put his index and middle fingers together, "Like this."

The phone rang then and there was a beep from the telex machine, which began spewing text on a roll of white paper. Jeb went over to it and read it as it continued to type. There was nothing earthshaking there. It was just another warning about snipers and possible terrorist bombings, nothing specific. He let go of the paper and the perforations caused it to bend and sway as it neatly piled on the floor beneath the machine. Jeb looked over at Sal and saw that he was busy. He waved to him and mouthed the words, "Good Night." Sal looked up and saluted him casually.

That was the last time Jeb ever saw him.

SIX

Return to the Woodshed

August 2006
Wilderness Campground, Crawford Notch, NH

**** Angie ****

I returned to the woodshed. No one was around now. I pulled the flashlight from my back pocket and flicked it on. In a second or two, my eyes adjusted to the darkness. I squatted down near where I had found the nickel. I moved the light slowly over the ground, sweeping away the chips of wood, pieces of leaves and a few stray pine needles. Except for where I had dug the nickel out, the ground was fairly smooth, packed down from years of stacked wood, people walking on it and who knows what else. I picked up a large piece of bark and swept it along the ground near the wall. I wondered if I would find anything by digging?

"Angie? You in there?" My dad was at the door, squinting into the darkness.

"Dad!" I jumped up and ran to the door. "Look! Look what I found in here!" I pulled the nickel from my pocket and handed it to him.

"Well, I'll be! You actually found something?" He set down his fishing pole and tackle box and wiped the nickel on his pant leg.

"Look at the year! It's a buffalo head nickel! 1937! And look at the back!"

He flipped the coin over. "What?"

"Look carefully," I said.

"Can't without my glasses and they're probably back at the lodge."

"Oh, Daddy," I said in disgust as I took the nickel from him. "Jeb could see it fine!"

"Ah, the competition continues," Dad said shaking his head in mock seriousness. "So, what is it that Jeb can see with his fine x-ray vision that I can't?"

I smiled. "The buffalo on the back - it only has three legs! Jeb says it might be worth something."

"Could be," Dad agreed. "Better keep it someplace safe." He looked around and saw the stack of wood. "You want some help putting the wood back into the shed?"

I grimaced, but saw he wasn't upset. I nodded. "I guess," I said.

He leaned his fishing pole against the shed and started carrying the logs back into the shed. In a little while we were done. He closed the shed door and put his arm around my shoulders and turned me towards the lodge. "Come on. We'll probably have some check-ins arriving soon and at any rate, we'll have to help Tessie with dinner. I think that family with the little girl will be coming up to eat with us again tonight."

"Melanie? The one I babysat yesterday?"

"The Jacobs. Yes."

"We have some hikers, too," I said. "Two guys doing the AT. They'll be sleeping in the bunkroom tonight."

"Trail hikers, huh? Did you get a chance to talk to them yet?"

"Just for a minute or two, then Kay took over," I rolled my eyes, and he laughed out loud.

"One of them must've been young and good looking I take it?"

"Well, the one named Joe is. I don't know about the other one. I didn't get to meet him. According to Joe, his hiking partner went into Bartlett to pick up his mail. He's supposed to be back here by dinnertime, I think."

I pushed the flashlight into my back pocket again. Dad picked up his fishing pole and I picked up the tackle box and with his arm still around me, and mine around his waist, we walked together to the lodge.

"What am I going to do with your sister?" he asked, although he didn't really expect me to answer. "She's 15 going on 30... whew!"

"What does that mean? 15 going on 30?" I asked, looking up at him.

"It means she's trying to grow up too fast and I've got to figure out a way to slow her down." He chuckled, but there was no real mirth in it. Instead, I could hear a note of weariness.

SEVEN

Dinner at the Lodge

August 2006
Wilderness Campground, Crawford Notch, NH

*** Angie ***

That evening we were seated around one of the dining tables that was covered with a white linen tablecloth. Cut flowers were in two plain glass vases at the center of the table; the food steamed in serving dishes on either side of the vases. Dad sat at one end of the long table with Jeb at the other end. Joe sat to Dad's right and, no surprise to me, Kay managed to seat herself right next to Joe. Keith Jacobs, Melanie's dad, was to Kay's right. Next to him was seated another camper, Lesley Stanhope, and finally Tessie, just to Jeb's left. Jeb was at the end of the table with Kevin to his right, then Lesley Stanhope's friend, Todd Carlyle sitting directly opposite Lesley. Next to him was Nora Jacobs, and next to her was their four-year-old daughter, Melanie. I was at Dad's end of the table, to his left and directly opposite Joe.

The first several minutes after we all sat down, we served and passed food around the table, everyone commenting on the wonderful aromas. We ate in silence for several more minutes then the conversation hopped lightly from the weather to fishing to the names of surrounding mountains and so on, as happens when people are getting to know each other and establishing rapport.

"Boy, it sure is good to have a real meal sitting at a real table," Todd Carlyle said.

"Not much for camping?" Dad quipped conversationally. The others smiled.

Todd shrugged. "It does seem an awful lot of work for such a small return in pleasure."

"Really?" Dad said leaning forward a bit. "Some people would say that the pleasure is in the work."

Todd snorted. "In that case, I guess I like to keep my work and pleasure as separate as possible."

Lesley shook her head but said nothing. I could see Dad watching her and we both saw a look get exchanged between Lesley and Todd. Apparently, the two of them had had this discussion before, and it wasn't a pleasant memory for either of them. To change the subject, Dad turned to Joe, "So, Joe, tell us how your hike has been so far."

Joe glanced down the table at Kevin and grinned. "It's been a lot of work, sure, but it's been an incredible five months."

"Five months of hiking? That's my idea of a nightmare," Todd interjected, but no one gave him more than a glance.

Joe put his forearms against the edge of the table and stretched slightly. "Well, for me, being in the woods like we've been is a dream come true. I've wanted to do the Appalachian Trail since I was twelve years old." Joe looked around at the interested faces. "Of course, we've had some tough times, but overall, it's been great. I wouldn't exchange the experience for anything in the world."

"Don't forget about our wet times...you want to talk about uncomfortable! There are a few of THOSE days I might exchange gladly!" Kevin added with a laugh.

"Yeah, that's true," Joe nodded. "The first month through northern Georgia, North Carolina, and the southwestern part of Virginia, it rained constantly. We were cold and wet to the bone nearly all the time."

"Spongy, is what we were...you know how that feels? Spongy? Everything was just saturated...." Kevin said.

Todd shook his head but said nothing.

"We nearly packed it in right then," Joe said. "Could've too, since we were coming up close to home in northern Virginia, where our folks live."

"Yeah," Kevin said with a chuckle, "and, of course, that's also the main reason we didn't quit."

Joe smiled. "Too proud to admit defeat." He looked at my dad and shrugged.

Dad nodded with a smile. "I know the feeling."

"So, when did it start drying out for you?" Keith Jacobs asked.

"Oh, probably the day we hit Skyline Drive in Virginia, which, by the way, is not more than an hour from home! We figured it was a sign."

Everyone, except Todd, laughed appreciatively.

"Anyway, we took our stuff home and dried out everything over one long weekend, then when Monday morning arrived, we set out again just like nothing had happened."

"That's right," Kevin said with satisfaction. "We didn't even complain much to our folks either. But, man oh man, did we eat! Oooweeeee! You can't imagine how hungry we were for home-cooked meals. My mother was so glad when I put my pack back on and left her kitchen table at the end of that weekend."

"That's so true!" Jeb exclaimed. "Isn't it amazing how much you can eat when you've been on the trail?" He snapped his fingers and looked at Dad. "Remember that little diner we went to, Alex? Let's see, somewhere in the Blue Mountains of Pennsylvania, I think it was..."

"God, yes! I'd nearly forgotten about that." Dad nodded, enjoying the reminiscence. "We must've eaten...what? Two or three stacks of pancakes and each stack had, like, ten pancakes in it."

"TEN pancakes?" I laughed and mimed choking. "Dad, how could you eat that much?"

"I don't honestly know, honey. Except we'd been walking for so long, all that hunger must've just gotten saved up, I guess."

"I'm surprised you didn't end up with a weight problem," Todd commented dryly.

"Well, you do walk it off pretty quickly," Dad replied, looking a little annoyed. I noticed Dad glance down the table at Lesley. He was probably wondering what she saw in this Todd fellow. I know I was. I saw Lesley catch Dad's look and shrug almost imperceptibly and then he relaxed and smiled at her. What was going on between them, I wondered?

"Alex, remember how you just kept going on and on about how good the syrup tasted?" Jeb hooted, loving to tease my dad.

Dad grinned sheepishly and nodded. "Well, if I remember correctly, it was pretty good."

I saw Lesley smile at him, and he almost seemed to blush. Dad was blushing? Ohmigod!

"We had the same thing happen to us," Joe said. "I don't think I've ever eaten as much as I have on this trip...at least when I've had the chance."

"Yeah, you can't call what we carry in our packs 'gourmet fare.' Heck, most of the time when we stop, we are too tired to fix anything, even when we have the ingredients!" Kevin said. "Man, am I sick of cold food."

"So, let me see if I have this straight," Tessie said leaning forward so she could see the faces around the table. "All of you would agree then that doing the Appalachian Trail comes down to two basic experiences: Hunger and exhaustion?" She paused for effect, then finished, "So explain to me again what the attraction is?"

Everyone laughed.

"Here, here," Todd said, toasting her with his beer. He apparently didn't realize she was kidding.

"Well, you may be right about the hunger and exhaustion," Joe nodded. "But it's been worth it, every minute."

"Yes," Nora Jacobs spoke for the first time. "It must be a remarkable experience to be off in the woods like that for days on end." Her voice was very quiet but friendly. She draped her arm around her daughter, Melanie's shoulder, as she looked across the table at Joe and then to her right at Dad. "I don't know, but I think it would be fabulous to be on the trail like that."

"You can have it, if you ask me," Todd said, draining the last of the beer from his bottle.

Ignoring Todd, Dad said, "I think you're absolutely right, Nora. There is no feeling like being immersed in Nature for days or weeks at a time. I thought I'd be tired of trees and forest noises, but you know, when Jeb and I finally got to Katahdin — I mean after we had finished patting ourselves on the back and all that bullshit — my first instinct was to turn around and get right back on the trail and head back to Stone Mountain in Georgia. I simply didn't want it to be over. I didn't want to leave the woods."

"Sounds like you were out there too long," Todd said with a chuckle.

Lesley frowned at him, "Well, at least Alex finished it. That's quite an accomplishment." Everyone else nodded in agreement.

"I think I'd be the same way," Keith Jacobs said. "I think I wouldn't want to leave the woods, either."

"Well, let's face it: my dad hasn't really left the woods, now has he?" Kay interjected dryly, her arms in the air taking in the lodge. I had to admit that Kay was right about that. Everyone laughed at the truth in it. Kay was always coming up with some dry comment that was true, but also humorous. I envied her being able to do that. I may be smarter than she was, but she had a ready wit; I had to give her that.

Dad chuckled. "Yeah, well, I've been lucky, that's true. I was able to come back and live in the mountains. Not everyone can do that," he said, then added, "Or maybe not everyone would even want to." He looked directly at Todd who toasted him with his empty beer bottle.

"You are lucky, sir," Joe said. "I'm envious of what you've got here."

Dad smiled, but from my vantage point, I could see the look exchanged between Kay and Joe, and I wondered if Joe was talking about the campground or Kay. Give me a break!

Dad didn't seem to notice what was going on between Kay and Joe. He was looking over at the huge fieldstone fireplace that dominated the center of the lodge. It would be another cool night and he and Jeb had brought in a few logs and set them in the woodbin by the fireplace grill. If the evening wore on late, as it sometimes did when there was good company at the lodge, they'd build a cozy fire. I couldn't wait. It was the best part of a late summer's evening.

"We'd like to take a hike tomorrow. Any suggestions?" Mr. Jacobs asked.

I looked at Dad, but he seemed to be off in another world. "What do you think, Dad?" I asked, nudging him.

"About what?" Dad looked at me and then down the table with a blank look on his face.

"Earth to Dad! Earth to Dad!" I laughed. "Mr. Jacobs just asked for a suggestion of a good half-day hike that they could take tomorrow."

Dad smiled, looking at Keith Jacobs. "That depends, Keith. Are you planning to take Melanie with you?"

Keith Jacobs glanced at his wife, Nora. "Hon, what do you think?"

Nora looked down at Melanie who was clutching her small brown teddy bear and squirming in her seat. Nora shook her head. "No, we'd rather not, Alex. But I guess that will depend on whether Angie can baby-sit her tomorrow?" She looked questioningly at me.

I shrugged. Melanie wasn't hard to take care of, so I said, "Sure, no problem. I'd love to." At least, I knew I'd get paid for it, and really, I wasn't lying, Melanie was easy.

"I want to go hiking, too," Melanie said, tightening her grip on the little bear and pulling at her mother's arm.

"But Melanie, we'll have fun!" I said, trying to be helpful, but Melanie wouldn't even turn her head to look at me.

"Melanie, Daddy and I want to do a long hike tomorrow and it will be too hard for you. You'll have to stay here and have fun with Angie." People don't usually put "have to" together with "fun" in the same sentence. I wonder if Melanie picked up on that?

"I want to go with you and Daddy," Melanie repeated stubbornly. She jammed the little bear on the seat for emphasis.

"Honey, don't hurt your little bear..." Nora said in her most soothing voice, hoping to distract the child.

"No! I want to go too!" Melanie said more loudly.

Nora sighed and stood up. "Say 'goodnight' to everyone, Melanie. You and I are leaving now," she spoke sternly. She smiled wearily at everyone and picked up Melanie, who was blubbering now. Melanie had the little bear by the leg and was swinging it against her mother's back, repeating "I go hiking," over and over again. Nora carried the sobbing child across the lodge and out the front door.

"Sorry about that," Keith said as the front door closed, and the sound of Melanie's crying grew softer.

Dad shrugged slightly. "She's pretty young. You'll be glad not to have her along tomorrow."

"That's what we figure. She wouldn't be able to keep up, and she's getting too heavy to carry very far."

"As for the hike, I'd suggest you try Mount Webster and Jackson. They're right down the road in the Notch, and you'll get really fine views, plus you'll actually be hiking part of the Appalachian Trail."

"Nora would love that!" Keith said with excitement. "That's sounds like just the ticket."

"What time are you thinking of leaving?" Jeb asked.

"I don't know. Nine or Nine-thirty."

"I could give you a ride to the trailhead. I'll be heading right past it on my way to Littleton," Jeb volunteered.

"That'd be great." Mr. Jacobs turned to Dad, "If we have to hike back, how far are we talking about?"

"Five or six miles. But people are pretty friendly about picking up hitchhikers if you look non-threatening enough."

"And you're not soaking wet," Kevin interjected with a laugh.

Joe agreed, "Nobody picks up wet hitchhikers. We learned that the hard way." He shook his head. "That whole month of rain we were telling you about? We never got one ride into town. In fact, the worse the weather, the faster they drove by us."

"That seems sort of mean," Kay said in her poutiest voice. It was enough to make me want to gag.

"I'd do the same thing," Todd interjected. "I wouldn't want a couple of dripping hikers in my car."

"I have to agree with Todd," Joe said seriously. "I mean, we were wet, really, really wet..."

"And we STUNK...really, really stunk!" Kevin added and everyone laughed.

Todd glanced at his watch. He looked across the table at Lesley, who he seemed to have noticed was looking at my dad. He held up his empty beer bottle until she glanced over at him. "Lesley, honey, I'm out of beer. I'm thinking of driving into... what's the name of that little hick town just down the road?"

"Where the grocery store is, do you mean?" Jeb asked.

"I guess."

"The closest grocery store is in Glen. It's located at the intersection of Route 16 and 302. But you can pick up a six-pack at the general store in Bartlett. It's not far from here."

"Great." He stood up. "Thanks for the dinner. I assume you'll add it to the bill." He glanced at Lesley who remained seated. "Are you coming?"

She shook her head. "No thanks, Todd, I think I'll stay here awhile longer. I'll meet you back at the tent later."

He glared at her for just a second then the look was gone. "Yeah, right." He turned and without another word, left. I think he'd already had too much to drink, but no one asked me for my opinion.

Dad watched him leave but said nothing. He turned to look at Lesley and so did I. She actually looked kind of relieved, and Dad smiled at her reassuringly.

Jeb stood up, "Well, Angie, I believe it's you and me doing KP tonight. Let's get to it so we can hear some more stories from these boys over coffee."

"Awwww. I forgot it was my turn," I said. "Darn!"

Tessie stood up, too, picking up her plate and Jeb's, "Come on, I'll help. In fact, why doesn't everyone carry their plates to the sink while I get the coffee started."

Keith Jacobs, probably feeling guilty about leaving Nora with a sulky Melanie, brought his plate in but said his goodnights and arranged to meet up with Jeb in the morning.

Soon it was me and Jeb standing in front of sink. Just my luck, the dishwashing machine was broken again, so we were washing, rinsing, and drying the dishes by hand, assembly-line fashion.

"Here," I said handing a wet dish to Jeb, who dried it and then handed it off to Tessie who put it away. Tessie wiped down the counters while she waited for Jeb to dry each dish. She couldn't stand just patiently waiting for the next dish.

Jeb took the dish from me and asked, "How'd your archeology project go today, Angie?"

"Archeology project?" Tessie repeated, her eyes lighting up with interest.

"Well, I was thinking more of it being for Social Studies, actually," I said to Jeb, then turning towards Tessie, "I've decided to do a Social Studies project on the Civilian Conservation Corps! Isn't that so cool? Dad says this campground used to be one of their camps."

"Really?" she said. "That is interesting, Angie. So how were you thinking of approaching the subject?" She was good about letting me design my own projects, which I liked.

"Well, first I wanted to see if they – you know, the CCC guys - left anything behind, so this afternoon I started looking in the old woodshed."

"The woodshed?" Tessie said with a laugh. "Why on earth start there?"

"Because Dad says it's from that time period; that it was here when the CCC was here. They might've even built it, although he wasn't sure about that. Anyway, I figured something might've been left behind."

"And did you look? Did you find anything?"

I nodded with a grin. "As a matter of fact, I did! A 1937 buffalo nickel! Here, look," I pulled the nickel from my pocket.

Tessie took it and squinted. "Well, that is pretty exciting."

"And, Jeb says it might be worth something, because...look at the back...see? The buffalo only has three legs."

I saw Tessie glance at Jeb and raise her eyebrows, "So, a coin expert, eh?" she said, teasing him. She turned the coin over and studied the back. "Well, it does seem to only have three legs. That is odd, isn't it? But, Angie, don't get your hopes up too high, you don't know if that's the way it was supposed to be on this particular coin."

Jeb agreed. "She's right, Angel. It could be nothing."

I nodded. "I know, but it doesn't matter. I think it's cool anyway. I'm not sure I'd want to sell it even if it turned out to be worth something." I finished another dish and handed it to Jeb.

"So, what about the project? Do you need some help mapping out a strategy?" Tessie asked. "We could go into North Conway to the library and do some research."

"Yeah, I plan on doing that, but I wanted to look around here a little more first."

Jeb handed the dish to Tessie to put away and he stopped. "You know, come to think of it, Angie, I believe the foundation of this lodge building might be pretty old, too."

I looked at him with interest, "What do you mean? I thought the lodge wasn't built that long ago."

"Well, yeah, we added on most of it after we moved up here, but if I remember correctly, there's a crawl space in part of the cellar here under the kitchen. There used to be a root cellar down there. It could've been from the CCC time. It's back behind the furnace, in the northeast corner of the cellar."

Tessie looked at him in amazement. "How on earth do you know that, Jeb?"

He shrugged. "Remember when we had to install the new furnace?" He turned to me, "It's one of those funky ones with half-wood and half-oil burners. There was a flue problem and we had to get a contractor in here to do some of the work to bring it up to code. We noticed the root cellar when we were down there banging around."

"What would she be able to find in a root cellar?" Tessie asked.

"Maybe some old vegetables," Jeb suggested with a grin.

"Yeah, that would be a find," Tessie replied dryly. "Petrified carrots."

I laughed. "Well, I found a nickel in the woodshed. Who knows what I might find in the root cellar!"

Tessie noticed the look on my face and said sternly, "Wait a minute, Angela Jackson, you are NOT going down there tonight to start looking."

"Awwww, come on, Tessie. Just for a couple of minutes?" I pleaded.

"No, it's dark and it's...creepy down there at night. If you want to take a look, I suggest you get up early in the morning, because don't forget you have Melanie to baby-sit all day tomorrow."

"Ohhhhh, darn! I forgot about that," I said. I looked at Tessie and saw she wasn't going to budge on this, so I shrugged. "Oh, all right. I'll go down in the morning, before I have to take care of Melanie. Darn! I wish I didn't have to watch her the whole day."

"You made a promise, and you must keep it," Tessie said. She pulled out a tray and carefully placed the coffee pot, mugs, milk, and sugar on it.

"She's right, babe," Jeb said. "Besides, it's nice to give the Jacobs a break. I doubt they've been alone much since Melanie was born."

I looked at him. "Really? I was thinking it might be just the opposite. I get the feeling they leave her all the time. Why else would she get so whiny about wanting to be with them?"

Tessie glanced over at me. "That's very insightful, Angie. I think I agree with you." She sighed. "But it's not meant as a criticism of the Jacobs. I think it's a sign of the times."

"What do you mean?" Jeb asked, folding his dishtowel over the edge of the sink, and turning to help her with the tray.

"Oh, it's just that parents are so busy these days, they don't really spend much time with their children, not nearly as much time as some children need. There's no such thing as this so-called spending 'quality time,' you know. With children, it's always been about quantity. That's what counts. Besides, how can a person know for sure when a quality moment is going to happen? You just have to make sure you're there when it does." With that she pushed through the door to the next room with Jeb following close behind, carrying the large tray.

I emptied the dirty dishwater in the sinks and rinsed them out, then looked around the kitchen. All done. I glanced at the door leading down to the cellar. I really wanted to see the root cellar, but then I remembered the chipmunk in the woodshed. Yes, on second thought, I'll wait until morning. Mice in daylight wouldn't be quite as awful as mice jumping out at you in the dark of night.

I pushed through the swinging door and paused, as it swung closed behind me. The others were relaxed in chairs around the fireplace where Dad had already built a fire that had caught and was now going very well, sending out a glow of warmth to the surrounding faces. There was the hum of voices and the occasional laughter. I watched the scene from the doorway as if I weren't a part of it but only observing it from the outside.

I could see Kay snuggled up close to Joe, practically in his lap, for God's sake. I wondered why Dad didn't say something about that? But then I saw Lesley Stanhope sitting on the couch with Dad practically hanging over her from his seat on the arm of the couch next to her. Lesley was looking up at him with an expression not unlike the one on Kay's face.

I couldn't hear what Dad was saying, but I could see the way they were leaning in towards each other. Something was definitely going on between them and I wasn't sure how I felt about it. It was so rare that he ever showed any interest in a woman. Of course, we didn't get all that many single women his age up here, either. Camping isn't much of a single woman's activity; even single mothers don't do much camping. Why was that? Maybe it is the whole setting up of tents, the macho woodsman sense of it all, or was it the sleeping out of doors? And yet, I liked to sleep outdoors.

I felt sort of funny about Dad and Lesley, I guess. After all, Dad was kind of old for all that lovey-dovey stuff, wasn't he? He was forty-six, after all. I hoped that he would act his age and not embarrass me by acting all silly and gross. God! Parents could be so embarrassing at times.

I looked at Lesley. How old was she, anyway? I studied her for a second or two. I'd say she's younger than my dad, at any rate. Maybe in her late 30's? Could be a little older? It's not that I had anything against the woman, but I liked things just the way they were. There wasn't any room in our lives for someone else. Besides, Tessie had Jeb, and now Kay had Joe, so if my dad had Lesley, who was left for me? OK, I know that doesn't make any sense, but that was what I was thinking as I stood there that night. But this wasn't about twosomes, it was about my family, and for now, I wanted to hang on to just the five of us, the way we were, even Kay.

Tessie and Jeb were setting out the coffee things on the table in front of the couch when Tessie looked up and noticed me standing there, and she waved me over. I felt better. It is always nice to be included. I still felt sort of isolated from them, as if by standing off and observing them, I had somehow detached myself from the group. And afterwards there was a feeling of loneliness in not being able to reattach myself. I wasn't sure why I felt like that. In the past year or two, ever so often a cloud of grayness would descend over me, and I'd feel disconnected and sullen over nothing and everything. Tessie said it happens to all teens. But I knew I wasn't a typical American teenager.

I didn't have a group of friends my own age and I didn't hang out with other teenagers. Home-schooling and living at the campground made it difficult to meet the town kids who attended school in Bartlett or Conway.

When I talked to Tessie about how weird I felt, Tessie just said it was all a part of growing up. She said your teen years were kind of like an emotional version of those growing pains I used to feel in my shins and ankles when I was younger. I knew what Tessie meant, though. I was already developing a woman's body; heck, I already started having my period and really it didn't turn out to be that big of a deal.

Besides I'd watched Kay go through it all, hadn't I? Everyone had! Let's face it; Kay couldn't shut up about herself. She seemed to think every bra size, every inch she added to her figure, were matters of public concern or celebration. I rolled my eyes at the memory. But I'm not Kay. No. And I will never be like Kay. I never really wanted to be. But on the other hand, who does that make me? Who would I turn out to be? That was the question.

I went and sat next to Jeb, and he automatically put his arm around me. He's good like that. It's one of the things I love about him. I curled up into his embrace and stared into the fire.

Kevin and Joe started talking about their hike and Jeb and Dad quizzed them about trail angels – people who left food and treats along the trail for the thru-hikers – and in turn, Jeb and

Dad talked about the sights that they remembered from their own hike. I could see Dad leaning towards Joe and Kevin as he listened to them talk about their hike and I suddenly longed to feel a real part of it all. Just wait until I hike the AT myself! I will stop here, too, just like the other thru-hikers. I could imagine my dad's face as I told my own stories from my trail adventures. He would be impressed, admiring, envious, even. I couldn't wait! For as much as I hated all the changes in growing up, I couldn't wait to actually be all grown up. How weird is that?

I looked over at my father and saw his hand resting on the couch behind Lesley. Jeb noticed me looking and he shrugged and then he smiled at me. He seemed to think it was a good thing for Dad to be interested in Lesley. But Lesley was with that jerky Todd fellow, wasn't she? I wondered again what Lesley saw in that guy?

"Scoot over, you two," Tessie said, nudging Jeb.

He smiled at her and pushed me a little to make room for Tessie. Tessie looked over at Dad and Lesley and exchanged a glance with Jeb. I saw it, but I couldn't read anything in the look. Instead, I turned and looked into the fire and lost myself in the gray smoke as it curled and twisted in on itself and then disappeared up the chimney.

Tomorrow I would check out the root cellar and see if I could uncover some big mystery. If those CCC guys had actually lost anything, I was going to find it. Maybe it wasn't as big a deal as hiking the AT, but it would be nice to get everyone's attention for a little while.

I looked again at Jeb and saw that he was staring into the fire now, too. It was funny how fires were so mesmerizing. I wondered what Jeb was thinking about. He had a sort of somber look to his face. He must be remembering something, but what?

After a while, the conversation lagged and there were intervals of quiet as the fire warmed us and made all of us feel content and sleepy. Eventually, Kay and Joe wandered out to the kitchen and didn't return, and Kevin said his goodnights a short while later and headed up to the loft bunkroom. The evening grew late, and Tessie nudged me awake and nodded her head towards the staircase. I groaned and got up.

"She's one tired kid," I heard Lesley say as I climbed the stairs. I heard a small thump as she set down her mug. "I should head back to my campsite, too. Todd must be wondering what happened to me."

Dad said, "If he found his way back from the store, you mean?" I smiled at that.

Lesley responded evenly, "Yeah, he doesn't belong out here, does he? I admit that I read him all wrong. I had no idea he would be so uncomfortable in the outdoors."

"Where'd you meet him?" Tessie asked politely. I paused outside my door and listened curiously for Lesley's answer.

"Oh, it was sort of a blind date. He's a friend of a friend, I guess you'd say."

"Have you dated him long?" Tessie asked with interest.

"A month or two, but the dates have been mostly double dates with our mutual friend and her husband, so..."

"You didn't really get a chance to get to know him?" Tessie finished for her.

"Well, it seemed like we were talking all the time, but apparently neither of us was doing much listening." I heard Lesley chuckle. "It's sort of embarrassing, given what I do for a living..."

"What do you mean?" Tessie asked. "What is it you do for a living?" I waited for the answer, too.

"You won't believe me," Lesley said, and I could hear the smile in her voice.

"What?" Tessie responded. I didn't have to look to know she was leaning in towards Lesley. She had a way of showing interest with her whole body.

"I'm a psychic," Lesley answered.

Tessie giggled. "Oh, that's what you meant about 'reading' him wrong."

"You're kidding, right?" Dad said with a snort.

Lesley replied with as much dignity as she could muster. "No, actually, Alex, I'm not. People come to me or call me on the phone, or now, they email me with questions about themselves and their futures. If I sense anything, I tell them."

Dad asked. "That's it?" He didn't sound impressed.

"Well, I charge them an arm and a leg for it, of course," she added, and everyone laughed. I smiled a little at that, too. She did seem to have a sense of humor about it, at least.

"And they don't mind paying you?" Dad asked.

"Of course, they don't." Lesley sounded slightly offended.

"What do you charge?" Jeb asked with obvious curiosity.

"Well, that depends. When I first started doing this sort of thing, I was in college, and I did readings for free for my roommates and friends. But then when they started referring their friends and acquaintances to me, it got sort of ridiculous. I found myself swamped with calls, so I started charging for my services, more as a way to get rid of them than to make any real money off them."

"Did it work?" Tessie asked. "Getting rid of them, I mean?"

"Some, but the ones who were serious, who thought I was sensing something true about them, were willing to pay me pretty much whatever I asked, and it gave me some much needed spending money. I stopped doing readings after I graduated; you know, when I got a job and got married, and all that."

There was a pause, but then Lesley continued, "After my husband and I divorced, he wasn't very reliable with the childcare payments, and I had my son to take care of. Oh, it wasn't that he didn't want to take responsibility, but he had moved out to California by then and was struggling for a while. I guess we both were. Anyway, I needed the extra money, so I started doing readings again for a few friends and neighbors. Word got around. And, to make a long story short, I do it full-time now."

"And you make enough to live on?" Tessie asked in wonder.

"Sure. Actually, more than enough. You'd be surprised what people will pay to get a glimpse of their future."

"I bet," Dad said. "So, you just make up a lot of vague stuff and they pay you to make them feel good?"

"No, actually, I don't make up anything, Alex. If I sense something, I tell them. If I don't, I tell them that, too – that I don't know. They don't have to pay me if I don't see anything."

"See?" Tessie repeated. "Do you mean you literally see their future?"

Lesley seemed to relax a bit. "Sometimes. Usually, it's more of a...a knowing...I feel it in my bones, I'd guess you'd say." She made a small laugh.

I heard Jeb chuckle. "If that doesn't beat all!" I didn't have to see him to know he was probably shaking his head.

Dad added, "I can't believe people are so gullible." A comment that made me smile. That's my dad all right; gullible he is not!

"Gullible?" Tessie said in Lesley's defense. "What's wrong with wanting to know what's going to happen? Think how you would prepare yourself if you knew how something was going to turn out ..."

Lesley paused and then said, "I don't know, Tessie. I sort of agree with Alex. I think people trick themselves into thinking they could fix something if they knew what was going to happen. But it doesn't usually work out that way."

"What do you mean?" Tessie asked.

"Well, let's say I told a person that if they continued on the path they're on they will push the person they love away. You would think they might make some changes, wouldn't you? But usually, they don't. They just continue doing what they're doing and when the other person actually does leave them, they congratulate me on how right I was."

"Well, you predicted it, so what changes could they make?" Jeb said.

"But that's the point! The future isn't set in stone, Jeb. It's not just one set path that you have no choice but to follow," Lesley replied earnestly.

"It's not?" Jeb asked in surprise.

"No, of course not! The future is...well, I think it's like you're standing at the hub of a wheel and there are spokes leading out in every direction. Those spokes are your potential future paths. Your decisions, the millions of decisions you make every moment of every day, determine which spokes or paths are available and you choose among them."

"Then what is it you see?" Tessie asked.

"Well, as they move down a spoke, I see where the path could lead, and that's what I tell them."

"But you think it could be changed?" Tessie asked.

"Of course, it can be changed! If you make or don't make a decision anywhere along the way, that will change where you're going to end up. There are choices at every step of the way."

"So, you don't really see the future then, do you?" Dad said after a moment.

"What?" Lesley asked.

"Well, you're not predicting the absolute future; you're just guessing at where they're heading."

"Alex, that's what I'm saying. There is no absolute future. We all make it up as we go along. And as for 'guessing,' I suppose maybe it could be considered an educated guess if I were in on all the details of the person's life, but I'm not. From my side of it, I just respond to what I see and feel after they ask their question; I don't have any great insight into their lives and what's led them up to that point."

"They just ask you something and you think about it and then you tell them what you think will happen to them?" Tessie asked.

"Pretty much. If I sense something, I tell them what I see. Otherwise, I tell them the truth: that I don't know." I could hear the rustle as Lesley stood up. "And now, I really have to get back to my campsite."

"I'll walk with you," Dad said.

"That's not really necessary," Lesley responded demurely.

"Maybe not, but I'd feel better if I did. We have a problem with bears and skunks this time of year."

There was a pause and then Lesley said, "Well, then if you don't mind. Thanks, Alex, I'd welcome your company."

Lesley said goodnight to Jeb and Tessie, and I heard her and Dad leave.

Downstairs I could hear Jeb and Tessie cleaning up. "Bears and skunks, eh?" Jeb said with a chuckle.

"Well, we have had a few roaming around the campground this summer..." Tessie said noncommittally.

"Uh yuh, t'is true 'nough," Jeb said in an exaggerated Yankee accent. I knew he was grinning. "Me thinks Alex is showing some interest in our Ms. Lesley Stanhope."

Tessie responded warmly, "That would be great, wouldn't it?"

Jeb's voice was soft, but I could still hear him. "It has been a while since he showed any interest in a woman, hasn't it?"

"Kathy's been gone for eight years. You know, I never thought he'd stay single this long."

"Yeah, but it's hard to swing a relationship with the girls and all."

"No, it's not the girls. Well, O.K., it's partly the girls, sure, but it's also living on a campground in the middle of nowhere. I never thought he'd stay away from Washington this long."

"Well, his old boss, Barrister, calls every couple of months, but Alex just tells him he won't go back into government security work. He says he doesn't have the heart for it anymore. I have to agree with him there. I don't know if I could go back to it either."

"Do you think he might after the girls are gone...?" Tessie asked.

Jeb answered, "I dunno. Maybe. I don't think he looks that far ahead, to be honest. But what about you, Tess? Do you miss Washington?"

"Sometimes, I do. I always liked the feeling of being close to the action, you know. There's excitement in being in a big city with the restaurants, shopping, and museums. And Washington is hard to beat with the government and decisions being made and the intrigues and all the rest." She nodded and then looked at him for a long second. "But the truth is, I'm pretty happy up here with you and Alex and the girls, too. What about you?"

"I'm content for now, I think," he said and paused. "And for a guy like me, that's about as blissful as it's ever going to get!"

They were quiet for several moments then I heard Tessie ask, "Should we wait up for Kay, do you think?"

Jeb snorted. "I'm not getting into the middle of that can of worms. Leave her to Alex."

I heard Tessie sigh. Sighing was about all anyone did anymore when it came to dealing with my sister, Kay.

They switched off the overhead light and Tessie headed up the stairs just as I slipped into my room. I listened at the door for a couple more minutes and I heard Tessie ask Jeb, "Are you coming to bed?"

He answered from somewhere downstairs. "In a little while. I'll walk around the lodge one last time. Night, Tess."

"Don't be long, OK?"

"Wait up for me."

I closed my door softly. There was a small nightlight above the desk that provided just enough light to change into my favorite sleep shirt. I looked over at Kay's neatly made bed. Where in the world was she? Still with Joe? Dad would go through the roof if he knew.

It's amazing to me when I think back over those days that Kay was the one doing all the irresponsible things, and yet I was the one who got blamed for Melanie's disappearance.

EIGHT

Treasure Hunt in the Root Cellar

August 2006
Wilderness Campground, Crawford Notch, NH

*** Angie ***

I was up earlier than usual on Thursday morning. Six wasn't as early as my father and Jeb got up; they were usually up between five and five-thirty. Nor was it as early as Tessie, who was invariably in the kitchen by five-forty-five each morning no matter what the season. But six was definitely early for me. I normally liked to sleep in until at least seven-thirty, and even later in the winter if I could get away with it.

But that day I had to baby-sit Melanie and I was hoping to get the chance to dig around in the root cellar before the little girl and her mother arrived. However, that idea got sidetracked when I looked up from my breakfast to see Jeb standing on the other side of the screen door.

"Hey Angie, could you come help me clean up around the trash dumpster?" Jeb said through the screen. "We had a visitor last night."

"Raccoon?" I asked sleepily.

"Nah, looks like maybe a bear. Could be that big one is back again," he said.

"Where's Dad?"

"He went to check around the campsites to make sure none of the campers had any furry visitors last night. But, just between you and me, I think he's checking on that woman, Lesley Stanhope. Bring the broom from the pantry when you come."

"All right. I'm right behind you," I said. I went to the pantry and grabbed the outdoors broom. The bristles were worn and dirty, but still serviceable.

I went around the corner to the side of the building behind the laundry/clean up area and saw the strewn garbage. It was always disgusting and smelly when animals got into the trash and in a campground, it happened pretty often in the summers especially when the campground was full. As I got closer, I saw the circle of tracks. They definitely looked like bear tracks; even I could see that.

"Someone forgot to latch the top again, huh?" I said as I began sweeping the garbage towards the dumpster.

"Maybe," Jeb said. "Or maybe this bear has figured out how the latch works. I think we need to put a bigger one on it with some kind of metal pin stuck through the latch. This bear is way too smart." He shook his head. "Ewwwww. What a stench!"

I grimaced and nodded. "So why is Dad checking on this Lesley woman?"

"Apparently, her boyfriend, Todd, went for beer last night and never came back."

"You're kidding!" I snickered. "Why'd he do that?"

"Who knows? He wasn't much of a camper. I think that was obvious at dinner. Anyway, when Todd didn't come back to the lodge last night, your Dad walked Lesley back to her campsite. That's when they discovered that Todd was gone, and he'd taken all his clothes and things with him. He obviously wasn't planning to return."

"But how's Lesley going to get back home to Boston? Didn't they drive up together in Todd's car?"

"Yeah. What a jerk, eh? She may have to get a car rental in North Conway, or more likely your dad will help her out."

I wondered about that. If Lesley had wanted to spend more time with my dad, she couldn't have planned things to work out any better. "So, Jeb, what do you think is going on with Dad and Lesley, then?" I decided I might as well ask him straight out.

Jeb stopped and looked at me, then started picking up the big stuff and throwing it into the open dumpster. "I'm not sure. Maybe nothing. It's been a while since he seemed interested in the opposite sex. Fact is, since your mother died, I haven't seen a woman that's turned his head much."

"Excepting now, you mean?" I asked.

"Except FOR now," Jeb corrected and nodded. "But let's wait and see, Angel. Could be it'll just peter out on its own. Give them some space, OK? If we all start pressing him, he may go and do something he'll regret."

"Like marrying her?" I ventured.

He frowned at me. "No; I meant like letting her get away."

I was silent as I continued to sweep. Jeb's comment got me to wondering if maybe my dad could get serious about Lesley, after all. I admit that I hoped not. I looked up at Jeb. "You gonna shovel this stuff back in?"

"Yeah. Just sweep it towards me."

We worked in silence for several more minutes.

"OK, Angel. Thanks for your help. You can get to searching your root cellar now. I'll finish up here."

I grinned. "How'd you know that's where I was going?"

"You seemed pretty anxious to check it out last night. To be honest, I thought you'd get up a lot earlier this morning."

"Nah. I didn't want to go down there when it was still dark out."

"Why? Scared of ghosts?" he teased.

"No. Mice. I hate the way they jump out at you. It gives me the willies." I shivered at the thought.

"Yeah. Don't like them much myself. And I've seen some big ones around this garbage dumpster." As he saw me glance around anxiously, he grinned and added, "Not this morning, though."

"That's good," I said as I turned away. "I'll let you know if I find anything interesting."

"Just don't make too big a mess."

"Now you sound like Dad!" I said over my shoulder.

I returned the broom to the pantry and saw by the clock over the doorway that it was already a quarter past seven. I was running out of time. I'd better get moving.

I grabbed one of the bigger flashlights from the top of the refrigerator and clicked it on and off to test it. I flipped on the light to the cellar as I closed the door behind me and trudged down the rickety steps that led to the dark cellar below.

Down in the cellar, it was cool and moist, although the air smelled stale. There was a single bulb dangling from a foot of electrical cord out of a hole in the ceiling near the furnace. The cellar floor was packed dirt, but as smooth and hard as a cement floor after being tamped down by decades of people walking on it. The ceiling was low, maybe six feet or so, not much more. My dad and Jeb had to walk hunched over when they came down. But no one came down very often anymore. Why would they? We didn't keep much of anything down here. Once we built the garage outbuilding, all the tools and campground equipment were kept there. It was more convenient, right next to the lodge and not far from the woodshed and was tall enough so that my father and Jeb didn't have to worry about hitting their heads going in and out; a big plus.

As I got closer to the furnace, I flicked on the flashlight and pointed it into the blackness beyond. It took a minute before my eyes adjusted to the darkness. Slowly I walked past the hulking brown furnace, ducking under its vents and pipes. The stone foundation of the massive fireplace was just ahead. It had old stonework and bricks at its base, then it rose up through the ceiling to form the double-flue chimney of the grand fireplace in the lodge above.

I flashed the light ahead of me just past the fireplace. It was then that I noticed the dark opening. I crept up to it and saw that the ceiling was even lower here; apparently the crawl space that Jeb had mentioned. I stopped and flashed the light through the opening and saw that there were two steps going down into a small room. So, this must be the root cellar! I skimmed the light along the floor, mostly looking for mice, but also to gauge the size of the space.

It was a small room with the doorway opening and two steps down on one side and built in shelves, literally dug into the walls, on the other. I took the steps one at a time and stopped at the bottom. It was cold in here, and the change in temperature suddenly gave me the creeps. I flashed the light along the floor again, but didn't see anything interesting, just dirt and old cobwebs.

I paused to listen. The furnace was humming behind me, and there was creaking sounds coming from somewhere above, probably someone walking around. Perhaps my sister, Kay, was up. Or maybe it was Jeb.

I shone the light along the dirt floor again. It took a while to scan the entire floor, even though it wasn't that large. I worked slowly and methodically; that was the way a real archeologist would work. I didn't want to miss anything. I squatted down to get a closer look as I moved the small circle of light along the dirt surface. The floor wasn't quite as smooth here as in the rest of the cellar. Certainly, it had less traffic. I picked up a small stone, then a dried, almost petrified leaf of some sort. There didn't appear to be much here, I had to admit. I let the leaf drop back to the floor.

I stood up slowly, stretching my legs and feeling the stiffness in my knees. Idly, I shined the flashlight along the dusty shelves. All were built at or below my eye level. For the lower ones, I had to stoop to peer along their surfaces.

And that was when I saw it. There was a bump in the wall behind the lower shelf. If it hadn't been for the shadows cast by the flashlight, I might never have noticed it. Excited, I knelt down and shined the flashlight directly at it. I couldn't tell if it was a stone lodged in the wall or something else. I scratched away some of the dirt with my fingernail. Whatever it was, it seemed to be hard but smooth. It could be a rock, but maybe not.

I leaned in closer and put the light right next to the bump. Immediately I could see that it wasn't a rock! It was brownish in color, but not like dirt or rock, more like...like shiny cardboard? I dug at it some more, but the surrounding wall was as hard as cement. I'd have to get a shovel, or maybe even a hammer and chisel. I leaned back on my haunches and stared at the bump. This was something. I felt the hair rise on the back of my neck and I rubbed at it absentmindedly. I didn't know what exactly it was, but it was definitely something. I just knew it.

"Angie, you down there?" Tessie called from the cellar door upstairs. She sounded far away, like she was hollering down a well shaft. The words even echoed a bit.

"Yeah," I said as I stood up and brushed myself off. "I'm down here. I'll be right up."

Tessie watched me as I climbed the stairs. "You are sure growing up," she said with a slight shake of her head, like she had suddenly just noticed. "So did you find anything interesting down there?" she asked.

"I'm not sure," I said, "but I think so." I could feel a growing excitement as I described what I'd seen. It's funny how it becomes more real when you share it with someone else. "There's something stuck in the wall behind one of the lower shelves in the root cellar. But I couldn't tell what it was." I reached over and turned off the cellar light and the cellar and stairs behind me were plunged into darkness.

"You sure it's not a stone or maybe even the brace for the shelf?" Tessie asked as she walked with me through the kitchen.

"A brace?" I stopped and looked at her. I hadn't thought of that. "If it was a brace, what would it be made out of do you think?"

"Hmmm." Tessie tapped her lip as she considered. "Wood, probably, depending on when it was built. If it was quite a long time ago, it might even be made of fieldstone or the smooth river stones."

"No, I don't think it's that big. But I'm not really sure. I want to dig it out and see."

"Well, be careful about digging. You don't want the shelves to cave in on you." Tessie looked at me for several seconds. "On second thought, maybe I should have Jeb or your dad take a look at it, just to be sure it's nothing dangerous."

"Aw, come on, Tessie," I said. Immediately, I realized I'd have to put off my investigating until either one of them had the chance to come down and take a look. Let's face it, this wouldn't be high on their priority list, and with the campground filling for the weekend, they probably wouldn't have the time. "I swear I'll be careful. I promise!" I pleaded.

Tessie looked doubtful, but she knew as I did, that Jeb or Dad probably wouldn't get around to looking at the root cellar anytime soon, certainly not today. "OK, but right now you have Melanie and her mother waiting for you in the front hall. You didn't forget about babysitting today, did you?"

"No, I didn't forget. I just didn't think it would be so early."

"Early? It's nearly nine o'clock," Tessie said, looking down at her watch.

"Really? Nine? Wow, I was down in the cellar that long?" My, how time flies, and all that.

Tessie and I walked together into the main room of the lodge, but then Tessie continued on upstairs to the office while I went over to Mrs. Jacobs and Melanie. They were waiting just inside the open front door. Melanie clutched her stuffed bear by its stubby little arm and stood staring at the floor as she glumly held her mother's hand.

"Hi, Melanie," I said in a cheerful voice. I saw that this could go either way. She could throw a tantrum, or she might give in peacefully. We'd just have to wait and see how it played out.

"Hi," Melanie answered softly, without raising her eyes. Well, at least, she was speaking to me; that was a start.

"She's not happy about being left behind, I'm afraid," Nora Jacobs said to me.

Boy, that was obvious. "Oh, we'll find plenty to do to keep her busy," I said as optimistically as possible to Mrs. Jacobs. "She'll be glad she stayed here with me by the time you get back."

"Well, I hope so, Angie. She had a good time with you the other day when you babysat her, didn't you, Mellie?" she said looking down at her glum-faced four-year-old. Then Nora Jacobs turned back to me. "Here's a lunch I packed for her. Melanie is sort of picky about what she'll eat." Nora handed me a small backpack covered with the picture of a cute little bear princess and a sparkly castle. I don't know if I mentioned it already, but the kid was bear-crazy. "Melanie's jacket is inside, and there's room to put her teddy bear in it later on if she gets tired of carrying him around."

I nodded. "Don't worry about anything, Mrs. Jacobs. And have a good time today. It looks like the weather's going to be nice for your hike."

"A little warm, I think," Nora said dubiously.

"Nice and cool up on top, though," I added.

"Yes, well. Good luck, Angie." She smiled and then knelt in front of Melanie so she could look her in the eye. "Be good for Angie, honey. Daddy and Mommy will be back this afternoon, after your nap, OK?" She took the child in her arms, but I could see that Melanie was stiffly refusing her mother's affections. Big crocodile tears sprung up in the little girl's eyes and got caught in her dark eyelashes. It would've been adorable if it weren't so pathetic.

"Now, don't cry, Mellie," her mother said, wiping away a tear from her daughter's cheek with her thumb.

"You better just leave," I said, knowing that in a few minutes this could escalate into a tantrum if Mrs. Jacobs didn't get away quickly.

"Yes, you're right," Nora said sounding a little relieved. She stood up once more. "Bye-bye. I'll see you both later. Have fun, Mel."

She hurried through the open door and jogged down the camp road towards the Jacobs' campsite not far away, apparently deciding it was better not to look back.

Melanie sobbed as she realized her mother was leaving and the sobs grew louder when she saw that her mother wasn't going to turn and come back for her. "Mommy!" she shrieked. But to my surprise, she didn't try to follow. She just pathetically put her little arms in the air and then dropped them in a forlorn gesture of defeat. Again, it was adorable, but also pathetic.

I took the little girl's hand and led her into the kitchen. Melanie gave little sign of resistance. I laid the backpack on the center island counter.

"You hungry right now, Melanie?" I asked softly. I knew food was always a good distracter.

Melanie shook her head. She wiped at her nose with the back of her sleeve.

I went over to the desk and took a tissue from the tissue box and wiped the little girl's face. "There, that's better." I smiled brightly at her. I stood looking down at the Melanie while she stared at the floor, her chin trembling and her bottom lip jutting out. "Hey, I know! Do you and your bear want to go on a treasure hunt?" I had an inspired idea if I could talk her into it.

Melanie glanced up at me, looked at her bear for a second and then shrugged her shoulders.

I walked over to the cellar door and flipped on the light. "Come on, I'll show you."

Melanie stood at the top of the cellar stairs and her eyes widened as she stared down into the relative darkness below. OK, I know my intentions probably seem a bit self-centered, but it was worth a try, wasn't it?

I leaned over and whispered, "Don't worry, Melanie, your bear might be a little afraid, but we'll take care of him, won't we?" I took her hand and guided her down the cellar steps. When we reached the bottom step, I glanced down at Melanie who was now huddled up next to me hugging her bear tightly to her chest. Her eyes were as wide as saucers.

"Is your bear scared?" I asked.

Melanie nodded very firmly and squeezed her eyes shut. She held on to my hand but wouldn't budge.

I looked at her for several long seconds then sighed. This wasn't going to work. "Oh, well. I'll have to do this another time, then," I said aloud. I glanced around one last time then led Melanie back up the stairs. "Well, we could go back to the woodshed. It's not that scary in there. We could pretend it's our little house in the woods." It was my Plan B.

Melanie looked relieved when we got to the top of the steps and back into the kitchen again. "Brownie no like it down there," the little girl said quietly pointing down the steps.

"Yeah, I know. It's OK. We're going to take the bear someplace else to look for treasure."

"What's treasure?" Melanie asked.

"Anything that's valuable. Here, let me show you what I found yesterday," I said. I pulled the nickel from my back pocket and handed it to the little girl.

Melanie took it and squeezed the bear against her chest so that she could hold the coin with the thumb and index fingers of both hands. She looked at it closely and then smiled a shy little smile of delight.

"It's a buffalo head nickel from 1937," I said. I pointed to the back. "See the buffalo?"

Melanie nodded. "Can I have it?"

I shook my head, "No, it's mine," I replied, but seeing the gloomy look on her face reappear, I added, "But you could hold it for me for a while. Would you like that?"

Melanie smiled again and nodded. "I won't lose it. I'll be careful," she added solemnly.

I grinned. "OK, you hang on to it for me. Let me grab a couple of flashlights and the shovel from the pantry and then we're off. Treasure hunting! Maybe we can find an old nickel for you to keep!"

Melanie followed me into the pantry and watched me get the shovel, then followed right behind me through the kitchen as I took the small flashlight from the top of the refrigerator and retrieved the one I'd used that morning from the table where I'd left it.

Melanie stopped when we got to the door. "I gotta go potty." Her eyes were squinted, and her mouth screwed into a tight grimace.

I looked at her for a second then had to laugh. "OK. Good timing," I said. "Come on. There's a bathroom right through here." I led Melanie back through the swinging door and into the dining area. Just to the left was another door that was hard to see because it was set flush with the wall. I opened it. Inside was a tiny powder room with just a toilet and sink. I flipped on the light. "Here it is, Melanie. Do you need some help?"

Melanie shook her head. She carefully placed the bear down on the edge of the sink and placed the nickel in his lap then turned and closed the door. I could hear shuffling noises and after a while there was the sound of flushing and water running.

Melanie opened the door and smiled up at me. "All done," she said proudly. She had the bear under her arm and the nickel cupped in her hands once again.

"Do you have any pockets?" I asked, looking closely at the little girl's clothes.

Melanie looked down at her overalls and then nodded. "I think so."

"Let's put the nickel in one of them, so you don't lose it. OK?"

Melanie watched as I took the nickel out of her hand and shoved it deep into her side pocket. She looked up at me and smiled again. I handed her the small flashlight, which she took greedily. She flicked it on and off over and over again as we walked out the back door and across the clean-up area and around the lodge to the woodshed. I had the shovel and the larger flashlight. I thought through what I wanted to accomplish. I'd rather be in the cellar digging at whatever it was in the wall down there, but I'd get back to that later. Besides, I did want to look in the woodshed again. There could be more coins or even something else in there. That was the beauty of treasure hunting, wasn't it? You never knew what you might find.

At the door, I propped the shovel against the side of the shed and unlatched the lock. I opened the door, staring in for several seconds before stepping inside. I took one of the logs and placed it up against the door to hold it open as I had done the day before. "There," I said with satisfaction. "That should hold pretty well."

Melanie watched me as I carried logs of wood out of the shed and set them in a stack beside the outside wall. Melanie flicked the flashlight on and off, making the light dance against the wall of the shed. She giggled and pointed at it. Well, at least she seemed happy enough, I thought.

"Hey, you're giving us a real light show, aren't you?" I said. I stepped into the shed. "Come on, Melanie. Come and see what's in here." I turned on my flashlight and aimed the beam at the floor. The ground was covered with wood chips, pieces of dried up old leaves, and twigs.

"What's here?" Melanie asked, staying very close to me as she followed.

"Well, I found that nickel in here yesterday," I said.

"Is there another one for my bear?" Melanie asked.

"There might be. I don't know. We'll have to look and see." I squatted down along the back wall, where I had found the nickel. I aimed the beam of light along the ground, sweeping the wood chips and pine needles away with my hand. Melanie squatted next to me in imitation, but she grew bored almost immediately and started moving her flashlight around so that the beam squiggled crazily along the ceiling and walls. There were huge cobwebs covering most of the corners and hanging down from the rafters, and she aimed the light at them and studied them.

We heard an engine turn over and get revved up once or twice. It must be Jeb leaving, I thought. I turned and looked at Melanie who had stopped bouncing the flashlight to listen intently to the engine outside. I wondered if the little girl knew what the engine meant: that her parents were leaving now. But Melanie just stared at the floor seeming to be deep in thought.

I crawled along the floor sweeping my free hand lightly over the ground.

"Brownie has to go potty," Melanie said, tapping me on the shoulder.

"You just went," I said incredulously.

"But my bear Brownie's gotta go this time," Melanie said more determinedly.

I sighed. "Oh, all right." I stood up and dusted off the knees of my jeans.

Melanie was already out of the woodshed and headed back towards the lodge.

"Wait up," I said, but that seemed to make her move even more quickly. Maybe she has diarrhea or something, I thought. "I'll be there in a minute, Melanie," I hollered at her retreating figure. I turned to pick up the shovel when I heard the honk of a horn. I looked up and saw that a van with a camper had pulled up in front of the lodge. I waved and headed over to the vehicle.

I could see there were a man and woman in the front with several small children in the back of the van; one was an infant strapped into a car seat.

"Hey!" the man said in greeting.

"Hello," I said as I came alongside the van's window.

"You have any vacancies? We're looking for a campsite, just for overnight. We'll be leaving tomorrow. We're on our way to Maine."

"As long as you're out by noon. We're filled for the weekend, but most of the weekend campers won't be showing up until late tomorrow afternoon."

"Sounds good to us," the man said jovially, smiling at his wife. He switched off the engine and climbed out of the van.

I led him inside. I looked around and wondered where everyone was. "Tessie? Dad?" I called out. There was no answer. I shrugged and turned back to the man. "Well, I guess I'll have to check you in." I pulled a registration form from the desk and handed it to him. "You need to fill this out. I'll need the license number on your vehicles, too."

"Oh gee," the man said. "Could you go out and check the camper's? I don't have it memorized," he added apologetically.

I nodded and jogged out to the van. "Have to check the license plate numbers," I said by way of explanation to the woman in the car, who was now in the back, taking the baby out of its car seat. The other two children were giggling in the rear seat.

I walked around the vehicles and stopped to write down the license plate numbers. When I was done, I returned to the lodge. The man was just finishing up and handed me the registration form.

"Mr. and Mrs. Glenn Fairfield?" I read from the form.

"And entourage," he added with a chuckle.

"Great! Everything looks fine here," I said. I handed him a map and circled the campsite, number 7. This is a good site. It has water and electricity."

"That sounds perfect. Can we take a look at it?"

"Sure," I said and showed him on the map how to get to it. "You just continue past the lodge and take the first left at the bathhouse. It's the second site on the left. The numbers are nailed to a tree at the entrance of the sites. You can't miss it."

"Fine."

"Now, I also have a Fish & Game Department brochure to give you with advice on keeping wild critters away. We have raccoons and bears around here that can be a real nuisance. They come looking for food, so you should always store your food securely where the bears can't get it and bag up your trash and bring it down to the dumpster behind the lodge before you go to bed in the evening," I said as authoritatively as possible, but I could see he wasn't impressed. I wished these tourists would take the bears more seriously. I'd seen the damage they could do to a tent or camper. "Anyway, if you have any questions, let us know."

"Sounds great," he said.

"Oh, we have bundles of wood for sale, if you need it for your fire. And, if you want dinner at the lodge, you have to notify us by one in the afternoon. Dinner is usually served at 6:30 p.m. and we just add the cost of it to the bill."

"No kidding, you have a restaurant here?" he asked looking around.

"Well, no, it's just that we rent out bunk space in the lodge to hikers and we provide them with dinner as a part of the deal. We didn't think it was fair not to offer the dinner option to our other campers, too; so, we do. We get one or two takers on most nights. You know, people who are tired of cooking over a campfire, or who forgot to bring their pots and pans."

"Ain't that something?" the man said with a shake of his head. "No, I don't think we'll need dinner, but it's nice to know it's there if we did. That's quite a nice service."

"Thanks," I said, although I wasn't sure what I was thanking him for exactly.

"Well, if that's it, I'll take this map and round up my family to set up camp. Thanks for your help."

I nodded and smiled, and then I walked him to the door. I returned to the desk and sat down on the stool to enter the registration form information into the computer and mark campsite number 7 as "reserved", the way my dad had shown me to do. Finally, I sat back satisfied. I glanced at the wall clock and saw that it was already ten-thirty. It had taken me nearly a half hour to check them in. That passage of time, as it turned out, would prove important later on.

I went back outside and watched as the Fairfield's van moved slowly down the driveway towards their campsite. I'd put them right next to Lesley Stanhope's campsite. We'll see how she likes little children and babies, I thought with a moment of glee. Maybe she'll decide to leave a little sooner.

NINE

Melanie is Missing

August 2006
Wilderness Campground, Crawford Notch, NH

*** Angie ***

I got back to the woodshed and saw that it was just as I'd left it. The door was still open with the log leaning against it. My shovel was there too, leaning up against the side of the shed. I saw my flashlight on the ground next to the shovel. I picked it up, flicked it on and entered the shed, shining the beam along the floor again. Then suddenly a panicked thought flashed across my mind. Melanie! Where was Melanie? She hadn't come back from the bathroom. That was odd. I had just been in the lodge and realized that I hadn't seen the little girl at all.

I glanced at my watch and realized that Melanie had gone to the bathroom more than forty-five minutes ago. Suddenly, I had an empty feeling in the pit of my stomach. I walked quickly over to the lodge. Kevin, Joe's hiking companion, was sitting in the kitchen at the center island.

"Hey," he said in greeting.

"Hi, Kevin," I replied. "Have you seen Melanie? The little girl that was at dinner last night?"

"Nope, the only one that's been around here this morning was Lesley. She was here a couple of minutes ago looking for your dad. Other than her, it's been pretty quiet."

"Where is everyone, anyway?"

"Well, my buddy, Joe, and your sister, Kay, went for a hike up to the ponds. I think they're going for a swim. Tessie left a while ago, heading down to the camp bathrooms. She said they needed toilet paper. Jeb took off for Littleton a while ago and I haven't seen your father. And me? I'm sitting here trying to get up the motivation to clean out and repack my backpack that's sitting out there," he pointed with his thumb over his shoulder towards the back door.

I smiled. "You're the message man today, huh?"

"We each have our parts to play in this life," he replied with mock seriousness. He stood up and stretched. "And now I'm really going to go out there and attack my pack." He paused. "Hey, that rhymes... 'attack my pack', get it?" He chuckled as he went out the backdoor.

I shook my head, then again remembered Melanie. I went into the dining room and knocked on the bathroom door. No answer. I opened it. It was empty, not that I had really expected her to be in there, but I had to check it, didn't I?

I went back to the woodshed and walked around it, looking in the bushes and behind a boulder, hoping the little girl might be hiding there. "Melanie?" I called in a loud voice. There was no answer. "Melanie?" I shouted even louder.

I wondered if the little girl might have walked back to the Jacobs' campsite. Yes, that's probably what I would do if I were her. Plus, I was running out of ideas. I took off down the road leading to the Jacobs' campsite, number 12, one of the furthest from the lodge. I went past the double site that Jeb and I had cleaned up the day before. Then I passed site 15 on my left. There was a small blue dome tent next to the picnic table, but no one appeared to be around. The site belonged to a man and his eleven-year-old son who were in the mountains for a week to camp and hike. They left early most mornings. I hadn't even talked to them except to nod when they drove past in the late afternoon as they returned from one of their hikes. They kept to themselves.

I continued walking and finally came to campsite 12. It was at the end of the cul-de-sac for this stretch of campsites. The Jacobs had a large two-room tent and there was a huge blue rain tarp stretched over the tent and picnic table. The fireplace had a grill on it, but it looked like it hadn't been used this morning. "Melanie?" I called out. "Are you here?"

There was no answer. Even the chirping crickets were quiet.

"Melanie?" I called a little louder.

I unzipped the tent and entered. It was stuffy inside and I could see the three sleeping bags lined up in a row in the center of the far room. The flaps between the rooms were tied off to the sides, so the two-room tent was a single open area. The Jacobs' clothes and towels were in several organized piles towards the front of the tent. It felt odd being in their tent like that, like I was invading their privacy. I looked around and not seeing the little girl, I quickly stepped back out of the tent and zipped the screen flap and the outer flap back the way they had been.

"Melanie?" I called again.

I turned and headed back to the lodge. Now what? What if the little girl had wandered off? My heart started beating harder. I began to jog. It seemed to take forever to get back to the lodge and when I finally arrived, I was breathing hard.

Tessie saw me and waved. "Hey, where are you going in such a hurry?" she asked, coming over to me just as I reached the lodge.

"Tessie, I can't find Melanie!" I said out of breath.

"What?" Tessie replied in alarm. "What do you mean you can't find her?"

"I mean I don't know where she is," I panted. "We were in the woodshed, and she had to go to the bathroom. I walked her over to the lodge. Some campers showed up and I got all involved registering them, and..." the words came out in a rush, and I couldn't seem to catch my breath.

"Slow down, Angie," Tessie said, putting her arms around my shoulders. "Here, sit down," Tessie said pointing to the steps in front of the lodge. "Now, take a slow deep breath."

I felt like I had just run a marathon. My lungs were bursting, and my heart pounded wildly inside my chest. But I knew it had nothing to do with jogging back to the lodge. It was quite simple and devastating. I had lost Melanie and like a stroke of lightning, I realized that it was all my fault.

TEN

Searching for Melanie

August 2006
Wilderness Campground, Crawford Notch, NH

*** Angie ***

It didn't take long for Tessie to organize a small search party. She and I started searching the campground, going from campsite to campsite, looking in bushes and behind trees and boulders, and calling Melanie's name. Tessie found Dad at Lesley's campsite and when he heard what had happened, he and Lesley joined the search, too. After an hour of fruitless looking, we all met back in the lodge kitchen. Tessie made sandwiches as the five of us — Dad, Lesley, Kevin, Tessie, and me — discussed what to do next.

"Let's go through this again, Angie," Dad said. "The last time you saw Melanie she was headed for the lodge to go to the bathroom, right?" he asked as gently as he could. He could see I was pretty close to tears.

I nodded.

"Did she get to the lodge? Did you actually see her go inside?"

I shook my head. Then I cleared my throat. "The Fairfields drove up and I went over to talk to them. I thought she went into the lodge, but I don't know for sure if she did. I saw her heading around towards the back door. That's all."

"OK. When you went into the lodge with Mr. Fairfield, you would've been able to see the powder room from the desk. Did you see her or hear anything?"

I shook my head. "No. Nothing."

He turned to Kevin. "Where were you when all this was happening?"

Kevin thought for a minute. "Probably in the shower in the clean-up area. I went in just after Jeb left and I heard the Fairfields' van pull away when I came out. I went back up to the loft room to put my stuff away and get my pack because I wanted to bring it down to clean it out and repack it. I brought it down and then came in here to the kitchen. Lesley was in here looking for you, Alex. Lesley left and that's when Angie showed up asking me if I'd seen Melanie."

"Lesley? Did you see Melanie when you were in here?" Dad asked, turning to Lesley.

She shook her head, "No, she wasn't in the kitchen when I was here. I only saw Kevin," she said nodding at Kevin.

"Angie, what time did you last see Melanie?" Dad asked.

Tessie set the sandwiches on the center island counter and Kevin and Lesley each took a half sandwich from the pile and began eating. Tessie went to the refrigerator and pulled out the pitcher of iced tea. She brought it over to the counter and set it down, returning with a stack of cups.

"I think it was around quarter to ten maybe," I said hesitantly. "If Jeb left with the Jacobs at nine-thirty, it couldn't have been more than fifteen or twenty minutes later when she said she had to go to the bathroom. I remember looking at Melanie when we heard the Jeep's engine. I wanted to see if she realized that her parents were leaving."

"Did she?" Tessie asked, looking up with interest.

"Yeah, I think so. She seemed to get really quiet for a second. But she didn't cry or anything." I reached for a sandwich and took a bite but set it down after a moment. I really wasn't hungry. Then I thought about Melanie. She would probably be getting hungry about now, too. Her mother had made her a lunch, I remembered. I glanced around then jumped up. "Hey! Where's her little backpack?"

"What backpack?" Dad asked with interest.

"Mrs. Jacobs packed a lunch and stuff in a little backpack for Melanie. We left it right here on the counter." I looked under the counter and glanced around the room.

Alex turned to Kevin. "You said you were sitting here earlier. Was there a kid's backpack here then?"

Kevin thought back then shook his head. "Nope. I'm pretty sure there wasn't. I'm certain I would have noticed it."

Lesley looked at my dad, "I didn't see it either, Alex. That means she probably came in and got it and..."

He nodded and their eyes met as he finished her thought, "... and she's gone for a hike."

"Oh my God!" Tessie said, her hand flying up to cover her mouth.

I'm sure I turned pale because I felt suddenly light-headed. "Her parents are going to kill me when they get back and find her gone," I said glumly. But "glumly" doesn't begin to describe how really horrible I felt at that moment.

Dad stood up. "I'm going to call the authorities. We're pretty sure she's not at the campground, which means she's gone off into the woods. I doubt she'll get too far, but she's been gone nearly two hours now and we're going to need help to find her before nightfall. I'll call the New Hampshire Fish and Game. They should be able to organize something quickly."

Kevin stood up. "Alex, I'm going to hike up to the ponds and get Joe and Kay so they can help look for her, too. Plus, I can look for Melanie on the way."

"Good idea," Dad said.

"Can I go with you?" I asked.

"No, Angie," Dad said, "I need you and Tessie and Lesley to walk up some of the other trails. And someone should walk to the highway and back to make sure she didn't go that way...."

"I'll do that," Tessie volunteered. She grabbed another half of a sandwich and hurried out the back door.

"We need to go up the river trail. You know the one that follows the stream, Angie, up past the Jacobs' campsite."

I nodded.

Lesley spoke up, "I can take that one, Alex."

"O.K., but Angie should go with you. It'd be better to double up so no one else ends up missing. Angie knows the trail pretty well."

I was going to object, but I couldn't think of a single good reason, other than simply not wanting to go with Lesley. Finally, I nodded. "OK, I'll go," I agreed less than enthusiastically.

Dad misread my subdued voice, though, because he said, "Angie, I'm not blaming you for this. Melanie was a stubborn little girl, and she obviously was determined to go hiking today." He squeezed my shoulders.

"I know, Dad. But it's still my fault. I was the one babysitting her."

Lesley stood up. "Well then, let's get going and find her before her parents get back."

That thought made me feel better. I followed Lesley to the door. I heard my father's voice on the phone behind me reporting Melanie's disappearance. A wave of guilt washed over me, and I felt really terrible again. The door slammed behind me, and I had to hurry to catch up with Lesley.

She slowed so I could fall in step beside her. We walked in silence for several minutes. When we got to the camp bathhouse where the camp road splits, Lesley halted and turned to me, "Angie, I want to get my pack and canteen from my campsite. Would you like to come with me or wait here?"

"I'll wait," I said, not meeting her eyes.

Lesley hesitated for only a second, and then she hurried away. I sank down in the shade of the oak tree next to the entrance to the men's side of the bathhouse. I closed my eyes and tried to imagine what Melanie might have been thinking this morning. I wished I'd listened to her more closely. But all I was thinking about this morning was searching the cellar and the woodshed for treasure.

We should've stayed in the cellar. Melanie wouldn't have heard the jeep leaving and she might not have gotten the idea to take off. Plus, I probably would've dug that thing out of the wall by now, too. Of course, Melanie might still have taken off, I reminded myself bleakly.

Lesley returned in a few minutes. "I packed a small blanket, too."

"A blanket?" I looked at her blankly.

"Melanie could be hurt. We might have to carry her out...."

I blinked. I hadn't thought of that. What if Melanie was hurt? That was one more thing to worry about. We started up the road, past the campsites that I had searched earlier.

We were quiet for a couple of minutes then Lesley said, "Angie, I can tell that you think I'm no good at this outdoor stuff, but I'm actually pretty handy in an emergency. My father was a fireman, and my mother was a nurse. I know my way around first aid."

I looked over at her. "Well, I'm sort of hoping we won't need any first aid."

"I know; me, too," she agreed quickly. "But it's always better to be prepared."

I led the way past the last campsite. "This is the Jacobs' campsite," I said, pointing. "The path over here runs from the camp road to the stream. Then it meets up with another path that follows the stream for about a mile or so. It's a little grown over in places, and there are no trail blazes to follow, so you have to watch where you're going. When you get a ways down, there's a place where the stream is shallow this time of year. It's filled with rocks and small boulders. That's where we cross, and the path climbs a bit into some rocky ledges. The ledges are as far as anyone goes, normally."

"Does the trail go further?"

"Yeah, but it's almost like bushwhacking. There's a small deer path that follows the ridge around Mt. Tremont. That's the name of this mountain." I pointed vaguely behind her. "It meets up with the Mt. Tremont Trail. The Mt. Tremont Trail goes to the top of

Tremont and then on to Owl's Cliff. But before you get to Owl's Cliff there's a small cut-off. It you take it, you'll eventually come out at the Sawyer Ponds. You know, the ponds where Kevin went to find Kay and Joe."

"I'm impressed. You do seem to know the trails around here pretty well. Have you hiked this trail all the way to the ponds by yourself?"

"Oh, yeah. Dozens of times," I said airily.

"When was the last time?" Lesley asked pointedly.

I glanced at her and after a moment shrugged. "I don't know, last summer, I think."

"So, then it may have changed? It may even be overgrown completely?"

I shrugged again, trying not to show my annoyance at being quizzed. "It could be, but I doubt it. These trails don't disappear that quickly. I've been on some that probably haven't been used in years and years, and you can still make out where the trail is."

Lesley studied my face for a second. "Maybe," she replied noncommittally.

It was a warm day, and I broke out in a sweat after the short hike to the stream where we stopped. Lesley scanned the bank, which was littered with rocks, large and small. There was an entire tree, from leafy branches down to its huge mass of roots, lying along the other shore, perhaps struck by lightning from a recent summer thunderstorm.

"What do you think?" Lesley asked.

I looked around and saw the path leading off to my left along the stream bank. "The trail is over that way," I said, pointing.

"No, I mean, do you think Melanie came up this way? We haven't seen any signs of her at all. Do you think she would try to cross the stream here?" Lesley pointed across the stream, which was fairly shallow and could easily be traversed by jumping from stone to stone.

"She may have come up this path, but I doubt she tried to cross here," I said.

"Why?"

"Well, the water is really noisy — hear it? — and moving fast out there in the middle, even though it isn't really very deep. Melanie's only four. I think she would've hesitated — it might sound scary to her — and with that big tree blocking the other bank, I don't think she would've tried going across. Besides, she wanted to go hiking, not swimming."

Lesley nodded approvingly. "You're probably right. I keep forgetting how little she is. This would've looked pretty wide and deep to her."

I felt proud of myself. "Ready?" I asked, pointing to the trail.

"Sure. Let's go," Lesley said with a smile.

ELEVEN

Holding Down the Fort

August 2006
Wilderness Campground, Crawford Notch, NH

*** *Tessie* ***

Back at the campground, the place was coming to life, as if from slumber as many serious-faced men and women began to arrive at the lodge. Tessie set up the big coffee urn in the dining room, as police with radios, forest service rangers, and search-and-rescue volunteers arrived and set up their command center in the lodge. They laid out huge topographic maps onto the tables in the dining room and talked into the radios to people who were already branching out on foot to search the surrounding trails.

Search dogs had been called in and the dog-handlers asked for some of Melanie's clothing to give the search dogs her scent. Tessie went down to the Jacobs' campsite and searched for the little pink t-shirt with the purple and fuchsia teddy bears on the front that she remembered Melanie wearing to dinner at the lodge the night before. She felt odd entering the Jacobs' tent, though, and searching through their piles of clothing. Luckily, she found the t-shirt quickly and hurried back to the lodge to hand it over to one of the searchers.

If all the search and rescue vehicles clogging the camp road weren't enough, the campground's normal influx of campers also began to arrive during the afternoon. Thank goodness it was Thursday and not Friday afternoon, was all Alex could think with a shake of his head. He gave up a silent prayer that Melanie would be found quickly so that all these cars and trucks would be gone before his normal weekend camper traffic started pouring in, adding to the confusion and the work.

Unfortunately, there was no good news all afternoon. The dogs arrived and were set to work. They had picked up Melanie's scent almost immediately, or seemed to, but they grew confused as soon as they reached the stream, where they lost the scent. A cadre of searchers trudged up and down the stream bank, morbidly looking for Melanie's body, figuring that she may have fallen in and drowned. But they found nothing, which was both good news and bad news – good that she wasn't found dead, but bad because that meant that she was still missing.

When Jeb got back mid-afternoon, he stood flabbergasted for several minutes trying to take in the changes at the campground. He stared at all the vehicles lining the camp road until he saw Tessie come out of the lodge and he hurried over to her.

"What in the world is going on here?" he asked.

"It's Melanie Jacobs. She's lost," Tessie answered tersely.

"Are the Jacobs back from hiking yet?" Jeb asked with a worried frown.

She shook her head. "We have been hoping that we'll find her before they get back."

"Who are all these people, Tess?" Jeb asked, looking around in wonder.

"Search and Rescue, police, a fire department or two, volunteers, you name it and they're here. They must've put the word out on the police scanner, because we've had people coming in to help look for her all afternoon."

"Jesus, this is unbelievable!" Jeb shook his head.

Tessie took his arm. "Jeb, listen. I think you should go to the trailhead and wait for the Jacobs. I don't think they should hear about this from total strangers."

He nodded, feeling a lump in his throat, as he thought about having to tell them that their little girl was missing. "How did it happen? How did she get lost?"

Tessie's mouth grew tight. "Angie was babysitting her. Melanie had to go to the bathroom just when some campers arrived to be checked in and Angie lost track of her. We're guessing that Melanie had already decided to follow her parents hiking, because she took her little backpack that was in the kitchen with her lunch and stuff Nora had packed for her. Of course, she might have seen it lying on the counter and got the idea to leave on the spur of the moment. Who really knows?" her voice trailed off.

"Poor Angie," Jeb said. "Where is she?"

"Looking for Melanie. She and Lesley set out around lunchtime to look down the stream trail. They're not back yet."

Jeb shook his head again. "All right. Tell Alex I've gone to the trailhead to wait for the Jacobs. Unless they've changed their minds, they will be coming out at the Webster Cliff Trail off Route 302, so that's where I'm going to wait for them. I've got the car phone in the jeep, so if you need to get a hold of me, you've got the number. Call if you get any word at all about the little girl, OK?"

She smiled. "I promise I will. Now go."

Tessie spent the next hour alternately pacing the front porch of the lodge and going inside to take care of the million tasks that now all seemed to be resting on her slim shoulders. There were campers arriving to be checked in, and volunteers with a thousand questions about what was going on, and she had to answer the lodge phone, which was suddenly ringing off the hook. She also tried to keep the coffee urn filled and handed out iced tea and filled water bottles for the searchers. She knew it was the community waking up to the emergency and responding as best it could, so although she was exhausted, she found it a comfort.

She was surprised and relieved when she looked up to see Jeb's jeep stopping in front of the lodge a while later. Her heart tightened in her chest when she caught sight of the Jacobs. Nora was hunched over in the backseat and Tessie could see when Nora glanced up that her face was streaked with tears; in the front passenger seat, Keith looked equally pale and drawn, his lips a tight thin line. Tessie went to the jeep and when Nora stepped out, she instinctively reached out and encircled the woman in her arms. The gesture of sympathy acted like a release of a dam and Nora broke down sobbing.

"No word then?" Keith asked seeing Tessie's somber face.

Tessie shook her head. "Come on in. You can talk to the search-and-rescue commander. His name is Stockman, uh...Jerry, I think his first name is. Yes, Jerry Stockman."

Tessie released the sobbing woman as Keith put his arm around Nora's shoulders and she let herself be led into the lodge.

Alex looked up from a map laid out on one of the tables as they entered. He stood up and tapped another man on the shoulder. The other fellow — tall, steel gray hair, and massively built — held a walkie-talkie to his ear. Alex mouthed the words "father" and pointed to Keith. The other man nodded and said something into the transmitter and then pushed it into a slot on his belt. He and Alex weaved their way through the throng of people surrounding the map-strewn tables.

"Mr. Jacobs? I'm Jerry Stockman. I'm heading up the search-and-rescue mission looking for your little girl."

They shook hands.

"This is all....all so.... I'm sorry, Mr. Stockman..."

"Please, call me 'Jerry'..."

"Jerry, this whole thing is just such a shock to my wife and me. Jeb just told us about Melanie being missing in the jeep on the way over here."

"No need to apologize, Mr. Jacobs..."

"Keith."

"No need to apologize, Keith. I understand how overwhelming this must be for you. I want you to know, though, that we're going to find that little girl of yours." He paused. "But, to do that we need some information about her, things that might help us to find her..." Stockman turned to Alex. "Is there someplace we could go that's a little quieter? More private?"

Alex nodded. "Sure, the office is just up the stairs. First door on the right. Come on, we can go up there."

Tessie touched Nora's arm. "Can I get you something, Nora? A glass of iced tea? A drink of water? Something to eat, maybe? Anything?"

Nora started to shake her head but stopped. "Actually, yes, a glass of iced tea would be nice. I think I'm a little dehydrated from the hike." She smiled almost apologetically.

Tessie smiled back and nodded. "Coming right up. And I'll get one for Keith, too." She was glad to have something to do for them. She felt so useless in the face of their fear and anxiety.

Nora followed her husband, Alex, and Stockman up the stairs to the office. They all went in, and they closed the door behind them.

*** *Jeb* ***

Jeb followed Tessie to the kitchen. "Tess?"

"Huh?" she asked distractedly as she scurried around getting the iced tea and some cookies for the group in the office upstairs.

"I think we should keep Angie away from the Jacobs until things settle down a little. They're bound to blame her and I'm sure she feels terrible enough."

She stopped and looked at him and smiled. "I was thinking the same thing," she said. "Do you want to watch for her? Maybe catch her before she comes inside?"

"Actually, I was thinking of hiking up and coming back with her. It will give me a chance to talk to her."

Tessie nodded. "Don't forget that Lesley's with her."

"Oh, yeah, actually I did forget," Jeb said. "But that's OK. She'll understand. She has a kid."

Tessie glanced at him. "She does? How do you know that?"

"Alex told me. Apparently, she's divorced and her son – he's eighteen, I think – moved out to California to live with her ex."

"Hmmm, I do sort of remember her mentioning being divorced." She shook her head. "Actually, I didn't figure her for the mother of an eighteen-year-old, though. She looks too young," Tessie said as she put the iced tea pitcher, glasses, and plate of cookies on the tray. "So, her son doesn't live with her, though, huh?"

"No, apparently not. But if my mother was a psychic, I think I'd hightail it for California, too." Jeb grinned.

Tessie chuckled. "Come on, she's not that bad."

"No, she's not," Jeb agreed. "I just don't get the whole psychic reading thing. It's sort of a weird occupation, don't you think?"

"Well, keep your thoughts to yourself," Tessie advised. "I think Alex likes her."

He snorted. "Think? Heck, I KNOW Alex likes her."

She looked at him quizzically. "Why? Did he say something to you?"

"Not in so many words. But you saw him last night..." He raised his eyebrows significantly. "...and he didn't come back from her campsite until way past two...if at all..."

Tessie's eyes widened. "Really? You think he...they...Oh boy, this could get serious, huh?"

Jeb nodded. "We'll see. I hope he's not moving too fast, though."

"Yes," Tessie said thoughtfully. "With Angie and Kay, things could get touchy." She nodded at the door, "Could you hold the door open for me?"

Jeb pushed the door open, and said as she passed by, "I'll see you later."

"All right. Be careful out there, OK?"

Jeb looked at her and grinned. "Aren't I always?"

Tessie smiled and headed across the busy room towards the stairs. Jeb stopped at the pantry and took a water bottle from the shelf. He filled it at the sink. As he was heading out the back door, he noticed the cellar door was opened a crack and he pulled it closed as he went by. It gave him an idea. He knew what he'd do with Angie when they got back. He'd help her in the cellar with her treasure hunting. That would keep her mind off of Melanie and away from Melanie's parents until they came to grips with the situation. Would they ever come to grips with it if she weren't found, though? He blew a soundless whistle through his teeth as the back door closed behind him.

Someone would locate the little girl, he reassured himself. She was only four, how far could she have gone? Probably not too far, right? And once she was found everyone would be so relieved that they would forget that it might be Angie's neglect that led to Melanie getting lost in the first place. Heck, even if Angie had been to blame, she was only thirteen — a child herself really — he wasn't going to let her get hurt by all of this.

TWELVE

Day 1 of the Search (Jeb)

August 2006
Crawford Notch, NH

*** Jeb ***

Jeb headed down the camp road towards the stream trail. Now he just needed to catch up with Angie and Lesley. He passed the Jacobs' campsite and was soon in the canopy of the woods. He listened to the buzz of insects, the chirping crickets, and the call of birds as they swooped from tree to tree in the sheltering branches above him. He heard the scurrying of a red squirrel in the underbrush, or maybe it was a chipmunk. He wasn't certain. He stopped when he reached the stream and listened again. He held very still and realized that it had grown very quiet. The crickets had even stopped chirping. A second or two passed then two men came out of the woods along the path.

"Hey," Jeb said softly to alert them to his presence.

They looked startled by his sudden appearance but recovered quickly.

"Looking for the little girl?" one of the asked.

"Yeah, I'm Jeb Wilcox. I'm part-owner of the campground."

"Too bad about the lost kid," the other one said.

"Yes, it is. Listen, I'm looking for a woman and a teenage girl who hiked up this trail earlier. Have you seen them?"

Both of the men shook their heads as one drank from his canteen while the other one mopped at his forehead.

"Didn't see anyone at all, as a matter of fact," said the one with the handkerchief.

"How far up did you two go?" Jeb asked.

"To the Tremont trail. We didn't pass anyone."

Jeb nodded. He realized that Angie and Lesley must have gone all the way to Sawyer Pond. That left him with a choice: he could go back and take the Sawyer River Trail to the ponds, or he could bushwhack over the western slopes of Mt. Tremont. It was steep, but he could shave an hour off the hiking time, he was sure.

"We're going to report back in. You coming back our way?"

"No," Jeb said. "I'm going to cross the stream here and search up that way," he said, pointing across the stream.

The two men scanned the other bank. "She might've gone over there, for sure, but don't you think it would've been a bit tricky for her to climb over that downed tree?"

Jeb nodded, "Yeah, you might be right. But I'm going to look just to be sure. Be a shame if she was there and we never looked, don't you think?"

The other two nodded. "All right, then. We'll let them know at the lodge where you're headed."

"Thanks. See you later."

They waved and turned to continue on the path back to the lodge that Jeb had come up. Jeb hopped from rock to rock across the stream. He leapt to the trunk of the fallen tree on the other side and scanned the woods beyond. After a moment he saw the deer trail he was looking for. He pulled his compass from deep inside his jean pocket and held still to read it. He looked up at the sun, down at the compass, and then up at the ridge of open rocks he could just make out between the trees. He hopped off the tree trunk and started up the trail. He kept his compass in his right hand and glanced at it every so often to keep himself on course, triangulating off the ridgeline.

Occasionally he stopped and listened to the woods around him. He thought about Melanie and tried to bring her face into his mind. He wanted to get a sense of her, a kind of gut reaction as to whether she had ever been on this trail. He closed his eyes and after a minute opened them again. No, he couldn't explain it, but he was positive she wasn't around here. And yet, the stream path was the one closest to the Jacobs' campsite. Wasn't it the most likely trail for her to follow? He turned the thought over in his mind as he headed over the shoulder of Mt. Tremont to the ponds. What would a four-year-old do? That was the question.

He hiked quickly and quietly. He had learned to move easily in the woods. His childhood hiking the Montana and Idaho mountains and his special services training in the Marines had served him well.

He heard them long before he could see them. In the distance he could hear Angie calling, "Mel-lan-nie!" in a kind of three-syllable singsong.

When he got closer, he shouted, "Angie!" just once.

"Jeb?" she answered with a mixture of relief and questioning in her voice.

"Be right there," he called back.

In a minute he stepped off the overgrown path and onto a wide trail. He soon saw Angie and Lesley coming towards him. They looked beat. Sweat beads traced soggy rivulets down the sides of their faces. Lesley's short dark hair was wet with sweat and her bangs looked black where they were damp and stuck to her forehead. Angie had pulled her light brown hair into a kind of loose bun with her elastic. She looked just as hot and sweaty as Lesley, more so even.

"You look mighty hot, babe," Jeb said as he gave Angie a quick hug. "You should've gone for a dip back at the ponds to cool off."

Angie smiled and shook her head, "Didn't have time. We came around Tremont from the stream path." She was panting slightly.

"Yeah, I figured. I cut across from there to catch up with you."

"Any word yet about Melanie?" Lesley asked hopefully. She slid the backpack from her shoulders and dropped it on the ground. The back of her shirt was soaked, and the outline of her bra left a weird dry pattern stretched across the middle of her back. She reached into the pack and pulled out her water bottle. It was one of those large double-quart ones, but Jeb could see it was nearly empty.

"No, not a sign of her," Jeb said. "Let's rest here a minute." He dropped down into a squat and leaned against a boulder at the side of the trail. He took his water bottle from its holder on his belt and unscrewed the top. He handed it to Angie. "Here, Angel, take a drink."

Angie dropped down next to him and took the bottle from him. "What a day!" she said with a tired sigh. She tilted up the bottle and drank thirstily.

Lesley sat on top of the boulder, just behind them. "What's happening back at the lodge?" she asked.

"Well, there's about a million search-and-rescue people there. I mean they are everywhere! It's a madhouse." He shook his head.

"No kidding?" Angie said with interest. "And what's Dad doing?"

"Directing traffic, I think."

Angie chuckled. "Yeah, right!"

"He and Tessie are trying to keep things under control. There's some guy, Jerry Stockman, heading up the search teams. I think he's from Fish and Game. Seems like a real take-charge kind of guy."

"What about media?" Lesley asked.

Jeb turned to look at her. "Media? What do you mean?"

"Well, once the word gets out, the media's bound to show up. This is a great human interest story — little girl lost in the woods...."

Jeb struck his forehead. "God, you're absolutely right. Those vultures are sure to show up. I wish I'd thought to warn Alex and Tessie."

"You guys should be getting your story straight, if you want my advice."

"What story?" Jeb asked her.

"Who, what, where, when...why....you know the drill," Lesley said with a wave of her hand.

"Actually, I never knew there was a 'drill.'" Jeb said dryly. He studied her for a minute. "How come you know so much about this sort of thing?" he asked.

Lesley smiled tiredly, as if recalling another lifetime. "One of my specialties, back before I started doing psychic readings full time, was media public relations. You know, spin control." She grimaced. "I used to go into companies and help them come up with plausible stories to cover up their mistakes," she chuckled, "or at least that's what it seemed like sometimes!"

Jeb shook his head slowly. "That sounds like a nightmare job, if you ask me."

"Yeah, it was, but it paid well, and I was a single mother trying to pay the rent," Lesley finished wryly.

THIRTEEN

Day 1 of the Search (Angie)

August 2006
Crawford Notch, NH

*** Angie ***

Angie was too tired to say anything. She just listened to Lesley and Jeb talk and the words ebbed and flowed over her, soothingly, but the meanings barely sunk in. She couldn't imagine the scene Jeb described back at the lodge. She wished she could just stay out here on the trail and not have to go back. If only they had found Melanie quickly. Why hadn't they found her yet anyway? She was a little girl. How far could she have gone?

Thinking of Melanie gave her thoughts urgency and a surge of adrenalin. Angie stood up. "We'd better get going," she said.

"Yeah, you're right," Jeb agreed as he slowly got up, too.

Lesley stood and put on her backpack. Angie watched her and had to admit the older woman didn't look half as tired as she herself felt. In fact, Lesley seemed to have a reserve of stamina that she'd barely tapped into. Angie took a deep breath and heard her stomach rumble. She realized that she was also hungry. She thought back and remembered that she hadn't eaten lunch, just a single bite of a sandwich. No wonder she felt so beat.

"Do you have anything to eat, Jeb?" she asked.

He shook his head, "Nope." He felt in his pockets, "I have some gum. Want a piece?"

She nodded and took the stick of gum he handed her. He handed one to Lesley, too.

"Thanks," Lesley said. "I should've thought to bring some food along. But we left in such a hurry."

They hiked down the trail in silence for a while. It wasn't long before they arrived at Sawyer River Road, an old fire road. It was wide enough that they could walk three abreast, with the women on either side of Jeb.

"Angie, you want to talk about this whole deal?" Jeb asked finally.

She looked over at him and grimaced. "I don't know how it happened, Jeb. One minute Melanie and I were in the woodshed, and she was saying she had to go to the bathroom then the next minute she was gone."

"Did she actually go to the bathroom?"

"I don't know. The last I saw of her, she was heading towards the lodge, but then the Fairfields—some new campers—drove up. It was Kay's turn to do check-in, but she wasn't around, of course," she added with a disgusted look before continuing. "Anyway, since I seemed to be the only one there, I had to check them in. When I got done with them, I went back to the woodshed, but Melanie wasn't there. That's when I started looking for her."

Jeb nodded as he listened intently. "Do you think she planned to run away?"

Angie thought for several moments. "I don't know. She was sad, crying a little when her mother dropped her off this morning. And she looked kind of...I don't know...quiet when we heard you drive off..."

"You heard us drive away?" he asked with growing interest.

She nodded. "I looked at her to see what kind of reaction she would have. I thought maybe she would say something, or cry, or – I don't know – react somehow."

"But she didn't react?" Lesley asked.

Angie shook her head. "No. It was odd. She just got very quiet. Then a little while later she said she had to go to the bathroom.... and, you know, that was sort of weird, too," Angie added.

"Why weird?" Jeb asked.

"Because she'd just gone to the bathroom maybe a half an hour before, when we'd first started to leave the lodge to go to the woodshed. I showed her where the bathroom in the dining room was and waited outside the door until she was done. I can't believe she had to go again so soon."

They walked in silence for a while as the three of them thought about the events of the morning.

"What about her backpack?" Jeb asked.

Angie's head jerked up as she looked at him. "How'd you know about that?"

"Tessie mentioned it. Do you remember what was in it?"

"Her lunch. Mrs. Jacobs said Melanie was a picky eater, so she'd made her a lunch. She also said she'd put a jacket in it. I didn't notice the jacket, but I did see a change of clothes when I looked in it. And there was room in it for her to store her teddy bear."

"What about water?"

Angie thought for a minute, then shook her head, "Maybe, but I don't think so. I mean, there could've been a drink in with the lunch, but I didn't see one. And I think if there had been one, Mrs. Jacob would've asked me to store it in the refrigerator until lunch time."

Lesley nodded her head, "That's probably true. Besides, she packed her a lunch because she was a picky eater. She'd probably figured you'd offer her something to drink for lunch."

Jeb agreed. "Well, it sounds like she won't be hungry until tonight, if she ate that lunch. And she may or may not get thirsty. She has a change of clothes and a jacket, so if it occurs to her, she could put them all on to stay warm."

"How cold is it supposed to be tonight?" Lesley asked.

Jeb glanced at her and said grimly, "Not below freezing. Around 50 degrees, I think. But it'll feel really cold to a four-year-old."

Lesley nodded.

Angie thought about Melanie lost and cold in the dark woods. She squeezed her eyes shut to get rid of the image of the four-year-old huddling against a tree in the dark, shivering. She nearly tripped.

"You OK, Angel?" Jeb asked as he caught her by the arm.

"Yeah," Angie replied. "I just don't know what I'll do if anything happens to her."

"Angie, people get lost and survive out here all the time. You know that. It's too soon to give in to those kinds of thought," Jeb reassured her.

"I know, Jeb, but she's only four."

"Let's think positively, O.K.? We're going to find her. It's just a matter of time."

Yes, Angie thought bleakly, time.

FOURTEEN

Return to the Campground

August 2006
Wilderness Campground, Crawford Notch, NH

*** *Lesley* ***

It was late afternoon when Angie, Jeb, and Lesley trudged back into the campground. From a distance, they could see the communications antennas on the tops of several vans, with radio and TV logos brightly painted on their sides. Lesley had been right. The media had indeed arrived. This would be a sensational story regardless of whether the little girl was found alive or not.

Lesley skirted the crowd of searchers, reporters, and the merely curious who had heard about the missing child. She went directly to her campsite to change out of her sweat-stained clothes and hoped to get a quick shower at the bathhouse. She was so glad that Todd was no longer around. He was a jerk. She could see that now. How had they ever ended up camping together? she wondered.

Alex Jackson was nice. She smiled and felt a warm tingle inside; that was something she hadn't felt in a very long time. Still, he had two daughters: and teenagers, to boot. That should give a person pause, she thought wryly.

*** Jeb ***

While Lesley was changing at her campsite, Jeb and Angie headed around to the rear of the lodge. Jeb had decided to slip Angie in the back way. He knew she wasn't prepared to meet the reporters nor the Jacobs, face to face. They hurried up the back stairs from the kitchen and into the loft. Thankfully, it was empty.

There was a line of bunks down one side of the room, with some cots recently set up along the other wall. They could see the pile of Kevin and Joe's gear around the bunk at the far end of the room near the window.

From the loft, they slipped unnoticed through to the upstairs hallway by way of a small door in the back of a closet that linked the loft to the family's side of the upstairs.

The little door was designed to be used as an additional exit in case of fire but was all but forgotten lying as it did at the back of the linen closet. When they were younger, Angie and Kay used to pretend it was the magical wardrobe from the *Chronicles of Narnia*. They were probably the only ones to use the linen closet access in order to get out of the lodge without going through the main area.

Angie headed for her room to change, and Jeb went downstairs to find Tessie and Alex. After scanning the crowd in the dining room, he finally spied Tessie near the swinging door to the kitchen and waved to her. Then he spied Alex near one of the tables talking animatedly to Jerry Stockman.

Alex looked up from the table where Stockman was pointing out search sectors on the map in front of them.

"Hey," Alex said to Jeb with a nod. "Meet me in the office in a couple of minutes. We've got to talk."

Jeb nodded and turned to go back up the stairs. He made no eye contact with the reporters who were strutting around the room with their microphones held before them like holy chalices. An entourage of cameramen lugging heavy mobile video equipment on their shoulders followed the reporters. Jeb took the last couple of stairs two at a time.

Alex and Tessie joined him in the office a short while later.

"No luck, huh?" Jeb said to Alex, in what was both a question and comment. Jeb was sitting behind the office desk, silently rocking the chair back and forth, as he watched Alex and Tessie through his long fingers linked together in front of him, forming a sort of pyramid.

Alex shook his head and sank into one of the two chairs in front of the desk. Tessie waved off his nod for her to take the other chair. Instead, she leaned against the wall next to the door, her arms folded comfortably below her chest.

You saw all the radio and TV reporters?" Alex asked Jeb.

"Yeah," Jeb replied. "Lesley predicted they'd be here sooner or later."

"Lesley? Where'd you see her? Is she back, too?"

"Yeah. I hiked from the stream trail across Mt. Tremont to the Sawyer Pond and caught up with Lesley and Angie there."

"How's Angie doing?" Tessie interrupted.

Jeb glanced over at her, "Feeling lousy and responsible for the whole thing, as you'd expect. I brought her in through the loft and told her to stay out of sight until dinner."

Alex nodded. "Good thinking. Those media fellows will grill her until they make it look like she lost Melanie on purpose."

Jeb grimaced and shook his head. "Alex, we can't let them talk to her."

"I don't know how we're going to prevent it," Tessie said wearily. "I mean as soon as the Jacobs mention her name, they're going to want to talk to her."

Jeb got an idea. "I wonder if Lesley can help us with this."

Alex looked interested. "Lesley? What do you mean? How could she help?"

"Well, on the walk back she said she used to do media relations consulting for big corporations. You know, helping them protect their asses when they screwed up...."

"No kidding!" Tessie interjected. "She's certainly a lady of many talents!" she said with a grin, then added, "She might know just what to say to them."

"I hate to get her involved," Alex said hesitantly. "This could turn into a real circus..."

Jeb and Tessie exchanged glances. Jeb stopped rocking his chair and leaned forward. "Alex, look around. It's already a circus. We'd be dumb not to make use of her if she's willing. She says she's done this stuff before. She knows how to handle those vultures. We sure don't. If she can figure out how to protect Angie, then I say we don't have a choice!"

"Alex, we could at least ask her," Tessie said more moderately.

Alex looked from one to the other. "All right. I'll ask her. But if she doesn't want to, we're not going to pressure her into it, agreed?"

Jeb and Tessie nodded, looking relieved.

There was a knock at the door and all three looked guiltily at each other, like junior high kids who'd been caught smoking in the bathroom.

Tessie opened the door a crack and saw Lesley standing there. She swung the door open wide. "Come on in." she said with a slight bow.

"Hi. Sorry to bother you, but they said Alex and Jeb were up here...."

Tessie smiled and nodded. "Funny, but we were just talking about you."

Lesley stepped inside and Tessie closed the door behind her.

"Alex," Lesley said, "I came to offer you my help." Jeb and Alex exchanged surprised glances.

Lesley looked from one to the other, "What?"

Tessie grinned at her. "Boy, that psychic stuff really works!" she said with a laugh.

Alex stood up and smiled at her, too. "We were just talking about asking you if you would help us. That's all. We don't know much about dealing with the press."

"And we'd really like to protect Angie from them," Jeb added.

Lesley nodded. "That was my thought, as well. They'll chew her up and spit her out."

"That's what we're afraid of," Alex said glumly.

"O.K., then let's get started," Lesley said as she sat in the chair opposite Alex. He sat down, too. "The first thing we need to do is to come up with our version of what transpired this morning; you know, how Melanie ended up lost in the woods. Then we need to agree on what and how much Angie should say. When we're ready, we'll coach her on what to say and then go down and set up a meeting with the press, on our terms."

"Coach her?" Tessie repeated suspiciously. "Isn't the truth good enough?"

Lesley smiled. "Of course, she should tell the truth. You'd think that would be enough, wouldn't you?" She shrugged. "But we need to plug up all the gaps, answer every question before it's asked. They will be looking for a bad guy, someone to blame. It makes their story more powerful that way. We need to make certain they don't pick Angie to play the scapegoat."

"Lesley, what about you personally? Do you believe that Angie is to blame?" Tessie asked her quietly.

Lesley glanced over at Tessie in surprise. "Does it matter what I believe?"

"Well," Tessie said with a nod. "I think it does."

Lesley eyed Tessie for several seconds. "Angie said that Melanie took off when she was busy checking in some new campers. I believe her. I think that Melanie wanted to get back at her parents for leaving her, in her own little girl way. She very definitely wanted to go with them. I was there last night at dinner, remember? I saw the tantrum she threw."

Alex and Jeb both looked relieved.

Tessie smiled warmly. "Good." Then she added, "I can't speak for Alex and Jeb, but for myself, I feel better that you believe Angie is not to blame for Melanie being lost."

"I understand," Lesley said. "But you know, this all comes down to perception and viewpoint. I'm sure the Jacobs feel differently than you or me. I know I'd want someone to blame if Melanie were my child and I'd left Angie in charge of her. After all, when all is said and done, she was the person responsible for Melanie when she disappeared."

Alex glanced out the window behind Jeb. It would be sunset in another hour or so. "Damn! I wished we'd found her this afternoon. That little girl is out there in the woods somewhere and she's probably going to be out there all night. Poor little kid."

"Are they going to continue searching tonight?" Jeb asked.

Alex nodded. "Jerry's started splitting the volunteers into groups and has established four-hour search shifts. I offered the bunks in the loft to as many as can fit. And I'm turning over one of the RV sites and the grounds around the lodge for any tents they might want to pitch. It could get nutty around here if they don't find her quickly, though."

"Yeah, don't forget the campground is booked solid this weekend," Tessie said.

Alex nodded. "And next weekend is Labor Day weekend. You know what that's going to be like. Labor Day Weekend's been booked up since April."

"Well, we'll make sure you get some sympathy and good press for the campground, too. No sense in throwing away a good PR opportunity," Lesley said.

Alex shook his head. "Thanks, but I'm not sure I want the attention."

"Well, my advice is for you to stay in control of what's being said, so that you don't end up with negative press. You really don't want that. You can't leave any wiggle room for the media to fill in the blanks on their own. We don't want them speculating and coming up with really off-the-wall ideas."

Alex looked at her. "All right. You obviously know what you're doing. I'll gladly leave the media to you."

"Good, then let's get to it. First, we need to prepare Angie for an interview with the press. How about this? The distraught babysitter tells the world how a headstrong four-year old was determined to go hiking after her parents had told her "No." What do you think?"

Jeb and Alex nodded at each other. "OK," Alex said. "That sounds about right. Do you want me to go get Angie?"

"I'll get her for you and send her in here," Tessie said as she moved to open the door. "I've got to go down and check on how my stew is doing. It looks like we may have fifty for dinner."

"Did Jerry get you some help in the kitchen?" Alex asked.

"Yeah, he sent me three cooks. I think they'll work out fine."

"Good."

"I thought I'd set up some dinner for the family in the kitchen," Tessie said. "Is that OK with you?"

"Thanks, Tessie. That sounds great," Alex said. "Now go get Angie, so we can get this media monster off our backs."

Lesley looked at her watch, "Yeah, we're getting close to their story deadlines for the six o'clock news. We want to make sure we control that first report. I'll go down and organize a press conference. We'll set it for — what do you say? — 20 minutes from now? That will give them a half an hour before airtime."

"Airtime?" Jeb repeated softly. "Who would've thought that would be part of our vocabulary, eh, Alex?"

Alex looked grim again, and he just shook his head slowly as Tessie and Lesley left the room. "It's a nightmare, Jeb. And I can't wait to wake up and find it's all been a mistake."

Lesley turned and went downstairs to meet with the reporters while Tessie went down the hallway to Angie's bedroom.

FIFTEEN

The Press Conference

August 2006
Wilderness Campground, Crawford Notch, NH

*** *Angie* ***

My door was closed so Tessie knocked. She was always good about respecting other people's privacy.

"Who is it?" I answered.

"It's Tessie, honey," she said softly.

I opened the door and Tessie came in. We hugged, maybe a second or two longer than usual. "How are you doing?" Tessie asked even though she probably could see the answer plainly enough on my face. Basically, I was tired, hungry and a little depressed and scared, but how do you dump all that onto someone who cares about you?

"I guess they didn't find her yet, huh?" I said quietly.

Tessie shook her head. "Not yet. But they will."

"I sure hope so." Tears sprang to my eyes, but I blinked them back. "Are the Jacobs really mad at me, Tessie?"

Tessie put her arm around my shoulders and sat me down on the edge of Kay's bed. "Honey, of course they're very upset about Melanie being gone. I think they feel a little guilty about leaving her today, especially after they knew how much she wanted to go with them. Remember the tantrum she threw last night at dinner?"

I looked up. "Gee, I had forgotten about that. That's right, isn't it? She really did want to go hiking with them."

"Yes, she did. And we think she ran away when you weren't looking, so she could follow them on their hike."

"Do you really think so?" I asked, feeling slightly better. "She might have thought she could catch up with her parents if she went hiking..." Little by little, it felt like the blame might be shifting from irresponsible teen to willful child and I must admit that I was already feeling slightly better.

Tessie nodded. "That's exactly what I think happened." She reached over and took my hands in hers. "Honey, your dad and Jeb and Lesley are waiting for you in the office. The reporters downstairs want you to tell them what happened this morning and Lesley says she will help you to figure out exactly what to say..."

"No, Tessie, I don't want to talk to any reporters," I said, shaking my head firmly.

"We think you should. And it's better to get it over with right away. Then they'll leave you alone."

"I can't, Tessie....I'd feel so stupid," I said plaintively.

"Of course, you can do it. You're quite a good speaker. And you shouldn't feel stupid. All you have to do is to tell them exactly what happened. Let them know how upset you are, and that you were out searching for her yourself all afternoon..."

I stood up. "Tessie, I really don't want to do this...."

Tessie stood up too, squaring her shoulders to emphasize her full five foot three inches. We were now eye to eye. "I know you don't, honey. But sometimes we all must do things we don't want to do. Come along."

I knew that tone in her voice. Tessie meant business and there was no fighting her now. I meekly followed her down the hallway.

I stopped where the railing overlooked the dining room and looked down at the scene below. It was the first time I'd seen for myself the buzz of activity inside the lodge. I was astounded at how many people were milling around below me. Could this really be the same quiet place I'd left just that morning?

I could see the bright lights following behind the huge TV camera on the shoulder of a burly cameraman. There were maps spread out on the surfaces of the tables and dozens of men and women huddled over the maps, talking and gesturing. And the noise! I couldn't get over the noise of cell phones buzzing, people talking on walkie-talkies pressed up to their mouths, and somewhere the static crackling of what sounded like a police scanner. It was organized pandemonium. I stopped and stared at the scene for several long seconds, trying to take it all in.

Lesley saw me and came up the stairs quickly. She put her arm around my shoulders shielding me before any of the reporters guessed who I might be. She led me, almost pulling me into the office. Tessie was behind us but at the door to the office she quickly turned and went down the stairs, creating a diversion, waving away the reporters when she reached the bottom of the steps.

"Was that the babysitter?" I heard one of them ask her.

I knew how Tessie would handle them. She would look blankly at the reporter, as if she couldn't understand him. That was one advantage to being Asian; I had to give her that. They would have no idea whether she could understand English or not. Tessie would enjoy the deception immensely, and she could keep a straight face better than anyone I knew. She would never let on.

Lesley pushed the office door shut and I turned around to face Jeb and my dad who were sitting on either side of the desk.

Fifteen minutes later, Lesley led us down the stairs. I was directly behind her, then Dad, and finally Jeb bringing up the rear. Jeb immediately drifted into the crowd hoping to find a place down in front so he could provide at least one friendly face in the audience for me to look at.

The news services had cleared a spot at one side of the dining room to hold the press conference. There were three chairs facing the center of the room where the cameras and press people were setting up. In front of the chairs was a small table that was now sprouting microphones of various shapes and sizes and sporting an alphabet soup of call letters.

Lesley sat in one of the chairs and indicated for me to sit in the chair next to her, with my dad on the other side next to me. She leaned forward and spoke into the microphones. "Are you folks ready?" Her voice reverberated through the room. She waited for a signal from the crew from the local New Hampshire TV station since they were the ones who would be running the story on the six o'clock news as a breaking local news headline. She told me in the office earlier that it was only a matter of time before the big national and international news services picked up the story, too. The print media only needed pictures, so Lesley said she was less concerned with them. I didn't like being concerned with any of them personally. My hands were balled up in my lap and I felt like I'd swallowed a lead weight. I tried to take a deep breath, but my chest felt tight. Could a thirteen-year-old have a heart attack, I wondered morosely?

Lesley began by introducing Dad and me. "This is Alex Jackson and his thirteen-year-old daughter, Angie. Mr. Jackson owns the Wilderness Campground here in Crawford Notch. His daughter, Angie, was babysitting the little girl, four-year-old Melanie Jacobs, when she wandered into the woods." She turned to me, "Angie, why don't you tell everyone in your own words what happened here this morning."

I cleared my throat and for a second I just stared out at all the people looking at me. It was very disconcerting to be on this side of the lights and cameras.

"It's OK, honey, just tell them what happened," Dad said softly, taking my hand in his and squeezing it tightly.

I glanced at him, felt slightly better, and nodded. "Um. Let's see. Mrs. Jacobs dropped Melanie off here at the lodge at around nine this morning. She and Mr. Jacobs asked me to baby-sit Melanie while they went hiking." I paused, remembering. "Melanie really wanted to go hiking, too. She cried and carried on last night at dinner when her parents were planning today's hike." I looked around. It was a little easier once I got started talking. I continued, "I thought she'd cry and throw a tantrum when her mother left this morning, too, but she didn't. She just got very, very quiet." I shifted in my seat. "It was a while later — maybe, fifteen or twenty minutes, I think — when Melanie and I went out to the woodshed to play a game. It was then that we heard the jeep leave with her parents. When she heard it, she stopped and got very quiet again. And then a short while later she said she had to go to the bathroom. I started to walk with her back here to the lodge, but just then a camper drove up. I went to check in the people while Melanie came into the lodge alone. And that was the last time I saw her." I glanced down and felt the relief that I had finished telling the story, but at the same time I suddenly felt like bawling. I don't know why. To cover it up, and not knowing what else to do, I said, "I looked everywhere for her. I was so worried. She's only four years old. All I can think about is how scared she must be. I spent the whole afternoon hiking the trails around the campground, yelling her name, hoping she might hear me." It was the truth, but somehow it just felt like I was trying too hard to convince them of how much I cared, and that never feels right. It felt like futile excuses.

The room was silent for several seconds. "That's great. I got it," the cameraman said to the female reporter, Robin Keller. Suddenly the room came alive again and the reporters scurried around asking questions and scribbling in their small notebooks. It was sort of bizarre, but suddenly it didn't seem to be about me anymore and I felt relieved.

"Manny," Robin Keller said to her cameraman, "Let's see if we can get a reaction from the parents, and then a few words from that Stockman guy about how the search is going, then that'll be it." She paused, thinking, and then said, "Let's start with a live shot from the outside the lodge for the broadcast, then we'll go with this taped stuff."

I saw Lesley walk over and stand at Robin's elbow. "Good to see you again, Robin," she said when Robin turned towards her.

"Lesley! Listen, thanks for arranging things with the kid. I appreciate it."

"No problem, Robin. Glad to help out. How do you think she came across?" I looked away so they wouldn't realize I was listening to every word.

"She looked good," Robin said. "Sincere, concerned. I think viewers will be sympathetic." Robin leaned towards Lesley. "Listen, Lesley, do you think they're going to find this little girl soon?"

Lesley shrugged. "I don't know, Robin. From what I understand, if they don't find her right away, then it could be a while."

"A while? Like another day? Two? Or more?" Robin asked her with growing interest.

"Who knows?" Lesley answered.

"What are her chances do you think?" Robin asked, her voice lowering slightly.

Lesley threw up her hands. "You'd better ask Stockman that question. I mean, like Angie just said, Melanie's only four years old. The question is how well can she take care of herself, isn't it?"

Robin nodded and scribbled something into her pocket notebook. "Yeah, I'm going to ask the parents about that. Then I'll see what Stockman has to say about her chances." She glanced at her watch. "And I'd better hurry if I'm going to wrap this up in time for the news at six." She turned and signaled to her cameraman, Manny, who nodded.

Robin said, "Thanks again, Lesley." Then she paused and touched Lesley's arm lightly. "So, are you handling things for the campground with this story? I mean, if I need any more information, should I talk to you?"

Lesley nodded. "Yes. I volunteered to help out. The owners are...friends of mine."

Yeah, some are closer friends to her than others, I thought as I stood up.

"They don't know how lucky they are to have you!" Robin said with an attempt at a sincere smile. "See you later." She waved her hand, or maybe she was signaling Manny, the camera guy; it was hard to tell which.

Dad came over to Lesley as Robin left with the cameraman in tow behind her. The cameraman was moving through the crowd like a rowboat in the wake of her ship. "You know her?" my dad asked Lesley, indicating Robin with the nod of his head.

"Yeah. We've worked together before," Lesley replied. "She's a sharp newsperson, but you have to keep an eye on her and on your back. The story and how she looks telling it are the only things she really cares about," she added.

Dad nodded.

Lesley glanced around and noticing me just behind my dad, she said, "Oh, there you are, Angie."

Dad turned around and he seemed mildly surprised to see me there, too. "Hey, honey, are you getting hungry? Tessie is making dinner for us in the kitchen." Before waiting for my answer, he turned to Lesley and smiled warmly, "You're invited, too, you know."

Lesley smiled back at him. "Thanks. I'll be there in a few minutes, Alex. I want to listen to Robin's interview with Nora and Keith."

"Keith?" Dad repeated. "Oh, he won't be there. I'm pretty sure he went out with one of the search groups."

"Nora's doing the interview alone?" Lesley asked in alarm.

"Probably. Why? Will that be a problem?"

"It could be if she's distraught. Distraught women say a lot of things they don't necessarily mean," Lesley said. "I'd better get out there."

"All right. I'll be in the kitchen. Meet me there afterwards, OK?"

She nodded and smiled at him. He touched her chin but said nothing. Then he turned to me, apparently remembering me once more. "Let's go get some dinner, OK?"

I nodded, but now I was curious about what Nora would say about me, so I hesitated. "I'll be there in a minute, Dad. I want to get something upstairs first, OK?"

He looked at me for a second, puzzled, and then nodded, "Sure, but don't talk to any of these news people without Lesley or me there, all right?"

"Sure, Dad, I know," I said. As if I'd even want to!

Dad moved through the crowd heading towards the kitchen. I turned and saw the bright camera lights out on the porch, so I headed in that direction. That must be where Nora was being interviewed. I squirmed my way through the crowd, but as I got closer, I hung back a bit. I didn't really want Mrs. Jacobs to notice me while she was being interviewed. There was no sense in reminding her that I'd lost her child, after all.

Instead, I climbed up next to one of the porch posts towards the back where I could see over the crowd and could hear well enough. And, unless she knew I was there, Nora Jacobs probably wouldn't notice me. From my vantage point, I could see that Lesley had found a spot between two reporters down in front. The newswoman, Robin, was sitting across from Nora on the wooden love seat at the far end of the porch. Nora, I saw, was weeping. Her voice was high and squeaky as she spoke to Robin, apparently answering a question.

Robin held the microphone tipped towards her own mouth and said in a soft, comforting voice, "Mrs. Jacobs, we understand that you left little Melanie in the care of Angie Jackson, the campground owner's thirteen-year-old daughter. Is that true?" My throat went instantly dry as she said my name and immediately, I wished I could turn invisible.

Nora nodded. "Yes. Melanie liked Angie, so we thought it would be OK to let her baby-sit while my husband and I went hiking for a few hours. We can't understand how Melanie could end up missing." Nora dabbed at her eyes with the edge of a tissue that she held knotted in her hands. I studied her for a minute or two and decided that she was not faking the tears, but then, why should she? Her daughter really was missing, after all.

"So, you think she may have run away from the babysitter and gotten lost?" Robin asked smoothly, almost as if Nora had actually said such a thing. Uh oh, I thought. She continued as if Mrs. Jacob had agreed with her, "But why would little Melanie run away? Do you think that the babysitter might have scared her somehow?" Scared her? I stared at Robin not really comprehending where she was going with this line of questions. Scared Melanie?

Nora looked up at Robin through teary eyelashes. "I...I don't know...We don't know what to think." Nora said through another bout of sobbing. "I just want my baby back, that's all."

"Cut." Robin said. "Thank you so much for talking with us, Mrs. Jacobs. I know how hard it must be at a time like this..." Robin stood up and patted Nora's shoulder lightly.

Nora just nodded without looking at Robin. She was hunched over, and her shoulders shook as she quietly sobbed into her tissue. Even I felt sorry for her, and I was apparently the one being blamed for all this.

Then I saw Lesley catch Robin's arm as she started to move by her. Lesley was not smiling. "Robin, will that whole interview with the mother air?"

Robin looked Lesley in the eye and shrugged. "It might. Depends on how much time the folks back at the station in Manchester have for this story. We're cutting it awfully close on time."

Lesley nodded. "You know you put words in her mouth back there...."

"It's a story and you know how little time we have on air," Robin replied rather defensively.

"But you tried to make it sound like it was all Angie's fault," Lesley responded.

"This isn't a court of law," Robin shot back. "I needed to speed it up, so I moved things along a little. Big deal. Besides, who knows what really happened?"

Lesley put her face close to Robin's, a real mano-a-mano move, I thought. "Robin," she said in a low but firm voice, "you and I can work together on this thing, and I can promise you all the story you can handle, or we can work against each other, and I will make sure you're the last one to get the story. You're choice. Do you understand?"

They faced each other for several long seconds. Then Robin broke the staring contest when she glanced down at her watch. Two points to Lesley, I thought grimly. Robin said by way of explanation, "I have an interview with Stockman. I'll talk it over with Manny about editing the mother piece. I might have been a little over the top," she added lightly.

"Yeah," Lesley agreed dryly. "A little over the top." I was touched. She was really coming to my defense.

Robin moved past her and signaled to Manny. The two of them stood near the door of the lodge, not far from my perch, talking in low voices and gesturing broadly. After a minute or so, Manny threw up his hands but then he shrugged. He pointed towards Stockman who was waiting for them just inside the door. They went through the door together and Robin was all fake smiles again when she reached Jerry Stockman. Boy, I could never be a newsperson. Were they all so artificial?

I heard Lesley sigh and I turned to see her next to me. "You saw all that, I assume," she said with weary smile.

I nodded as I hopped down.

"I can't promise that Robin really will edit the interview with Nora, you know."

I nodded again.

"But I'll ask your dad if I can go up to the office in a short while to watch the local TV news broadcast out of Manchester. We'll know soon enough, I guess."

"Thanks for trying to help," I said, rather lamely. "That Robin lady really made me sound like the babysitter from Hell, didn't she?"

Lesley sighed again as we walked towards the kitchen together. She didn't really have to answer me. I knew.

Lesley stopped but when I looked up, I saw that she was glancing back towards the porch. Nora Jacobs was walking down the steps. Lesley frowned a bit and then turned back to me. "Angie, I want to make sure Mrs. Jacobs is all right. Why don't you go ahead and get some dinner in the kitchen?"

I nodded. "OK. See you later," I said. I made a beeline for the kitchen door. Now that the press conference was over, I was starving.

SIXTEEN

Reaching Out to Nora

August 2006
Wilderness Campground, Crawford Notch, NH

*** *Lesley* ***

Lesley went out onto the front porch, but Nora was nowhere to be seen. She thought about going back inside and listening to Robin's interview with Stockman, but she wasn't in the mood. She'd hear it later on TV in any case. Suddenly she just wanted to be away from the shuffle of people and cameras and microphones. There was tawdriness to it all that made her skin feel gritty. It was the reason she'd gladly left her PR consulting job. How could it not sully her soul?

She went down the stairs and stepped out onto the dirt driveway. She took a deep breath and smelled the pungent aroma of pine. It was then that she noticed that the sun was setting somewhere beyond the mountains. The shadows were lengthening, and it was already growing dark in the valley, particularly here in the campground with its canopy of leafy trees blocking the sky. It was all so beautiful and peaceful in the growing twilight. She closed her eyes for a moment to just enjoy it for a moment.

With her eyes closed she noticed the hubbub of voices coming from the lodge. When she set that sound aside and listened a little harder, she could hear the crickets and buzz of insects. The whine of a mosquito close by made her open her eyes again and she sighed. She decided to walk around the lodge and get to the kitchen through the back door.

As she passed the storage shed, she thought she heard the sound of someone crying. Her heart missed a beat. Could it be that Melanie was still here in the campground?

"Hello?" she said into the darkening trees. "Is someone there?"

"Sorry, it's just me," Nora said as she emerged from behind one of the pine trees. She touched a tissue to her nose.

"Oh, Nora!" Lesley hurried over to the other woman. "I heard someone crying...I guess I was hoping it was Melanie...." She stopped, not wanting to make the other woman feel worse. "I'm so sorry about..." she paused and gestured to the lodge, "about all this."

"I know," Nora said, her eyes casting around. "Everyone's sorry, aren't they?" Her hands jerked spasmodically for a second. "Well, you know, Lesley, I'm sorry, too. Jesus knows I'm sorry! And what about Keith? He's not even around to be sorry. And now, you're sorry... I guess we're a sorry lot, aren't we?" she attempted a laugh, but it came out pinched and bitter.

The two women faced each other in the growing gloom. Lesley couldn't discern Nora's features, but she didn't have to. She knew what she'd see – the swollen, red-rimmed eyes, the raw nostrils, and the streaks of tears on the freckled cheeks. "Is there anything I can do for you, Nora?" Lesley asked softly, reaching a hand towards the other woman.

Nora pulled her hand away as if stung. "Find Melanie," she said bluntly. "That's about all I want from anyone." Her body was rigid with emotion.

Lesley nodded, wondering what she could possibly say that would help. "I can't imagine what you're going through, Nora. I'm a mother, too, and if something like this had ever happened to Jake when he was a little boy....God, I don't know how I would've handled it."

"Jake?" Nora repeated the name as if from a dream. Then her shoulders sagged as she lifted her eyes and looked at Lesley. "So, you have a son? I didn't know that. I'm a little...a little strung out, I guess," Nora said shakily. "Your son...How old is he?" she asked.

"He's eighteen. In fact, he just turned eighteen in May. He lives out in California now with his father...my ex-husband." She paused and then continued, almost forgetting the other woman as she thought about her son. "I miss Jake so much sometimes." She shook her head and crossed her arms, wrapping them around her body as if she were chilled. "He lived with me until he was fifteen." She shrugged. "Then he got a little wild, and mouthy, as only an angry teenage boy can. So, his father offered to take him for a while. I think that's what he needed, but I don't know." She looked into Nora's eyes. "I don't think Jake has forgiven me yet for letting him go." She laughed, but it came out hollow and hard. She realized it was the truth. Jake hadn't wanted to go. He'd wanted something from her, but she didn't know what it was or whether it was something she even had in her to give him.

Nora looked at her with sympathy. "I'm sure you'll work things out with him. Eventually."

Lesley shrugged. "I thought raising a child would get easier the older he got. I worried about him so much his whole life, years and years of silly worries. Nothing like any of this, of course...." Lesley gestured helplessly. "I'm so sorry this has happened to you, Nora."

"Yes, I know. Thanks for that." Nora nodded slowly. She glanced at Lesley then and asked, almost shyly, "When you first found out you were pregnant with Jake, were you...were you happy about it?"

Lesley looked at her in surprise. What an odd question. "Happy? Oh, yes, definitely! You see, I got married when I was 25 — I know it doesn't sound all that old these days, but it sure did back then. All my friends got married either in college or right after graduation. It seemed all I was doing was either going to bridal showers or baby showers in those days." She chuckled. "And I wanted a baby badly! I was so ready. But you know how it is sometimes. I had trouble getting pregnant. It ended up taking us another two years and a lot of doctors for me to get pregnant.

I've often wondered since then if my body knew something about my marriage that I didn't."

"You mean that you thought you couldn't get pregnant because your relationship with your husband wasn't sound?"

"Something like that," Lesley said dryly. "We'd lived together all through college. Neither of us had ever really dated anyone else. We were comfortable together, but looking back, I don't think we were really in love. I think we got married because it seemed like the next logical step; you know, when you move in with someone, it just seems the next step is to get married and have kids."

"Well, it was different for Keith and me," Nora said with a sigh, "We weren't trying to get pregnant. It was a total shock!" She paused and looked at Lesley. "The truth is that Melanie wasn't a wanted child. We were both sick about it when we found out I was pregnant. We'd just gotten married and neither of us wanted children."

"It's hard on a marriage having children right away."

"No. You don't understand. We didn't want children ever. We'd talked about it before we got married. We agreed not to have any children."

"Agreed?" Lesley looked at her. "Oh, Nora." She took the other woman's hands. "But I saw you with Melanie the other night... You...she..."

"Oh, don't get me wrong! I love her dearly. More than anything in the world. Once I had her, took her in my arms...."

Lesley nodded with a knowing smile.

"But that doesn't change the fact that I very nearly had an abortion," Nora said quietly.

Lesley took a deep breath and let it out. "That must have been such a difficult time for you."

"Yes, but it's more than that. It's like I've never been able to make it up to her," Nora said. "I nearly threw her away once, and look what's happened? Now she's really gone." A sob escaped and her voice cracked. "It's like I'm still being punished."

"Punished?" Lesley repeated. "You can't be punished for something you never did. You can't be punished for thinking about doing something, Nora!"

"Oh, yes you can! Intention is every bit as important as action. Check out the Bible. I have." Her voice quieted as she continued, "Besides, it was more than just intention. It was a fluke that I didn't go through with it. I hemmed and hawed right up until the end of my first trimester, but I finally decided to go ahead with it. I went to the clinic the morning of my appointment, and..." she let out a laugh and quickly covered her mouth, "it was closed! Some nut had tried to blow up the clinic that morning. Can you believe it? If my appointment had been an hour earlier, I might have been killed."

"My God!" Lesley exclaimed.

"I never did get the abortion, of course. I was very intimidated by the whole thing. It was difficult enough to get up the nerve to go the first time. So, I took the path of least resistance and just had the baby."

"And you were happy about it, in the end, weren't you?"

Nora nodded. "Oh yes, I was very happy. I'm not sure if Keith was, though. He knew I was shaken up about the clinic thing. But having Melanie changed everything for us. And now...she's gone."

Lesley put her arm around the other woman's shoulders. "Come on, honey. You and I need to get something to eat, and we need to talk some more. Because when they find Melanie, she's going to need a mother who's not all black and blue from beating up on herself."

Nora laughed despite herself, although it came out as a sort of snort. She fell into step beside Lesley. "Do you really think they'll find her?"

Lesley nodded. "Yes, I do. There's a lot of praying going on around here, and I'm a great believer in prayer. So yes, I think God will help us find her."

"But they say you're a psychic. Don't you know for sure?"

Lesley stopped and looked at Nora. "It isn't that simple."

"Well, I understand that maybe you don't know exactly where she is, but can you sense whether she's all right, at least?"

"Listen, Nora, I just don't know." Seeing the slump of the other woman's shoulders, she added, "But I promise that I'll meditate on it and see if anything comes to me. OK?"

Nora looked relieved, "Oh, thank you! It would mean so much to me. I could pay you. Is that how it works?"

"Don't worry about it, Nora. If I sense anything - anything at all – I'll let you know. But you must understand, it's not something I can turn on and off. Do you understand? Sometimes, I just don't sense anything, and if I don't, it doesn't mean she's not OK, it just means that I don't know one way or the other." She reached out and hugged the other woman. "Nora, we'll need whatever help we can get on this search and rescue, I think. So don't give up on praying."

"If He can ever forgive me for what I nearly did," Nora said glumly.

"No, for that, you need to forgive yourself," Lesley said as they walked slowly towards the back door.

When the two women reached the clean-up area, they heard giggling coming from one of the showers, then one of the voices shushed the other. Lesley and Nora exchanged glances and Lesley shook her head and shrugged. It was when Lesley replayed it in her mind that she realized the shushing voice had said "Kay". Oh, boy, Lesley thought. If Kay is in there with Joe, this may be a night of fireworks. The shower door opened a crack and she saw Joe's face as he peeked out to see who was there.

"Hello, there," Lesley said. "Coming into dinner?"

"Uh, yeah," he said, quickly shutting the door. He added a muffled, "Be there in a jiffy."

Lesley could hear shuffling sounds from inside the shower room. But she didn't intend to wait for them to come out. Joe wasn't her son and Kay wasn't her daughter. Thank goodness! She caught up with Nora and followed her into the kitchen.

SEVENTEEN

Dinner in the Kitchen

August 2006
Wilderness Campground, Crawford Notch, NH

*** Angie ***

When I got to the kitchen it was warm and filled with the aroma of stew and just baked bread. There were two men at the double sinks. One was taking dirty dishes from the stack on the counter to his right, and in a single motion, scraping food into the trash can by his right thigh, then handing off the dish to the second man who rinsed it and placed it in the dishwasher. They worked well together like choreographed dancers. Had they fixed the dishwasher?

At the center island, Dad and Tessie were sitting opposite each other; Dad was hunched over his bowl of stew eating hungrily. Tessie was apparently already done. She looked exhausted as she sat watching him, her elbows on the counter, her shoulders slumped and her chin resting on her hands. I sat down next to Dad and in seconds was wolfing down my own bowl of stew. I swear I don't think I even chewed more than two or three times. By the time I was scraping up the last of it, I could feel a warm fullness settle in the bottom of my belly. I also drank two tall glasses of iced tea and realized then that I must be more dehydrated than I thought. But I was definitely feeling better. It's odd how your perspective improves when you have a full stomach of good stew. I wondered about that as I leaned back in my chair.

Just then, Nora and Lesley came in the back door and Dad smiled, his eyes lingering on Lesley.

Tessie stood up and stretched a little. "Come and sit. Have some dinner. You both must be starved," she said warmly, waving them in to sit on the stools around the center island with us.

I got up and carried my bowl over to the sink and handed it to the man who was rinsing dishes and stacking them in the dishwasher. He nodded without really looking at me. There was still a tiny bit of iced tea left in my glass, so I sipped at it and caught an ice cube with my teeth, as I turned to watch the others.

Nora sat next to my dad, while Lesley sat in the seat Tessie had vacated, directly opposite Dad. Then Kay and Joe came in, the back door banging loudly behind them. Kay giggled, grabbing Joe's arm and he laughed, too. "What's the matter?" he said to her. "Did it scare you?" He tickled her, looked up and only then noticed everyone in the kitchen was watching them. There was an awkward moment of silence, and I had the urge to laugh out loud, but managed to keep silent.

"God, did we have a day!" Kay said as she linked arms with Joe, and they strolled over to the counter.

I saw Dad's eyes narrow as he studied the two of them. "Where've you been all day, anyway?" he asked Kay.

Kay looked up at Joe. "We started out at Sawyer Pond, but when Kevin came and told us about Melanie being lost, the three of us headed further down the trail to look for her. God! We ended up on the Kanc and had to hitchhike back! That's what took us so long."

"You hitchhiked from the Kancamagus Highway?" Dad asked, "Kay, we've had this discussion before about hitching...." Dad said sternly. Boy, had we! I know I'd heard it at least three times in the past couple of months myself. It was high on his list of things we weren't allowed to do...ever.

"But, Dad, I was with Joe and Kevin. There were three of us. Besides, we ended up walking most of the way because no one would pick us up."

"Yeah," Joe added. "We did get a ride over Bear Notch Road into Bartlett, though. I sure wasn't in the mood for hiking up that zigzagging mountain road at the end of the day."

"That's for sure!" Kay agreed.

Dad looked from one to the other. "All right, but Kay, you know how I feel about you hitchhiking."

Hmmm, he seemed to be letting her off easy this time around. It must be because of all the company, I decided.

"I know, I know," Kay answered impatiently.

"Why don't you two go sit down, and I'll get you some stew," Tessie said, to change the subject. "By the way, where's Kevin?"

"Oh, he ate with the men outside," Joe said, nodding his head towards the door. "He said he was beat and was going to hit the hay early. He's joined up with one of the search parties and they're heading out at 4:30 tomorrow morning."

"What about you, Joe?" Dad asked. "What are your plans for getting back on the Appalachian Trail?"

"Well, if it's all right with you, Sir, Kevin and I would like to hang out here and help out until the little girl is found." He glanced at Kay.

I think we all knew why he really wanted to stay.

"It's OK if they stay, isn't it, Daddy?" Kay asked, touching Dad's arm.

Ah, yes, I thought facetiously, and this personality would be the meek-yet-sweet-little-girl Kay. We haven't seen much of her in a long while.

Dad nodded gruffly. I'm sure he didn't know what to make of this particular Kay avatar either. "Of course. The more help, the better. And I'm sure Stockman will be glad to have experienced hikers like you and Kevin."

"They won't let me go out with them," Kay said in a pouty voice. "Mr. Stockman said you have to be eighteen to be a volunteer searcher."

"He's the boss, Kay," Dad said. "Besides, we need your help around here. We'll have a bunch of campers showing up tomorrow who will need to be checked in. Jeb and I have volunteered to go out with the searchers, so I'll need you and Angie to help Tessie with the campground."

I nodded, but no one seemed to notice that I was even there.

Kay sighed her agreement, "All right. Joe will be gone all day, anyway."

I saw that Lesley looked at Tessie whose mouth twitched slightly. Kay was nothing if not funny.

Joe and Kay sat down next to each other – practically in each other's lap – and Tessie served them steaming bowls of stew. Everyone was quiet for a minute or two while Joe, Kay, Lesley, and Nora ate.

Jeb brought his dishes over to the sink and stood next to me surveying the scene. "Hey, Angel," he said nudging me a little. "How about if I take a look at that root cellar with you?"

I grinned. "You mean it?"

He smiled and nodded. "Guppy that I am."

I didn't give him a chance to change his mind. I went and took two flashlights from the top of the refrigerator.

Dad glanced at us, "Going downstairs to the cellar?"

Jeb nodded and grinned.

"What's in the cellar?" Joe asked.

"Jeb's helping Angie with her social studies project," Tessie said.

"The CCC thing?" Lesley asked.

"Angie's latest obsession!" Kay said with a derisive laugh.

Thanks for the stunning support, sister dear.

Jeb and I went down the cellar stairs, but we'd left the cellar door open and could still hear the chatter from the kitchen, although it became more muffled as we descended further.

I heard Nora saying, I guess to my father, "Oh, no, Alex, I blame myself. I shouldn't have left Melanie. We should've taken her with us."

Then out of nowhere I heard Keith Jacobs' voice. He must've come into the kitchen from the other room. In a biting tone, he said, "No, you're wrong, Nora," His voice was loud, but cool and controlled. "Angie should've done a better job of watching her." He paused then added, in a bitter voice, "After all, everyone assured us that she could handle it." I felt my face flush, even though I was downstairs and no one but Jeb was even around. Jeb patted my shoulder but didn't say anything.

Next, we heard Nora say, "Keith? I was beginning to worry about you! Come and have something to eat."

Mr. Jacobs sounded angry. "That's OK. We can get our own food back at the campsite."

"Keith? Are you alright?" Nora's voice had an odd submissive tone to it.

"No, Nora, I'm not. Have you forgotten? Our child is missing. I'm tired. I've hiked probably fifty miles today. And just now I walked in and heard my wife absolving everyone of any responsibility. No, I'm not feeling all right."

"Keith," Nora said quietly, "please, come and have something to eat. You'll feel much better...."

Mr. Jacob's voice sounded tight with understatement, "I'll feel much better when Melanie's back with us, OK? Come on. Let's get out of here."

Then I guess they left, or at least, we didn't hear their voices again. In fact, no one was saying much of anything, and it was silent for several long seconds. Even Jeb and I stood stock still in the dark of the cellar below them.

Finally, I heard Lesley's voice. She said, "That poor woman." She let out a deep sigh. After a second or two, she said. "Oh my, it's almost six! I want to see the six o'clock news. Alex, do you mind if I use the TV in the office upstairs?"

"Go ahead, but it only picks up the local stations: Manchester, occasionally the PBS station out of Durham, and if the weather's calm, a station in Portland. We don't have cable out here, and the truth is I'm too cheap to buy satellite for the TV."

"Yeah, he wouldn't buy cable even if they offered it here," Kay said.

"You're right," Dad answered. "I don't miss it and you don't need it."

"That's OK," Lesley said before Kay could reply. "I just want to see the local Manchester news broadcast. That's the one Robin will be on."

"I'll go with you," I heard Dad say and he added, "I'd like to see that, too."

Tessie said, "You'd better hurry if you're going to get up there before it starts. I've got to go and check on Jerry Stockman and his people to see how they're doing with dinner."

It was rather quiet upstairs and Jeb nodded to me and we turned to walk further into the cellar towards the root cellar in the back. It was then that we distinctly heard Kay's giggle. "A romantic dinner alone," she said, apparently to Joe. Jeb nudged me and grinned. I rolled my eyes.

Then one of the dishwashers piped up and said, "Let us know if you two need some privacy, OK? We embarrass easily, you know." He gave a wolf whistle and then he and the other dishwasher laughed. Jeb and I chuckled at that, too.

EIGHTEEN

Return to the Root Cellar

August 2006
Wilderness Campground, Crawford Notch, NH

*** Angie ***

Jeb and I moved through the cellar and the beams of our flashlights bounced off the ground and walls as we walked. I led him back to the root cellar and excitedly showed him the hard thing stuck in the wall between the shelves.

"So, Jeb? What do you think it is?" I asked after a second or two. I noticed I was speaking in a hushed voice. It's funny how you do that when you're in a darkened place like in a theater or a tent at night, or, in this case, a creepy dark cellar.

He held the flashlight closer to the bump and dug at it with his fingernail. "I'm not sure, honey. It has a little give to it. Not much, but a little. Hmmm. You know, it feels like, I'm not sure, maybe like paper? ....No, more like cardboard. See how my thumbnail leaves an imprint? Let's get the lantern in here. That should help us see it better."

I went out by the furnace where I'd left the rest of the equipment that I'd accumulated for this excavation. This included a camp lantern, a shovel, a pick, a hammer, a screwdriver, and a broom. I picked up the lantern and rocked it back and forth near my ear. I could hear fuel sloshing around inside, a good sign. I set it down on the ground and pumped the air pressure knob about thirty times the way Dad and Jeb had taught me to. Then I flipped the lever and felt in my back pocket for the book of matches I had stuffed in there. I pulled out a single match, ripping it from the booklet. I struck the match and when it flamed, I quickly lifted the glass and lit the mantel inside. It flared up and then in a second began glowing, as it should. I blew out the match and adjusted the brightness of the light. When it was all set, I carried it back to the root cellar. I was rather proud of myself, I admit. Sometimes it takes a few tries before the lantern stays lit and I had done it on the first try. That was a good sign, I decided.

Jeb was digging with his fingers around the object. Now it looked like a tiny pyramid sticking out of the rough dirt wall. He looked up as I brought the lantern into the little room. It cast wild shadows stretching and bouncing on the walls. "That's much better," he said. "Angel, you're right. It's definitely something, but I can't tell what yet."

"You want the shovel?" I asked, as I set the lantern down on the floor.

He shook his head and thought for a second. "How about the hammer and the screwdriver? I might be able to chisel it out with them."

"O.K., I'll get them for you." I hurried back to the other room to get the hammer and screwdriver. I brought them back and handed them to Jeb.

For several minutes, Jeb hammered the screwdriver into the plaster-hard dirt of the wall around the object. Little by little, clumps of dirt fell away and the object began to take shape. "It looks like a box," Jeb said, squinting through the dust he was creating with his digging. He brushed the dirt away with his fingers and blew on it to get rid of the extra dust.

Finally, he stopped and stared at the thing. "Well, I'll be!"

"What?" I asked leaning in to get a better look.

He took the edge of the object in his hands and jerked at it until he could pull the rest of it out of the wall. Dirt clumps tumbled to the floor as the object slid out. "Look! It's a cigar box; a really old cigar box!"

I took it from Jeb and brushed more of the dust and dirt from its lid. "Wow! Let's open it!"

"Could just be cigars, you know," Jeb teased. "And, if that's the case, I get first dibs on them." He put his fingers along the edge of the box, trying to pry the top loose. His fingertips turned white with the effort. "Boy, this lid is really stuck on."

"Here, use this," I said handing him the screwdriver.

"Yeah." He scraped the head of the screwdriver along the edge of the box, and more dirt and dust fell to the floor. Again, he tried to pull open the top of the box. "Whew!" He tried again, and it finally gave way. "There!" he said with satisfaction.

Slowly he opened the lid. If this wasn't exactly like discovering a treasure chest, I don't know what was. We both leaned in closer to look, causing a shadow to fall over the box and its contents. "Let's put it down here near the light," I said as I squatted next to the lantern.

Jeb kneeled down next to me and placed the open cigar box gently on the dirt floor next to the lantern. Suddenly, we could see that the box was full of stuff.

"Wow," I said, staring at the contents of the box without touching any of them. "Look at it all!" From what I could make out in the shadowy light cast by the lantern, I saw an old-fashioned ink fountain pen, some ancient curled and brownish papers, a marble, a black-and-white photo with a white frame border, and a small book.

I picked up the photograph. It was of a young woman in a wide skirt sitting on a bicycle. The woman had one foot on a pedal and the other on the ground. Her hands were relaxed around the handlebars, and she was smiling into the camera. Her brown hair was curly and full and was held back with a white hair ribbon. Behind her was a wooden building, with three steps going up to a door that was closed. I turned the photo over and saw handwriting in smeared blue ink on the other side. It said simply, "Lorraine, Sawyer River Camp, June 1941."

"This is great! Perfect!" I said triumphantly. "It's definitely from the CCC camp. Look! It even says 1941!"

Jeb glanced at the woman on the front and then flipped the picture over to read the back. He grinned at me. "I think you're right!" He glanced down at the cigar box and looked over the other contents. "What else do we have here?"

I took the picture from him and placed it back in the cigar box. "What's this book?" I asked, picking up the small book.

"Can you make out the title?"

I dusted off the front, and turned the cover towards the light and read, "Your CCC: A Handbook for Enrollees." I glanced at Jeb and grinned. "This is so awesome! It's exactly what I wanted to find."

"Really?" Jeb asked. "I think some old cigars were what I was hoping for."

I ignored him as I thumbed through the book. I read from the table of contents out loud. "What It's All About....It's Not All Work....Safety Regulations... Hey, listen to this, Jeb! The last section is called 'Diary.'" I flipped the book to the end and thumbed through the pages from the back forward. Most of the pages were covered with handwriting, front and back. "Hey," I said with a frown. "Jeb, this writing doesn't look like English...."

Jeb took the book and squatted next to the lantern, tipping it towards the light. After several seconds, he looked up at me. "You're right, Angel. The front part of the book's written in English, but this handwritten stuff at the end here is in French."

"French? But why would someone write in French?"

"Well, keep in mind where you are.... New Hampshire is full of French-speaking Canadians that moved down here from Quebec to work in the mills. Whoever wrote these entries was probably French-Canadian."

"Wow!" I said.

"Why don't you have Tessie translate it for you? She speaks fluent French."

My face brightened. "Great idea! Yes, I will ask Tessie. This will be so cool."

"What do you say we take the box upstairs and show it to your dad and Tessie?"

"Yeah." I glanced around the root cellar. "This is probably all that's down here anyway. What do you think?"

"Probably. Let's make sure we don't leave any of our tools down here, though."

I brought the cigar box up the stairs and into the kitchen while Jeb gathered up the tools. Tessie was wiping the counters with a sponge, but the two dishwashers and Joe and Kay were gone. Tessie turned when she heard me coming up the cellar stairs.

"Hey, what do you have there?" she asked.

"Tessie, look what we found in the root cellar! It's a cigar box full of stuff from 1941." I gently placed the box on the counter of the center island as Tessie came over to take a look. Jeb came upstairs and closed the cellar door and flipped off the cellar light as he stepped into the kitchen.

"See what Angie's found?" he asked Tessie.

"You actually dug this box out of the wall down there?" Tessie asked in amazement. Until then, I didn't realize they hadn't expected me to actually find anything. I guess I showed them.

Jeb nodded. "She said something was there, and she was sure right."

Tessie's fingers glided lightly over the items. She stopped and picked up the photo and looked at it, studying the young woman in the picture and then turned it over to read the inscription. She glanced up at me and smiled. "Congratulations, sweetie, this really is a find."

"I know! Isn't it just so cool?" I said, my voice filled with excitement. I picked up the CCC handbook. "But we do have one problem."

Tessie looked at the book in my hand. "What problem?"

"This handbook has a diary section that someone's written in, but it's all in French."

"Really? French?" Tessie said with interest. "Let me see."

I handed her the book and pointed to where the diary section began. Tessie studied the first page, then flipped through a few more pages, then went back to the first page again and began reading. She nodded. "His handwriting is pretty good, although the ink's a little smeared." She glanced down and began reading, "'I have just arrived at the special camp at White Ledge Park in Albany, New Hampshire.'" Tessie read aloud and she looked up. "That's the first line."

"Albany, New Hampshire? That's on the other side of the mountains," Jeb said. "I wonder how the book ended up here."

"Maybe the later entries will explain," Tessie said as she thumbed to the front cover. "Hmmm. Here's the owner's name. Uh, let's see, it looks like Jean-Louis Duclos, and there's an address for him in Lowell, Massachusetts. St. Pierre Avenue, Apt. 2-A." She looked up and smiled.

"What a name. Yep, I'd say he's French-Canadian, all right!" Jeb said with a laugh.

Tessie nodded. "Lots of French-Canadians ended up in Lowell — and Lawrence and Manchester, as well — they worked in the mills."

"The Industrial Revolution. Right? When everyone left the farms and went to the cities to work in factories," I said, as if quoting from a textbook.

Tessie chuckled. "Very good, Angie! That's correct. Apparently, you did learn something in Social Studies last year."

"So will you translate this diary for me?" I asked.

Tessie looked at me then at Jeb. "Actually, I've got a much better idea..."

"Oh no," I said, seeing the look in Tessie's eye. "This can't be good."

"Yes, it is good, and will fit perfectly into a great lesson plan for the fall semester. We can combine your French language skills with your new CCC project..."

I just shook my head in mock dread.

"I'm going to have you translate it," Tessie said triumphantly. "I'll help you when you get stuck, but it will be a great way to improve your French."

Jeb nodded approvingly. "That's a good idea, Tess."

"Some good idea!" I said in anguish. "It will take me forever."

"Not if you apply yourself. And if you want to know what this fellow has to say," she said pointing to the book, "you will have to apply yourself. I've made up my mind."

"Made up your mind about what?" Dad said as he and Lesley came in from the dining room. They looked weary and grim.

"Oh, Dad, come and see!" I said with renewed excitement.

Dad and Lesley came over to the counter and saw the cigar box.

"What's all this?" Lesley asked, picking up the photo.

"This is the box that Jeb and I dug out of the wall in the root cellar!"

Dad looked at me in surprise. "No kidding! You actually found something?" He picked up the box and opened and closed the lid. "You found an old cigar box?"

"Yeah, isn't it so cool?" I said coming around to hug Dad. "There's even a diary in it."

"A diary?" Lesley said with interest. "Now that is quite a find."

"Yeah, except the whole thing is in French and Tessie says I have to do the translating myself."

Dad and Lesley laughed. My dad reached out and put his arm around my waist and squeezed me, "It won't kill you, Angie." He glanced at Tessie with a nod of approval. "Besides, I think I have to agree with Tessie. It's a great project for you, and it will give you something to do. Things are going to be a little crazy around here for a while and Jerry tells me that he's only allowing volunteers who are eighteen and older to go out on the searches, so you and Kay can't do any more looking."

I glanced up at him guiltily. "Oh, gosh, I feel terrible. I nearly forgot all about Melanie."

The room fell silent as everyone else realized they had forgotten about the lost little girl, too. At least, it wasn't just me.

"Well, the rest of the world hasn't," Lesley quipped. We all looked at her as she continued. "Alex and I just finished watching the news. It must be a slow news day because the story made both the local and the national news."

"Wow!" I exclaimed.

Tessie looked at Dad then at Lesley. "What happened with that interview?"

"What interview? Angie's, you mean?" Jeb asked.

"No, she's talking about the Nora Jacobs one," Dad explained to Jeb grimly. "And yes, it went on air completely unedited.... unfortunately." He shook his head.

"What does that mean exactly?" Jeb asked. "What did she say that was so bad?"

Dad and Lesley exchanged glances then Dad looked down at me. He let out a sigh. "You may as well hear this, Angie. Why don't you sit down?" He patted the stool next to him. When I did, he said, "The woman who interviewed Mrs. Jacobs asked her some very leading questions about how Melanie got lost. The result was that she made it sound like Melanie ran away from you, Angie."

Of course, I knew about that because I had heard the actual interview, but I pretended to be surprised. "But why would Melanie run away from me?"

Jeb touched my arm. "She wouldn't, Angel, but that lady doing the interviewing doesn't know you or Melanie. She just wanted to make it a more exciting story."

"But Melanie's lost in the woods....isn't that exciting enough?" I didn't have to pretend to be serious about that question. I really didn't get it. Why does there have to be a bad guy to blame whenever something awful happens? Sometimes awful things just happen, don't they?

"Yeah, you'd think that a lost little girl would be enough, wouldn't you?" Dad said dryly. "But don't worry about it. Once Melanie's found, it won't matter what they said or think."

NINETEEN

The Basics of Search & Rescue

August 2006
Wilderness Campground, Crawford Notch, NH

*** Angie ***

The door opened to the dining room, and a weary Jerry Stockman stood in the doorway. "I hope I'm not interrupting anything private."

Dad waved him in, "No, come on in, Jerry. What can we do for you?"

Stockman walked over and nodded to everyone around the counter. "I just wanted to update you on the search and to thank you for letting us use the lodge."

Dad nodded. "No problem. We'll do whatever it takes to help find Melanie."

Stockman nodded. "I wanted to talk to you while Keith Jacobs isn't around," He put up his hands in mock surrender. "Don't get me wrong, Alex, I'm sure he's a good man, but he's also the little girl's father. As the commander of this search operation, I have to make objective, unemotional decisions, and that's easier to do when the Mom and Dad aren't around trying to second-guess me." He shook his head, his lips pursed in irritation as he added, "He had his group moving into sectors that they had no business being in this afternoon, and they didn't even do that good of a job in the area they were assigned to search." He shook his head. "I'm sympathetic to how tough this must be on both of them, but..."

Dad nodded his agreement. "I understand, Jerry. So, what's the outlook?"

"Not great, I'm afraid. The Weather Service is predicting fifty-degree weather tonight with the possibility of rain for tomorrow and tomorrow night. Believe me, that's not good news. From what the parents and Angie here have told me, all Melanie has is a lightweight jacket in her backpack, which we assume — but can't be positive — she has with her. We could be talking about hypothermia, especially if she gets wet tomorrow." He paused as he let the information sink in.

Jeb stared at the floor, while Lesley nodded grimly, and we all waited for Stockman to continue.

"I've called out the Civil Air Patrol. If the weather holds, they will begin an air search tomorrow. A special K-9 search team from Pennsylvania will arrive some time tomorrow, as well. Until then, we will have to rely on our ground crews to do the bulk of the searching."

"Did they find any trace of her today at all?" Tessie asked.

Stockman shook his head. "No, and although I am a little surprised, it's not entirely bad news. This may sound like a joke — but I assure you I'm quite serious — not finding a trace is just as important as finding something."

"What?" Lesley said. "How can that be?"

Stockman smiled. "Well, let's see if I can explain it clearly. When we're searching for someone, there are four relevant pieces of information," he said, holding up four fingers. "The first is the person's present location, which we don't know; the second is any and all previous locations which we can discern from the presence of clues or traces; the third is the person's plans which would give us a hint as to where to look for clues or traces; and the last is the locations where the person has not been. And those we discover..."

"By NOT finding any traces," Lesley finished for him.

"Exactly." Stockman smiled broadly at her. "You get an 'A' for Search and Rescue information theory."

"So," Tessie said with a frown of concentration, "by NOT finding any traces of her, you know where she ISN'T..."

"And the more places she's not, the closer we come to discovering where she is." Lesley finished.

"It sounds like semantics, to me; you're just playing with words," Tessie said dismissively.

I added, "It sounds totally nutty to me, too. I mean, these are pretty big mountains around here and there are a lot of places where she could be. Isn't it like trying to find a needle in the haystack?"

"I can understand why it might sound nutty to you," Stockman agreed. "But if we can take our maps and grid out search sectors, like we've done today, and have searchers go as close to shoulder-to-shoulder as possible through each of those sectors looking for any kind of trace of her, we can find out if she's been there in the past ten or eleven hours. If she hasn't, we can cross that sector off and try another one. Eventually, we will find something. She didn't just disappear into thin air, after all. She had to leave behind something, even if it's only a little footprint in the mud. And once we have any kind of trace of her — and I mean anything. A wrapper from her snack, a tissue, a hair elastic, a thread caught in a sticker bush, anything! — Then we have a clue as to where she went, and we have a chance of finding her."

I nodded, but I wasn't really convinced. I didn't want to admit what I was thinking — what I really wanted to ask him — and that was whether he thought we would find Melanie alive. But I didn't ask it. I couldn't.

"We'll be glad to have your help tomorrow, Alex. I've put you in the Sector 3 group. John Brett's the leader. I think you know him," Stockman said.

"Yeah, he teaches rock climbing over in North Conway. I've climbed with him a few times. He definitely knows this area."

Stockman nodded. "Sector 3 will take you north towards Nancy Brook. It's bushwhacking and steep on the side of Mt. Saunders and Bemis, as you know. I wanted to put my most experienced group into that sector. It's not the most likely area for her to be found, in my opinion, but I need people who can climb and won't get lost or hurt themselves."

Dad nodded and smiled. "Thanks for the vote of confidence."

Stockman returned the smile. "I let John pick his own team. He wanted you on his team, so you can thank him for the compliment." He turned to leave. "I'm going to monitor the teams that are still coming back in and after they report in, I'll try to grab a couple hours of shut eye. Any bunk space left in your loft?"

"I can go up and reserve you a spot," Jeb said, standing up.

"Thanks. I appreciate it, Jeb." Stockman said and then he turned and headed back into the dining room.

Jeb went up the back stairs to the loft to set aside a bed for the operations leader.

"Come on, Angie," Tessie said. "Let's take that box and diary up to your room and start setting up your research project."

"Can we start translating the diary right now?" I asked with excitement. I couldn't wait to find out this guy Duclos' story. And who was the woman in the picture?

"Aren't you exhausted?" Tessie asked with a sigh. I think that's called "projection". It's when you project your own feelings and sensations on to other people; something tired adults do a lot.

"Not if we can translate some of it!" I answered with a laugh. "Come on, Tessie, please. Just the first entry, that's all!" I pleaded.

Tessie eyed me. "If you promise when we finish one page, you will go right to bed. We have a big day tomorrow and we're all going to need our sleep."

"I promise," I said solemnly. Inside I was screaming, "Yes!"

Tessie and I said goodnight to Lesley and Dad. As we were heading towards the door to the dining room, I overheard Lesley say, "Alex, what do you want me to do tomorrow? Should I volunteer for one of the search groups?"

I paused to hear his answer.

"No," he said, "I think you should hang out here and deal with any media issues. Maybe volunteer to act as a liaison between the press and Stockman and take some of the pressure off him."

Lesley responded. "O.K., I'll be glad to help out. I wish I'd been more effective in handling that Jacobs interview."

"Are you kidding?" Dad said, "You did a great job helping prepare Angie. Don't blame yourself about Nora's interview. You did the best you could. Who knew they were going to pick on Angie so early in the game?" he said with disgust.

"Well, tomorrow's another day, right?" Lesley said and I heard the stool scrape the floor as she stood up. "I think I'm going to head back to my tent now."

Then I heard Dad say very softly, "I'll walk with you. It's pretty dark out there."

The door closed behind me before I could hear her response, but I didn't really need to, did I? No doubt it was some flirtatious come-on. Geez, Dad was falling for her. I could tell.

TWENTY

Translating the Diary

August 2006
Wilderness Campground, Crawford Notch, NH

**** Angie ****

Upstairs, I quickly forgot about Dad and Lesley and was soon bent over the diary, squinting at the first of the handwritten diary entries. I was at it for a while, maybe a half-hour or more when I started feeling frustrated. "Tessie, this is too hard," I finally said with a huge sigh. "My French isn't good enough for this!"

"Then perhaps it is late, and we should try again tomorrow?" Tessie answered lightly. I hate it when she says stuff like that.

"No, I want to do it now, Tessie. Come on. You said you'd help me if I needed it," I said petulantly. O.K., I know it's not all that attractive to be so whiny, but sometimes it wears them down and they give in. Sometimes. Of course, it works much better on Jeb or my dad than it does on Tessie.

"The deal is that you must translate it. If you don't want to begin tonight, that's fine with me. We can wait and start tomorrow. I think we'll both be in better spirits after a good night's rest anyway."

"No! I want to do at least the first page tonight. OK? I promise I'll try to do it myself." I frowned at the computer screen before me. I had already typed the first page of French text into the word processor. Now I loaded in my French-English dictionary, and I laboriously did a look-up of the words I wasn't sure of. I also had a huge dictionary laid out next to the keyboard for any words but especially phrases my online dictionary couldn't deal with.

I'd studied French with Tessie over the past couple of years and I was fine with simple conversational French and could probably manage in a tourist area of France if they agreed to speak slowly and to enunciate clearly. But reading and writing French is harder for me because my vocabulary isn't that large. I found I usually have to look up nearly every multi-syllabic word, and most of the colloquial phrases are beyond me. If this guy used any of that sort of phrasing, I'd definitely need Tessie's help to figure it out.

Tessie has never let me use one of those translation sites on the Internet. That would be cheating, she says. Besides, they didn't do that great of a job anyway. They translate way too literally to the point where the sentences don't make sense and are sometimes hilariously wrong when you translate them back into English; an activity I highly recommend for its comedic potential.

Tessie sat next to me reading the words on the screen as they appeared. As she grew bored waiting for me to decipher them, she casually picked up the diary and read ahead. As she turned to the second page, the air caught in her throat and her left hand fluttered slightly in the air. She took a deep breath. That was odd.

"What's the matter?" I asked, glancing over at her.

"Nothing, honey," Tessie said shaking her head. "Go ahead and finish the page and then we'll go over it together." When she saw me go back to my translating, she took the book and sat on the edge of my bed behind me. I figured she was reading ahead again. I know that I would do that if I could read French as well as she does. Heck, she went to a French convent school as a child in Vietnam, so this diary was probably no challenge for her at all.

I could hear the pages being turned behind me and finally I couldn't stand it any longer and I turned around to see what she was doing. I saw that she was bent over the diary so intently that she didn't even notice me looking at her for several long moments. "Tessie?" I said and her head shot up.

She quickly shut the small book.

"What's the matter?" I asked. "Geez! You look like you've seen a ghost!"

"Nothing, honey," Tessie said, her voice sounding a little queer. "It's just been a long, long day, hasn't it?"

I gave her a quizzical look, then shrugged and yawned. "Yeah, it sure has." I nodded at the screen, "petit jeune fille" that means little girl, right?"

Tessie nodded, watching me intently, sort of the way she had been looking at the diary a few minutes ago. In fact, if I didn't know better, I'd swear she was holding her breath.

I turned back to the screen and read and then reread the paragraph. Then suddenly I understood! I spun around. "It says there's a little girl lost in the woods! Just like NOW! I translated it right, didn't I? But how can that be?" Then I saw the look on Tessie's face. "Hey! You already knew about this!"

"I just read it myself, honey," Tessie said with a tired smile, gesturing at the diary in her lap. "It is a very odd coincidence, isn't it?"

I stood up and started pacing excitedly around the room. "But what does it mean? Did a little girl really get lost back in 1941, too? Just like now?"

Tessie stood up and put her hands up, "I don't know anything more about it than you do, Angie. But we can certainly go to the library and look up the old newspaper stories on it. We have the dates..." She looked down and flipped through the book. "Yes, here. From September 30th and into the beginning of October of 1941."

"Wow! This is so cool!" I said, hugging myself. I sat down next to Tessie and then it hit me. Did I really want to know how their search for their little girl back in 1941 had turned out?

"What is it?" Tessie asked me softly. She must've noticed my face change.

I shrugged. "Oh, I was just wondering...you know...what if they never found that other little girl? Or what if it didn't turn out all right, if she was found but was hurt...or...or worse?"

Tessie nodded. "Either way, there may be something we could learn from their experiences. There must be some reason why you found this book just now. Of course, how much we'll learn depends on whether this Jean-Louis talks some more about the search in here." She tapped the book lightly.

"Why? Did you notice that he stopped writing about it?" I asked nodding at the book.

Tessie grinned. "Oh, no you don't! You're not going to get me to translate this for you!" She stood up and lightly touched the top of my head. "You need to get some sleep, sweetie. We'll tackle some more of this tomorrow. OK?"

I shrugged. She was right. I was really tired. "Oh, all right." I glanced at Kay's bed. "I wonder when Kay's coming to bed. Where is she anyway?"

Tessie shook her head, looking perturbed. "Probably with Joe, and I don't think that is a good thing. He's a bit too old for her, I think."

"Why? He's eighteen and she's fifteen, that's not such a big age difference."

"It is when you're talking about a high school girl and a boy who's already graduated high school."

"Why? Because they might have sex?" I asked bluntly, wanting to shock her a little.

Tessie looked at me speculatively. The truth is she is a very hard person to shock. "My, you are growing up, Angie, aren't you?"

I eyed her, "So, what's the big deal?"

Tessie shrugged. "Sex shouldn't be taken lightly, is all."

She noticed my interested look and she continued.

"Of course, there are a lot of good reasons why teenagers shouldn't have sex. But my ancestors originally came from China, and I was taught to believe that when you make love to a man, you give your souls to each other. The two souls become intertwined so that you and your lover are forever connected."

"So?"

"So, think how complicated...what a spiritual mess you make when you have many...uh, liaisons."

"Yeah, I guess that could be messy all right." I laughed and she smiled, too. "But I like that idea about giving your souls to each other. It's very romantic, you know," I said and then impulsively asked, "Tessie, is your soul connected with anyone's?"

Tessie blushed slightly, something she didn't do very often. I honestly thought she was nearly impossible to embarrass, and it always took me by surprise when I noticed that something had actually gotten to her.

"That's a very personal question," she said lightly. She looked at me for several seconds, as if deciding how to answer me, and then she shrugged. "My parents arranged my first marriage when I was fifteen. I never met my husband—my Vietnamese husband—until the day of my wedding when I was nearly seventeen."

"Were you a virgin?" I asked.

Tessie arched an eyebrow but smiled. "Yes, of course, I was a virgin." She chuckled then and added, "I was brought up in a Catholic all-girls convent boarding school and didn't have much opportunity to be anything other than a virgin, so I can't take all the credit for my purity."

I grinned.

"You've heard the rest of my story dozens of times. You should get to sleep." Tessie said softly.

"Tell me again." I said, wrapping my arms around my knees. I loved it when Tessie told me of her past, particularly of her childhood. It was so different from mine and yet seemed so familiar to me, too. Maybe because we both had lived most of our childhood overseas and not in the United States.

Tessie sighed and sat down on the edge of the bed next to me. "My husband was killed in a bombing at the restaurant we owned in Saigon, or Ho Chi Minh City, as it was known at that time. We'd only been married a little more than a year. A few weeks later, what was left of our families – my mother-in-law, my grandmother, my two sisters – were on a boat trying to get away from the Communists. I gave birth to a baby boy, born on the boat prematurely. He died a few hours after he was born." She stopped and her eyes took on a faraway look, sad but like it had all happened to some other Tessie.

I took her hand gently and Tessie glanced at me, coming out of her reverie. "Sorry, I haven't thought about all that for such a great while. I'd forgotten how very young I was...only a little older than Kay actually." She smoothed my hair and cleared her throat. "So, we ended up in a refugee camp on the border between Cambodia and Thailand where I met your Uncle Tim and that was the beginning of my second life. Through him, I met your mother who was his sister, and your father, and Jeb, and then later, Kay and you. I lost one family and found another."

I thought about that. "Weird how things work out, huh?"

Tessie nodded. "Yes, it is. But enough of this talk, young lady. You need to get to sleep, and so must I. We're in for another very full day tomorrow." She glanced over at Kay's bed and shook her head. "I don't know what's to be done about your sister." She shook her head again with a frown. "I hate to add another burden to your father's life right now." She sighed.

"Kay's just an airhead. He already knows that." I said with a laugh.

Tessie smiled wanly. "Sometimes she is."

Tessie closed the door gently as she left. I heard her soft steps as she walked down the hallway. Jeb's door creaked open at the end of the hall and then closed quietly with a little click. I thought about the two of them, how kind and loving they were to each other, and I wondered if they would ever get married. I'd asked her, naturally, dozens of times, and she always answered that she'd been married twice before and both husbands had died in accidents, she just didn't see the sense in tempting fate. She said she was content with life the way it was. I wondered if her soul and Jeb's were intertwined. I thought that they probably were. It made me smile to think of that and that was the last thought I had before I fell asleep.

TWENTY-ONE

Night in the Campground (Kay)

August 2006
Wilderness Campground, Crawford Notch, NH

*** *Kay* ***

On the other side of the campground, Kay and Joe had found a place to be alone. Because of the extra people needing places to sleep at the lodge, Joe had graciously given up his bed in the bunkroom to one of the female searchers. It was Kay's idea to set up his little two-person backpacking tent on an empty campsite at the far end of the campground; in campsite 17. Kay knew the site wouldn't be used until campers began arriving for the weekend and she'd make sure to clean up the area before then.

Of course, Kay was nervous. She couldn't be sure whether her father or Jeb had noticed she wasn't in her room at the lodge, and they might be out looking for her. Every scratch of branches or change in the sound of the chirping crickets made her pause and listen intently or watch for the bobbing light of a flashlight being carried along the dark camp road. Still, it made it more exciting to be snuggled in this tiny tent next to Joe wondering if at any second, they would be found out.

"God, you're beautiful!" Joe whispered in her ear as he kissed her neck, his left hand moving over her shirt tracing the outline of her breast.

Kay could hear his breathing growing more ragged. She wasn't sure if she was ready for this. But they were in love, weren't they? If he says he loves me, she thought, I will go all the way with him tonight. That will be the test. She held him and returned his kisses and waited. After a while as his kisses became more insistent and she wondered how she'd stop him if he didn't say it? But of course, he loved her. Look at him. He was obviously crazy about her.

"God, I love your body, Kay," Joe whispered into her hair. It wasn't exactly what she had been waiting for, but then she was her body, wasn't she? If he loved her body, he loved her, right? Surely it was a sign. It was fate, wasn't it? If he loved her, then it was as if the decision was out of her hands completely. Or was it? She just wasn't sure.

TWENTY-TWO

Night in the Campground (Lesley)

August 2006
Campground, Crawford Notch, NH

*** *Lesley* ***

Alex wasn't looking for Kay. He had walked Lesley back to her campsite. They talked quietly while he built a fire in the fire pit. Then they laid a blanket on the ground in front of it and huddled together watching the sparks and new flames wrap their fiery yellow and orange tongues through the dry logs. Their talk was spaced with long periods of silence, while they listened to the night sounds, the hoot of an owl, the chirping crickets, the swish of some scurrying animal in the bushes.

The Fairfield family in the next campsite was quiet and the lights in their camper were off. They'd had a long car trip coming over from upper New York state that day, and with all the excitement around the campground, they must have gone to bed early.

"Where do you think she is right now?" Lesley asked, as she stared into the fire.

"Melanie?" Alex sighed. "I cringe thinking of her out in the dark alone. I remember the way Kay and Angie were about the nighttime when they were little. Even with night lights in their bedroom, and the bathroom lights left on the whole night, even then, they still had nightmares."

"All kids do," Lesley said quietly.

"Yes, that's true, but later I began to think when they wandered into my bedroom in the wee hours of the night, what they were looking for was reassurance that I was still there, that I didn't just up and disappear from their lives the way Kathy did."

"You might be reading more into it than there was. Scary dreams are a normal part of coping with change."

"It hasn't been easy for them," Alex said.

"You sound almost angry at her about it."

"Do I?" he asked. "I guess there were times I was pretty angry; left behind with two little girls, and all. But I got beyond that eventually."

"Did you? And yet you're up in these mountains holed away in a campground."

"I'm not holed away!" he said a little defensively. "I mean, this is what I'd always wanted. But I thought I'd have to wait until I retired to live like this."

Lesley watched him as he spoke. "So, Tessie home-schools both of the girls?"

"Yes, for most of the past eight years. We started it to get them caught up after being out of school for a month or two after Kathy's death and the move back to Washington. Then later when we moved up here, it just made a lot of sense." His voice drifted off.

"I understand that Kay will be starting high school this fall, but you're not thinking about sending her to a regular high school?"

"Why should I? She's getting a good education from Tessie," he said. He leaned in and moved a log in the fire and a shower of sparks rose in the air.

Lesley paused for a moment, then nodded. "But high school isn't just about academics, Alex. There's so much...I don't know, so many other things they need to learn from the other kids. The social aspects are important, too. Kids need to learn to deal with their peers, work in groups, be a part of a team, you know, all those being-a-part-of-a-community skills."

"I don't know. With all the drugs, sex, and violence in schools today, I'm not sure I want them exposed to some of the stuff their peers could teach them," Alex said.

"But, Alex, that's the world they'll have to live and work in some day. They have to learn to deal with it."

Alex laughed. "Did Kay put you up to this? She's been bugging me for a year to let her go off to high school."

"But you tell her you think she's better off hidden away on this campground?"

"She's not hidden away. She and Angie get into town as often as they like. I'm not a recluse, you know. None of us are!" He sounded defensive again.

She eyed him. "I didn't say you were, Alex. I understand what you see in this place, in these mountains. I think it's one of the most idyllic places I've ever been."

"But?" he added.

"But," she said with a smile, "You have two teenage daughters. How is it going to help them learn to deal with the real world?"

Alex sighed. "I just want them to be safe."

Lesley nodded and touched his hand. "I know. But taking them away from society doesn't teach them to develop their own sense of safety."

Alex poked at the fire, and it flared up for a second. "I know that's the goal. To let them go."

Lesley smiled and nodded. "Well, if it's any consolation, you've done a great job raising them so far. Your girls are terrific. You ought to be very proud of how they've turned out."

"If I survive their teen years, I'll be very proud!" he said with a laugh.

Lesley was quiet for a minute then she made up her mind. "Alex, I don't want to stick my nose in your business, but I've noticed there's something going on between Joe and Kay."

"Going on?" Alex's eyes narrowed. "Why? What did they do?"

"Alex, you know I don't want to interfere. It's really none of my business..."

"Lesley, go ahead. You won't hurt my feelings no matter what's she's done."

Lesley studied his face, watching the reflection of the fire flicker across his cheek.

"Well, when I was coming into the kitchen with Nora this evening before dinner...remember?"

He nodded.

"I heard some giggling and whispering going on in one of the shower rooms when we walked past."

Alex's eyebrows rose slightly. "And?"

"And I think Kay might've been in there with Joe," Lesley said and then quickly looked away towards the fire.

"Jesus," Alex said and took a deep breath and let it out slowly. He stared into the fire; his look grim. "You think she's having sex with him?"

She shrugged. "I don't know. Maybe. Maybe not."

"Oh, Christ! I'm going to kill the both of them." He leapt to his feet.

"Yeah, that'll work," Lesley said dryly.

Alex began pacing, his hands thrust into his pockets, his head down like a bull's. "She's just a kid. Joe's taking advantage of her."

"Yeah, right." Lesley rolled her eyes.

He stopped in front of her. "What? You don't think he's taking advantage of her?" he demanded.

"Alex, maybe he is, I don't know, but she's probably taking advantage of him, too."

He stared at her quizzically. "What's that supposed to mean?"

"Alex, Kay is a beautiful, sexy young woman...."

"She is not!"

"Yes, she is," Lesley repeated slowly. "A young, very sexy fifteen-year-old woman."

"So, you're saying she led him on?" Alex asked, his voice rising.

"Well, yes, I guess I am," Lesley nodded. She patted the dirt next to her. "Come on, calm down, Alex. Sit."

He stopped in front of her but did not sit down. "Lesley, this is my daughter we're talking about...."

"Yes. I know. We're talking about Kay." She patted the dirt again. "Sit. Please." He sighed and plopped down next to her. "Alex, you're right: Kay is very, very young. But she is also well built, beautiful, and yes, to an eighteen-year-old boy, quite a sexpot."

"If he so much as..." he swallowed without finishing the thought.

"There's not a whole lot you can do, you know."

"So, I should do nothing?" Alex asked, the exasperation rising in his voice. "Let them screw their brains out?"

She blinked and then said, "No. I would suggest being more practical. First, get her on birth control."

"Birth control?"

"Yes, birth control. You and I both know that by the time kids are in their teens, you can't stop them from doing whatever the hell they want. But you can try to protect them from the consequences. There's no way a fifteen-year-old can understand what it means to be a parent. Heck, I was twenty-seven when I got pregnant with my son and I don't think I really understood what I was getting myself into." She shook her head and a smile tugged at the edges of her lips.

"God, what did I do wrong?" Alex said slowly shaking his head.

"Nothing! And don't write her off yet. We don't know if anything has happened," she reminded him.

"I guess I'm not as optimistic as you are, but then I'm privy to some of the dumb decisions Kay has made in the past."

"I don't know about that. But then, I have a son, so the discussions I had with him went a bit differently. You know: same theme, different song. With him, it was more about respecting females, how to interpret the come-ons and teases, how to learn to respect yourself, that sort of stuff. These days, boys are treated like sex objects and notches on the bedpost, too, you know."

"Notches on the bedpost?" Alex snorted. "You're kidding!"

"No, I'm not. Jake was fourteen when he came home one Friday night to tell me he'd been asked to bed by a girl who was in competition with a girlfriend to see how many guys they could lay in a month. Alex, he was in junior high! And so were they. Believe it and weep!"

"Things have changed a lot from when I was fourteen."

"And you think it would've been great having a girl bed you down, eh?"

Alex smirked.

"Well, with AIDS and STD's and all the rest of the stuff that's out there today, wouldn't you hesitate when confronted with a girl who's trying to get in bed with as many guys as possible?"

"Did he?"

"My son? Hesitate, you mean? I don't know. I think so. I hope so. Actually, though, I think he was too shy, maybe too insecure to be compared to however many other notches the girl had already collected."

"Yeah, I could understand that. I would've been a little insecure at fourteen, too, being faced with a really experienced girl. Most guys like to think they're the more experienced one, or at least, hope the girl won't realize how inexperienced they really are."

Lesley shook her head and laughed. "I'm trying to imagine you at fourteen," she said.

"Why? Do I seem too world weary now to ever have been that young?"

"Yeah, that might be it. But it's more like I can't imagine you not being able to handle a situation or a person."

"I can't handle my own daughters, though..." he added with a resigned air.

"Well, that comes with the territory."

Alex studied her face for several seconds, then suddenly he sat bolt upright. "Christ!" he said.

"What?" Lesley asked.

"He gave up his bunk space to one of the female searchers."

"Who?"

"Joe, that's who! He and Kay are probably in his tent together somewhere right now." He stood up. "Look, Lesley, I'd love to spend the evening here with you, but I've got to find my daughter."

"Alex...." Her voice died out as he hurried away into the darkness. In a minute, he was gone, and it was as if he had never been there. "Damn," she said, her fist smacking her thigh. "Kids!" She made it sound like a cuss word.

TWENTY-THREE

Night in the Campground (Nora)

August 2006
Wilderness Campground, Crawford Notch NH

*** Nora ***

There was no whispering at the Jacobs' campsite that night. Well after the other campsites had grown quiet and dark, Keith was still pacing. He walked from the lantern lit area at the picnic table, to the dark edge of the campsite just beyond their parked van. Back and forth, his footsteps pounded out his thoughts of anger, worry, and frustration.

"We could sue them, you know," Keith said, pounding one fist into the palm of the other hand.

"Sue who?" Nora asked weakly.

"Sue Alex Jackson! Sue this campground, goddammit!" Keith spat the words. Half of his face was in darkness as he walked out of the arc of lantern light.

Nora watched him. "Who cares about getting money from them?" she asked.

"I don't care about the money, don't you see? But if they don't find Melanie, I'm damn well going to put this place out of business!" He turned at the van and returned. "This is all their fault. Who knows what that daughter of his did that made Melanie run away."

"What?" Nora's eyes widened. "Keith, what are you talking about?"

"I saw the news on that little TV the reporters had on. That lady reporter was right. We don't know what went on after we left. Melanie may have run into the woods to get away from that girl!"

"That girl? You mean, Angie?" Nora shook her head. "Keith, Melanie liked Angie. You know that. You're talking crazy. We wouldn't have left Melanie with her if we didn't think we could trust Angie with her. And I don't believe Angie would ever hurt or scare Melanie."

"Whose side are you on, Nora?" Keith's voice was filled with biting sarcasm.

"I'm on Melanie's side! That's whose! I just want her back." Her voice broke and she jumped up and hurried to the tent. She unzipped it and stepped in before Keith had a chance to respond.

Nora lay down on her sleeping bag and put her arm across her eyes to block out the lantern light that lit up the tent. She would prefer darkness. It was unnerving to see Keith like this. Of course, he'd always had a temper, but normally he was able to control it. She didn't like the icy meanness that sometimes resulted from that control, but this explosive anger was something new and far more frightening. She hoped leaving him alone would allow him to get himself under control again. She closed her eyes and thought about her daughter. All she could see was Melanie's frightened face. She prayed fervently. *Please, God, please.*

The lantern was still lit at 2:30 a.m. when Nora woke with a start. She had dreamt that Melanie had wandered back into their tent and was curled up in her own little sleeping bag. Groggily Nora reached for the sleeping bag and felt for the solid little body she hoped was there. Her shoulders sagged when she realized it had just been a dream.

Outside she heard the sound of Keith's boots as they scuffed the ground. His pacing was not as even now. She heard him trip and curse. Perhaps he was finally growing tired. She hoped he would come to bed. Morning would be here soon, and everything always looked better in the daylight, didn't it? They both needed their strength to endure this. She reminded herself that God never gave more than a person could bear. She hoped that was true.

TWENTY-FOUR

Night in the Campground (Alex)

August 2006
Wilderness Campground, Crawford Notch, NH

*** *Alex* ***

Alex headed back to the lodge. He'd find the campsite map and look to see which sites were empty and furthest away from the lodge. He knew Kay and that was where she and Joe would be. He would rustle Jeb out of bed and the two of them would go and find her. He fumed as he marched towards the lodge. How could she be so stupid? God, what if he was too late?

"Alex?"

Alex turned to find Jerry Stockman standing by the long table with a coffee mug in his hand. He could see the weariness lining the man's face.

"Hey there, Jerry! Any news?"

The other man shook his head. "No. All the teams have reported in. I sent everyone off to bed. We'll have an early morning tomorrow."

"You ought to get to bed yourself," Alex said.

"I tried. But I have a niece about the same age as Melanie. I can't imagine her sleeping in the woods by herself at night. Heck, she wouldn't even sleep in a tent with her sister in her own backyard this past summer!"

Alex smiled. "I know what you mean. You've been on these search and rescue missions before, right? What do you think her chances are?"

"Honestly?" Stockman shook his head again. "Probably not good. Hypothermia is the real danger. It's cold out there tonight and at best she has a windbreaker. The forecast is calling for rain tomorrow. And that's not good. Not good at all."

They were both quiet for a minute. Stockman continued, "The key to these types of searches – where small children are involved – is to find them quickly." He glanced down at the table and his eyes glazed over for a second. He jerked his head up and sighed. "Heck, I don't know...."

"Yeah. Can I do anything? Do you need anything?" Alex asked.

"Nah. Go to bed. I'll let you know if I hear anything."

"OK, see you in the morning then."

Jerry Stockman nodded.

Alex turned and went upstairs. He reached for Jeb's door, but just as he touched the knob, he heard the muffled voices inside. He pulled his hand away. It was Jeb and Tessie. He considered for a minute then he shook his head. No, he wouldn't bother them. They thought they had this great secret with these clandestine meetings. He smiled. He'd watched them for years, as they slowly became friends and then lovers. He wasn't sure why they felt the need for the secrecy, but he would respect their privacy. He turned and went back down the stairs. Jerry Stockman was gone.

Alex went over to the front desk and touched one of the keys on the keyboard and the computer monitor sprang to life. He waited for his eyes to adjust to the light, and he traced the campground map on the screen with his finger, noting which campsites were occupied and by whom. He found what he was looking for: site number 17, the smallest campsite and the furthest away. If he knew his daughter, and he thought he did, that was the one that Kay would choose.

Alex went into the kitchen and grabbed a heavy-duty flashlight. It could double as a weapon, if need be, although he didn't think he'd have to grapple with Joe. He was just a kid, after all. Still, he wondered what he would he say to them when he found them? *Hey, get off my daughter?* Yeah, right. That sounded more like a line from a British farce. If it weren't so serious, the absurdity of his position would make him laugh.

Alex started towards the backdoor when it unexpectedly opened and Kay came in, looking slightly disheveled. He stared at her as if she were an apparition.

"Hi, Daddy!" Kay said as she looked down and tucked in the ends of her shirt into her jeans and straightened her sweatshirt.

"Where have you been?" Alex asked.

"Oh, Joe and I went for a walk," she said, not quite meeting his eyes.

Alex looked behind her. "So, where's Joe?" he asked.

"Asleep," she said. "He said he was beat from all the hiking today. Me, too," she said and yawned. "I'm going to bed. Goodnight, Daddy," she said and stood on her toes to kiss his cheek.

He kissed her forehead. "Night, sweetie. See you in the morning."

She nodded and walked past him and through the dining room door to reach the staircase to the bedrooms upstairs.

Alex watched her leave then he glanced down at the flashlight in his hand and breathed a sigh of relief. His body felt wound up and he knew there was no way he would be able to lay down and go to sleep. He tapped the flashlight lightly against his leg, thinking.

He headed out the backdoor, stopping for a second to let his eyes adjust to the hazy starlight. It was still cloudy and threatening rain. He started to click on the flashlight, but on second thought, he left it off. He knew the camp roads well enough to navigate in the dark. He heard the rumble of low voices and paused at the unexpected sound before remembering the searchers and news people who had set up tents and parked their RV's out behind the lodge. When would things get back to normal around here, he wondered?

He walked at a slightly slower pace than usual because of the dark but soon found himself walking past the bathhouse. If he turned here, he would be back at Lesley's campsite again. Would she still be awake, he wondered? What the hell, he told himself. He would check. If she were asleep, he'd go back to his own bed in the lodge. However, if she was still awake....well then.

He walked closer to her campsite and saw the glow of the last embers of her campfire. All was quiet, though. He should at least put that out before returning to the lodge. As he walked over to the fire, he was surprised by a voice coming from the darkness.

"Alex?" Lesley whispered. "You came back!"

He could hear the surprise and joy in her voice and that made him feel incredibly glad that he had come back. "Well," he said, "I was walking past, and I thought I'd check to see if you were still up."

She stood up and came over to him. "I'm glad you did. Did you find Kay?" she asked quietly, taking his arm as she pulled herself in close to him.

He put his arms around her and kissed her lightly on the lips. "Yeah. I was just getting ready to search the campground when she came strolling into the lodge. She said Joe fell asleep in his tent."

"And so, you didn't need to play the over-protective father?" she teased.

"No, thank God. Still, I can't quite believe he fell asleep with her around."

She chuckled. "Yeah, what's that all about?" she said and kissed him back.

He grinned. "Youth is wasted on the young, huh?"

"I doubt you wasted anything when you were young," she countered.

"You either," he said. He let her go and reached over to pick up the water kettle sitting on the rocks that surrounded the fire pit. He poured the hot water on the coals, and they hissed, smoked, and finally went out. He turned and saw that Lesley was already at the tent flap unzipping it. He smiled and followed her in. As he stepped through the tent flap and turned to zip it back up, he had the sensation that all this had happened before. Certainly, it had been a while since he felt so comfortable with a woman, but this sense of connection and easy friendship was something new and yet old and familiar, too.

TWENTY-FIVE

Kay & Angie Lost at Lake Langano

June 1998
Lake Langano, Rift Valley, Ethiopia

*** *Alex* ***

It was full dark when Alex and Kathy made their way back to the campsite. They were holding hands and the beam of light from Alex's flashlight bobbed carelessly before them. They could see the low flames of the campfire through the trees. When they got closer to the tents, they were struck by how quiet it was. Certainly, it didn't seem to contain five American children under the age of eleven.

"Where is everyone?" Kathy asked hesitantly.

Alex frowned. He knew that something wasn't right because they'd been gone less than an hour. The others couldn't have gone to bed that quickly. Certainly, Kay and Angie wouldn't have fallen off to sleep alone in a darkened tent.

"Hello?" he called tentatively.

"Ishi (*Yes*), Mr. Alex," Arage said as he materialized from beside a tree opposite the fire pit where the campfire burned low. He was carrying a long stick that in the dark looked almost like a spear.

"Arage, where did everyone go?" Alex asked in English.

"They go there," Arage said in his broken English and pointing with his free hand towards the lake.

"The lake?" Kathy asked. She switched to Amharic and asked him again where everyone had gone. He answered, now speaking more quickly and with broad gestures. "Did you get all of that, Alex? He was speaking a bit too fast for me. Did he say 'hippo'?"

"He says they saw a hippo or wanted to see a hippo. Well, actually the word he used translates as 'hunting', but I doubt that hunting hippos is what the Daniels and Olivers might actually be doing," he said with a smile.

"Hippos?" Kathy repeated incredulously. Suddenly, she felt an apprehensive chill. "They shouldn't be looking for hippos at night when the animals are out foraging. That could be dangerous, couldn't it?"

Alex nodded. "If they're not careful. Come on. We'd better go find them. At least, we'll bring our girls back."

"They should be getting to bed, anyway," Kathy said in agreement.

They headed down towards the lake. They hadn't gone far, not even to the edge of the water when they heard voices. Alex initially felt relief, but then he thought he heard a note of alarm in Stan's voice, and it stopped him in his tracks.

Kathy, who had been following closely behind Alex, nearly bumped into him. "What's wrong?" she whispered.

"I'm not sure," Alex said. "Stan?" he called into the darkness.

"Alex? Is that you?" Stan Daniels called back. In a second, he appeared out of the dark and was next to them. "Alex! Kathy! God, I'm glad to see you! Your girls are lost!" Stan's voice held a creeping note of hysteria.

"What? What do you mean 'lost'?" Alex asked.

Kathy froze, her nails digging unconsciously into the palms of her hands.

"Everyone went down near the lake to follow the hippos. We saw a mother and a little baby one just over there in the weeds along the edge of the lake. We heard them snuffling around and we collected our flashlights and went to have a look. Our Tina was with your girls and somehow in the growing dusk and confusion they got separated from the rest of the group. As soon as we noticed, we called to them, and our Tina came right back." There was an unmistakable note of pride in his voice. He continued, "She said that Kay told her that she and Angie wanted to see the baby hippo one more time, so Tina came back without them."

"She left them? Oh my God!" Kathy breathed out in horror.

"We've got to find them," Alex said.

But Kathy was already heading towards the lake. "Kay? Angie!" she yelled as she jogged towards the shrubs and weedy area to the right.

Alex caught up to her and grabbed her arm, "Honey, don't go off alone. We must stay together." He turned to Stan, "Where's your wife and kids and the Olivers?"

"They went up along that way. We're supposed to meet back at the tents in fifteen minutes," Stan said, pointing the flashlight at his watch on his wrist so he could check the time.

"They went in here, you said?" Alex asked pointing to an area of downtrodden grasses.

"Yes, right about there," Stan answered. "Are you going in to look for them?"

"Of course!" Alex replied.

"Then I'll go back to the campsite and get Joseph. He and I will come back with a couple more flashlights and we'll help you search for them," Stan said. Without another word, he trotted off back through the trees towards the campsite, his flashlight beam bouncing along the ground as he went.

TWENTY-SIX

"1941's Little Miss Courage"

September 1941
White Ledge State Park, Albany, NH

It was September 28, 1941, and the Hollingworth family had driven up from Massachusetts for a day trip in the mountains to look at the season's spectacular foliage. The parents: Joseph and Blanche, and their two children, Teddy, age seven, and Pammy, age five, along with the family dog, Shag, an English setter. The family had planned a day of looking at the autumn leaves. Over the previous weeks, the hardwood forest had turned into a magnificent display of reds, yellows, and golden oranges, like a candy store filled with multi-colored lollipops.

There was a drought in the White Mountains that season, but the campfire ban was only in effect north of Conway. They picnicked just to the southeast of Conway, at White Ledge State Park in Albany. In the distance they could see the single peak of the 3400-foot Mount Chocorua, a mountain of mystery and legend. It was said that white men were cursed from its peak by the Native American chief, Chocorua, in response to the poisoning of his son, which he blamed on the white family in whose care he'd left him. But on the late September day in 1941, there was no thought of Indians or old curses.

After a day in the mountains, the Hollingworth family planned to grill a few steaks in the park's picnic area and relax with friends and relatives before returning home.

Five-year-old Pammy loved these day adventures to the mountains. They had come up to visit her aunt in North Conway during the summer and she felt comfortable in the woods, particularly when she was with her big brother, Teddy. She followed him everywhere, and unlike many older brothers he didn't seem to mind her company; or perhaps he just tolerated it.

"Mom, I'm going down to the brook to fill my water bottle. The water here is too warm," Teddy said.

Blanche looked up and smiled. "O.K. But, take Pammy with you, why don't you?"

He shrugged as Pammy grinned up at him. "Come on then."

The two turned and headed through the trees. The brook wasn't far. Pammy skipped along behind Teddy. She hummed a little as she noticed the crunching of the fallen leaves beneath her sneakers and the glow of the sun coming through the yellow birch leaves above.

When they reached the brook, Teddy stopped. He studied the water and looked downstream and then glanced upstream, as if considering. He handed one of the bottles to Pammy. "Better get the water further upstream where it's deeper and cleaner."

Pammy nodded and turned upstream. She hesitated when she noticed that Teddy wasn't behind her. "You coming?" she asked.

"In a minute," he answered. "I want to check on the dam I started earlier. It's just down near those rocks," he said pointing a little ways downstream.

"OK, I'll go fill my bottle," Pammy said happily.

She turned around and followed the bank upstream. She noticed occasional leaves falling into the water and she squatted down to watch them float by. She could imagine little ant sailors onboard the magical leaf-boats as they spun in the current, rounding rocks and getting caught up in twigs floating alongside.

She hummed as she picked up a long stick and splashed it in the water. She glanced up and saw another leaf caught on a rock a little farther along and she reached out with her stick and freed the leaf. It twirled and floated downstream.

She turned and headed farther up the bank. Parts of the brook were shrouded in thick bushes and boulders, and she had to take a path through the woods until another path would lead her back to the stream bank. It was fun going from the sunny brightness of the dancing water to the shadowy cool woods and back again. There were paths going in every direction, some leading further into the woods, others leading back to the brook.

After a little while, the brook widened slightly, and she saw a deeper pool surrounded by small boulders. "Perfect," she thought. She decided to fill the water bottle with its cool clean water. She sat on the bank and took off her shoes and socks. She rolled up the bottom of her overalls, the way she'd seen Teddy do when he was going to wade in the water. Then she hopped on the rocks to get as far into the center of the brook as she could before stopping to uncap the bottle. She squatted down and nearly lost her balance. She grinned as she swayed with her arms outstretched, "Whoa!"

She filled the bottle and carefully stood up. She retraced her steps from boulder to rock; carefully testing each to make sure it was firmly in place before placing all her weight on it. It took a lot of concentration, and it seemed like a long time before she was on the bank next to her socks and shoes again. She sat down with a sigh and brushed off the bottoms of her feet before putting her socks and shoes back on. She had recently mastered the art of tying her shoelaces and she carefully went through the steps, just as her mother had taught Teddy. Pammy had wanted to learn too, and she had watched her mother's instruction with intense interest. She could hear her mother's voice, "Tighten the laces, then make a bow. The other lace is a bunny who comes around the bow tree and down through the bunny hole. Pull the two bows tight and you're done." She looked down and smiled. On her left foot one bow was quite a bit bigger than the other, but at least both shoes were tied, and she was ready to go back and find Teddy.

She stood up and picked up the water bottle that was heavier now that it was full. She checked the cap to make sure it was on snugly and set off. She followed the bank a little while until the bushes were too thick to get through and then she turned to take a path into the woods. She smiled remembering going back and forth from the woods to the brook on the way upstream. There was a clearing up ahead and she thought she saw something duck into the bushes. A bunny? She wondered. She went through the bushes and trees where she thought she'd seen the movement and looked around. A chipmunk sat on a stump frozen like a small statue.

She giggled. "Hello, little guy," she crooned softly. He watched her as she slowly crept towards him. She reached out her hand and in a flash, he shot down the stump and into the shrubbery behind. "Oh!" she said, backing up in surprise.

She knelt down to look under the bush, but she didn't see the chipmunk. She stood up and brushed the pine needles off the knees of her overalls and then wiped off her hands. They felt sticky from the pine sap. Perhaps she'd wash her hands in the brook, she thought brightly. She turned around and saw that there were several paths she could take. She shrugged and followed the nearest one. Even if it didn't take her back to the brook, she reasoned, it would surely take her back to the picnic grounds and her family. She began to walk.

Pammy walked and walked, first taking one path and then another one. She always believed that in a minute or two, the path through the trees would open up to the picnic clearing and she would see the glint of metal from the car bumpers or hear the soft chatter of her aunt and her mother, their heads bent companionably together over the picnic table. She wasn't going to just sit down and cry, she told herself. Her brother, Teddy, would call her a crybaby and she would hate that. No, she would be brave, she told herself, and she would find her family if she just kept on walking.

The shadows were growing long, and although she wasn't sure what time it was, she could see that it was getting late. Her mother would be angry that she was taking so long getting the water bottle filled. She would have to confess that she had made a mistake and had taken the wrong path. She sighed. But still, it would be all right if she got back soon. She skipped a little to increase her pace and sang a song softly under her breath. It made her feel better.

By nightfall, she was growing colder. She tucked her arms under the straps of her overalls. She had returned to the stream. Well, she thought it was the same stream. It looked a little different though. It wasn't as deep, she thought.

As the sun set and the evening darkness closed in around her, she shivered a little. She didn't like being in the woods at night. She glanced around warily and noticed there was a stand of huge hemlock trees with their branches and needles draping over the ground not far away. Pammy thought it would be a good place to hide from any scary animals that might be moving about in the woods at night. She went over to the nearest and largest tree and lifted the bottom boughs. It looked warm and inviting in there. Pammy squatted down and dug deep under the lowest branches and she discovered a thick mat of needles. She burrowed under them and reached up and pulled more on top of her. She curled into a little ball and with a mound of needles piled up as a pillow, and then she said her prayers – or what she could remember of them – and closed her weary eyes. Tomorrow she would find her family. She was sure of it.

TWENTY-SEVEN

Day 2 of the Search (Angie)

August 2006
Wilderness Campground, Crawford Notch, NH

*** Angie ***

When I got up at 5:30 a.m. on Friday, Melanie had been missing for nineteen hours. There was a fine drizzle falling in the predawn darkness. Tessie and Jeb were in the kitchen quietly setting up for breakfast when I came downstairs. There would be roughly fifty people to feed, perhaps more, as additional volunteers made their way to the campground to help with the second day of the search.

Tessie was preparing a pancake, bacon and sausage breakfast and she and Jeb needed to get the butter, syrup, juice, and coffee ready for the buffet style serving. The pungent aroma of bacon, sausage, pancakes, and sweet maple syrup already wafted through the lodge. It made my stomach growl.

We couldn't seat all the searchers for a meal in the lodge so at mealtimes the volunteers had to find spots on the steps or floor to eat, not an easy task to manage with pancakes. But it was a small inconvenience in exchange for a full stomach before going out on another long day of searching, a day that would be that much harder because of the cool light drizzle falling outside.

If there was any good that might come from the drizzly weather, it would be that we probably would have some cancellations at the campground. Many, maybe even most campers are fair-weather campers at heart. I understood. Camping just wasn't quite as much fun in the rain and it was positively horrible when it was cold, too.

"Need some help?" I asked with a yawn as I came into the kitchen from the dining room.

Jeb tousled my hair. "Morning, sleepyhead! What're you doing up so early?"

"Why? What time is it?" I asked.

"Nearly a quarter to six. Your dad's already left with the first group."

"Geez, it's not even light yet."

"The sky is starting to lighten. Anyway, they took flashlights."

I went over to the back door and peered out. "Is it raining or just drizzle out there?"

Jeb paused and nodded. "It goes back and forth; and that is not good news."

"Poor Melanie," I said, knowing that was what he was thinking, too. I stood there staring out for several more seconds. I tried to imagine Melanie huddled, probably asleep, under a tree or curled near a bush or beside a boulder. I hoped she was asleep for it was worse thinking of her awake and scared and crying, or maybe wandering aimlessly in the dark. I squeezed my eyes closed to get rid of that pitiful image. *Oh, God, please help her, wherever she I,* I prayed. I wondered if God answered prayers from people who didn't pray all that often? Was it like you earned points for praying regularly, sort of like frequent prayer points? I hoped not. I hoped He was more likely to help the ones that hadn't bothered him too much, maybe as an incentive to focus on what is important.

"Honey? Are you OK?" Tessie came over and put her arm around my shoulders.

I shrugged and then linked my arm around Tessie's waist. "I'm scared for her, that's all."

"I am, too," Tessie said quietly. We stood for a moment just looking out at the darkness then she pulled on me slightly. "Come on, why don't you have some breakfast? Then you can get your chores done quickly so you can get back to work on your translating."

That gave me a great idea. "Can we go into North Conway to the library today to do some research on the CCC and the 1940's, and see if there are any newspaper articles about the other little girl?"

"It doesn't open until eleven today," Tessie replied absently.

"Could we go after lunch, then?"

"Sweetie, I don't see how I can leave the campground today. It's bound to be a zoo here once the weekend campers start arriving this afternoon."

"Aw, please, Tessie," I pleaded.

"How about if I find you a ride to the library? You could go without me," Tessie suggested tentatively.

I sighed heavily as I plopped on to the stool at the counter. "Oh, all right," I said, but I wasn't feeling very optimistic about my chances.

Jeb took the seat across from me. "You can hitch a ride in with Mr. Dooley when he stops by with the mail. I called him yesterday and told him we wouldn't be in to check our box and he offered to bring our mail out to us. I think he's looking for an excuse to come out here, anyway. I'm sure he's curious about how the search is going."

"Everyone is," Tessie said as she turned from the stove. "I heard a report about it on the radio this morning, and that was a station out of Portland, Maine." She set a plate of steaming pancakes in front of me. "What about you, Jeb? You want some more coffee or anything?"

He shook his head. "No, thanks. I'm done." He glanced across the counter at me. "So, what are you going to research at the library, Angel?"

"Well, last night, Tessie and I translated the first page of the diary, and guess what?"

"What?"

"You really won't believe this...." I said, putting a forkful of pancakes into my mouth before realizing that he didn't know about the little lost girl in 1941.

"What?" he asked again, waiting patiently with an expectant look on his face.

I put a finger in the air to indicate for him to wait a moment. I swallowed, then continued in such a rush that my words tumbled over each other, "Well, it turns out there was a little girl lost in the woods back then, too! Back in 1941!"

"Whoa! Slow down! Did you say that there was another little girl lost, in the diary?"

I nodded and continued, "And the guy writing the diary was the cook at the search camp. Isn't that totally amazing?"

"You're kidding!" Jeb really did look amazed. He glanced over at Tessie, "Hey, how come you didn't tell me anything about this?"

She chuckled, "I knew Angie would want to be the one to tell you, that's why."

"Thanks, loads," he said and returned his attention to me. "So, what do you think you'll find out at the library?"

"I want to see if the library has copies of newspapers from back then so I can find out more about the search and rescue of the little girl."

"So, she was rescued, then?" Jeb asked hopefully.

I grimaced. "Well, we don't know about that yet. But I sure hope so."

Jeb nodded. "Yeah, me, too." He glanced at Tessie, and they exchanged a look, but said nothing.

Jeb stood up. "I'm going up to get my heavy socks and wool sweater. With this rain, it's going to be cold and wet out there in the woods. My group is set to leave just after six."

"Be careful today, Jeb," Tessie said.

"Yeah, it is nasty weather for hiking, isn't it?" He looked at her, then at me, then back at her again and smiled. "Thanks for the concern, though." He saw the look on her face and added softly, "I'll take care of myself, Tess. Don't worry." He touched her arm briefly then left.

Tessie stared after him for several moments then she shook herself slightly and sighed. I smiled at her and shrugged.

TWENTY-EIGHT

Chores at the Campground

August 2006
Wilderness Campground, Crawford Notch, NH

*** Angie ***

Tessie gave me all sorts of chores to do that morning. I guess she was trying to keep me busy. I helped out with the breakfast, making sure there was coffee in the urns, and ran errands and answered questions for people. Kay showed up for breakfast late. So, what else is new? I wondered what time she had finally come in the night before. She was in her bed when I got up in the morning, but I know she must've gotten in really late because I hadn't slept all that well and woke up a number of times. Each time I'd glance over at her bed and each time I'd see that it was still empty.

Lucky for her that Dad was so preoccupied right now; not just with the crowd of searchers that had taken over the lodge, but with Lesley, too. I'd seen them leave together the night before when he said he was going to walk her to her campsite. What a gross thought, him with her in her tent. I mean, it's not that she isn't good looking and nice enough, but geez, he is my father. It wasn't something I wanted to contemplate any further and I shook my head to clear the uncomfortable images.

After breakfast, Kay helped clean up without being asked and checked in a couple of early arriving campers. She didn't even complain when Tessie came up with one task after another for her and me to do. Kay not complaining was more than just unusual;

it was weird! It was like a zombie had taken over her body or something. I actually studied her for a few seconds, wondering if that were possible.

After watching her for a while, I had to ask her about it. "Kay, what's going on with you?" I asked. Subtlety thy name is not Angie, that's for sure! But this was so unlike my sister that it was driving me nuts.

"Huh?" she responded. At least, that sounded like the old Kay.

"You haven't complained once about the chores Tessie's been giving us all day. What gives?"

She smiled, Mona Lisa-like. "I figured something out, that's all."

I waited, but when she didn't say anything more, I asked, "You figured out what?" If she's figured something out, I wanted in on it; that was for sure. She was normally so clueless.

She stopped and studied my face for several seconds, as if deciding whether to let me in on her big revelation. "Well, obviously, all I want is for the night to come when Joe will be back, right?"

I looked at her and saw she wasn't trying to put me on, and that she really was waiting for an answer from me. So, I nodded.

"Well, I can't make time go by faster obviously. But if I'm busy it seems like it's going by faster. So, the more stuff Tessie has me do, the quicker Joe will be back." She shrugged and smiled serenely. "That's all." When she finished, she started humming. God, I hate it when she's that happy. It's like the world has slid off its axis and everything is suddenly out of kilter.

"Time plods along at the same rate whether you're busy or not," I said, knowing that it was scientifically irrefutable.

She nodded agreeably. "I know that. But it doesn't matter what time does in reality; all I care about is what it feels like it's doing. And if it feels like it's crawling, then it's unbearable. If being busy makes it seem like it's going by quicker, than I'd rather be busy. That's all. Tessie's taught me that."

I stared at her. Was this really my sister, Kay? "What time did you get home last night?" I asked, not that I really cared, but more to change the subject and maybe throw her off a little.

She frowned. "Why? What's it matter to you? Dad doesn't care."

I shrugged. "He's too busy with Lesley to notice what you are doing. But Tessie was helping me with translating the diary last night and she noticed you weren't back."

She saw the look on my face, and she frowned. "You know, it's no one's business what I do."

"Kay, you shouldn't be out in the middle of the night with Joe."

"Angie, mind your own business, OK? I know what I'm doing."

"Do you? What is it that you're doing then?" I asked and I actually was really curious. I assumed they were out somewhere kissing and making out, but I only had the vaguest of notions about what that entailed exactly.

"Like I said, it's none of your business."

"Tessie says he's too old for you," I said, trying to get some kind of rise out of her.

"When did she talk to you about me?" she asked testily.

"Last night. I asked her if she was worried that you were having sex with Joe, and she said she thought he was too old for you."

There was a funny look on Kay's face that I couldn't quite read, and then she looked angry. "Well, I'm not having sex with him, but even if I was, it's no one's business but mine."

I was taken aback. It hadn't occurred to me that she might really be thinking of having sex with Joe. She'd only known him for one day, for God's sakes! "Kay! You can't be serious! He'll think you're a slut."

Kay spun around and there was venom in her eyes. "You take that back!" She practically spat the words at me.

I took a step back, but like any true sibling, I retaliated, "If you're not sleeping with him, then there's nothing to take back, is there?" I know my voice had a childish tit-for-tat tone to it, but I couldn't help it. She brought that out in me.

"Well, I'm not, but at least it's better than being responsible for losing a four-year-old," she lobbed back at me. That was a low blow, and she knew it.

I was so furious that I sputtered, "I did not lose her. She ran away."

"Yeah, she ran away from you!" Kay shot back at me, triumphantly.

I felt like she'd slugged me in the stomach. She was my sister, and it didn't occur to me that she might not be on my side. I felt tears spring to my eyes, but I blinked them quickly away. I wasn't going to let her see how much she had hurt my feelings. But as I looked at her, I couldn't think of anything to say back to her – which was fine, because I wasn't sure I'd be able to keep the shakiness out of my voice anyway. Instead, I turned and walked away as fast as I could.

"Angie," Kay called behind me. I don't know what else she was going to say. If she said something, I didn't hear it; the blood was pounding too loudly in my ears.

I hurried through the dining room, ignoring the busy sounds of people on mobile phones and walkie-talkies, and huddled over maps that were stretched out across the tabletops. I jogged past them all and took the stairs two at a time. I just wanted to be alone, which wasn't easy to manage anymore.

I went into our bedroom and closed the door behind me. I sat down at the end of my bed and felt the anger and sadness that I'd been fending off since Melanie disappeared suddenly envelope me. I could barely swallow as my throat squeezed shut and a few tears escaped, making wet tracks down my cheeks.

Kay was right, of course. It was my fault. Melanie was out there somewhere, and I was most definitely to blame. I closed my hands into fists and dug my nails into my palms to force back down the sobs I could feel rising in my chest. I wouldn't cry. I would not cry.

After a couple of minutes, breathing deeply and waiting for the intensity of my feelings to pass, I finally got up and sat in the chair in front of my computer. Maybe I would take another crack at the translation. No one would miss me. Let Kay handle my chores for a change. She was the one who was so happy being so bloody busy, wasn't she? I hoped my chores made her positively ecstatic.

TWENTY-NINE

Day 2 of the Search (Alex)

August 2006
Wilderness Campground, Crawford Notch, NH

*** *Alex* ***

Alex switched off his flashlight. It was dawn, and the sky had lightened slightly although the drizzle and clouds promised a gloomy day. He felt his heart beating strongly as he brought up the rear of the six-person search team. There was John Brett, his rock climbing buddy from North Conway, who was head of this group of searchers; Carl Langdon, an EMT from Jackson; Tina Graves, a nurse volunteer from Maine; Janice Stoughton, a part-time gym teacher from the high school in Conway; Stan Fairbanks, a retired military man; and young Kevin Westerman, Joe's AT hiking partner.

Brett led the group and they quickly fell into a comfortable single file order, suited to their hiking pace and the length of strides. The group was assigned to hike over the back side of Mt. Saunders and then along the valley between Saunders and Duck Pond Mountain. There wasn't a real trail. They were bushwhacking along old deer trails and the path they were on was narrow, rocky, and now muddy from the rain. They went slowly because of the dark, the weather, and not wanting to lose the trail. Alex had volunteered to bring up the rear of the column of hikers. He knew the least about search and rescue techniques, of course, but he was also the least likely to get lost. He had spent the past five years tramping on trail and off in these mountains and valleys around his campground, and he knew the area well.

They'd been hiking about a half an hour and would come to the edge of their search sector shortly. Once there they would slow down considerably and begin to look for traces of Melanie's presence carefully and very methodically. Alex remembered Jerry saying the night before that this sector was the least likely area for Melanie to have gone and Alex had to agree. It was too steep, too rocky, too unfriendly for a small child, and today, it was too slippery and dangerous for anyone, adult or child. He would have to be alert, he reminded himself.

He looked at the soft boot imprints in the mud between the rocks on the thin width of trail before him and let his boot step into the footprints left by the others. How would it have been stepping along this rocky path in moccasins as the Native Americans did two centuries before, he wondered, not for the first time? It was something he liked to think about when he was out in the woods. Did they search for their own small children who went missing? Did they have some trick to finding and rescuing them?

He thought about his own children, Kay and Angie, glad they were older and that he didn't have to worry as much about them getting lost. It could happen, of course, but they had been taught mountain safety: not to hike alone, to stay on the trails, how to read a compass and map, how to pay attention to their surroundings so they could retrace their steps, and finally, if lost or hurt, how to hug a tree and survive in the wilderness until they were found. No, he didn't worry about them getting lost in the woods anymore but getting lost in life was another matter.

How ironic that you teach your children to hike in pairs and groups, but in life, you want them to stand alone and be an individual. When hiking, you teach them to stay on the trails; but in life, you want them to be creative and forge new paths. In the woods, you teach them how to use a compass and how to read a map, but in life, there is no map, and their compass is pretty much whatever morals, values, and beliefs they carry with them. He had taught them to survive in the wilderness, but had he taught them to survive in life?

Not paying attention, he nearly lost his footing. He stumbled and quickly caught himself and recovered. For several moments he re-focused on following the footsteps of Carl, the searcher in front of him. But before long, Kay's face drifted into his mind. Kay. What should he do about Kay and Joe?

"This is it." Alex heard John Brett's voice from the front of the column. They came to a halt and Alex quickly caught up with John.

"What now?" Alex asked.

They were in a wide ravine, the sides rising over their heads, covered with boulders and bushes, loose rock, and ground ferns.

We'll spread out and walk towards the other end of the ravine where this deer trail we've been following goes back into the hardwoods. We will continue on until we reach Nancy Brook Trail. Then we'll call in and see if they want us to take Nancy Brook Trail between Mt. Nancy and Mt. Anderson or if they want us to bushwhack around Bemis. It may depend on the weather, but I'll leave it up to them."

Alex nodded. "What should I be looking for?" he asked.

"Anything that looks like a human left it. A footprint, a piece of fabric or threads, a gum wrapper, anything that looks like it doesn't belong out here. Call out if you find something. Leave it in place until we've had a chance to take a look. And listen, everybody, if you find something, don't try to decide on your own if it might've been Melanie's or not. It doesn't matter. We want to know about it, whatever's been found."

"Won't we find a lot of that kind of stuff anyway?" one of the searchers asked. "These mountains are pretty popular places, especially in the summer."

John nodded. "That's true. But we're off the network of National Forest trails here. There should be a whole lot less human sign. What we've been following here are deer trails. They zig and they zag, and they tend to go around the mountains, not to the tops of them." John smiled. "Only humans care about the views and bagging peaks, you know. The deer just want to get from here to there with the least amount of energy expended."

"Why would the little girl go this way?" asked Kevin.

"Because it's a path, and for a child, it doesn't need to make sense, nor does it need to lead to the mountain peak. She's little and will tire easily, so it's a good guess that she'd probably take the path of least resistance just like an animal would. Besides," he said added with a smile, "we've been asked to check out this area, so that's what we're going to do."

They spread out and searched, bent over so they could see under the bushes and squatting down to look closely at things on the ground. It didn't take long for Alex find the bending over excruciating on his lower back. He didn't like being hunched over as he reached down to pick up small rocks that looked like kid-sized buttons, to pull at spider webs that suddenly resembled nylon thread from a blue windbreaker, and to stare through the gloom of the foggy morning at dried up wildflowers that, for a second, looked like candy wrappers.

Alex hoped they'd find something because it was hard to continually focus on searching for traces when there didn't seem to be any. Of course, if they did find something, what would that mean? That Melanie had walked this far yesterday and might be lost in a labyrinth of deer tracks somewhere in this vast wilderness? Perhaps it was better to find nothing, and know that she had not gone this way, thank the Lord.

"Find anything?" Kevin asked Alex as he moved crab-like, his arms out before him, moving aside bushes and small branches as he went. He was no more than an arm's length to Alex's right.

"No," Alex shook his head. "And the more I don't find anything, the harder I find it to focus on looking."

"This is tougher than it sounded back at the lodge, isn't it?"

Alex stood up and rubbed his aching back. He let out a groan. "I, for one, have a new respect for search and rescue professionals."

"Yeah, me, too," Kevin said with a grin. He stood up but didn't seem to be bothered with the same painful back muscles as Alex. Must be his youth and the shape he's in, Alex thought, looking at Kevin's tight muscular body. Man, to be eighteen again!

"Sleep good?" Alex asked as he watched Kevin pull his water bottle from its holder on his belt.

"Yeah. It was nice to be in a bed again, although it sure took some getting used to!"

Alex laughed. "I remember going through the same thing when Jeb and I were doing the Trail. As a matter of fact, I remember pulling my sleeping bag out and curling up on the floor, because I just couldn't get used to sleeping in a real bed again."

Kevin nodded. "Joe and I talk a lot about what it's going to be like after we're done. Geez, we'll be done in less than a month. It's hard to believe we're so close to the end."

"You guys are real good friends, huh?"

"Yep. Of course, we were friends before, but more like friendly acquaintances, you know, compared to now. I mean after going through this trip together....well, now we're more like family, like brothers." He searched for another description, but he realized that there wasn't a relationship that described their kind of closeness. Kevin knew Joe, he understood him, and depended on him with a kind of trust that only grew out of shared danger and time together. "I've never been in the military, but I would guess we're probably like they describe foxhole buddies." He paused and smiled, liking that description the best. "My dad was in Korea when he was my age. He's a big-time government lawyer now, but even now his closest friends are still the guys he went through the Korean War with. When they get together, man, that's real friendship..." He shook his head. "It's the real thing, you know what I mean?"

Alex nodded. "Yeah, I wasn't in a war either, but Jeb and I have been buddies since we were in the third grade, back in Montana. I know what you mean, we were never as close as we became hiking the Trail together."

Kevin smiled. "Yeah, that's how Joe and I are, too." He tucked his water bottle back into its holder.

They went back to searching. It was another half-hour before they'd gone through the entire ravine area. John Brett had radioed back to the lodge letting them know their location and negative results.

Kevin and Alex were resting against a boulder waiting for the signal to move out. The sun was up, although it promised to be a dark, dreary day. There was a fine mist of rain, turning occasionally to drizzle, but not a hard driving rain that might have made them give up the search. There were low hanging clouds blocking the view of the mountain ledges and peaks surrounding them.

"No search planes out today, what'd you think?" Kevin said, looking up at the wispy clouds moving slowly just above the treetops.

"I think you're right. They wouldn't be able to see a thing on the ground on a day like this. Too bad, though. It's probably better to throw every resource at the search early on."

Kevin nodded. "Alex? Tell me the truth. How long do you think it's really going to take to find her?"

Alex shook his head. "I haven't got a clue. I figured we'd find her yesterday, like right away. She couldn't have gotten very far when we first started looking for her. I think she was gone less than an hour when Angie first noticed her missing."

"Yeah, it's weird, isn't it? Like she just vanished."

"And yet, she went in and got her backpack, like she had planned it."

"If you can say that a four-year-old actually plans ahead," Kevin added with a laugh.

"Yeah."

"How's Angie taking the whole thing?" Kevin asked.

"She feels responsible and guilty."

"Kay said that Angie's a good babysitter."

Alex looked at him and smiled. "Kay said something nice about her sister?"

Kevin grinned. "You know how it is. You fight with your siblings but defend them to the death if anyone else tries to say anything bad about them."

Alex nodded. "Nice to know she cares enough. Sometimes you'd never know it."

"Actually, she talked a lot about Angie when we were hiking over to the Kancamagus Highway yesterday. How smart she is and all."

Alex shrugged. "Angie is bright. But, so is Kay, if she'd apply herself. She's a little...flighty."

Kevin laughed. "She said you'd say that! She said you'd say she was bright but didn't apply herself. She sure has you pegged."

Alex looked a little sheepish. "Well, I'm glad she hears me."

"She's a nice girl. Better than some I've seen Joe go for."

"Oh?" Alex said. "He's had a lot of girlfriends, then?"

Kevin eyed him with an *Uh Oh* look on his face. "Nah. Joe's only been serious about one or two girls since I've known him. He's the kind that's afraid of committing himself to someone, I think. To him, the whole relationship thing is sort of large and scary."

"It is when you're in your forties, too. But he's only eighteen, pretty young for a committed relationship, anyway."

"Yeah, probably," Kevin agreed readily.

"Tell me something, Kevin. The truth, OK?" Alex paused and Kevin sat stiffly waiting for the question. "Is Kay going to end up getting hurt by Joe?"

Kevin studied Alex's face. He shrugged. "I don't know. Joe and I haven't been alone since they met, so he hasn't said anything to me, one way or the other. But watching them...I don't know, he looks pretty whipped..."

"Whipped?" Alex repeated.

"Like he's falling for her. You know what I mean?"

"And what happens when you guys leave?"

"I guess that's the test of time, isn't it?" Kevin nodded. "If they still feel the same and all."

"They're too young for any of that," Alex said definitively.

"Too young to fall in love, you mean?"

"Too young to do anything about it," Alex replied gruffly.

Kevin nodded but said nothing.

"O.K., folks, just got the word for us to move on. We're heading over to Nancy Brook Trail," John Brett announced.

Alex stood up as everyone began hefting their packs onto their backs and scanned the area one last time. Then they followed Brett into the woods. Droplets of rainwater collected on leaves and sprayed them as they brushed through the branches of the small trees and bushes along the path. Alex was glad they were moving again because the dampness of the day and temperature hovering in the low sixties made him feel chilled, even through his wool sweater. He thought about how cold a little four-year-old might be feeling today and the thought made him focus on the footfalls of Carl in front of him. Instead of Melanie, though, he could imagine Kay's face at four years old: sweet, trusting, innocent.

THIRTY

Day 2 of the Search (Jeb)

August 2006
Wilderness Campground, Crawford Notch, NH

*** Jeb ***

By mid-morning, Jeb and his group, which included many of the less experienced and younger volunteers, were spread out along the Signal Ridge Trail. They were going slowly and doing as thorough a search job as they could under less than ideal conditions. Soon they would turn northward onto the Carrigain Notch Trail. Another group that had passed them earlier in the morning was following the Signal Ridge Trail to the top of Mt. Carrigain. That trail was steeper, and in these conditions, more treacherous. Jeb was glad he wasn't with that other group.

To be honest, he didn't want to be with any group. It gave him the creeps being on the trail with a group of people, marching along. It was like being in the military again. It made him want to start whistling the tune from the movie, *Bridge On The River Kwai.*

He was used to hiking alone or with Alex, but never in a group. He had a superstition about groups that he knew came from his Marine days in Beirut. He learned the hard way that groups equaled large targets and being in one was just plain bad luck. Sure, no one would be shooting at him from behind the brush here or standing next to him with a suicide bomb ready to blow, but bad luck was bad luck, wasn't it? Whenever he thought about bad luck, he thought about Beirut.

THIRTY-ONE

At the Marine Barracks in Beirut

October 23, 1983
Marine Barracks, Beirut, Lebanon

*** Jeb ***

The last time Jeb had seen Sal Solvino in Beirut was Saturday night. What he remembered was that he hadn't slept well after he'd returned to the barracks that night. There had been a lot of sniper fire from the slums on the hillside above them well after dark. He woke early Sunday morning, around 5 a.m., and couldn't get back to sleep. He tossed and turned for a while, then finally got up and decided to get some coffee and check on Sal who would be coming off duty at 6 a.m.

Even when Jeb wasn't on duty, he liked being around the operations center, checking the telex machine for status messages or reports, or just hanging out with his buddy, Sal, in the radio room. Sometimes they tuned in to the chatter between the naval vessels anchored offshore. It passed the time and Sundays were usually slow days.

It was five minutes after six when he poured his coffee and sipped gingerly at the steaming cup, hoping not to burn his lip. There were a few others lining up at the coffee machine, but, as usual, not much talk. Jeb headed down to the lower level to find Sal, walking slowly as he continued to sip at his coffee. He stuck his head in Sal's area, but he saw at once that Sal wasn't there. He must've already gone off duty, which meant he might be in his cot back in the barracks.

Jeb headed back upstairs, deciding to go over to the barracks for breakfast. He thought that Sal might've decided to eat before he went to get some sleep and he might catch up with him there. But Jeb never made it back to the barracks building. At 6:22 a.m. there was a terrific explosion, the lights dimmed, glass shattered everywhere, and Jeb was thrown to the floor, his coffee splashing on the wall opposite him. He sat on the floor stunned for several seconds still holding the empty Styrofoam cup. He couldn't register what had just happened.

Slowly, he rose to a half-crouch, expecting another explosion. He heard shouts from outside and although he didn't remember how he got there, the next thing he knew he was outside the building along with several other shaken soldiers. The air was full of smoke and dust and now there were small explosions going off nearby. He crouched down again, thinking it might be snipers. When he looked up, it was several moments before he realized that through the smoke and dust, he could plainly see the Air Traffic tower, which normally was blocked by the BLT Headquarters building. The building was no longer there.

It was then that he realized that it must be the headquarters building that had exploded, or more accurately, imploded. Its four stories were now compacted into a heap of concrete and rubble. He saw that the other men around him were running towards the destroyed building and not knowing what else to do, he joined them. That was the last coherent memory he had of that day until sometime late in the afternoon when he found himself carrying another litter with another body still in its bloody and gore speckled sleeping bag to the outdoor morgue they had set up on the tarmac.

He placed his end of the litter down and, like a robot, turned to trudge back towards the still smoking HQ building. His next disjointed memory was near sunset when he found himself wandering along the water's edge on the other side of the runway tarmac with a huge jet lifting off near him. He remembered thinking that he could almost reach out and touch the metal skin of the fuselage of the departing aircraft, so close was he to it. Then in a roar the exhaust from the jet engine knocked him down and everything went black.

Someone must have found him and put him in a helicopter to be taken out to one of the ships offshore. He arrived, covered with soot and blood and gore from the day's work of scrambling around in the rubble of the building. A doctor sedated him, and he was later told that he had slept with only occasional breaks for nearly two days. When he finally woke up, he saw that they had cleaned him up, probably looking for the source of the blood, most of which turned out not to be his. Because he wasn't wounded – just cuts and abrasions - he was sent back to the Command Operations Center on shore. Arriving back there was like entering a weird looking-glass world where everything seemed familiar, but slightly askew.

Still, in his heart he knew that he was meant to go to Beirut, to be there when the Mercedes truck rigged with 12,000 pounds of TNT drove into the BLT Headquarters building and killed 241 Marines, Navy, and Army personnel. He was meant to be witness to this first horrifying terror attack on American personnel overseas. It was the largest loss of life for the Marines since the first day of Iwo Jima during World War II. Perhaps he was meant to be where he was, but if that was true, then why? That was the question that haunted him. Could he ever live up to the luck of surviving it?

But then he thought, maybe he had been meant to die in the Marine Barracks. He often wondered about that because it certainly was fate that he had decided to get up early that Sunday morning and grab a cup of coffee in the Command Operations Center just 250 yards from the barracks. His cot, his sleeping bag, his photo of his mother and father, his favorite pair of socks - all were crushed under thousands of pounds of concrete when the four-story building was blown up and collapsed in upon itself. He had left the building for a cup of coffee and was saved, while his friend, Sal, had returned early for a bite to eat and died. Where was the sense in it?

A month later, Jeb was sent back to the U.S. with the remnants of his group and by February he'd heard that President Reagan had ordered the Marines to withdraw from Lebanon completely. No retaliation was taken, no perpetrator identified. It was a humiliating and catastrophic defeat and Jeb came back to the United States a lost soul.

THIRTY-TWO

Montana Homecoming

November 1983
Missoula, Montana

*** *Jeb* ***

It was Jeb's fault for going into the Marines rather than into the Peace Corps the way Alex and Kathy had. But at the time, he had wanted action, and action is what he got. When he returned from duty in Beirut, having helped dig the more than two hundred bodies from the rubble of the Marine Barracks after the bombing, he took his honorable discharge and quickly lost himself trying to adjust to "real" life. If he and Alex hadn't hiked the AT, he'd probably still be lost. Alex and the AT had saved him. He had no doubt of that.

Jeb was out of the Marines by the end of October of 1983. So sudden was his separation from the Marine Corps that he felt like he had suddenly been dumped back into the U.S. He could've used some time to absorb the trauma he'd been through in Beirut with the bombing and its aftermath, but the military made it difficult to get psychiatric help without the fear of having a mark on his permanent record that might haunt his job prospects forever. When they asked how he was handling what he'd been through, he had smiled and said, "Fine, Sir! No problems!" When asked if he had experienced any nightmares, he had lied and said, "No,

Sir!" All he wanted was to be out of the Marines as soon and as quickly as possible.

Once he was out of the Marines, though, he was suddenly at a loss as to what to do next. He'd never looked beyond just getting out of the uniform. He knew he should go home, but he wasn't ready to face being treated like a hero by his family and friends when he felt like he didn't deserve to even be alive. So instead, he anesthetized himself with Scotch, lots of grass, and the occasional line of coke. And he rode his motorcycle fast, very fast.

Over the days and weeks that followed, he began to notice that when he was out at night in the bars, normal women shied away from him. Perhaps it was his crew cut that hadn't quite grown back in yet, but it felt like it was something deeper than that, as if they sensed his profound unease with himself. He knew it wasn't his imagination either because he had to pay for sex when the urge for it became too strong; something he'd never had to do before. He found it oddly humiliating.

Jeb felt disgusted with himself and made excuses on the few phone calls with his parents when they asked him when he would be coming home. Not yet, he'd tell them. He'd be home soon, but not quite yet. And that turned out to be a big mistake, one he would regret for the rest of his life. Because one gray Saturday the week before Thanksgiving he called his parents to make another excuse for not coming home for the holiday, only to have his mother tell him in a high cracking voice that his father had died the day before of a massive heart attack.

They'd tried to locate Jeb, she assured him, but hadn't been able to find him. She had been beside herself; he could hear the frenzy in her voice. She'd called everyone, she said, including Alex, to help locate Jeb. She was so relieved that he had called. Her prayers had been answered.

"I'm on my way home, Ma," Jeb told her. He was a mess, and he knew it. But, for the first time since the bombing, he felt he was doing the right thing. It was a hollow commendation.

The funeral was somber and crowded with his father's friends, all their neighbors and their extended family of relations from around Montana and Idaho. No one seemed to mind that Jeb was drowning in drink. They felt sorry for him and said they understood, assuming that he was falling apart because of his father's death. Alex was the only one who saw through the haze Jeb was wallowing in and he was deeply concerned about him. Jeb, for his part, found he couldn't even meet his friend's eyes.

"What's eating at you, old buddy?" Alex had asked when they met for drinks at a once-familiar bar in Missoula two days after the funeral. They were sitting at a small table against the wall far from the crowded line of stools at the bar. The scratched tabletop was bare except for a small wooden bowl of stale corn chips and their drinks – Alex's beer and Jeb's Scotch.

Jeb picked up his drink and took a long sip, more to forestall having to answer the question than from thirst. He'd already had two Scotches before he left his mother's house; it wasn't like he needed more. "I didn't get a chance to see my dad, you know, before he died..." Jeb said and let his voice trail off. It was true, but not what Alex was really asking. He looked up and saw that Alex was still waiting for an answer. "Christ, Alex! I don't know what's wrong with me. I'm a fucked-up mess, that's all."

Alex nodded and took a sip from his beer. "Well, at least you're being honest with me." He watched the young ranchers laughing and shoving each other at the bar. Those guys must've been little kids when he and Jeb used to come here during college. He glanced back at Jeb and nearly winced at the pain he could read in his friend's face. "Jeb...Jeb, you can't do this to yourself, the drinking and drugs and all that shit. Come on, man, that's not what you're about!"

Jeb shrugged. "Maybe I've changed, Alex. Maybe this is what I'm about now."

Alex slammed his fist on the table and made the drinks and the little corn chip bowl jump. "No, dammit! Don't ever say that, do you hear me?"

Jeb looked up in surprise, but picked up his drink and sipped from it, looking at Alex over the rim. He swallowed and set the glass down again. "Alex, I'm burned out inside. It's like…I don't know, like I'm just a black hole of emptiness. I don't know if I can ever get right again. I really don't." He nearly whispered the last words and he saw that Alex was leaning towards him to hear him.

"I know, man, I know. I can see you're fucked up. But that doesn't mean we can't figure out a way to…to…I don't know, to bring you back, make things right again…"

Jeb smiled, the ends of his lips barely turning up, but a smile, nonetheless. "We? You and Kathy, you mean?"

Alex looked directly into his eyes, "Yup, me and Kathy and you – the three of us. She's my wife and you're my best friend. The three of us made it through college together and we're going to get through this together, too. That's how it is now and how it's going to always be, so get used to it, Bud."

Jeb's shoulders drooped and he sighed. "Ma's thinking of moving in with her sister in Billings."

Alex nodded. "I figured she might."

"What the fuck do I do about the ranch, Alex? I can't run it, but I don't want to sell it, either. Shit, I'll belong nowhere if I do that."

Alex blinked. "Sell it? Of course, you're not going to fucking sell it! Heck, I'll buy it if you sell it! You promised it to me when we were ten, don't you remember?"

Jeb chuckled and felt himself relax. He would probably end up blubbering into tears if he drank any more or Alex said one more nice or sentimental thing to him. He cleared his throat. "So, what do I do with it until you're able to come up with the scratch to buy it from me?"

Alex took a long sip of his beer, his eyes distant as he considered. He set the bottle down and furrowed his brow, idly tracing the scratches on the surface of the table. Finally, he looked up. "Let's lease the land out. The Camdens' ranch borders yours. Let's see if they will lease the upper pastureland for their cattle. You can sell off your dad's cattle or make some kind of arrangement with Cal to fatten them up and take them to market with his herd next year. When we're ready to split from Montana, we'll rent the house out. It's close enough to town, so we might be able to get a college family to rent it. What do you think?"

Jeb studied Alex's face for a minute or two as he thought about it. He shrugged and nodded. "That might work. I'll talk to Cal Camden about it."

"No, WE'LL talk to Cal. I'm coming with you." Alex's voice would brook no discussion.

Jeb started to say that Alex didn't have to baby-sit him, but seeing the look on his friend's face, he decided that perhaps he could use a babysitter after all. He'd be glad to have Alex watching his back again. Finally, he nodded. "Thanks." And he lifted his drink in salute.

Alex toasted Jeb with his beer bottle. "I won't leave you hanging, Jeb. Not ever."

Jeb felt tears sting at the corners of his eyes, but he blinked them back before Alex could see. He was falling apart, he thought again. It was embarrassing. If he'd tear up in front of Alex while drinking in a cowboy bar in the rougher part of town; shit, then he was definitely falling apart.

"What are your plans for the future, Jeb?" Alex asked a while later. "You didn't re-up in the Marines, so I assume you're not planning to go back into the service."

Jeb shook his head. "Nope. I was fooled by that whole peacekeeping thing. I forgot there's a difference between peace-making and peace-keeping." He shrugged. "Let's face it: if you have to send in the Marines to keep the peace, then there probably isn't any peace there worth saving."

Alex chuckled. "You're right about that. So, what's next?"

Jeb shook his head. "I don't really know."

"Care to go on a hike with me then?" Alex asked.

Jeb heard something in Alex's voice, and he studied his friend's face for a second. "What sort of hike did you have in mind exactly?"

Alex grinned. "The AT, man! We need to hike the Trail! We always said we would, you know. Now's our chance!"

Jeb sputtered, "Are you kidding me? You and Kathy just got married! Is she really going to let you just up and leave her for six months?"

"More like seven or eight months, but who's quibbling?" Alex laughed. "Besides, we've already talked about it. She wants to go to grad school at Georgetown. I was thinking of applying for a job at the State Department, but she's fine with you and me taking some time off and doing the Trail first. She even volunteered to drive down and re-supply us when we get within driving distance of D.C." He stopped and looked at Jeb. "So, what do you think? I don't know if we'll ever get another opportunity like this when neither of us is tied down to a job or the Marines or whatever."

Jeb stared at him for several long seconds. He shook his head, but it wasn't in refusal, it was in wonder. "The Appalachian Trail? Shit, Alex! I'm...I'm flabbergasted."

"Yeah. We always said we'd do it, didn't we? And like I said, now's the perfect time!"

Jeb turned it over in his mind. He could see them with packs on their backs, sweaty, boot sore, but...happy. He nodded. "What the hell, man? I've got nothing else going on. I'm in!"

And that was the beginning of their AT saga. They spent the next month through the Christmas holidays of that year together buying supplies and equipment, breaking in their hiking boots, and getting their bodies ready for the physical endurance test that the AT would undoubtedly be. Jeb quit drinking, they worked out, and they hiked for miles in the mountains around Missoula. They hiked the Hellgate Canyon Trail, then to the top of Lolo Peak, and on a few trails in the Bitterroot Mountain Range just to get their bodies ready. Then when the three of them moved to Washington, D.C. so Kathy could start classes in January, they scouted out the

Virginia portion of the trail and did some day trips and a couple of overnighters to test out their equipment.

Luckily, Jeb hadn't been out of the Marines very long so even though he hadn't done his body any favors with the abuse he'd laid on it in the months since he'd been back from Beirut, it wasn't hard to rediscover the underlying muscles and stamina that had always been there. Alex was in decent shape and except for some days of intensely sore muscles, he adjusted quickly to the increased physical activity.

At the end of February, they finally set off from Springer Mountain in Georgia, two of the hundreds of hikers to begin the hike that year. Only a quarter of the hikers that set out would actually complete the entire thru-hike end-to-end. And some hikers did the trail in reverse, starting from Mt. Katahdin in Maine and hiking south. But since Alex wanted to be close enough to see Kathy on weekends, he was happy to start in Georgia and follow the spring northward, the usual way.

When they got back after the hike eight months later, Jeb found he was once again able to get his life back on track. He returned to school and got his master's degree in computer science. He thought it would be a nice safe and lucrative career. Any bombs would be in the application software code, not in the building next door; or so he thought.

He couldn't remember the exact sequence of events that put him into harm's way again. How did he end up working for the State Department in embassies overseas? How did he end up working for the CIA? He wasn't exactly sure. He never applied for any of those jobs, never went on an interview, never negotiated a salary, none of that. He was sure it had something to do with Alex. Most of the major turns in his life had Alex written all over them, after all.

Alex and Kathy had both taken jobs and started careers at the State Department. One day, Alex mentioned that the Department was looking for some computer savvy help and that he had mentioned Jeb's name to his boss. The next thing Jeb knew he was working not only for the State Department, but for the CIA, as well.

They liked that he had been in the Marines, and they loved that he had worked in Communications and understood how intelligence operations worked. For his part, he was glad to be working near Alex and Kathy. After his mother passed on, they were the closest things he had to family.

It had been interesting work; he would have to give it that, but neither as safe nor as lucrative as it would've been in the private sector. Most of what he did involved analyzing the security of communication traffic between Washington and a particular overseas embassy. It required a lot of travel to some very remote and dangerous places, but he found it challenging and very compelling work. It was sometimes like a giant puzzle whose detail he had to fill in slowly and carefully, step by step. Maybe it wasn't so different from trying to find a four-year-old girl in the woods of northern New Hampshire, he realized.

THIRTY-THREE

Day 2 of the Search (Jeb)

August 2006
Wilderness Campground, Crawford Notch, NH

*** Jeb ***

"Hey, Jeb," Joe called out. He was hiking further behind Jeb and had to holler to be heard.

Jeb came out of his reverie, stopped, and turned. "Yeah?"

"Wait up." Joe jogged to Jeb's side. He held up a wadded white tissue. "Could this be something?"

"Let's see," Jeb said taking the muddy white tissue from Joe's hand. He studied it. It looked yellowed and ancient to him, but he was no expert. "Let's show it to Travis." They passed the word up the trail to Travis, the group leader, who was leading the group of searchers. Everyone stopped and Travis came back to see what Joe had found.

He took the tissue from Jeb and he, too, studied it. He shook his head. "I doubt it was hers, but we'll take it back with us. Let's mark on the map where you found it, Joe." He pulled a map from his vest pocket and spread it on a flat boulder near the side of the trail. "How far back did you find it?"

Joe pointed, "Just back there to the left, a couple of feet off the trail. There, near that tall paper birch. See it? The one there, just past the trail blaze."

"Let's take a look, then," Travis said as he put a small mark on his map and folded it back up and stuffed it back into his vest pocket. Travis and Jeb followed Joe to the spot he'd pointed out. The three of them spread out and looked carefully to see if there was anything else.

Travis crouched down and then lifted his head and looked around. He smiled and shook his head.

"What?" Jeb asked.

Joe stopped and looked quizzically at Travis, too.

"I don't know, but I think that tissue might have been someone's toilet paper. See how secluded this spot is? Good tree cover, not too far off the trail, nice big boulder blocking the view from the back...." He smiled. "We'll take it in with us, but..."

Jeb and Travis grinned at Joe.

Joe shrugged. "Don't they teach hikers up here that the only thing they're supposed to leave behind are footprints?"

"Sure, ON the trail. Off the trail's another matter entirely," Jeb teased.

"Apparently," Joe answered dryly.

"Nice going, anyway," Travis said to Joe, punching him lightly in the shoulder. "Let's get moving," he said a little louder for the others to hear.

Soon the group was hiking up the trail once again.

"Man, that was embarrassing," Joe said to Jeb, who was just in front of him.

"Yeah, but funny," Jeb replied with a grin.

Joe chuckled. "I guess it's another story for my book."

"Are you writing a book?" Jeb asked.

"Thinking about it," Joe said. "I'm keeping a journal of my trip. I should have a few weeks to work on putting it together before I start college in January."

"It's a good idea, even if you never publish it. Wished I'd kept more notes on what I saw. You forget after a while. You don't think you will, but you do."

"That's why I'm keeping my journal. I've made entries just about every day. Missed a few at the beginning because I was just too damn tired and overwhelmed. Now, I'm better about it."

Jeb nodded. "I read about a guy...I think he lived down in Boston...that wrote in his journal every single day of his adult life. His whole friggin' life! Published the volumes, too. It made quite a story in the paper." He shook his head.

"What? You don't think publishing it was a good idea?" Joe asked.

"I dunno." Jeb shrugged. "Who'd read it? You know? It's just the daily life of some guy."

They hiked in silence for a while then Jeb turned his head slightly. "Joe, is Kay in your journal?"

Joe didn't answer right away. "Why do you ask?"

"I'd hate to see her written up as a passing attraction in this book of yours, that's all."

"I wouldn't do that!" Joe said defensively. "Anyway, she isn't a passing attraction to me."

"No?"

"Does she think I see her that way?" Joe asked tentatively.

"I don't know," Jeb responded truthfully. "But she's pretty young and gullible. She'd probably believe whatever you told her."

"You think I'm just trying to score with her?"

Jeb shrugged. "Why not? She's a beauty. As I'm sure you've noticed."

"Yeah, she is," Joe said with a smile. "But, it's not like that. I really do like her. As a matter of fact, I think she's one of the most incredible girls I've ever met."

Jeb stopped and turned. "Joe, I'm not trying to put you on the spot about Kay. It's just that I don't want her to get hurt when you pack your stuff and move on. That's all."

"Yeah, I know. But you got to believe me when I say I really do care about her, Jeb. I'm not just trying to get my jollies. You know, love 'em and leave 'em and all that crap."

"Good. Because, you may as well know that Alex and I will follow you up the Trail and get you if we find out you were just messing with her."

Joe stared at Jeb for several long seconds. He couldn't tell if he was serious or not. Finally, he decided Jeb was serious. He nodded. "Uh, yeah. O.K. I understand, sir."

Jeb smiled and patted Joe on the back. "Good boy! As long as we understand each other then."

They hurried to catch up with the rest of the group. As they hiked on, Jeb thought about Joe and Kay and wondered what was going on between them. He suspected it was more serious than any of the rest of them realized. He couldn't put his finger on it, but he sensed that Joe wasn't telling him the whole story. But then, was it really any of his business? He thought about that. Then he nodded to himself. Yup, as a matter of fact, it was his business. She was as much his responsibility as she was Alex's or Tess'. That was the way they had worked things out after Kathy died and that was the way he wanted it. This was his family; however unconventional it might be. He'd die for any one of them.

Jeb heard a thud and scramble behind him, as Joe tripped and then caught himself.

"Hey, are you OK?" Jeb asked, turning to survey the young man. It was obvious his mind was somewhere else.

"Yeah," Joe replied. "I let my mind wander for a second. I should know better."

Jeb nodded and turned back to the trail. We should all know better.

THIRTY-FOUR

Back at the Lodge

August 2006
Wilderness Campground, Crawford Notch, NH

Kay

Back at the lodge, Kay was thinking about Joe. She was busy, though, checking in campers, hurrying from one task to the next as Tessie came up with one thing after another for her to do. She wasn't complaining; she was glad to be so busy. She couldn't stand just sitting around waiting for Joe to get back to camp. How did women do that? Waiting for their men? Like those sea widows pacing the shores, waiting for their sailor husbands to return, not knowing even if they would return? How did they stand it? She could barely get through five or six hours. But weeks? Months? She thought of Joe, his smile, his hands reaching for her, holding her. She was not good at waiting. It made her feel all wound up and anxious. She knew she should be worrying about Melanie, but her mind was stuck on a single track. And that track was named Joe.

The dining room hummed with the busy sounds of people on mobile phones and walkie-talkies. Maps were stretched across tabletops. There was the incessant clicking of keys on the keyboards of laptop computers as calls from the field were recorded. In a day and a half, the search and rescue had become a full-scale operation, a self-contained enterprise, with bosses and employees — albeit all volunteers — and information received, processed, and returned, decisions made and the distinctive buzz of a hectic office wherever one turned.

They had ordered the press out of the lodge, only allowing them access twice a day: once in the morning and once in the late afternoon when Jerry Stockman would provide an official update and would conduct a Q-and-A press conference. It was Lesley's idea to get the news people barred from the lodge and out from under everyone's feet. Organizing two press events also kept them at bay for most of the day. People could work without a camera or microphone in their faces. The relief was palpable.

Tessie

Tessie was overwhelmed by the change in their quiet home. On most days, before this onslaught, she had been able to hear the clock tick-tocking on the mantle; now she could barely hear herself think.

Earlier, she'd seen Angie go up to her room to work on translating the diary for the morning. She was surprised that Angie hadn't wandered back down, though. She had expected the teen to get quickly bored and frustrated with working alone. Of course, she was glad that Angie had stayed in her room. If she were walking around, they took the chance that some errant reporter might begin hounding her, particularly since they had little else to report.

The civil air patrol planes were grounded due to the weather and the special canine dogs from Pennsylvania hadn't been able to pick up Melanie's scent at all, probably because of the rain. Jerry Stockman said the dogs had been trained to seek out human cadavers, as well, but if they were actually conducting such a ghoulish search, it was being done surreptitiously, because no one was talking openly about it. Everything was focused on the ground search, and that effort wasn't going well. So far there hadn't been a single sign of Melanie. Nothing.

With great relief, Tessie had watched Keith Jacobs go off with an early search team. He didn't look good. His eyes were rimmed dark purple and had the sunken look of exhaustion. She wondered if he would be able to keep up with the other more rested volunteers.

It was obvious that Jerry Stockman was not happy about Keith going out again. Still, Tessie was sure that the thought of having Keith hanging around the lodge and second guessing his every move weighed heavily in the decision to let him go.

"Take him with you," Stockman had told Pete Daigneault, the sector leader. "Why don't you have him walk the trail with a megaphone. Tell him to repeat, *'Melanie, if you see some men near you, go to them.'* If she's out there, she's sure to react to her father's voice."

Tessie thought it was a good idea, because Melanie might indeed hide from strangers. Children were taught not to trust adults they didn't know. Still, she wondered if Melanie would understand and follow the instructions. Perhaps it would've been better to have Nora on the megaphone instead of Keith's harsh voice.

Tessie tried to imagine where the child might have gone, what she was doing at that moment. Was she wandering the woods? Had she stopped? Did she find a place to keep warm through the cold, rainy night? Tessie felt chilled at the thought. Would they find her alive? How would Angie handle it if Melanie were dead? How would any of them handle it? She shook away the thoughts. She mustn't jinx the search by pulling such dark thoughts into reality. She must concentrate on Melanie alive, Melanie warm, Melanie found.

Nora

Not far from the lodge, Nora paced at her campsite, her arms folded tightly across her chest. She hadn't slept much. She wasn't hungry. Earlier, she had made herself some dry cereal in a red plastic bowl, but she found she couldn't swallow it.

All she wanted was to hold Melanie, to feel her small solid body tucked warm and safe within her arms. The emptiness of

Melanie's absence was hard to bear, impossible to bear. Now, as never before, she understood women wailing their grief in ancient times. Keening, wasn't that the word? She, too, could wail, she could scream, she could cry until there were no more tears. And she would do any of it, all of it, if only it would bring Melanie back safely.

She knew the dangers of the woods. They were vivid in her mind's eye. The wild animals that chase, frighten, and strike a child down, the rocks and crevices that trap small legs, the deer paths that confuse and lead a child astray, the ever confounding mazes of trees and bushes that mesmerize, and the cold that would surely overtake and numb. She thought she could hear the hysterical cries of a lost child, of all lost children. She held her hands over her ears. She knew it was her imagination. Or, she wondered, was she losing her mind? She marched towards the lodge. She couldn't be alone with these thoughts.

THIRTY-FIVE

Research at the Library

August, 2006
Library, North Conway NH

*** Angie ***

I came downstairs later that morning looking for Tessie to see if she'd found me a ride to the library. I wished I were old enough to drive because I really wanted to get away from the campground and from everyone in it. With Dad and Jeb out searching, I felt a little bereft. If my mood were a color, it would've been a shade of gray when I got up that morning but after my encounter with Kay it had turned positively black. Yes, I know I was feeling sorry for myself. After all, no one had come upstairs to check on me to see how I was doing. Apparently, no one had even noticed that I hadn't been around.

I began to wish that I were the one lost in the woods. Yeah, that's how pathetic I had become. Next, I'd be imagining everyone at my funeral expressing regrets about not being nicer to me when I was alive. My thoughts were on a definite downward spiral.

Downstairs, the lodge was still bustling with people, of course, and everyone was very busy. Still, I was surprised when the media types didn't stop me on my way to the kitchen looking for Tessie. I pushed open the door and peered in. There were a number of people in the kitchen, sitting at the counters and standing around. I immediately homed in on Lesley and Tessie. They were huddled together, apparently, in mid-conversation. I quietly stepped inside and let the door gently close behind me. Neither of them looked up. Good. I was curious what they were saying because I was wondering if they were talking about me.

From my spot near the door, I could just make out their words. It turned out that Lesley was telling Tessie about how she organized the press by explaining to the band of reporters already camped at the lodge that although Jerry Stockman would be providing them with regular updates, if they had any questions, they were to come to her. She would serve as the go-between from now on. As Dad had predicted, Jerry Stockman welcomed her offer of help. Stockman had already been worn down with the second-guessing and persistent questioning from the media.

"You know what he said to me?" Lesley asked Tessie with a laugh.

Tessie shook her head, smiling back at Lesley. They were certainly getting chummy, I thought.

"He said 'I don't know how you do it, Lesley. They drive me up a wall! It's like battling a bunch of black flies. You know what New Hampshire's black flies are like? They're persistent little devils that won't leave you alone until they draw blood.' I thought that was hysterical, and oh, so true," Lesley said with a knowing nod.

Tessie nodded, too. "That's as good a description of the press as I've ever heard," she agreed.

"Of course, I'm glad to help out," Lesley said. "The goal is to make sure that there is only one story going out over the air waves. I may not be able to control what the news is, but at least I can try to make sure it's coherent and consistent, and with a little bit of luck, make it favorable."

"We're lucky to have someone like you who knows what they're doing," Tessie said.

"It feels good to be doing something constructive," Lesley nodded. "Besides, I know Alex thinks my being a psychic is on par with being a snake oil salesman or a carnie. I'd like to show him that I'm not a total New Age nut."

"Oh, he doesn't think you're a nut," Tessie responded.

"Really? Has he said anything to you about me?" Lesley asked hopefully.

I rolled my eyes when I heard her ask that. God, she sounded just like Kay.

Tessie shook her head. "To be honest, Lesley, I haven't had a chance to talk to Alex much in the past couple of days. Not with all this going on," Tessie said with a wave of her arms, taking in the hubbub in the next room.

Lesley nodded.

"I would've liked to talk to him about Kay, though," Tessie said with a sigh. She folded her dishcloth in front of her.

"Kay? Oh, you mean about her and Joe in the shower room?"

Tessie's head snapped up, and I'm sure mine did, too. Kay and Joe in the shower room? What was that all about?

"Huh?" Tessie responded. (Expressing my sentiments exactly.)

Lesley seemed to cringe a little as she put her hand to her mouth. "Oh, God! You don't know about that. I probably shouldn't have said anything."

Tessie smiled maliciously, "Come on, Lesley, you know you can't leave it like that!"

Lesley paused, took a breath, and then shrugged. "All right, but just remember to act surprised if Alex mentions it to you, OK?"

Tessie grinned and nodded. "Go on," she said, pulling her stool closer. I started to move a bit closer too but stopped myself. I didn't want them to notice me now before I heard what she was going to say about Kay. There were a few volunteers sitting on stools at the long counter between me and the two of them, so I felt pretty sure that unless they turned completely around, they probably wouldn't notice me. Not yet anyway.

"Well," Lesley started. "Yesterday evening, do you remember when Nora and I were coming into the kitchen for dinner?"

Tessie nodded. "Yeah, I remember. It was just before Keith showed up and made that little scene and then took Nora away."

"Right!" Lesley agreed. "Well, as Nora and I were coming through the outdoor clean up area, we heard giggling coming from one of the shower rooms."

"Giggling?" Tessie repeated, and then her eyes grew wide. "No! You mean Joe and Kay were in the shower together?"

Even from a distance I could hear the shock in Tessie's voice. To be honest, you could've knocked me over with a feather, too. And Kay had been so vehement when she told me that she and Joe weren't doing anything! What does she call showering together? Now I was growing incensed with righteous anger. If she had been in the kitchen, I think I might've even punched her. And I doubt I've hit her since I was five and she was seven!

Lesley nodded and shrugged. "It could've been fairly innocent, I suppose..."

"Innocent?!!!" Tessie repeated indignantly and more loudly than she had meant to. She immediately quieted her voice a decibel and continued, "In what way could it have been innocent?"

"Oh, I don't know," Lesley shrugged. "You're right, of course. I don't think it was innocent either, but Alex seemed to need that illusion when I told him about it last night."

"You TOLD him about it?" Tessie asked breathlessly. "Oh my God! What did he say?"

"Well, he stormed around my campfire a bit, and then took off into the night to find her and Joe. He assumed they were together somewhere; you know, maybe at one of the campsites."

"Did he find them then?"

Lesley smiled and nodded. "Sort of, but it's not what you think." She put her hand out and touched Tessie's arm.

"What do you mean? What happened?" Tessie asked, leaning in towards Lesley so as not to miss a single word.

I leaned in, too, praying that Lesley wouldn't start whispering or something and I'd miss the whole thing. While wondering how I was going to hear this next bit, another part of my mind was reviewing the scene with Kay that morning. I was having difficulty reconciling the idea that Dad might've caught her with Joe the night before and yet she was playing all innocent with me. That really seemed beyond the acting capabilities of the sister I thought I knew so well.

"That's just it! Nothing happened!" Lesley said. "Alex came back about an hour later. He said he'd gone to the lodge to get his big flashlight and to find Jeb to ask him to go with him after Kay and Joe, but instead he ran into Jerry Stockman who gave him an update on the search. Then when he turned to head out, Kay came waltzing in...alone."

Tessie looked disappointed. "Really? That's it?"

Lesley nodded. "Yes, thank God!" She laughed. "Come on, Tessie, you didn't really want a family homicide at the campground, did you?"

Tessie chuckled, but I wondered if she was putting two and two together the way I was and realized that Lesley had just admitted that Dad had gone back to her campsite after running into Kay. I wasn't sure how I felt about it. It was hard to picture my dad as some kind of Don Juan; that was for sure!

Instead of pursuing the discussion about Kay, Tessie suddenly snapped her fingers. "Oh, Lesley, before I forget; I need to ask a big favor of you. Could you drive Angie into town to the library? I was going to send her with Mr. Dooley, the postmaster, but it turns out he won't be coming out here until late this afternoon."

"Sure. I'd be glad to. The media folks won't need me until later this afternoon when the search teams start coming back in. I'd be glad to take Angie. Which vehicle can we use?"

"The jeep has gas, and the keys are hanging on the board above the desk in the kitchen; and the registration is in a folder in the glove compartment. You know how to drive a stick, don't you?"

Lesley nodded. "Who said I don't have some useful skills?" She smiled. "When do you want us to leave?"

I straightened up and pretended I had just come into the room. "Hi," I said to them.

"Oh, there you are," Tessie said. "Lesley has agreed to take you into North Conway to the library. Are you ready to go now or do you want to wait until after lunch?"

"Now," I said. "I'll go get my stuff." I turned and hurried upstairs to grab the diary and my notes. When I got back to the kitchen a few minutes later, Lesley was waiting for me.

We stepped out into the drizzly cool day and hurried around the lodge to the storage building. The door was unlocked, and we stepped through into the relative darkness of the garage. After a second or two, my eyes adjusted to the dim light coming through the small dingy window of the garage door.

The jeep was the vehicle closest to the door and Lesley motioned for me to get in. I pointed at the garage door and mimed lifting it to indicate that it was a manual garage door not an electric-powered door. Our electricity wasn't that dependable out here, so my dad opted for the old-fashioned manual door system. Lesley nodded that she understood, and I went to the door and lifted it. It glided silently overhead.

I climbed into the passenger seat next to Lesley. She was already looking over the dashboard to locate the lights, wipers, and other controls. Then she snapped on her seat belt and glanced at me to check that I had mine on, too. It was a motherly thing to do. No doubt she was one of those drivers who would karate chop my midsection if she stopped suddenly, too. But then I remember hearing that she had a teenage son living with her ex-husband in California. Having a child gave her those protective instincts, I suppose.

Lesley smiled and gave me a jaunty thumbs-up. I rolled my eyes and looked away. Adults could be so weird, at times. Just when you were enjoying something together, they would use a cringe-worthy slang word or would make a gesture that was either way too urban chic or was from a previous century. Their actions were anachronistic, which, if my vocabulary builder program on my computer was correct, means they are chronologically misplaced. And I'm not talking just about their actions, either.

I've seen older women dressed worse than streetwalkers, with low slung tight skirts showing the top of a thong in the back and their wrinkly bellies and abs all hanging out in the front. I mean, come on! It's gross. Don't they see that? 'Chronologically challenged' is putting it mildly. I hoped Lesley wasn't like that.

Lesley started the engine. Immediately, we saw two reporters pointing at us from the porch of the lodge. "Uh oh," Lesley said under her breath.

We watched them as they turned as if to come over to the jeep, but Lesley waved innocently as we drove by and then she sped up. She smiled a little to herself and didn't say anything, but she was obviously enjoying it.

She slowed down a short distance up the camp road, which was rutted and muddy due to the rain. That was wise since you never knew whether there would be campers – and I'm referring to the vehicles, not just the people – coming up the road, which was only about one and a half vehicles wide. As if thinking about it conjured it up, the headlights of a camper appeared about 100 yards in front of us. Lesley flashed the headlights and pulled over to let it crawl by.

As the vehicle passed, the driver nodded to us. There was a man and his wife and at least one child, a little girl who waved from the backseat. I waved back at her. She looked a little like Melanie, although her hair was shorter. Probably all little girls would look like Melanie to me from now on.

Lesley stopped when we reached the highway. "You can give me directions to the library when we get into North Conway, right?"

"Yup," I nodded. "It's on Main Street, just past the railroad station. I'll show you where to turn when we get there."

We were quiet for most of the trip. The windshield wipers were going nearly the entire time, but it was frustrating with the drizzle. The wipers had to be set to high when there was a car or truck in front of us because of the spray from their tires, but as soon as we passed the vehicle, Lesley had to turn the wipers off for several minutes until enough moisture collected to make the wiping effective. If she left the wipers on, they squeaked and squawked against the glass.

Soon we were driving through the town of Glen at the crossroads of Route 302 and Route 16. Up the road from Glen through Pinkham Notch were the AMC Visitor's Center, Wildcat Ski Area, and the Mount Washington Auto Road. South on this road another fifteen or twenty minutes, depending on traffic, was North Conway.

"What are you going to be researching, Angie?" Lesley asked as she turned the jeep towards North Conway. She glanced at me and then lifted her eyes to look out the passenger window behind me. Normally, there would be an awesome view of the entire valley from this vantage point, but today the clouds hung low, and it was foggy and dreary. That was too bad.

"I want to find out about the little girl who was lost back in 1941. That's the main thing," I said.

Lesley frowned. "What little girl?"

"Oh, I forgot! That's right! We didn't learn about her until we started translating the diary last night. You and Dad haven't heard this part at all!" I relished having a story to tell.

"So?" Lesley said encouragingly.

"Last night Tessie and I translated the first page of the diary. The guy who wrote the diary – his name is Jean-Louis Duclos, by the way – was in the CCC at Sawyer River Camp. The camp used to be right where our campground is located now. Anyway, he begins by saying he is writing from a temporary camp down at White Ledge Park in Albany on the southern edge of the mountains and that he is there to help search for a little girl who had gotten lost in the woods."

"A little girl lost in the woods, just like now?" Lesley asked in amazement.

"Yeah." I nodded. "I know. Isn't the coincidence so weird? The stuff I translated this morning says that on the second day of the search, they think she might've headed towards the highway. On the other side of the highway is a lake, so he says they dragged the lake, figuring that she may have drowned. He also mentions there's a rumor around the camp that an ex-convict might have kidnapped the little girl."

"You're kidding! It sounds like something from TV news today, doesn't it? So, what happened? Did they find her?"

"Well, that's the thing. We don't know yet. That's why I wanted to see what the newspapers from that time say about it. Actually, I'm just hoping the story is even mentioned."

"Yeah," Lesley agreed. She shook her head. "What are the chances that you'd find a diary that talks about a little girl lost in 1941? It's such an odd coincidence."

"Dad says that in Nature, there are no coincidences." I don't know why I said that. I mean it was true. Dad did say that; but I guess I said it because I just wanted to sound smart.

Lesley glanced over at me. "What on earth does that mean?"

I didn't expect that reaction from her. Especially since she's the psychic, right? But after a moment's thought I answered, "Well, Dad and Jeb call strange coincidences 'Trail Magic.' You know, from when they hiked the AT. It means that once you are in tune with Nature and with the Universe around you, things that you need to happen just happen. You attract them to yourself on some cosmic level."

"So how does that negate coincidences?"

"Well, calling something a 'coincidence' makes it sound like it wasn't supposed to happen, but it did. 'Trail Magic' says that it was all supposed to happen, so it does."

Lesley shook her head. "I'm not sure I get the distinction. I mean, I believe in a lot of supernatural stuff – heck, being a psychic presupposes that, I guess – but what you're saying is that there's some sort of Fate or God out there controlling everything..."

"No, that's not it at all. It's not 'out there,' you see. It's inside, in each of us." As I explained it to Lesley, it dawned on me that I believed in it myself. Things DO happen for a reason, at least, I believe they do.

Lesley eyed me for a second and then returned her attention to the road. "So, what you're saying is that we each control what happens to us?"

"Yes. But it only works when you're in tune with Nature, with the Universe around you. If you're all out of whack, then all bets are off, I guess." I smiled. "In this case – in my case, I mean – it means that I was meant to discover this diary right now."

"I don't know. It seems a little too neat an answer to me. It's like 20-20 hindsight; after something has happened you wrap it up in a neat little explanation that fits." She shrugged. "Although, I admit, I can't explain it. It is very weird."

"Well, it happened, so there it is." I said and shrugged. I looked out the window for a minute or two then turned back to Lesley. "I think it's funny that you're a psychic, but you don't believe in Trail Magic." I guess I felt like she was spurning what I was saying, and I wanted to turn the tables a bit.

"Let's just say that I resisted the whole idea of the psychic realm for a long time."

"Really?" I said. "You didn't want to be a psychic?"

Lesley shook her head. "God, no!" She glanced at me then back at the road. "Who wants to be thought of as a freak? Or a witch?"

"I don't know about that. I think it'd be cool to be psychic," I said. "How did you end up doing readings then? I mean if you didn't want to be a psychic?"

"I kept having these strong feelings about people, about things that were going to happen to them. I'd dream really vivid dreams at night. Sometimes I'd wake up and I wouldn't know if something had actually happened or if I'd just dreamt it. It was sort of scary, actually."

I nodded. "So, you didn't have a choice, huh?"

Lesley shrugged. "It was give into it or go nuts!" she added cheerfully.

I studied her for a minute then looked out my window again. I wasn't sure how I felt about her. She wasn't like any other adult I knew. Of course, I didn't really know very many grown-up women.

Just Tessie, and Tessie wasn't like anyone else. First of all, she was Vietnamese, so she looked at things differently, and secondly, I had known her since I was a baby so there was no way for me to be objective about her; and thirdly, well, thirdly, Tessie wasn't in love with my dad!

I thought probably if Lesley wasn't interested in my father, I might've liked her more. After all, she was interesting, and nice, too, but then I'd see an image in my mind of the two of them kissing, and a surge of...of what? Anger? Repulsion? Discomfort! That's what it was. I sighed. Anyway, a surge of something came over me and I just couldn't be friendly to her.

I saw that we were getting close to the library, and I was glad to have something else to think about. I gave Lesley directions – a couple of left turns and a right that brought us into the parking lot. Lesley parked the jeep, and we went in.

The librarian sat behind a large wooden counter. She looked up as we entered and gave us a thin smile of welcome. I glanced around. It was a small library. At the table closest to the door, two older women sat side-by-side. One was studying a huge book laid opened before her, the other was reading from a dog-eared paperback that she had bent back so that the cover and first forty or fifty pages were curled around. It was hard to tell if the two women were together or merely sharing the table.

Behind the women was an older gentleman hunched over and sound asleep, his short white hair stood bristly on the top of his head. His breathing was deep and even. Slowly his head drooped on to his chest, and he jerked up with a start and glanced around. He stared at us through a furrowed white brow, as if accusing us of wakening him. I looked away.

Lesley nudged my arm and led me over to the librarian's counter.

"Excuse me," Lesley said quietly to the woman. "Do you carry newspapers from 1941?"

The librarian blinked once and nodded. "Oh sure. Of course, we do. On microfilm. There's a reader machine back in the corner. Do you know how to operate one?"

"Yes, I think so," Lesley replied. "Where can we find the newspaper files?"

The librarian paused and studied Lesley's face. "1941, did you say?"

We both nodded.

"Hmmm," the librarian turned and typed something into her computer. She studied the screen. "We have the Boston Globe, the Conway Daily Sun, and the Manchester Union Leader. Which ones are you interested in?"

"Maybe all three, we won't know until we take a look at them."

"Are you looking for something in particular then?"

I nodded. "Yes. It's a story about a little girl who got lost in the woods in September of 1941."

The librarian nodded and frowned. "Hmmm. Sounds sort of familiar." She looked thoughtfully into space for several long seconds. "Not sure why though."

I looked at Lesley with the barest of smiles.

"Could we see the newspapers?" Lesley interrupted the librarian's reverie.

"Certainly. Follow me." The librarian stood up slowly and groaned, as old people are wont to do. "I'll show you the cabinets where we keep them and explain how they're organized."

We followed her through the bookshelves towards the back of the building. In a dim corner sat the table with the microfilm reader sitting next to an older model computer terminal. Several file cabinets lined the wall beyond.

"Here you go," the librarian said. She glanced at me and studied my face for a second, "Why, I know you, don't I? You're the girl that was on the news last night, aren't you? The story about the little girl lost at the campground out on 302."

I swallowed hard and nodded, feeling vaguely guilty.

"Hmmm. That must be why it all sounds so familiar then. So, tell me, did the little girl run away from you or what?" She leaned in close and peered at me over the top of her wire-rimmed glasses.

I took an involuntary step back. "No, of course not. She didn't run away from me. We were...we were playing and then one minute she was there and then next I turned around and she was gone."

Lesley put an arm around my shoulders. "We think the little girl was trying to follow her parents who had just left to go hiking."

"I see," the librarian said. But she didn't. She stared at me as if she might be able to discern the truth from my face. She glanced at Lesley. "So have they found anything of her yet?"

I grimaced at the image her words conjured up as Lesley shook her head. "No, no trace yet. But I'm sure we'll find her soon. She couldn't have gone too far."

"People always say that, but my grandson got lost in that big mall over in Maine last year. He was only two and a half and you wouldn't believe how far he got in just a few minutes. We were lucky nobody tried to grab him."

Lesley winced. She quickly turned away and went over to the first file cabinet. It contained issues of The Union Leader newspaper. She dragged the first drawer out and started reading through the index tabs for the years dividing up the boxes of microfilm.

The librarian came quickly to her side. "Here," she said, peremptorily closing the drawer Lesley had opened. "The 1940's are in one of these bottom two drawers. Down here," she said, pulling one of the bottom drawers out. She leaned over and her fingers ran confidently over the tops of the index tabs. She made little sounds of question and approval under her breath. "Yes, here we are," she said as she stood up and held out a box of microfilm records. "The 1940's. September of 1941 will be in here."

Lesley took the box and carried it over to where I was seated in front of the reader. She thumbed through the boxes of film and pulled one out, "Here, this one says September 1941. Let's take a look at it."

The librarian stood behind us, which was a little disconcerting. But then a phone rang in the distance. "Oh," she said, sounding disappointed. "I'll be back shortly in case you need anything," she said over her shoulder, as she hurried away.

Lesley made a face. "Saved by the bell," she whispered.

I moved the microfilm around until I found the page one headings for September 29, 1941. "Look at this," I said to Lesley. "'Bay State Girl, 5, Wanders off in Albany Woods,'" I read aloud. I grinned. "Hey! That's it! That's our story!"

"Shhhhh," Lesley whispered, with a nod to the front of the library. She returned my smile. "I think we're on the right track."

We read through the articles, not just for September 29th but for the next nine days, as well.

"Finally! Here it is!" I said. "Look! They did find her. And she was alive!"

"After nearly nine days?" Lesley said, shaking her head in disbelief.

"And look at this!" I said, pointing. "The newspaper only cost 3 cents! Wow!"

Lesley grinned and nodded. I felt positively lighthearted, as if it was Melanie who had been found. I was certain it was a sign, and I didn't care if Lesley believed in signs or not.

THIRTY-SIX

The Pamela Hollingworth Story

September 1941 White Ledge State Park, Albany, NH

(A summary of the facts of the case, as reported in the newspapers at the time)

Sunday, Sept. 28, 1941. *A little girl, Pammy Hollingworth, got lost while on a picnic with her family at White Ledge State Park in Albany. Around 2 p.m. she disappeared. At 2:20 p.m. the family noticed her missing and started searching for her. By 7 p.m., the Forest Service rangers had been called in and they established a base camp at White Ledge Park. Temperatures dipped below freezing at night.*

Monday, Sept. 29, 1941. *The first report of the event was reported in the Boston newspapers. The search was extended to top of Middle Sister Mountain, and included an air search, flying low over mountains, meadows, and bare rock. Pammy's father rode in a sound truck over rough and narrow mountain roads through the forest calling into the loudspeaker "Pammy, this is Daddy. If you see some men near you, go to them."*

Tuesday, Sept 30, 1941. *At dawn the temperature was 22 degrees at the base camp at White Ledge Park on Route 16. The search included soldiers from Fort Devens, MA, and was more than 300 strong. 200 were concentrated* around Iona Lake because footprints had been seen leading to within a half-mile of the campground there. No other evidence was found. It rained later that day. 130 enlisted men from Fort Williams, Maine, arrived at 7 p.m. and went directly into woods to search.

Wednesday, Oct. 1, 1941. At 6 a.m. searchers began dragging Iona Lake. Ground search didn't stop at dark as 500-million candlepower Coast Artillery searchlight flashed over the area while men and dogs continued searching in the woods all night.

Thursday, Oct. 2, 1941. Men moved slowly an arm's length apart. It was a slow and difficult search. Gov. Robert O. Blood of New Hampshire visited the search area to commend and encourage the weary men. He added $500 to the reward of $350 that was offered for information.

Friday, Oct. 3, 1941. The Hollingworths stayed in a donated trailer at the scene. Later, Blanche Hollingworth, Pammy's mother returned home to Dunstable, MA. Slim Baker, who was in charge of the search, believed the parents that it would be uncharacteristic of Pammy to have been playing in the area where she was supposedly sighted, and he moved the search area northwest of White Ledge where he found a child's footprint. More searchers were sent to the area. Cellar holes, closed summer camps, and swamps were checked. Psychics were consulted.

(One was correct in predicting that Pammy would be found 2 miles off a mountain trail). A bloodhound from the RI State Police failed to find any scent it could follow because of rain and was returned home.

Saturday, Oct. 4, 1941. The search reached 14 miles out from the White Ledge picnic grounds. Mass. State Guard sent 100 men and another 200 volunteers from Lowell. National concern shared media space with the war in Europe. The reward was up to $1000. More than 6000 automobiles clogged the highway near White Ledge. Searchers were on 24-hour shifts. 300 people were treated for minor injuries.

Sunday, Oct 5, 1941. *Prayers were offered in all the churches for Pammy, although hope is waning.*

Monday, Oct. 6, 1941. *Pammy was found on this day, the eighth day of the search.*

THIRTY-SEVEN

Return from the Library

August 2006
Library, North Conway, NH

*** *Angie* ***

Lesley and I made copies of the articles, and it was just after noon before we were done. The sky was brighter when we emerged from the dimly lit library, but only just. Clouds rimmed with dark bands rolled low in the sky. Mount Cranmore, which is located behind the town and whose mountainside contains the local ski area, was hidden completely in clouds. In fact, if you had never been to North Conway before, you wouldn't be able to tell that the town actually sat in the bowl of the very scenic Saco River valley, surrounded by mountains.

"Want to grab some lunch?" Lesley asked as we climbed into the jeep.

"Sure. I'm starving," I said without a second thought. I was feeling pretty good now that we knew the 1941 girl survived her ordeal. It seemed to cast a glow of optimism over everything.

"What's good in town? And I mean a place that doesn't serve just fast food...!"

"Oh, well, Horsefeathers is good. It has soup, salad, and sandwiches, that sort of thing. It's just past the train station, and on our way."

"It sounds perfect. Let's go there."

The town was bustling with summer tourists, but Lesley managed to find a parking spot along the park near the train station and we hurried across the busy Main Street to the restaurant.

After we got settled and placed our order, Lesley sat back looking speculatively at me. "Well, you had a pretty successful morning, don't you think?"

I nodded. "I'm so glad they found that little girl in the story. I can't wait to finish the translation to see what the French-Canadian guy has to say about it."

Lesley smiled. "This is quite a project you've picked."

"I'm glad it turned out to be this interesting. It's hard to believe it all started with an old nickel, huh?"

Lesley nodded in agreement. "I'm amazed by everything that's happened over the past couple of days. If someone had told me last week what I'd be doing right now, I wouldn't have believed it."

"So does that mean you don't you get any psychic messages about your own life?" I asked. I was genuinely curious. I mean, what's the use of a psychic talent if you can't find out what's going to be happening in your own future?

Lesley shrugged, "Even if I did, I wouldn't trust it. I mean, how could I tell if it was real or just me wishing something would happen? I think it'd be too easy to trick myself."

I nodded. "That's true. So then, how does it work?"

We were interrupted by the waiter who set down our drinks, plunked down silverware and then slid the plates of food in front of each of us. I ordered a hamburger with a huge mound of fries. She can say what she wants about fast food, but I was still a big fan, probably because I didn't get a chance to order it very often. Lesley asked for a bowl of broccoli soup and a tossed salad.

When the waiter left, we ate, each of us lost in her own thoughts. As Lesley was finishing her lunch, she seemed to remember that we had been in the middle of a conversation. "Sorry. What were we talking about before?" she asked.

I glanced up at her. "I was asking how being a psychic works. Like, can you really see into the future?" I studied her. I wasn't sure if she really looked the part of a psychic, to be honest. She seemed too – I don't know – up-to-date and modern somehow. I guess my idea of a psychic runs more towards an aging hippie in a tie-dye grannie dress with a headband, wild hair and smelling of incense and marijuana. OK, it's maybe a little predictable, but it's what the word "psychic" conjures up for me. Although I might be confusing the word with 'psychedelic.'

"Well," Lesley said, "I don't know if what I see is the future. It's hard to describe. The way it usually works, though, is the person I'm doing a reading for will ask me a question and after a minute or two, I get a feeling about it. It seems to be quicker and more accurate if I don't try to consciously think about it, so I just let the images come to me. Sometimes thoughts or pictures of things will flash in my mind, like, for instance, the name of a place where they're going to live, or maybe I'll get an image of a child in their future, that sort of thing. It's just a brief glimpse, though; and sometimes not even that. Sometimes it's just a sense of knowing."

"So, have you received any of these images about Melanie? Like, do you know if we're going to find her?" I asked, leaning forward with interest.

Lesley paused and looked at me. "Of course, I've been thinking about Melanie ever since she disappeared, Angie. Nora asked me the other night if I sensed anything about where to look for her. I hadn't at the time, but I guess I do sort of feel like she's OK. I mean, I don't think anything bad has happened to her yet."

I let out my breath, not realizing that I had been holding it. "Wow! That's a relief! Did you tell Mrs. Jacobs?"

"No, I haven't yet." I could hear the hesitation in her voice.

"Why not?" I asked in surprise.

"Because the thing is…I don't know if what I'm feeling is real. I don't know if I'm really sensing it or if it's just my own wishful thinking. I don't want to give Mrs. Jacobs false hope."

I frowned. "Well, it seems to me that false hope is better than no hope, isn't it? It could make her feel so much better right now if you told her."

Lesley frowned. "But it's just a feeling, and I don't know if I can trust it." Lesley shook her head, and it was obvious that she was very uncomfortable. Still, it just sounded like a bunch of excuses, and it didn't make any sense to me.

"Is the reason you haven't told her because you're afraid of being wrong?" I asked bluntly. OK, I know that was kind of rude, but it's honestly what I was thinking.

Lesley stared at me and then she shook her head again. "No, Angie, I'm not afraid of being wrong. I always tell people right up front that I could be wrong."

"Yeah, but that's really a cop-out, isn't it? If you're wrong, you tell them that you warned them you might be? Maybe Dad and Jeb are right. Maybe this whole psychic thing is just a big fake," I said bitterly.

Lesley swallowed. "Your dad and Jeb told you I'm a fake?"

I shrugged. "Not in those specific words, but I'm pretty sure it's what they think. Actually, the whole thing sounds kind of fakey to me, too." All right, I admit I might've been trying to get a rise out of her. I felt a little pissed off about her not reassuring Nora that Melanie was all right. And, I guess, I felt that by doing that – or rather by not doing that – she wasn't backing me up either. Yeah, I know, in the end it came down to being all about me, I guess. What can I say? I'm a teenager.

"Angie, I'm not going to defend what I do. You can call it fake or not. Don't you think I'm used to people being skeptical? The truth is, I really don't know for sure about Melanie. I promise, though, when I feel more certain, I will tell the Jacobs. I'll tell everyone."

"Because it's all about you being right, is that it?" I asked coolly.

She didn't answer. To be honest, I can't believe I actually said that out loud to an adult. Anyway, she didn't answer. Either I was right, or she wasn't going to dignify my rudeness by answering me. Either way it was a quiet ride back to the campground.

I didn't feel like talking, but boy, my mind was sure churning. I was thinking about how maybe Lesley had this psychic gift but instead of sharing it with people where she might make them feel better, she hid it away and kept it to herself. Wasn't there a biblical passage about the folly of hiding your light under a basket? When she was right, she could feel all righteous about knowing that things would work out; but if she were wrong, no one would ever know. Heck, it was worse than a scam; it was a total waste.

We arrived back at the campground mid-afternoon and as we neared the lodge, we could see that more cars and trucks had arrived, as well as several camper vehicles, each stuffed to the roof with camping gear.

The garage bay door was open, and Lesley drove the jeep right in. We climbed out and I hurried, walking stiffly ahead of her, to the kitchen door at the back of the lodge. As we stepped inside the kitchen, we could literally feel the hubbub of the large group of people in the next room. The walls were positively vibrating with the energy.

There were three men – volunteer searchers - hunched over the kitchen counter slurping soup. So intent were they on their meal and so exhausted from their physical exertion of the day that they didn't even look up when we came in.

I glanced around. "It doesn't look like they found her," I commented, looking at Lesley with a note of challenge.

Lesley shook her head. She looked at the exhausted faces of the men and the slump of their shoulders. "No, it doesn't look like it," she agreed glumly.

Just then Tessie came in through the swinging door. She paused when she saw us and smiled wanly. "Boy, am I glad to see you two!" she said with an exaggerated exhale. "Angie, sweetie, I need your help checking in the arriving campers. We're swamped out there," she said and then turning to Lesley, she added, "and I need you, Lesley, to get those reporters off our backs. They're clamoring for a statement!"

Lesley nodded. "Right. I'll see what I can do." She left.

Tessie turned to me, "So?"

I looked at her blankly then suddenly I remembered. I grabbed Tessie's arm and said excitedly, "They FOUND her, Tessie! They found her alive! It took nine days, but they found her!"

The men at the counter looked up with interest. "Did you say they found her?" one of them asked.

I glanced over at them and shook my head. "Oh, no. Sorry. Not Melanie. This was a little girl who was lost in the woods back in 1941."

The man frowned, "1941 did you say?"

I nodded. "But that little girl was found! And she was only a year older than Melanie is."

The man shrugged. "Well, I guess you could look at it as a good sign." He shrugged and returned to the bowl in front of him.

Tessie smiled, "That's wonderful, honey! Thank God!"

I nodded. "I know. I was kind of worried that...well, you know..."

Tessie examined my face for a moment. "I'm glad they found that other little girl." She squeezed my shoulder.

I smiled. "Yeah, me, too." We were quiet for a minute then I made Tessie stop before entering the other room. "Tessie, can I ask you a question?"

Tessie studied my face and nodded. "Sure, honey. What?"

"Do you believe that Lesley can really see the future?"

Tessie eyes grew wide. "Did she say something about Melanie?" she asked in a tense whisper.

"So, you do believe she can then!" I said accusingly.

Tessie blinked, taken aback by my reaction, and shrugged. "I don't know. Maybe she can, maybe not. But I do believe that some people can."

I looked at her for another moment. "Well, I don't think she can."

Tessie frowned. "Angie, what's this all about? What did Lesley say to you?"

I shrugged. "I asked her about Melanie, and she said that she thought Melanie was all right. So, then I asked her why she hadn't told everyone that. And she said that she wasn't sure if it was just wishful thinking. I think she's just a fake," I said with finality.

"I see," Tessie said. She glanced into the other room and saw a family of campers looking in wonder at all the activity around them. "Honey, I don't know what to tell you. It's too long a discussion for right now. Let's talk about this later, perhaps with your father. But for right now, could you get those campers checked in for me?"

Tessie gave me a gentle push in the direction of the registration desk. I sighed, resigned to the work ahead of me. Maybe Kay was right about being busy, though. Maybe it would make the time pass more quickly.

THIRTY-EIGHT

Search Status Press Conference

August 2006
Wilderness Campground, Crawford Notch, NH

**** Angie ****

The search status press conference was conducted from the front porch of the lodge. Even if they had wanted to hold it inside, there was no longer enough room in the lodge for the number of media representatives that were now following the story. Over the past twenty-four hours, their ranks had swelled with national and even a few international news services. There was now a fleet of RVs with mobile satellite dishes, emblazoned with local and regional TV stations call letters, parked under the trees behind the lodge.

I stood at the back of the group of reporters to watch the session. Jerry Stockman came out and took his place on the porch in front of the large group. He looked tired but utterly capable. He stood there calmly waiting until the crowd grew quiet and then he modestly introduced himself. I was struck by how he handled himself with such unexpected ease before the reporters. I wish I could look half that relaxed in front of them.

He had a friendly, down-home style that seemed to make the reporters feel superior and respected. I watched him with interest, studying his mannerisms to figure out how he achieved the effect. I was amazed at how the reporters seemed to soften their questioning and responded to his offhanded bantering between questions. He was a natural, I thought with wry amusement. Go figure.

As I stood in the back of the throng, listening to the questions and Jerry's answers, I noticed Robin Keller had sidled up next to Lesley who was standing off to the side. Lesley looked up, startled.

"Hi, Lesley," Robin whispered. "Could I ask you some questions, one-on-one, after Jerry finishes?"

"For the camera?" Lesley asked with a frown.

Robin shook her head quickly, "No, no. Off the record," she added with a smile.

Lesley eyed her for a second, and then nodded. "Sure, Robin. I'll be right here."

Robin nodded then turned back to listen to Jerry's answer to something about the areas already searched. She moved forward a step or two and then put her hand up. She turned her head ever so slightly towards her cameraman, Manny, and he aimed the camera directly at her.

"She's making sure he films her best side," Lesley said into my ear. I looked up in surprise. I didn't think she'd noticed me standing here.

When Jerry pointed to Robin, she smiled as she asked her question, "Mr. Stockman? Robin Keller, from WMNH-TV. How are little Melanie's poor parents holding up? Our hearts and prayers certainly go out to them."

I saw Lesley look up quickly and she shot a look at Robin, but Robin was totally intent on Jerry's response. "Leave it to Robin to bring up Nora and Keith," Lesley muttered bitterly.

However, Robin wasn't finished. "And the babysitter?" She said into her mike, "Uh, let's see...Angie Jackson, right? Could you tell us if Angie Jackson has revealed any more about what really happened Thursday morning?"

My head jerked up at the sound of my name. I felt the blood race to my face. I saw Jerry Stockman frown, but he responded evenly, "I believe Angie has already given us the whole story, Miss Keller. There was no reason for her to anticipate that Melanie would go into the woods on her own."

"And yet, according to her own words yesterday, Angie said that Melanie had a tantrum at dinner the night before when her parents told her they were planning to go for a hike without her and would be leaving her behind with a babysitter. Isn't that true?"

I felt like crawling away, and I would've if it were possible to do it without being noticed.

Jerry smiled thinly, "And what is your point, Miss Keller?"

Robin smiled, "Only that perhaps the babysitter should've anticipated that Melanie would attempt to run away from her. That's all I'm saying."

Jerry smiled thinly. He put up his hands. "Thanks for your attention, ladies and gentlemen, but I really have to get back inside. If there is any news concerning the search, we will let you know. Otherwise, we'll meet back here tomorrow morning at 10 a.m. for the next search status update."

Several reporters tried to get Jerry's attention to ask another question, but he had already turned away and was quickly stepping back into the lodge. I hurried towards the lodge myself. I turned at the door and looked back when I heard Robin's voice.

"Lesley?" Robin called out.

Lesley spun around and I could see the angry blood rise in her neck and face. "What was that all about, Robin?" she asked coldly.

Robin's smile didn't reach her eyes. "It's simple, Lesley. I know something's going on here and I aim to find out what you and your friends are hiding."

Lesley stared at her. "What are you talking about?"

"Oh, come on, Lesley," she said. "No one hires a spin consultant like you unless there's a story that needs to be spun. I get that." Robin watched her guardedly. "So? Are you going to tell me what's going on or do you want me to speculate on the air?"

Spin Consultant? What was Robin talking about, I wondered.

Lesley paused and then said in a level tone. "You are way off the mark on this, Robin! It would be funny if it wasn't so serious." She shook her head slowly.

Robin's lips curled and she raised her eyebrows. "All you have to do is tell me what's up. Is Angie a mental case? Is that it? I heard she's being home-schooled. Is it because she can't be sent to a regular school? Do they think she hurt the little girl?"

Lesley put up her hands, "Stop it! For chrissakes, Robin, you are so far off the wall that I don't know where to begin!" She took a deep breath. "First of all, Angie is an extremely bright, wonderful thirteen-year-old. She's being home-schooled because...because her father believes that home schooling will give her the best education, at the moment. No, she did not hurt Melanie. She's heartbroken that Melanie is lost. She spent yesterday hiking the trails with me looking for her."

"So why did they hire you, then?" Robin asked suspiciously.

Lesley blinked. "Is that the kind of reputation I had?" she asked, shaking her head slowly. She sighed. "I quit doing PR consulting a year ago, Robin. I'm just helping these people out because I care about them," she said and added, "And that's the truth."

Robin looked dubious. "I heard you quit. But when they said you'd become a psychic, I figured it had to be bullshit." She watched Lesley's face for a second and so did I. "OK, maybe you're shitting me now too; maybe not. I don't know. But I'm not leaving this godforsaken place until I have the truth. If there's nothing up with your babysitter, you've got nothing to worry about, right?"

"There's nothing up with Angie. Nothing at all," Lesley said firmly. "The story here, Robin, is about a four-year-old lost and alone in the White Mountains of New Hampshire. Remember?"

Robin smiled coolly. "Yeah, right." And she turned and walked away.

Lesley watched her go, and so did I. To be honest, I wasn't sure what to make of the exchange I'd just overheard. It was nice of Lesley to defend me, but I couldn't help but feel deflated by all those hateful things that Robin had said about me. Is that what's being said about me on the air? Is that what people will think of me? That I'm some kind of nut that hurts little children?

THIRTY-NINE

Translating More of the Diary

August 2006
Wilderness Campground, Crawford Notch, NH

*** *Angie* ***

I went back into the lodge and checked in several families and filled out the campground map layout with the names of the campers and the plate number and make of their vehicles. When I finished with the last group, I decided to sneak upstairs to do a little more translating of the diary before dinner. Now that I had copies of the articles about the little girl, I figured it might help me understand Monsieur Duclos' journal entries a bit better.

I also suspected that Tessie had seen something interesting in the journals the night before when she clearly was reading ahead in her fluent French. I wondered what she had read that was so interesting and I intended to find out.

I tiptoed past the office door that thankfully was now closed. I could hear Lesley's voice on the other side, talking – on the phone? – to someone about media coverage or media "feeds" or something like that. I was glad I didn't have to deal with Lesley again right now. I still felt upset over our lunch conversation, but I wasn't sure why it had bothered me so much. After all, who really cared if she could see the future, anyway? And I didn't know what to make of Robin's calling her a "spin consultant." I wondered about that. Maybe she wasn't who she pretended to be?

I moved slowly down the hallway so that my footsteps wouldn't be heard, but when I opened my bedroom door and saw the room was empty, I hurried in and quickly closed the door behind me. I flipped on the light and then went to the desk and turned on the computer. I found the translation document that I had started the night before. It flashed on the screen, and I sat down and began to read through the paragraphs I had already translated.

I pulled the journal from the old cigar box where I had left it and I thumbed through the stiff pages of the small book. It still seemed hard to believe that this guy had written in it sixty-five years ago. I smoothed the surface of the cover with my hand. "Jean-Louis Duclos, St. Pierre Avenue, Apt. 2A, Lowell, Massachusetts," I read from the inside cover.

His handwriting was small and even, good handwriting actually – legible and easy to decipher, except that it was in French. People took more pride in their handwriting in the olden days, I reflected. Heck, they even received grades on their report cards for handwriting. That seemed so odd; like being given credit for a trick you could do well.

I read through the first paragraph again. This Jean-Louis guy was a camp cook apparently. He mentioned there were 300 "hungry" men at the search camp. Three hundred! Did we have that many in the woods today looking for Melanie, I wondered? Maybe. I wasn't sure. Still, three hundred seemed like a lot.

I started by typing the next paragraph of French text into the document on the computer then followed it with my attempts at translation. I looked up the French words and phrases that I didn't know (which turned out to be more of them than I care to admit). I would ask Tessie to check if I had captured the true meaning. You have to be very familiar with a language to understand its nuances. I was learning that.

The first entry was for September 30th, 1941. I thought about the date. I knew that Pearl Harbor took place December 7, 1941, so this was just a couple of months before America got involved in World War II. It was odd reading the diary and knowing what was about to happen. Maybe that is what it was like for Lesley when she caught a glimpse of the future? It was all so confusing. The journal continued,

> *It is good to be so busy. I have little time to think*
> *the dark thoughts that I cannot speak to anyone.*
> *I have decided that I will pour out my heart in the*
> *writing of this journal. Then when it is captured*
> *between the book's covers, I will dispose of it.*
> *Would that I could dispose of my pain as easily!*
> *My heart is in Portland with my dearest Lorraine.*
> *If only she would've let me go with her!*

When I finished translating those six lines, I looked up at the screen. I had been at it for nearly an hour with only a paragraph completed. I read it again. This time I tried to see it as not just a word-by-word, line-by-line translation, but as a story. He mentions a woman named Lorraine. Lorraine, I remembered, was the woman with the bicycle in the picture. I opened the cigar box and took the picture out. I looked at Lorraine more closely this time, really studying her face. She wasn't standing close enough to the camera to see the expression in her eyes, but her faint smile and the slight hunching of her shoulders made me think that perhaps she was a shy woman. She was pretty although her hair and clothes were quite plain. Apparently, this Lorraine had gone to Portland, Maine and Duclos wanted to go with her. So why hadn't he? I tackled the next sentence and the next and soon thought I had the gist of it.

> *I don't know how I will explain to my mother*
> *what has happened to my savings. I gave all my*
> *money to Lorraine. To think if things had been*
> *different, she might've been a grandmother. Ah*
> *well. I have arranged for my friend Roland to*
> *send me a note letting me know when Lorraine is*
> *recovered and back in Conway. That, at least, will*
> *be a relief.*

I read the sentences again. He mentions his mother. He gave all his money to Lorraine, and she went to Maine with it? But what about this mention of becoming a grandmother? Did I translate that correctly? Did he mean that his mother might be a grandmother or Lorraine? It couldn't be Lorraine; she was too young. I sighed. I wished I were more fluent. I sat back and casually traced the white border around the black-and-white photo with my finger. Suddenly, I sat up straight and read the entire paragraph aloud. Could it be that Lorraine was pregnant? Was she going to Portland to...to have the baby? Or more likely, to get rid of the baby? Did they do that sort of thing back then?

At that moment, Kay appeared, banging the door wide open and kicking it closed as she breezed in. She caught sight of me and stopped in her tracks. "Oh, you're here," she said. "I thought you were down checking in the new campers."

"I was, but I came up to get some work done on the journal."

Kay glanced at me with interest. "What journal?"

"Oh, I forgot. You weren't around last night when I found it. Jeb and I dug an old cigar box out of the root cellar wall...down in the cellar under the kitchen. There are all kinds of cool stuff inside and it's from 1941. Here, look," I said opening the lid of the box.

Kay came over and fingered some of the stuff in the box. "So, where's the journal?"

I picked it up from my desk and passed the book over to Kay who thumbed through it.

"Ugh, it's all in French!" Kay said in disgust.

"Yeah, the guy who wrote it was French-Canadian. At least, that's what Dad and Jeb think."

Kay looked over my shoulder at the computer screen. "So, you're translating it?"

"Yeah, it's going to be my fall social studies project for Tessie. I'll be learning about the Depression, the CCC, and all about the camps they built up here in the White Mountains," I said, as if I knew all about those things already.

Kay pursed her lips in distaste, "God, I'll be so glad when I don't have to do any more of Tessie's stupid home school projects!"

I shrugged, "Sometimes they're interesting," I said without conviction.

Kay rolled her eyes. "Yeah, interesting. Right. You're so... young."

"Like you're so much older," I said, hoping she wouldn't realize how much her words stung.

Kay continued in her most patronizing tone, "You'll understand one day when you have a boyfriend."

"I understand just fine, thanks," I said. "But I think I'll get to know my boyfriend a little better before I sleep with him." I retorted.

Kay sat up, her mouth agape for just a second too long. "You don't know anything about it!" she hissed; her face flushed with anger.

I stopped dead and stared at her. "God! You DID, didn't you? Oh my God, Kay! I was kidding, but I can tell you really did something!"

"I did not!" Kay responded hotly.

I plopped down in the desk chair and turned away from Kay. I stared unseeingly at the screen as I mechanically closed the translation document and put the journal and the photograph back into the cigar box. I turned around again. I lowered my voice to a whisper, "I hope you know what you're doing, Kay."

"I haven't done anything yet," Kay said. Her cheeks were crimson, and it was a second before she added, "Besides it doesn't matter because I'm in love with Joe and he's in love with me." She nodded her head as if my comment had been a question, "Angie, I know what I'm doing."

For a second I glanced down at the cigar box then up at Kay, "Do you?"

FORTY

The Duclos Diary

September 1941
Sawyer River CCC Camp, Crawford Notch, NH

On the inside cover of the Diary: Jean-Louis Duclos, St. Pierre Avenue, Apt. 2A, Lowell, Mass.

Mardi, 30 septembre 1941 - Je suis juste arrivé au camp spécial au White Ledge Park à Albany, NH. Le tour de camion était *lent et inégal. Nous avons entraîné une réduction par le camp de fleuve de Sawyer. Une petite fille est perdue dans les montagnes. Le commandant de camp m'a demandé si je viendrais à Chocorua pour faire cuire pour les chercheurs à leur camp de base au White Ledge Park. Il y a beaucoup d'hommes de l'autre CCC, comme me, aidant avec la recherche. Je, aussi, entrerait heureusement dans les montagnes recherchant l'enfant, mais ils me disent que je peux mieux aider en tant que cuisinier de camp. Il y a plus de 300 bouches affamées à alimenter.*

Translation:

Tuesday, 30 September 1941*. I have just arrived at the special camp at White Ledge Park in Albany, NH. The ride in the truck was slow and bumpy. We came from the Sawyer River Camp. A little girl is lost in the mountains. The camp commander asked me if I would come to Chocorua to cook for the searchers at their base camp at White Ledge Park. There are many other CCC men, like myself, helping with the search. I, too, would gladly go into the mountains to search for the child, but they tell me I can best help out as a camp cook. There are already more than 300 hungry mouths to feed.*

I arrived just before lunch and was immediately put to work making hundreds of sandwiches. We are using the chicken that a local chicken farmer in Conway donated. This evening it was beans and sausage. The beans burned a bit on the bottom, but no one seemed to notice. At seven, several trucks arrived from Fort Williams in Maine with over one hundred soldiers to help with the search. We didn't have to cook for them. Thank goodness. They went directly into the woods to begin searching.

It is good to be so busy. I have little time to think the dark thoughts that I cannot speak to anyone. I have decided that I will pour out my heart in the writing of this journal. Then I will dispose of it.

The truth is that my heart is in Portland with my dearest Lorraine. If only she would've let me go with her! I don't know how I will explain to my mother what has happened to my savings. I gave all the money to Lorraine. To think if things were different she might've been a grandmother. Ah well. I have arranged for my friend Roland to send me a note letting me know when Lorraine is recovered and back in Conway. That, at least, will be a relief.

It is raining.

Wednesday, October 1, 1941. *The searchers arise early. They spent the better part of the day dragging Iona Lake, just across Route 16. There was an earlier report the little girl was spotted playing near the road on the day of her disappearance. Footprints have been found leading towards the lake. She may have fallen in and drowned. There is also a rumor going around the camp that an ex-convict may have been involved in the disappearance of the girl. Oh, that it is not so! To harm a child! It is unspeakable. And yet, I remember the poor child in Lowell last year. Ah well.*

I've heard nothing from Roland. It is a cloud hanging over me. Lorraine left Conway last Friday. I'm certain she said she was to see the man in Portland on Monday morning. Certainly, all should be well by now?

As I lay here in my cot writing this by the light of my lantern, the questions spin around in my head. Nothing makes sense when I am away from the love of my heart. Why couldn't she marry me and have the child? The questions swirl in my head and haunt my dreams. Now it is too late. She said I am too young to marry. But is 18 so young? My own mother was 18 – even younger! - when she married, and even my father was but 19. Lorraine said the difference in our age was too much, but she is only eight years my senior. It means little enough to me, after all. What matters of age? I must see her again soon or I shall die. I wonder if I could stop in Conway on the way back to the Sawyer River Camp after the little girl is found? Ah, and when will that be, I wonder? Only the Father in Heaven can know.

Thursday, October 2, 1941. *Governor Blood came to camp today. I didn't get to shake his hand myself, but I overheard him commend and encourage the men as they arrived back into camp after many hours of weary searching. We made flapjacks for breakfast and made hundreds of sandwiches for the mid-day meal. I couldn't eat a sandwich myself after making so many of them. For dinner we made a hearty stew. Several men complimented me, personally, on it.*

Again, no word from Roland. I've sent a note to Sawyer River Camp asking after him. Surely, he has returned to camp by now. His leave was for the weekend plus two days, therefore he should have returned Tuesday, or yesterday at the latest. What's happened? I'm sick with dread.

Friday, October 3, 1941. *The reward money is now up to $850. I wish I knew where the little girl is. I could find many uses for the reward money. They brought in a bloodhound from Rhode Island, but he found no scent of the child. They think the rain erased her scent entirely. Peter, one of the other cooks, told me today that they have called in some psychics to find the girl. I wish I could consult one to find out what's happened to my Lorraine. Still no word from Roland. What could be happening?*

Saturday, October 4, 1941. *Finally! Today a note arrived from Roland! He is coming down to see me. He has news, but he does not want to relay it in writing in a note. I will see him tomorrow. Could it be bad news? Certainly, it won't be good news if he feels he must relay it in person. Ah, my heart is heavy.*

It is chaotic around here. Every day more and more automobiles show up. They are filled with curiosity seekers, although some help with the searching, it is true. Perhaps they are after the reward of $1000. If only I knew where she was, I would collect it myself. Perhaps that would solve everything. I could afford a wife then. I could convince Lorraine to marry me and we would have a new start. I shall dream of it tonight.

Sunday, October 5, 1941. *Roland arrived in an old Edsel. He says he borrowed it from his uncle who works at the garage. When I saw his face, I knew it was not going to be good news. But, to say she is gone from my life? Forever? Impossible!*

He says that his sister in Conway has told him that Lorraine is not planning to return to Conway from Portland. She is in a hospital. I feel that I have committed murder, first of our child and now even of my sweet Lorraine. I pray without ceasing for her recovery. But why is she not returning to me? Why?

FORTY-ONE

Keith Jacobs Confrontation

August 2006
Wilderness Campground, Crawford Notch, NH

*** *Angie* ***

Dinner was a haphazard affair that night. Kay, Tessie, Lesley, and I worked in the kitchen getting dinner ready for a hundred or so searchers. We put together sandwiches and placed them on platters and heated up a large vat of vegetable soup. One of the restaurants in town had sent over the soup and some deli meats along with several dozen loaves of bread. Just as in the olden days when neighbors would bring over casseroles in times of trouble, the surrounding towns had responded to this crisis in like manner.

Soup and bread for dinner weren't all that the community had provided either. In the morning several coffee urns had arrived from the church hall in Bartlett, muffins and rolls were sent down from a bakery in Jackson; a pizza place in Glen provided boxes and boxes of pizza, pre-sliced and ready to heat up.

Tessie thought we would have enough food for a couple of days. If it went much longer than that, she wasn't so sure. But could it go on longer than that? We just didn't know. I wondered if there was a point at which we would have to give up if no trace of Melanie had been found. For now, I was content not to ask because I wasn't sure I was ready to think about that possibility.

Tessie stirred the soup and watched Kay and me. I knew what she was thinking; that we were unusually quiet tonight. That wasn't like us. Even when we weren't getting along, there was usually a good deal of banter between us, whether it was friendly or not. Well, she would just have to wonder, because I certainly wasn't going to talk to her about Kay and what I thought my sister and Joe were up to, that was for sure!

Back when we were seven and nine, the disagreements had been about who touched whose dolls or who hadn't done her chores or whose turn it was to sit in the front seat of the car. It was simple and usually the bad feelings between us would vanish like soap bubbles popping in the air.

Now that we were older, though, our fights could be about anything – the war in Afghanistan and Iraq, Kay accusing me of reading her diary, or whether Kay took the last maxi-pad from my box in the bathroom. Well, maybe the disagreements are the same really – and maybe that's true of all sibling fights – they are about privacy, responsibility, and privilege. Who gets it, who keeps it, who violates it, and who never had it to begin with.

Tessie turned off the soup and started ladling it into individual Styrofoam bowls, setting them in orderly rows on the trays. When all the bowls on a tray were filled, she set the tray on the counter behind her ready for the men and woman who would shortly come through, buffet-style, to get their dinners. Lesley had put out a basket of rolls next to the trays of soup bowls, with the platters of sandwiches piled in little pyramids just beyond. I saw Tessie look around at the spread and nod in approval.

"Coffee done?" Tessie asked Kay, who was at the sink at the other end of the kitchen.

"Huh?" Kay looked up startled.

"The coffee, honey. Is it ready?" Tessie repeated, eyeing my sister speculatively.

Kay turned around to the urn and checked the light on the front. "Yeah, it looks like it's done, Tessie. Shall I tell the men in the front room to come in and get their dinners?"

Tessie nodded. "Sure, let's get them started. I expect the rest of the searchers will be in soon. It's starting to get dark." She glanced out the window above the sink behind Kay.

Kay turned and looked out too. The dark and the mention of the returning searchers obviously reminded her that Joe would be back soon, too. I saw her smile slightly. As if she felt my gaze, she turned to look at me and our eyes met. We both immediately looked away. What more was there to say, after all?

At that moment there was a huge bang outside the back door. We all spun around to look.

"What in the world?' Tessie exclaimed, hurrying to the door to look out.

The rest of us were there a moment later peering over her shoulder into the growing shadows in the outside shower area.

We heard voices, and then a shouted "Go screw yourself!"

I shrank back, immediately recognizing the voice. "That's Mr. Jacobs' voice!" I whispered, loud enough for the other women to hear.

Before anyone could react, he was there standing in the doorway before us, his red plaid wool hunter's hat pulled down low on his forehead. Kay and I both took a step back away from the door. Tessie reached out and pulled it open just as Keith Jacobs leapt up the two steps.

"What's happened?" Tessie asked him.

He ignored her. He squinted his eyes as he swung his head back and forth, looking around the room like a predatory animal. When he finally spied me, he took a step towards me. I fell back against the edge of the sink and Lesley stepped in front of me blocking his way. But he didn't look at her; his eyes seemed only intent on me. I was standing stock still backed up against the sink. I could feel the cool weight of it pressing into the small of my back.

"You!" he said spitting the word at me. "This is all your fault, isn't it?" The vicious tone made the words spew out of his mouth like a curse. His index finger pointed like a dagger inches from my face. "If you had watched Melanie like you were supposed to, she'd be here right now!"

"Mr. Jacobs, please," Tessie said taking his arm to turn him, but he shrugged her off. He leaned in towards me menacingly. "I just want you to know that if she dies out there, her death will be on your head." He glared at me, and I tried to shrink even further away from him. My heartbeat in my throat and my face burned with indignation and fear.

Just then Jerry Stockman came through the door from the lodge's main room to my left. He immediately took in the scene before him and acted. "Hey! Jacobs! What's this all about?" he said, roughly pulling Keith Jacobs away from me, and knocking his red hunter's hat to the floor. Jerry Stockman glanced at me and then back at Keith Jacobs. He jabbed at the man's shoulder, "For chrissakes, man, are you out of your mind? She's thirteen years old! She's a child, too, just like Melanie!"

Another man that I didn't know came through the kitchen door glaring angrily at Keith Jacobs. He turned to Stockman, "He's not going out with my team again, you hear me, Jerry? That frickin' guy's insane! I knew he was going to be bad news when I saw what kind of condition he was in this morning. I'm through being the nice guy!" He slapped his hat against his leg so hard that it made a cracking sound.

Jerry Stockman patted the other man on the shoulder, "It's OK, Pete. Don't worry, he won't be going out again."

"You can't tell me what to do!" Keith Jacobs hissed back. "That's my daughter out there, remember? You can't stop me from trying to find her." He snorted. "Not that your maps and grids are of much help. They're all a bunch of bullshit!" He spat on the floor for emphasis and Tessie jumped but swallowed her angry reprimand.

Lesley stepped forward, "Mr. Jacobs? Keith. Melanie is going to be fine. I...I'm certain of it." She laid a hand on his forearm in a gesture of comfort.

He shook her hand off as if had stung him and he turned on her, "You? What? You're some kind of psychic, so I hear," he sneered. "You think she's fine, do you? Well, if you're such a great psychic, tell me where she is right now." He paused. "If you can't do that, then what the hell good are you?"

Lesley took a step back as if she had been slapped. "It doesn't work like that..."

"Not for you it doesn't! Because you're a phony!" With that, he reached down and picked up his red hat and then took the two paces to the door and was out it before anyone could say anything. The door slammed against its frame behind him.

"What a jerk!" exclaimed Pete, the search and rescue team leader. He leaned down and recovered his own baseball cap and wiped it once or twice against his thigh as if to clean it.

Jerry Stockman sighed and shook his head. "He is. I know. But he is the father, and you have to give him a little leeway for that. It can't be easy when your four-year-old is facing a second night in the woods." The room went quiet as we each contemplated the truth of that. Two nights! Was Melanie okay? That's all I could wonder. I couldn't let myself picture how cold and scared she might be.

Pete let out his breath and his shoulders sagged. He combed his fingers through his hair and sighed tiredly. "Yeah, I know, I know. But you have no idea what a friggin' dick he was out there."

Jerry Stockman chuckled, "Like the one he's just been in here, no doubt. Come on, Pete, how about some dinner for you and your team?"

Tessie nodded and smiled, relieved. "Yes, let's get everyone fed." She turned to me. "You okay, honey?" she asked gently.

Lesley started to reach out to me, too, but she pulled her arm back as if she had had second thoughts. She probably saw that my eyes were swimming with tears.

Tessie took me in her arms. She glanced up at Lesley and I felt her nod to her. Lesley turned and took over getting the people who were now entering the kitchen organized into lines and handing out silverware and napkins. I heard Lesley ask Kay to start filling the cups with coffee.

Tessie led me out of the kitchen. We passed Robin Keller by the door, and I saw that she was busily writing in her notebook. She barely glanced up as we passed, but I knew she was aware of us.

FORTY-TWO

Message from the Diary

August 2006
Wilderness Campground, Crawford Notch, NH

*** Angie ***

Tessie left me at the door to my bedroom. She had to get back down to the kitchen to help out with dinner for all the volunteers. It was all right with me. I didn't want any company anyway and was glad that Kay hadn't followed us upstairs.

Probably, Joe had returned. If that was true, I wouldn't see her for the rest of the night, I thought with a cynical smile. I shook my head at the thought of Kay. What was she doing? Had she really slept with Joe? But she's only fifteen! I thought I knew her. Could she have changed that much without me realizing it? Were we actually that different now?

I was shaken by the confrontation with Keith Jacobs, shaken and frightened. Did he really hate me as much as he seemed to? I could hear the hubbub of the searchers in the rooms below and it made me feel protected and lonely at the same time. Lately, I'd felt like my life was veering off into some chaotic and uncharted direction and I didn't know how to stop it or what to make of it. How could people believe that I might harm Melanie?

I glanced around the room and the framed photo on the nightstand caught my eye. For a second, I felt a deep calm come over me. I went over and picked it up and sat down on my bed. It was a picture of my mother holding me and Kay in her lap; in the photo I was almost five and Kay was seven. There was an African thorn tree in the background, and she was sitting in a camp chair in front of the flaps of a dust brown tent. She was smiling happily at my father who was taking the picture. She was squeezing us in a hug that looked so tight and wonderful that I could almost feel it if I stared at the picture long enough.

My dad had given Kay and me each a copy of the photo, framed in identical heavy wooden frames the Christmas after my mother died. When he gave them to us, I remember being confused at first, thinking that perhaps she wasn't really dead because she looked so alive in the picture. He explained that the picture had been taken on our last camping trip to Lake Langano in Ethiopia a month before she went to Nairobi and died and that he wanted us to remember her happy the way she was in that picture.

She did look happy in the photo. The picture was taken the day after Kay and I had gotten lost in a swampy area near the lake and my parents had searched for us and finally found us. So maybe almost losing us gave a little extra edge to her joy.

Dad had found the picture when he got the film developed. It must've been a shock for him to go through that roll of photos after they had been developed. How hard it must've been for him to see my mother, happy, relaxed, and so unaware that she would be taken from us so soon. Poor Dad. Poor us.

I sighed. It was times like now when I most wished she were still alive. If she were, we wouldn't be here in New Hampshire; we would be overseas someplace and none of this would've happened. And we would all be together, like a regular family – mother, father, children – as our family and our life was meant to be. Sure, I would miss not having Tessie and Jeb around all the time, and for as much as I complain, I love the campground and would miss it. But given a choice, I would choose having my mother back. I sighed again. But no one ever gets to make those kinds of choices, do they?

I glanced over at my computer. I set the photo back on my nightstand and went over to my desk. Idly, I touched the keyboard and the black screen disappeared and was replaced by the translation document for the journal that I had been working on earlier. I sat down and looked at the next lines of French and after a minute or two I got back into the flow of translating. After a while I read through the last paragraph that I just completed. It read:

> *I have decided to go and help with the search for the little girl. She may not be alive now – it has been so long – 8 days! – but if we could at least bring her little body back to her parents, that would be a blessing, too. Of course, we pray for the impossible. But I cannot in good conscience stay behind and not help these poor weary searchers.*

I read the passage again, and then a third time. Then it came to me in a flash. I must go find Melanie myself! The journal, the lost girl from 1941, all of it was a message showing me what I must do. It was so obvious to me now! It was like a command from the beyond that a psychic might receive. Did Lesley get this sort of clear direction?

I stood up and began to pace, thinking through what I would need for supplies. Some food, warm clothes, an extra pair of socks, a flashlight...what else? Quickly, I changed my clothes, layering long underwear under my jeans, shirt, and sweater.

I'd have to wait until everyone was asleep before leaving, of course. I couldn't take the chance of anyone seeing me leave or suspecting what I was planning to do. I wondered how long I'd have to wait. Would anyone stay up late tonight?

FORTY-THREE

Dinner at the Lodge

August 2006
Wilderness Campground, Crawford Notch, NH

*** Kay ***

It was nearly eight before dinner was served to the last of the searchers as they straggled back to the lodge, tired and dispirited. The weather hadn't improved – it was wet and chilly in the woods and the heavy grey clouds and mist hung low even when it wasn't raining. The gloomy sky and dark misgivings spread a pessimistic mood over them all. Jeb, Joe, and Alex were among the last groups to return, and they were so exhausted that they barely grunted answers to questions.

Tessie had set up one end of a table in the dining room for them and they headed directly for it. Kay could see the tiredness and frustration of the day etched in the lines of their faces. There was a hollow look to their eyes and a sag in their shoulders as they hunched over their bowls of soup and tore chunks from the rolls that they dipped sloppily into the broth.

Kay sat close to Joe, leaning her head against his shoulder as he ate. She loved to feel the roll of his arm muscles as he lifted the spoon to his mouth and slurped the soup. When he momentarily put his arm down, she tucked her fingers in at his elbow and was rewarded when he squeezed her hand against his side.

She glanced up warily but saw that Jeb and her father weren't looking at her and Joe. Their attention was on something Jerry

Stockman was saying at the other end of the long table. For a second, she felt like she was alone with Joe, and she smiled happily at the thought. She hoped they'd get a chance to be alone tonight. Maybe after dinner, she wondered?

She had been so bored all day waiting for Joe's return. Sure, she filled the time being busy, but she spent a lot of it just watching the hands on the clock as the hours slowly crawled by. She was glad he was back now. She squeezed his arm again and when he picked up the spoon, she slipped her hand down along his thigh, feeling the warmth of him through the coarseness of his jeans under her fingers. He pulled away with a half-smile and whispered, "Hey, I'm ticklish."

She smiled back. "I know," she said. She hoped she sounded inviting and sexy to him. But he turned his attention to something that Jeb had just said, and she felt shut out again.

Tessie came out of the kitchen and paused by the table waiting for a break in the conversation. When it came, she spoke up. "Alex? Jeb? You want more to eat? I have a little soup left in the pot if you want it."

Jeb smiled lazily, "Thanks, Tess, but no. All I want is to wash up and let my head find my pillow."

"We're getting too old for this kind of stuff, Tessie," Alex added with a tired smile of his own.

Jeb grinned, "This stuff would tire out even a young guy. What do you say, Joe?" He nudged the younger man.

Joe nodded, glad to be included as an equal, "Yeah, I'm beat, too. God, what a long day!"

"And you're certainly used to long days on the trail," Alex added.

"True." Joe yawned a long, wide-opened mouth yawn that made his eyes water. "Man!" He shook his head slightly. "What time are we heading out tomorrow, Jeb?"

"First light is my guess. What do you think, Jerry?"

Stockman looked over at Jeb, "Yeah, first light. There's no moon with all these clouds so it'll be too dark to try to start out before then."

"Where's Kevin, by the way? Is he back?" Joe asked.

Jerry Stockman nodded, "Yup. He's already eaten. He took one of the beds in the bunkroom upstairs and is probably sound to sleep by now."

Alex nodded and stood up slowly. He stretched his arms above his head as if he could stretch the tiredness out of them. "Kevin's got the right idea. I'm off to bed too if anyone's looking for me."

Tessie glanced at him in surprise, "But it's only just eight o'clock!" she said.

"And five will come too soon, I'm sure." Alex shook his head. "Sorry, Tess, but I'm just exhausted."

Tessie nodded. She seemed to be looking at Alex speculatively but shrugged and said, "Go to bed then. Goodnight, Alex," she added warmly.

"Night, Tess." He looked around the table and nodded to the others.

"Night, Dad," Kay said sweetly.

He looked at her and paused as if he was going to say something, but instead nodded. "Night, Kay. Joe." He turned and headed for the steps. He paused as he reached the first step and turned back, "Hey, where's Angie tonight?"

"Must be up in her room," Tessie said after a second. "I haven't seen her since before dinner."

"She's probably doing more translating of that diary she found," Kay said offhandedly.

They all nodded in agreement. That sounded like just the sort of thing that Angie would be doing.

"What a kid," he said, almost to himself. He waved a hand over his shoulder and trudged up the rest of the stairs.

Just then Kay saw Lesley come through the kitchen door with a dishtowel in one hand. Lesley stopped and watched Alex climb the last of the stairs but she didn't say anything. When he was out of sight she shrugged slightly, then turned and went back into the kitchen.

Kay wondered what that was all about.

Then she noticed Tessie glancing at Jeb who had been watching her. She smiled and he returned the smile. Kay felt there was a lot not being said around this table tonight. What was going on? She looked at Joe and noticed that his eyelids were nearly at half-mast. She sighed. She'd waited the whole day for him to get back and now it looked like he was too tired to be any fun. And worse, she knew he'd be going out again tomorrow. How would she ever get through another long day?

FORTY-FOUR

Making a Decision

August 2006
Wilderness Campground, Crawford Notch, NH

*** Angie ***

I heard footsteps coming up the stairs and hurried to the door. I flipped off the overhead light before slowly pulling the door open just a crack. I peeked out and saw my father come up the stairs, pause, and then go into his own room. I could see deep lines etched into his face. He looked exhausted. After a moment I heard the sound of the water running in his shower. Good, he's taking his shower and probably...maybe...would be going straight to bed afterwards. I hoped so. I glanced at my digital clock glowing the time from the nightstand. It was five after eight. Early for him to be going to bed, I thought, but it had been a long day and he'd been out on the trail since dawn. I'd have to be patient.

I went over to my bed and lay on top of the bedspread and thought through my plan. When it was quiet, I would leave through the linen closet crossing over to the sleeping loft and then down the back stairs. In the dark, I figured I would be an indistinct shape and mistaken for one of the searchers going to the bathroom perhaps.

From there, I would sneak into the kitchen and pack some food, the flashlight, and whatever else I could find that might be useful. I'd listen at the backdoor and when I was sure no one was about, I would quietly go out along the edge of the woods until I reached the camp road that went out past the Jacobs' campsite. Lesley and I had hiked that trail the day before. This time, though, I would follow it around the base of the mountain, the way a four-year-old child might. This time, I would find her. I had to.

FORTY-FIVE

Heart to Heart

August 2006
Wilderness Camp, Crawford Notch, NH

*** Tessie ***

Tessie got up from the table and went into the kitchen, resting her hand lightly on Jeb's shoulder as she passed. He touched her hand and she felt as if he'd communicated everything in that slight touch. It pleased her to have these moments when they seemed to be so completely on the same wavelength. She smiled as she pushed open the door to the kitchen.

She wanted to see if there was anything more that needed to be done in the kitchen to clean up tonight's meal or to prepare for tomorrow's early morning. She was anxious to get back to Jeb before he went upstairs and fell asleep. As she came through the door, she saw Lesley sitting at the center island on one of the stools. There was a cup of coffee in front of her, but she didn't seem to be drinking it. She had a faraway look in her eyes as she rested her chin on her arms that were crossed in front of her.

"Long day, huh?" Tessie said by way of greeting.

Lesley looked up, only her eyes moving. "Uh-huh." She sighed and closed her eyes for a moment, then sat up, stretching. She climbed off the stool. "I should get back to my campsite and get some sleep myself. We're all beat tonight."

"That's true. And the rain doesn't help raise spirits, either," Tessie said with a shake of the head.

Lesley nodded. "Funny how weather affects us like that, isn't it? Sunny blue skies make us feel great, even when life is going lousy; but a little bit of rain can put a damper on even the best of moods."

"How true. Well, that is unless you're living through a drought; then maybe rain might be a cause for celebration." Tessie smiled.

Lesley chuckled, "You have a most interesting perspective on things!"

Tessie shrugged. "I try to remind myself now and then to step back and look at things from a little different viewpoint. We're the ultimate creators of our reality, after all."

"Oh really? How so?" Lesley asked, interested.

Tessie smiled and sat down opposite Lesley. It was nice having another woman to talk to for a change. "Well, when something happens, it's up to a person to define whether the event is a good thing or a bad thing. In and of itself, an event is just an event, after all, isn't it? But to a particular person, that same event could be an auspicious piece of luck, or a terrible tragedy, or maybe even a bit of both at the same time."

"Both?" Lesley asked. "I can't think of an event in my life that was both good luck and tragedy at the same time."

"Oh, you could if you thought about it," Tessie said with a laugh. "My life has been filled with tragic good luck!" She grinned and seeing the questioning look on Lesley's face, she continued. "I grew up in Vietnam during the Vietnam War. It was not an easy life, as you can imagine. I was twelve when the Americans left Saigon in April of 1975. In the next few short years, I was to go through a lifetime of misfortunes. By the time I was seventeen, I had been married, pregnant, widowed, then I lost the child, and I myself was orphaned; all that and I ended up in a refugee camp on the Thai border. Tragedy, right?"

Lesley nodded.

"Yes, it was tragic. It was hard and ugly, and at times, horrifying. But you see, if all that had not happened, I would never have met and married Tim, my second husband, and I would not have found this family that I am a part of now." Tessie smiled a sweet slow smile. "Much happiness has come out of much unhappiness, do you see? The same events were both tragedy AND the seeds of future happiness."

Lesley shook her head slowly, "Tessie, how did you withstand all that?"

"It's not a choice one gets to make, is it? You take the life you're given. How does Jeb say it? 'You play the hand you are dealt.' Yes?"

Lesley whistled slowly. "Well, I'm in awe of you. What a strong woman you must be!"

Tessie smiled shyly at the compliment. "Yes, I suppose that is one of the side benefits from a very hard life, isn't it? But it's not as if I'm a saint, you know! Believe me, I complained, I bitched, I whined the whole time just like anyone else...!"

They laughed together. For a few moments they were silent.

Then Lesley said, "Tell me about Tim. I know he was Kathy's brother, Alex' brother-in-law, right? How did you meet and marry him?" Lesley sat forward on the stool and leaned towards the other woman.

"Tim?" Tessie said the name quietly, with a smile of fond remembrance. "He was working for the UNHCR..." She paused when she noticed the look of question on Lesley's face, and explained, "The UN ran the refugee camps along the Thai border. UNHCR stands for UN High Commission for Refugees."

Lesley nodded. "So, he worked with the UN?"

"Yes. We met because they needed interpreters, and I was fluent in several languages, so I volunteered. There were extra rations and a small stipend that went with the job, but more importantly, it gave me something to do. No one realizes how boring a refugee camp can be! I was assigned to Tim's group. My job was to help them communicate with the people in the camps.

I really enjoyed the work. I traveled everywhere with him," she smiled at the memory. "Being thrown together so much, after a time, we... fell in love," she added quietly.

Lesley smiled. "How romantic! Did you marry him there in Thailand?"

"Yes, twice!" she laughed.

"Twice?"

"It was very difficult because I had visa problems and we needed permissions and all that," Tessie said with a shake of her head. "We were married the first time by a local priest – I'm Catholic and my grandmother was adamant about having God's blessing. But we had to get married again later once we got the official American marriage license. Then, even though we were married, I couldn't leave the camp until the visa difficulties were resolved. That took quite a long time. Two years, I think."

"Two years?" Lesley repeated. "That's awful!"

"But Tim was working, and I was working alongside him, and we were together, and we were very happy, so except for sending in papers and being interviewed by many people, we didn't let it bother us. We knew it would be resolved in our favor eventually. My working as a translator turned out to be the key."

"Really? How so?"

"Well, Tim's boss was an important man at the UN office in Bangkok and he spoke for me...uh, vouched, yes, 'vouched' I think the word would be...he vouched for me. Then I got my visa to come to America and we were able to get married officially."

For Tessie repeating the story brought those years back in a flood of memories. She could see the little shack they had turned into their first home, the daily Land Rover rides over muddy tracks between the camps, the sweet relief at the end of a long day of work, of being tired but together. For a second, she had a strong sense of Tim's presence as if he were standing right behind her and if she sat back she could lean against him and feel his warmth and solidity. She almost didn't want to breathe so she could hold on to that feeling a little bit longer.

"How did he die?" Lesley asked softly, breaking into Tessie's thoughts. "No one has said, and I wondered."

Tessie glanced up at her. "Oh. Well, that is not a happy story. No one likes to speak of it. Another tragedy, you know." Tessie shook her head grimly.

"Tragedy?"

"He was on his way back to the U.S., to meet me. I had flown ahead the month before to get my grandmother settled in this country. He and Jeb had arranged to meet in London to fly back together. Jeb was working in the Middle East or, no, maybe Cairo? I forget now. Anyway, Jeb was delayed and missed the flight, but Tim decided to go on ahead. They planned to meet up in Boston for New Years. That was December 28, 1988."

Lesley frowned. The date didn't have any significance for her.

"He died on the Pan Am flight over Lockerbie, Scotland," Tessie said quietly.

Lesley stared at her as it sunk in. "Oh my God!"

"Strange, isn't it?" Tessie said with a distant look in her eye. "No rhyme or reason. Jeb was supposed to be on the flight, too. It took so long to come to terms with it." Tessie wiped at her forehead, even though there was nothing there.

Lesley reached out and touched Tessie's wrist lightly. "How awful for you, Tessie! And for the rest of his family."

Tessie nodded. "And for Jeb. He arrived in London the next day only to find out that Tim had died on a flight he was supposed to be on, as well." She shook her head again and then sighed. "It was so surreal...I don't know, I can't think of another word to describe it." She looked up, "How does one describe something so unexpected happening that blasts you out of your normal ordinary life so completely?"

Lesley shook her head. "'Tragedy' is as good as any other word, I guess."

"Yes, I suppose." Tessie agreed.

"So, then what? What did you do?"

Tessie smiled sadly. "I was lucky to have Kathy and Alex, and Jeb, of course. They took me in and eventually helped me get a position at the Foreign Service Institute in Washington. I taught languages there for several years. Then when Kathy had Kay and later, Angie, I helped out as much as I could. I still had my job, but we became a sort of extended family. I stayed behind in Washington when they went to Ethiopia in 1998 for their two-year tour." She paused and sighed at the memory. "And then, of course, eight months later, I got the word that Kathy had been killed in the bombing at the embassy in Nairobi. What are the chances that two siblings would each be killed in terrorist bomb blasts?"

Lesley stared at her, shaking her head. "Unbelievable! Alex told me that when they got back to the States you started home-schooling the girls."

"Yes, it was supposed to be a temporary measure; to catch them up with their schooling." She looked thoughtful for a moment. "Kathy's death was hard. After she died, Alex brought the girls back to Washington. We all lived in a townhouse in Arlington, Virginia, not far from the Foreign Service Institute where I worked, but it was also less than a mile from the Pentagon. After the plane hit the Pentagon on 9/11, something in Alex snapped. It was like the last straw for him. I can't explain it but within a month he had quit his job with the government, and we all moved up here."

"Just like that?"

"Yes. He and Jeb already owned the campground. They'd bought it together a number of years ago. I think they'd always planned to retire up here someday."

"And he never looked back? Alex, I mean."

"Looked back? You mean reconsidered quitting his job and all that?"

"Yeah."

Tessie shook her head. "Not that I know of. Lesley, he was pretty burned out by then; maybe even a little paranoid and superstitious. Kathy was killed in August of 1998 thanks to a terrorist bomb at the embassy in Nairobi; he moved back to the States and three years later a plane flown by some terrorists goes into the Pentagon not far from his home. No, I don't think he's had any regrets about his decision, at least, he's never hinted that he has."

"Doesn't he miss his old life? I mean, running a campground isn't..."

"Isn't very intellectually challenging?" Tessie finished.

"Well, yeah."

"Has he told you what type of work he did when he worked for the State Department?"

Lesley shook her head. "I don't think he's ever actually said."

"No, he wouldn't; not unless you specifically asked." She paused. "He used to set up security systems for embassies and other American facilities overseas."

"So, what are you getting at?"

"The embassy down in Nairobi wasn't very secure. Neither was the one in Tanzania that was bombed the same day. Alex was one of the security experts who made recommendations for those two embassies, recommendations that were never acted upon."

"You mean he feels responsible for Kathy's death?"

"In a way, I suppose. He's not naïve. He knows he did his job and if they had put his security measures in place in time, it would've saved many lives, including hers. So even though he knows it wasn't his fault, still...." Tessie's voice lingered.

Lesley shook her head. "It's like my son says, 'sometimes life just sucks.'!"

Tessie smiled. "That's putting it mildly, but it's so true, isn't it?" Tessie looked at her watch. "Oh my! It's getting late."

Lesley yawned. "I thought it might be. I'm getting sleepy."

"Me, too," Tessie said as she got up. "It was nice talking to you, Lesley. I don't get the chance to sit and talk with another woman very often. Kathy and I used to do it all the time. I'd forgotten how much I miss that."

Lesley nodded. "Let's do it again soon." She touched Tessie's arm and Tessie patted her hand.

"Yes. We will," she said. "Do you need a flashlight for the walk back to your campsite? It'll be pretty dark out there. Unless you want to see if there's a bed available in the bunkroom?"

"No, I'll take your offer of a flashlight and sleep in my own sleeping bag tonight. Thanks, anyway," Lesley said. "See you tomorrow."

"Tomorrow," Tessie repeated. Tomorrow.

FORTY-SIX

Night at the Campground

August 2006
Wilderness Campground, Crawford Notch, NH

*** *Lesley* ***

Lesley walked slowly back to her tent thinking over all the things that she and Tessie had discussed. She found herself mesmerized by the bobbing beam of light from the flashlight as it bounced on the dirt and bushes along the road. She looked up between the leafy branches of the trees overhead, but she couldn't make out any stars. It was too cloudy, apparently. The night was cool and dark and although it was no longer raining, drops of moisture still fell off the sodden leaves from the canopy of trees above.

The dirt road was easy enough to follow, edged as it was by thick bushes and trees. It was a left turn at the bathroom building and then a quick right and it wasn't long before she saw the black outline of her tent and she was back at her own campsite again. It seemed sort of forlorn and bleak without the warm glow of the campfire, and Alex, of course. She smiled. She would be so glad to be snuggled inside her sleeping bag.

She paused before unzipping the tent flap. Crickets buzzed and there were some eerie sounds of night insects she didn't recognize and in the far distance the hoot of an owl. She couldn't help but think about night creatures that might be in the surrounding woods. She knew there was an errant bear that visited the campground occasionally looking for any food that wasn't properly stashed away. Jeb had mentioned that he and Angie had to clean up the mess left by it around the trashcans in back of the lodge just the other day.

She held herself still and closed her eyes. She felt certain that she could sense it if there was a large animal around. She closed her eyes and listened not just with her ears for the sounds of snuffling or heavy footfalls, but with all her senses for the...the what?...the essence of the animal? She wasn't sure. She knew, though, that she could sense these things. She'd done it many times before.

She waited, breathing slowly, calming her mind. After a minute, she just knew. Not that there was no bear around here now. But she sensed that there had been one close by recently. Maybe it was the one that Jeb and Angie had cleaned up after? She relaxed and smiled. So, she used her gift to comfort herself about wild animals. Was that so bad? With a grin she unzipped the tent and climbed inside.

*** *Kay* ***

Not far from Lesley's campsite at the outer edge of the campground, Kay had set up campsite 17 for Joe's tent. It was far away from the lodge and bordered the stream along the western edge of the campground. It was considered an iffy campsite, at best. In the spring when the stream flooded its banks, the site sometimes disappeared completely. It was usually the last site to be rented because it was smaller than most and was only able to handle a two-person tent. Not enough room for a dining tent on the site, either. It was perfect for Joe, Kay decided. Perfect for them.

All that day as campers had checked in, she managed to keep his site protected for another night. She marked it as 'taken' and made up a name of a fictitious camper so that no one would be able to tell that it was Joe whose tent was pitched on the site. She figured her father and Jeb would assume that Joe was sleeping in the bunkroom with Kevin and the other searchers. And Joe would assume that they knew that Kay had given him one of the campsites to put up his tent. Kay congratulated herself on thinking of everything.

She had thought of everything, that is, except how tired Joe would be when he got back from a day of hiking the trails searching for Melanie.

"Come on, Joe," Kay cajoled as they walked hand-in-hand to the campsite after dinner.

"Kay, come on! I'm beat! I wasn't kidding back at the lodge," Joe said as he trudged along next to her. He complained that every muscle in his body ached with the need to lie down and rest. He said he had pushed his body all day long for the past two days and he was just plain exhausted.

"I don't want to let Jeb and your dad down tomorrow," he said.

She squeezed his hand and he looked at her. She could see that he was in a struggle with himself.

They reached the campsite.

"Want to build a fire?" Kay asked.

"Nah," he replied. "Really, Kay, I'm not kidding. I need to get some sleep tonight."

She giggled. "Eventually," she said suggestively. At least, she hoped it sounded suggestive to him. This was all new to her. She'd dreamed of saying these kinds of things to a guy, but she had to pinch herself to believe that it was all actually happening now, for real. She was with a guy who liked her, and she was saying all the things she'd heard in movies and read about in sexy novels. It was incredibly intoxicating; like living out a fantasy.

"Kay, maybe you should go back to the lodge. What if they notice you aren't in your bed?"

"No one is going to notice anything. Didn't you see everyone go off to bed before we left?"

"Tessie and Lesley weren't in bed. They were still in the kitchen talking."

"They don't check my room, silly."

"What about Angie? She'll certainly notice you're not there tonight."

"Angie's probably asleep right now, too. Besides, she won't say anything to anyone."

"You're sure?" Joe leaned towards her and whispered, "I want you here, but I really, really don't want to get on Jeb's bad side or your dad's, OK?"

"You won't get on anyone's bad side, Joe," Kay said earnestly. She stood on tiptoes and kissed him lightly on the mouth. "I'm going to stay tonight, Joe, so just deal with it, OK?" She unzipped the tent flap and crawled inside. He could hear her rustling around.

She looked out and saw him smile wearily as he crawled in next to her. In the dark she couldn't see his face, but she felt his hands reaching for her and pulling her closer. He leaned over and kissed her. She was sure that after a few more moments of this, Jeb and her dad would be the last thing on his mind.

FORTY-SEVEN

Day 3 of the Search (Tessie)

August 2006
Wilderness Campground, Crawford Notch, NH

Tessie

It was still dark out when Tessie roused herself. She moved and almost at the same moment felt Jeb stir next to her.

"Morning," she said groggily, by way of greeting as well as information.

He grunted, but she thought she heard a smile in it.

She swung her feet over the side of the bed and sat up. She breathed out, a long slow breath. "God, I hate early mornings," she said almost to herself.

"You always say that," Jeb mumbled sleepily. He reached over and patted her buttock, the only part of her he could reach without rolling over or sitting up himself.

"Come on, you've got to get up, too. It's not going to be just me facing the pre-dawn dark," she said with a small laugh. She could feel the fog of sleep lifting from her brain.

She got up and headed for the small bathroom. She thought she heard the creak of Alex's bed from the bedroom next door. Good, he's up, she thought as she turned on the shower and let the warm water stream across her face. She was a morning person and would be fine once she shook off the night's vivid dreams.

Alex

Alex took a quick shower and changed into a pair of jeans and a wool shirt over a warm pair of silk long underwear. It was his secret pleasure to have the silky soft material next to his skin all day, so much better than the non-wicking cotton and wool blend he used to wear years before.

His muscles still ached a bit from overuse the previous day, but not badly. Not as badly as he had anticipated anyway. Not too bad for an old guy, he thought grimly. He had fallen asleep almost as soon as his head hit the pillow the night before. He needed the sleep, he was sure, but he regretted not spending the evening with Lesley. He hoped she'd forgive him, but he wasn't as young as he once was. Maybe when all this was over, he could make it up to her. He liked the sound of that, and he smiled.

He left his room and turned towards the staircase down to the main floor when he thought about Angie. He'd never had a chance to talk with her the night before and he was wondering how she was doing. He paused and turned around towards her room. He took several steps, and then turned away again. If she wasn't up, he should probably let her sleep a little longer, he thought. So instead, he retraced his steps and went downstairs to have breakfast.

There were already a number of men and women crowded into the kitchen. Tessie was there, her hair still wet from her shower and wound up and clipped to the back of her head, the ends were wet but no longer dripping. Tessie's a real trooper, Alex thought. She had one coffee urn set up and it was already providing coffee to the lucky men with cups to put under the spouts. He suspected the urn was filled with warmed up coffee from the night before, though, so he decided he'd wait until a fresher batch had been made in one of the other urns. He went over to Tessie.

"Need some help?" he asked.

Tessie smiled, "Sure do!" she said. "Could you finish filling these coffee urns with water, so I can pull out the eggs and get some toast started?"

"Are you frying eggs?" he asked.

"Scrambled, I think. That should work out better for a crowd like this."

"Here, little lady, let me help," one of the guys said, stepping forward from the milling group of men. "I used to be a cook in the army. I know my way around feeding crowds," he said, taking off his sock cap.

"You're hired," Tessie said over her shoulder.

Alex slapped the man on the shoulder, "I'm Alex Jackson," he introduced himself.

"My name's Chip Doherty," the man said shaking Alex' hand. "Down from Whitefield to help out."

"This is Tessie – she runs the kitchen. Whatever she says goes," Alex said.

"Gotcha. Hey, Tessie," he said with a wave. "I'll get the eggs going if you want to rev up that toaster."

Tessie went to the refrigerator and pulled out a carton of eggs and handed them to Chip. Soon they were standing side-by-side at the stove scrambling eggs and buttering toast. Alex finished the two coffee urns and had them pumping out black coffee even before the other one went dry. He refilled the empty one and got it started on a new batch of coffee, too. He found that he was whistling. There was something about having a chore to do and getting it done that felt very good, he thought.

Jeb came in and after sizing up the situation, started lining up the plates and serving platters for the rest of the searchers who would be coming through shortly.

"Where's Angie? Shouldn't she and Kay be down here helping out?" Jeb asked over his shoulder.

Alex looked around, half expecting one of his daughters to appear. "You're right. I can't believe they're sleeping through this," he said, half to himself.

Tessie had been listening. "I'll go and check on them, if you want," she said.

Alex saw that she was busy. "No, I'll go up. I want to grab my other pair of socks anyway, to take with me today." He turned and left the kitchen, heading through the main room of the lodge.

Kay and Joe came in through the front door just as he reached the stairs. He looked over at them in surprise. "Kay?" he said.

She was equally surprised to see him. "Uh, hi, Dad!" she said.

"Hey, Alex," Joe said with a small wave. He unlaced his fingers from Kay's and paused, then not knowing what else to do, he walked on through to the kitchen mumbling something about finding Jeb and breakfast.

Kay started to follow him. "Breakfast," she said pointing towards the kitchen.

But Alex stopped her. "How come you're coming in through the front door with Joe?" Alex asked, in confusion. He had thought she was asleep upstairs.

"Uh, no reason. I saw him walking towards the lodge and I went out to meet him, that's all," Kay said brightly.

Alex nodded, accepting the explanation. "Is Angie up?" he asked.

Kay looked at him, as if she suddenly didn't recognize the name. "Angie?" she repeated.

"Yes, you know, your sister? Is she up?"

Kay frowned, "How would I know, Dad?" she said with as much attitude as she could muster and walked quickly past him. "Where's the food? I'm starved," she said as she headed towards the kitchen.

Alex turned and watched her. He knew something wasn't quite right, but he just wasn't certain what. He glanced upstairs and saw that Angie's door was closed. She must still be in bed. He walked up the stairs. When he got to her door, he knocked softly. Should he let her sleep, he wondered?

He knocked again. No answer. Finally, hesitantly, he turned the handle and pushed the door open a crack. It was dark inside. "Angie?" he said softly. "Honey, it's time to get up."

No answer. He reached for the light switch and flicked it on. For several seconds, he stood just looking into the room as he tried to make sense of it. Angie's bed was neatly made. Kay's bed was neatly made. Angie wasn't in the room. After a moment, he realized - somewhere inside he must've already known - that she was gone and that she had not slept in that bed at all the night before, and that Kay had not slept in hers, either. He didn't like where his mind was going.

He turned to go downstairs to have it out with Kay when he noticed that Angie's computer was on. The power light was green and pulsing although the screen was black, in sleep mode. He went over to it and gently touched one of the keys. The computer screen flashed on, and he saw that a document was open on the screen. It was Angie's translation of the diary. He sat down in Angie's chair and started reading her translation.

The language was stilted, and the translation probably needed Tessie's review and correction, but still, Angie had done a pretty fair job of getting to the gist of each of the entries. He read through the several paragraphs until he got to the last one that she had translated: The end of it read:

> *I have decided to go and help with the search for the little girl. She may not be alive now – it has been so long – 8 days! – but if we could at least bring her little body back to her parents, that would be a blessing, too. Of course, we pray for the impossible. But I cannot in good conscience stay behind and not help these poor weary searchers.*

"Oh my God!" Alex said aloud. "She's gone out to search for Melanie!" His voice sounded strained and melodramatic even to his own ears.

He didn't remember making a conscious decision, but in a moment, he was down the stairs and in the kitchen. Jeb and Tessie looked up at the same moment and seeing the expression on his face, they both rushed to his side.

"Alex? What's the matter? What's happened?" Tessie asked, her hand at her throat, ready to cover her mouth in fear or in shock.

"Alex?" Jeb said, touching his friend's shoulder.

"It's Angie," Alex said in a voice suddenly gone hoarse. "She's gone."

Tessie's intake of breath was the only sound in the kitchen. "What do you mean...gone?" she asked in a low voice.

Alex looked from Tessie to Jeb and back again. Then catching sight of Kay and Joe at the counter just behind Jeb, he swung around and marched over to stand in front of Kay. "Where's Angie?" he demanded. "When was the last time you saw her?"

Kay went pale. "Angie?" she repeated blankly. "She's not in our room?"

Alex studied her face and then looked at Joe. The realization of where she had been coming from when he saw her and Joe earlier came crashing in and filled his mind with snapshot visions of the two of them sharing a sleeping bag in Joe's tent. "Oh Christ!" he said in disgust, and he turned away, his eyes closed and his fingers combing through his hair. "Christ," he repeated with a shake of his head.

He turned to face Jeb. "I think Angie might've been translating the diary when she decided to go out and search for Melanie herself," he said quietly.

"But why would she do that?" Jeb asked.

"Because of Keith Jacobs," Tessie interrupted. The two men turned and looked at her in bewilderment.

"What do you mean?" Alex asked for both of them.

"Last night. I meant to tell you about it, Alex, but you went to bed so quickly, I never got the chance," Tessie said by way of apology. She ducked her head. "I'm sorry. I should've told you about it right away."

"Told him what?" Jeb asked.

"Last night, while we were preparing dinner in the kitchen, Keith Jacobs came back with one of the groups of searchers. He started yelling at Angie that it was all her fault. He tried to attack her." Tessie said as calmly as she could manage. Her arms were crossed in front of her chest and her hands were nervously kneading the silky material covering the opposite elbows.

"Oh, Christ! That asshole!" Alex said. He breathed out. "Sorry, Tess. But the poor kid! I just wished I'd known."

Jeb nodded. The only thing that belied his calm was how he held his fists so tightly that the knuckles had turned white at his sides.

Lesley

Just then Lesley came in through the back entrance. She stopped and looked around at the tableau before her: Alex and Jeb, both obviously upset and angry; Tessie standing nearby looking nervous and anxious; Kay and Joe at the counter looking pale and guilty. What was going on? Quietly, she pulled the door closed behind her and waited.

Alex looked up and saw her and smiled weakly. "Angie's gone," he said quietly.

"Oh no!" She closed her eyes for a second. "When?"

"I think maybe last night. Her bed hasn't been slept in." As he said it, he turned and eyed Kay making it clear that he'd noticed her bed hadn't been slept in either. But he said nothing to her. That would be for later when he had time to think about it. Right now, he had no idea what to say to her or how. His initial reaction was to beat the shit out of Joe and lock up Kay in her room for a few months of grounding. He was pretty sure that was a logical reaction, but not exactly the "correct response" from an enlightened father; not that he really cared at the moment.

Jerry Stockman stepped forward. "Alex, she may have left a trail we can follow," he said.

Alex nodded. "I hope so, Jerry. But I think the rest of you should continue with the search for Melanie. I'm sorry but I have to go after Angie."

Jeb spoke up, "Me, too. I'm going with you Alex."

Jerry nodded to the two of them. "Yeah, I understand. We won't be at cross-purposes – we'll all be on the lookout for Angie and Melanie. You're right; we can't give up on searching for Melanie. I'm going to keep my search groups working their search sectors from yesterday. I'd hate to pull out and change course now."

"OK," Alex agreed. "Jeb and I will leave right away. We'll see if we can find any trace of which way Angie might've gone. If you don't mind, we'll take one of the walkie-talkies with us. We can use it to keep you updated on our progress and to find out from you if there's any news here, OK?"

Jerry nodded. "Sounds good. Let's go over the maps before you leave. I'll show you what we have scoped out for the search today. It might help you figure out where to start looking for Angie, too."

The three men – Jeb, Alex, and Jerry – turned and went into the main room of the lodge to pour over the maps.

Kay glanced at Joe and shrugged with a small smile. "When it rains, it pours," she said meekly.

"They're going to kill me, aren't they?" Joe said under his breath as he watched Jeb and Alex leave the room.

Their conversation, quiet as it was, wasn't lost on Lesley. She watched them for several seconds and realized what Alex had seen. She shook her head. Poor Alex. This couldn't be easy for him to deal with on top of everything else.

She saw Tessie looking at Kay and Joe, as well.

"Tessie?" Lesley said, touching the other woman's arm.

Tessie looked at her and smiled weakly. She shook her head. "Unbelievable, huh?"

"How much danger is Angie in, do you think?"

"Well, hiking at night is always a problem – there are gullies to fall into, she could get lost, not to mention, hypothermia if she gets wet, and then there are wild animals..." she said, her voice trailing off.

"Wild animals?" Lesley repeated.

"We've had a scruffy bear, maybe two of them - could be a mother and a cub, we're not sure – who have been around the campground recently. They're after trash mostly. But this time of year, when they're trying to get their last big meals in before winter, you never know how they'll behave."

Lesley held still for one long moment, closing her eyes. She rubbed her forehead and frowned. When she opened her eyes, she blinked once or twice. "Wow! When you mentioned the bears, for a second there I had this very vivid...image." She smiled tentatively at Tessie, "I'm not positive, of course, but I think she's OK."

Tessie eyed her for a moment, and then returned the smile. "All right, then. That's a start," she said squeezing Lesley's wrist.

FORTY-EIGHT

Going after Angie

August 2006
Wilderness Campground, Crawford Notch, NH

*** *Alex* ***

Jeb and Alex were ready to leave. They had each packed some extra supplies in their backpacks because they knew that if they didn't find Angie quickly, they would probably spend the night in the woods rather than return to the lodge.

They also knew that searching for Angie would not be like searching for Melanie. Angie was an experienced hiker, and she had a lot more physical endurance. She would hike faster and longer than a four-year-old child and would only stay put if she was hurt or if she felt she was truly lost, an unlikely scenario at this point.

While Jeb was saying goodbye to Tessie, Alex went out the back door to give them some privacy. Lesley followed him. She caught up to him and touched his arm. He turned and smiled.

"Good luck," she said softly.

Alex nodded. "Thanks, Lesley. We'll find her," he added, more to reassure himself than her.

"Sure, you will," Lesley said with a nod. She was quiet for a moment. "Alex?"

"Yes?"

"I...I had a strange dream last night," she said.

He frowned. "Is this one of your psychic things?" he asked a little nervously.

"I don't know," she answered with the hint of a smile. "Maybe. Most of it didn't make any sense. You know the way dreams can be."

He nodded.

"But there was an image towards the end of it, just before I woke up. It stayed with me, and it flashed into my mind this morning when I came into the kitchen, and you said that Angie was gone."

"An image?" he asked with interest. "What sort of image?"

"Look, I know you think this whole psychic reading thing is a bunch of mumbo-jumbo. That's fine. I don't have time to convince you otherwise right now. But my dream was very vivid, and I think it meant something."

"OK. What did you see?"

"Well, I saw... What I saw was Melanie's stuffed bear."

He blinked. "Her stuffed bear?"

Lesley nodded.

Suddenly, he chuckled. "So...that would mean what exactly? That we should keep an eye out for her little teddy bear?"

Lesley frowned. "I don't think it's likely to be that straight forward. I think it is more of a clue...or a warning, maybe."

He grinned. "A warning? Of a stuffed animal?"

She shook her head with irritation, knowing that he wasn't taking her seriously. "Alex, bears are meaningful in dreams. The Native Americans considered bears to be messengers. They can portend trouble..."

He took her hands in his and she stopped speaking. He looked into her eyes. "Lesley, I promise I'll be careful, OK?"

She looked back at him for a long moment and then nodded. "Good. Yes, please be careful, Alex."

He leaned over and gently kissed her on the lips. "I may not believe in all your signs and wonders, but I know you do. That's good enough for me."

She closed her eyes for a moment. "Thanks, Alex."

Jeb cleared his throat as he came out of the back door. "We'd better get going, Alex," he said.

Alex nodded. "I'm all set." He turned back to Lesley. "We'll call to check in."

Lesley nodded.

Alex turned and fell into step beside Jeb, but they stopped when Tessie came running out the back door followed by Jerry Stockman.

"Wait," Tessie called. They waited for her to reach them.

"What's up, Tess?" Alex said, feeling his heart speed up.

Tessie placed her hand over her heart as she tried to catch her breath. By then Jerry Stockman had joined them.

"It's Keith Jacobs," Jerry said without preamble. "Nora just came in and told us that she thinks her husband headed into the woods when he heard that Angie was gone." He shook his head. "After that scene in the kitchen last night, I don't think he's up to any good."

Lesley had joined them by now and overhead Jerry's information. "Will he hurt Angie, do you think?" she asked, looking from one face to the next. The hair on the back of her neck prickled.

Tessie looked at her and said grimly, "He would've hurt her last night if you and I and Jerry here hadn't been there to stop him." She added, "I think he will."

"If he finds her," Jeb said quietly. The others turned to look at him. "Don't forget that Angie's a good hiker and experienced in the outdoors, plus she has youth on her side. As tired as he must be, Keith will have a hard time keeping up with her."

Alex nodded in agreement, but his face looked drawn and pale. How had his life barreled so far out of control again? he wondered. He shook off the thought. They must find Angie quickly, certainly before Keith. "Come on, Jeb, let's get moving," he said, suddenly feeling that every moment counted.

FORTY-NINE

Remaining Behind

August 2006
Wilderness Campground, Crawford Notch, NH

*** *Tessie* ***

Tessie watched the two men until they disappeared in the trees beyond the lodge, then she turned back. Lesley was standing a few feet away. She had also been watching Jeb and Alex as they left.

"I hope they find her quickly," Lesley said.

Tessie nodded. "I hope they find her before Keith does," she said. "But if anyone can take care of it all, it's those two men." She nodded towards the trees where Jeb and Alex had been just minutes before. Having said it she felt better. While she feared for Melanie's survival, she thought that Angie could probably take care of herself in the woods, at least for the short term. But if she became lost or hurt, or if Keith found her, then all bets were off.

Tessie looked up and saw that several of the search and rescue groups had come out the back door and were preparing to leave. They stomped around in their hiking boots, perhaps to wake themselves up or more likely to keep out the chill of the dawn. The only talk was in murmured undertones.

Tessie noticed Robin Keller at the edge of the searchers. Robin was staring at Lesley and when Lesley finally glanced up and saw her, Robin walked over.

"So, what's going on?" Robin asked with a friendly smile.

Lesley looked at Robin. "Nothing much. Searchers going out, as usual," Lesley said with an unconcerned shrug.

"No, I mean with Alex and Jeb going off like that alone...what was that all about?" Robin asked.

Lesley looked at Robin, a thin smile on her face. "It's nothing, Robin. Just forget about it. It has nothing to do with the search for Melanie." Then Lesley turned away and fell into step with Tessie. Tessie could see the resolute look on Lesley's face.

Tessie and Lesley made their way through the milling people and back into the brightness of the kitchen. It took only moments to reacclimatize themselves to the morning tasks waiting inside. Tessie immediately went to see whether the coffee urns needed to be refilled. She was glad to be busy. It would give her little time to fret about Angie, or Alex and Jeb.

She said a quick prayer for their protection and safety. She made a quick sign of the cross and kissed her fingertips and then pressed them to her heart. When she looked up, she saw that Lesley was watching her. She smiled and shrugged slightly.

"Catholic schooling," she said by way of explanation.

Lesley smiled as she helped Tessie remove the lid off the big urn and peer inside. "There's no atheist in fox holes, eh?" she said.

Tessie nodded. "But lots of rabbits' feet and lucky charms, to cover all bases."

They spent the early morning hours working together to get the groups fed, sandwiches made and wrapped to be packed in backpacks, and canteens filled with water.

Joe and Kevin had departed with one of the early search groups and Tessie noticed that Kay was wandering in and out of the kitchen, helping for a few minutes, and then frenetically going to the back door to look out, then pacing into the dining room and back to the kitchen again.

The third time through, Tessie rolled her eyes and hissed at her, "Kay, would you stop the pacing and get something done, please?"

Kay stopped and looked up at Tessie. "What can I do? I feel like I'm going out of my mind!"

"You act like it, too!" Tessie responded, as she pulled off the rubber gloves she'd donned to wash the dishes. She slapped the wet gloves on the sink for emphasis and left them there to dry. "Come into the dining room with me," she said putting her arm around Kay's shoulder and leading her into the next room. "To the registration desk."

When they reached the desk, she touched a key, and the monitor woke up. "I want you to go through all the reservations and count up how many groups are supposed to arrive today then match them up to the campsite map to make sure everything is in order. Then I want you to go out and double-check each of those campsites to make sure they've been swept, the garbage picked up, and everything is ready for the new campers. Could you do that?"

Kay sighed, letting out a long breath. "OK," she said without much enthusiasm.

Tessie smiled, "Remember what I told you about being busy making the time go by faster? It requires you to apply yourself to the task at hand." She eyed Kay for several long moments. "You want to tell me anything, Kay?"

Kay looked at her blankly. "Like what, Tessie?"

"Oh, like why you weren't in your own bed last night?" Tessie watched the girl's face and knew that she had guessed right.

Kay feigned innocence. "That's ridiculous."

"So, you want to go that route, eh?" Tessie said, raising her eyebrows in disapproval. "Kay, we can talk around this for a while, if you'd like, honey, but in the end, you know and I know that I'm going to get to the bottom of it." She paused and eyed Kay sternly. "Your dad and Jeb are worried about you and are ready to kill Joe. So, what's really going on between you and Joe? That's what I need to know."

Kay was silent for several long moments, then her shoulders fell, and she whispered, "I slept in Joe's tent last night, Tessie."

Tessie nodded. "I know. So? What happened?"

Kay looked up in surprise. "Nothing happened, Tessie."

Tessie looked unconvinced. "What happened, Kay?"

"Look," Kay said, "I admit it. I wanted something to happen, Tessie. It's true. But nothing happened. Really!"

Tessie squinted her eyes. "Well, why not?"

"What?" Kay asked.

"You're a beautiful girl. You have a good body; big boobs, 'sexy' the boys call you," Tessie said. "So why did nothing happen?"

"Tessie," Kay said, embarrassed.

"Tell me," Tessie said sternly.

"Because he fell asleep, OK?"

"He fell asleep?"

"Yes. I was with him in his tent. We were kissing...and he fell asleep."

Tessie grinned and her hand flew to her mouth. "No way!" she said stifling a laugh.

Kay grimaced and nodded, looking mortified.

Tessie patted Kay's shoulder and headed back to the kitchen, shaking her head. "I only hope your dad believes you," she said over her shoulder.

"Yeah, me too," Kay agreed bleakly.

Just as she reached the door to the kitchen Tessie saw Nora standing at a window at the far side of the dining room. She took a few steps towards her. "Nora?"

Nora lifted her eyes, "Oh! Hi, Tessie."

Her voice, the downward slope of her shoulders, the defeated look in her eye broadcasted how miserable she was, but Tessie asked anyway, "How are you doing?"

Nora smiled but it didn't reach her eyes, "Fine," she replied automatically. She took a deep breath and then blew it out with a sigh. "Well...no, actually the truth is I'm not doing well, but that's to be expected, huh?"

Tessie nodded sympathetically as Nora came over to her. When she reached Tessie's side, Tessie opened the door to the kitchen for her. "Come, have a hot cup of coffee and something to eat," she said patting the other woman on the shoulder.

Nora nodded. "Coffee sounds good. No food, though. I'm really not hungry."

Tessie leaned in solicitously. "Nora, Jerry mentioned that Keith went back into the woods this morning," Tessie said, hoping to get the full story for herself.

Nora's face looked strained. "He...he's not handling things – any of this," she said gesturing at the tables covered with maps in the dining room behind them and the kitchen with groups of searchers around them, "very well, you know."

"Did he go after Angie?" Tessie asked, point-blank.

Nora looked as if she'd been punched. "Tessie, uh, he...well," she stopped then shrugged, "To be honest, I'm not sure what he intends to do. He's like a crazy man right now. He came back to the campsite this morning at full tilt, saying how Angie had headed into the woods after Melanie sometime during the night. He's not thinking clearly, Tessie. He seems to think that Angie went after Melanie to make sure that Melanie wouldn't say anything about Angie scaring her and causing her to run away."

Lesley came up behind them, obviously having overheard what Nora had said.

"Will he try to hurt Angie?" Lesley asked taking Nora's hand in hers and looking into her eyes.

Nora returned her look, straightening her shoulders slightly. "I...I don't know. The Keith I've been married to for the past seven years certainly wouldn't hurt her, but this new angry Keith?" she shook her head. "I just don't know."

Lesley nodded. "The stress of it all," she said, almost to herself.

"He has a gun," Nora whispered, her eyes brimming with tears.

Lesley and Tessie looked at her in shock.

"A gun?" Tessie repeated, her eyes widening as the ramifications of this piece of information slowly sank in.

Nora nodded. "A handgun. I don't know what kind. He bought it several years ago," her voice grew stronger as she explained, "There were some burglaries in our neighborhood back home and he wanted a gun in the house for protection. He used to leave it in the night table drawer until Melanie got old enough to be curious. Then he moved it to the top shelf in his closet. He always brought it along on long car trips. He said it made him feel safer. He kept it locked up in the trunk of the car in a special toolbox."

They stared at her. Lesley finally broke the silence, "We'd better tell Jerry Stockman. He can let Alex and Jeb know that Keith is armed when they call in."

"Oh, God," Tessie said. It came out like a prayer.

Nora looked at the other two women, "He wasn't a bad man," she said quietly as if speaking of someone who is irretrievably gone. She shook her head slowly and turned away.

FIFTY

Day 4 of the Search (Angie)

August 2006
Crawford Notch, NH

*** *Angie* ***

It wasn't until the first light of dawn broke through the treetops around me that I saw the bear tracks clearly. I had been walking most of the night; a steady pace, not fast because I didn't want to tire myself out nor did I want to fall down a steep drop-off and get hurt. But I also wanted to go slowly in order to try and sense which way Melanie had gone and where she was now. Heck, IF she still was, I thought glumly.

I reminded myself that the lost little girl, Pammy Hollingworth, in the diary pages had survived, and that had taken place later in the year and for twice as long as Melanie had been missing, and yet she had been found alive. That was good news; that was reason to be optimistic. But maybe that little girl was smarter about the woods than Melanie was, I worried. After all, it happened in 1941. Weren't kids more woods-smart then than they are today? Would Melanie think of doing something clever to stay warm during the cold nights? Her parents didn't seem to think so, but I know Melanie watched a lot of TV and for all its faults, a kid could get a lot of good information from TV shows, particularly from the PBS and Nature shows. Was I grabbing at straws?

I squatted next to a really good set of footprints. Yes, these were definitely bear paw prints. The ground here was muddy from the drizzle the previous day and the prints were deep and softly rounded. The rear prints were slashed with the impressions of the bear's claws as they dug into the ground as the bear had ambled along the path. A second, indistinct set of prints appeared alongside the other set. Sometimes, they were superimposed on top. That meant that a second animal might be with the bear, or perhaps following it.

I couldn't make out the other prints clearly, though. The second animal was obviously much lighter because it didn't leave as deep an impression in the ground. Could it be a bear cub traveling with its mother? Jeb had guessed that there had been an elusive mother bear and cub around the campground over the summer months. No one had seen them for a while, but there had been plenty of evidence – scratch marks and scat.

I stood up and stretched. My muscles were sore, especially along the top of my shoulders where the weight of the backpack had made the straps dig in. I pulled my navy blue jacket around me closer and zipped it up so that my neck was protected from the early morning chill. Having paused to look at the paw prints, the cold was already beginning to seep in, and I knew it was important to stay warm.

I was wearing an old black sock cap pulled down low with my braids hanging down on either side. I had found the cap in the mudroom off the lodge and had chosen it because I knew it was important to keep my head covered to stay warm. I also liked it because it was dark in color, and I knew it would make me less visible when I left the night before. I'd seen the old World War II movies of the commandos dressed all in black, their faces covered with charcoal so that only the white of their eyes and teeth were visible. I felt a little like a commando with all this sneaking around in the night. I had to admit that it was actually sort of exciting.

It turned out not to be that difficult getting away without being seen. I had waited a while after everyone had gone to bed. It was lucky that Kay had not returned to our room before I left because I was able to get an earlier start, not having to wait for her to get to sleep. I snuck down through the bunkroom and into the kitchen and filled my backpack with rolls, a plastic container of honey and a jar of peanut butter to make my favorite sandwich – peanut butter and honey. I also threw in a couple of granola bars and several oranges.

I brought along two large water bottles that hung from loops snapped to the sides of the pack. If I was careful, the water would last a while and I wouldn't have to resort to drinking from the streams, which were mostly questionable in the forests these days.

Too many people hiked and camped in these mountains and so the woods were not as pristine and pure as one would expect from a National Forest. I remembered reading that 70-million people lived within driving distance of these mountains. When you think about it, it was ironic that someone could even get lost in the woods so close to such a large number of people.

As I hiked, I replayed the scene in the kitchen from the night before. Mr. Jacobs had been right, of course. Melanie's disappearance was my fault. I had agreed to watch the little girl and I had failed that task miserably. I had been mesmerized by the thought of finding treasure and it had kept me from acting responsibly. I realized all that now; but it was too late.

It was sort of lame, I thought. I was going to be fourteen in December. I should be a lot more mature than I was. And what did I have to show for it? I didn't even have the three-legged buffalo nickel because Melanie had taken it with her. I remembered handing it to her and had seen her stick it deep in her overall's pocket for safekeeping. That was the last time I had seen the coin. Of course, I didn't know if it was valuable, but now I was hoping that maybe it would prove to be lucky, at least, for Melanie.

Birds were beginning to wake up in the treetops above me. They were trilling and calling to each other and occasionally swooping down from their roosts in the boughs above. The woods seemed friendlier now in the daylight as the air filled with the sounds of birds and woodland life.

I had hiked down the same trail past the campsites that Lesley and I had passed the first day of the search, but instead of following the trail around towards Owls Cliff and on to the ponds as she and I had done, I decided this time to go across the stream and follow an unused side trail that rounded the base of the mountain and into a swampy area beyond the ponds. It wasn't a popular trail because the soggy ground meant there were swarms of mosquitoes during the summer months. Even so, I thought it might be the preferred choice of a small child since it was not all that steep, and although it was muddy, it was not a difficult hike. That was the trick – to think like a four-year-old. If I could remember that I would find her for sure.

All night as I walked, I tried to imagine what Melanie might've done, if she had indeed followed this trail. Which way did she go when the trail split with one path leading up towards a distant peak and the other meandering along back and forth across a bog? Jeb said that animals tend to take the path of least resistance. I guessed a child would do that, as well.

Before the sun came up it had been too dark to notice any traces of Melanie, even if she had left something behind. I hadn't really expected to find anything, anyway. I figured that if there was anything to find, the professional search and rescue teams would've already found it, assuming that they had already searched this particular trail. My search plan was different, but quite simple. I was hoping to follow Melanie by mentally becoming Melanie. That was it.

The woods were thick in this part of the White Mountains. People had been lost out here many times in the last couple hundred years. Some were legendary stories like the young woman for whom the Nancy Brook Trail was named, who became lost in a snowstorm. In more recent times, airplanes had crashed in these woods, and it was months, sometimes years, before the remains of the flyers were found. Missing hikers, missing hunters, missing pilots, missing children, missing pets, all had wandered and sometimes died in these mountains. But many survived and were found. It wasn't hopeless.

Still, in some areas, the undergrowth was so thick you could miss even a small plane that might be within a stone's throw of where you were standing. One plane, a few years ago, had been trying to land at a small airfield in a snowstorm. No one really knows what went wrong, but the plane ended up crashing in the southern part of the White Mountains. They searched for the plane for three years. It was a mysterious tale that grew like an urban legend with the passage of time. UFO enthusiasts took an interest. Psychics were called in and many weekend hiking groups scoured the forests. Then one fall day, the crash site was found – covered in autumn leaves having crashed 20 miles from the airport into a thick stand of trees. Mystery solved.

The thought of psychics immediately brought to mind Lesley. I wondered if Lesley could actually locate Melanie with her psychic powers? Had she tried? What exactly were her so-called 'psychic powers' anyway? And, if they really existed, what was it like to have psychic powers? I wondered. Would it be like a séance where a group of interested people sat at a table in a dark room and waited for other worldly visitors to come and answer questions for them? I smiled at the thought of my father and Jeb participating in such a thing.

It didn't matter now, though. I would find Melanie all by myself. When I had started out from the campground the night before I had had a strong sense of Melanie walking on the trail that bounded the edge of the campground, so that was the one I had followed. When I came to the bear prints, I once again felt a strong kinship with the girl. But was that feeling of kinship a result of thinking more and more about Melanie or did it mean I was actually on the right path? I didn't know. Maybe that is what Lesley meant when she said she wasn't always sure if what she felt was true or if she was fooling herself. Was I fooling myself?

But what else was there to do? I couldn't go back now and face everyone empty-handed. What if I went back only to hear that the little girl was dead, or more likely, forever missing, never to be found? Melanie was still alive as long as I continued to look for her, at least to me she was. So, I would continue on. If that was what it took to keep Melanie alive, then I would continue to search for her.

As I walked, I thought about what it was like being lost. I had been lost once, too, when I was just a little older than Melanie. I had been luckier than Melanie, though, because I hadn't been alone. Kay had been with me. It's too bad that Melanie didn't have a big sister.

There is something mesmerizing about hiking, moving step after step for hours on end. You soon forget your surroundings and your mind becomes free to wander and sometimes to remember. I thought about that last family camping trip in Ethiopia when Kay and I got lost.

FIFTY-ONE

Getting Lost at Lake Langano

June 1998
Lake Langano, Rift Valley, Ethiopia

*** *Angie* ***

I remember when Kay and I got lost while camping in Ethiopia. We were looking for hippos.

My parents went for a walk after dinner the first night of our camping trip and left us to play with the other children in the Daniels' tent.

While they were gone, Mr. Daniels and Mr. Oliver heard some snuffling sounds down by the lake and went to investigate. They came back very excited.

"There's a mother and baby hippo down by the lake!" Mr. Daniels had said.

Immediately, all of us kids pleaded to be able to go down and see the hippos. Imagine! Hippos that were not in cages or seen from across a moat in a zoo!

"OK," Mr. Daniels said, "but we must all stay together, and no one should try to get too close. Mother hippos are very protective of their babies," Mr. Daniels explained.

Arage, our Ethiopian servant, wasn't happy. He touched Kay's shoulder and shook his head, "No go," he said, shaking his head again for emphasis.

Of course, we understood what he was saying, but we were determined to go and see the hippos. "It will be all right, Arage," Kay said, patting his hand. "We'll be with the Daniels and the Olivers. Mommy and Daddy won't mind."

He shook his head again, but he must've realized that it was futile. Maybe he figured it would be all right since we would be with the other adults.

It was still light out although the late afternoon sun was casting long shadows. We were giggly with excitement. Lauren and I played a game of tag as we skipped along, squealing, and leaping this way and that down to the water's edge. The adults shushed us, telling us to quiet down or we'd scare the hippos away.

We became quieter as we got closer to the lakeshore. At first, I didn't see anything – just the murky water of the lake reflecting the growing sunset with dazzling effect as a breeze rippled the surface of the water. We stopped and I looked up at Mr. Daniels who had his finger up to his lips and his index finger pointing into the grassy area just beyond the gravelly beach area from where we stood.

Kay grinned. "I see it," she said in a stage whisper. "Look, Angie, there!" She held my shoulders and pointed my head so that I gazed in the direction she wanted. "There! Do you see it?"

At first, I didn't. But then, suddenly I did! The huge rear end of the hippo blended into the brownish color of the grasses around it. I had to stare hard at the spot to make out where the mother hippo's body ended, and the tall grass began. Her head dropped as she ripped up a huge tuft of grass and chewed it, looking almost like a cow languidly chewing its cud. She moved a bit further into the grass and stopped. Her head swung around, and she seemed to look right at us. Actually, I remember thinking that she was looking directly at me, in particular, and I was transfixed by the notion. Her eyes were huge and watery, but soft in some mysteriously maternal way. I can't explain it, but I recognized intelligence in them looking back at me.

It was several seconds before I realized that the others – the adults and Peter, at least - had moved off to the right, going around the hippo and giving her wide berth. They assumed we girls were coming along behind them. But we weren't. Kay and I stayed where we were with Tina and Lauren, all of us engrossed in watching the mother hippo. Soon, the hippo moved and the four of us followed her at a distance. She was lumbering on, close to the water, but still moving along the lakeshore. Flies buzzed around her face and along her back, but she didn't appear to notice. Periodically, she would stop and nibble at the grasses or at some plant or other that grew in the swampy waters along the edge of that part of the lake. But we still hadn't seen the baby hippo.

Soon we were well within the thicket of grasses and the path we were on was growing more and more muddy. It sucked at our sneakers with each step, but still the four of us followed the hippo. After a while – I don't have any idea how long – we heard Mr. Daniels' voice in the distance calling to us. "Tina? Lauren? Where are you?" He sounded a long way away.

Tina's head perked up immediately. "Here, Daddy! We are here!"

"I told you to stay with us," he said sternly. "Come along now."

Tina took Lauren's hand and then mine, but I pulled away. "I don't want to go! I want to see the baby hippo!" I said stubbornly.

"Me, too!" Kay said.

"My daddy said we have to go back now," Tina replied authoritatively.

Kay shook her head. "Angie and I are going to see the baby first. Then, we'll go back," she said, with some authority of her own. Her tone implied, *"You're not the boss of me."*

If it had just been me, no doubt I would've gone with Tina and Lauren. If adults said to come, obediently, I listened. But I really wanted to see the baby hippo. I really, really did. And then there was my loyalty to my big sister, whom I worshiped at the time.

Tina's father called again. And Tina called back, "We're coming!"

With that, she and Lauren turned and ran hand in hand back along the path in the direction of her father's voice.

Kay saw me glance around indecisively towards their retreating backs, but she quickly took my hand. "Come on, Angie, you and I are going to be the only ones who get to see the baby hippo! The mama hippo has been just waiting for the others to leave so she can show us her baby."

I liked the sound of that, plus I loved that Kay was giving me so much solicitous attention. It was a rare treat, and I was like a desert bloom taking in a long withheld ration of raindrops. Kay and I were so different. She was always such a social girl, extroverted and gregarious and always the center of attention. At those rare times when she deigned to notice me, I became her rapt lieutenant.

Kay and I walked further, always keeping the mother hippo in sight. The shadows were lengthening, but I kept hold of Kay's hand, my eyes on the mound of hippo flesh ahead. At one point, the mother hippo stopped and so we did too. We faced each other across an expanse of low grasses, perhaps 20 yards apart. Then something magical happened. The baby hippo came into sight. He moved next to his mother, nuzzling up against her, his head down. She nuzzled him back and looked up at us, not meanly or anything, she just looked at us the same way we were just looking at her and her baby.

We stayed like that for what seemed like a very long time. She was chewing something and looking at us and we were standing perfectly still looking back at them. It was an enchanted moment.

Afterwards, she turned and lumbered into the lake with barely a splash and the baby hippo followed. We watched as they sank into the water, the reeds bending and swaying around them. It had grown dark by then, not pitch black yet, but certainly dusk. I felt Kay move next to me.

"Kay?" I said in a small voice.

"Huh?" she answered in her own hushed voice.

"How do we get back to Mommy and Daddy?" I asked.

"Probably that way," she replied confidently, pointing behind us.

I didn't see a path there; in fact, I didn't see a path any which way, except for the bowed grasses where the hippos had gone into the water.

Kay pulled me along behind her, saying, "Come on. Let's go this way."

I stumbled along behind her and felt the grasses rub against my face and tickle my neck. Mosquitoes buzzed close to my ears, and I waved my free hand around to make them go away. I could feel my throat tightening up as tears grew there. I didn't want to start crying because I didn't want her to call me a cry-baby, but I wasn't sure how long I could keep the tears inside before they would just burst out of me.

I followed blindly along as Kay pulled me in another direction and then another. Once, I took a step and when my foot came down there wasn't any land underneath me at all, only mushy dark water. Kay yanked me back at the last moment, but one sneaker was squishy with water after that. My throat burned with the sobs I wouldn't allow to come out and I wiped at my eyes hoping that Kay wouldn't be able to see the tears streaming down my cheeks. We were lost, it was getting dark, and I was scared.

FIFTY-TWO

Bear Paw Prints

August 2006
Crawford Notch, NH

*** *Angie* ***

It was noon, or thereabouts; I wasn't sure exactly what time it was because I'd forgotten to put my watch on before I left the lodge. The morning hours had been cool and cloudy and that made it hard to judge the time. Plus, I'd been walking since an hour or two before dawn, so my sense of time passing was totally messed up. But I was getting a little hungry now, so I thought that it might be close to lunchtime.

All morning I had continued to follow the small deer path that I'd found at dawn in the swampy area beyond Owls Cliff and Mount Tremont. I followed the path because I could see from the paw prints that it was the way the bear and its cub had gone. I wasn't sure if it was a smart thing to do, following the bears. After all, what if I suddenly came upon them? But I still had a strong feeling that this was the way Melanie had gone, too. The only problem was that if Melanie indeed had followed this trail, I wondered if the bear was ahead of Melanie or behind her? I hoped ahead of her.

Occasionally, I'd seen claw scratches and once even a large perfect paw print in the mud. And there were the smaller prints that I assumed belonged to the cub. They weren't like the sow's prints, though. They were more even and consistent, which seemed a little odd. But then again, what did I know about bear cub's prints?

I hadn't found any sign of Melanie, and that worried me a little. People always left traces, didn't they? Were children different?

As the morning hours had gone by, my mind had drifted. I grew used to the sounds of the forest: the scrape of my hiking boots on the ground, the clink of my water bottle against the straps of my pack, the buzz of the insects all around me and the chirping of birds overhead. There was monotony to it all, but not a bad monotony. It must be what a meditative trance was like.

I felt a little removed from my body as my thoughts shifted from Melanie to the bear, then back to the lodge as I wondered about Kay and Tessie, and about my dad and Jeb. Had they noticed that I was gone? Were they worried about me? Did they understand why I'd left? Did they know why I had to come out here myself to find Melanie?

When I grew thirsty, I stopped and unhooked the clasp on my water bottle, unscrewed the lid and took a long sip. I hadn't realized how thirsty I was until I took the drink, but once I tasted the cool water, I swallowed several more, long gulps before reluctantly putting it away. I reminded myself that I had to be careful not to become dehydrated. When the weather was changeable like this – cool and cloudy – it was not always easy to tell when you were getting dehydrated. But I also wanted to conserve the water as much as I could because I had no idea how long I'd be gone. I wanted to make sure I had water left for Melanie, and food, too, if and when I found her.

The thought of food reminded me again that I was also getting hungry. I may as well eat while I was stopped, I decided. I took hold of the left shoulder strap and wriggled my right shoulder free and then swung the pack around to set it on the ground in front of me. I squatted down, unzipped the pack, and reached inside to pull out the plastic bag containing a half loaf of bread. I felt around for the jar of peanut butter and a couple minutes later I was biting into a peanut butter and honey sandwich with great satisfaction.

I sat down on the ground with my back against a small birch tree and drawing up my knees I rested my elbows on them. I munched on my sandwich and looked vaguely around the small clearing I was in, seeing a blur of greens and browns but not really noticing the individual trees and bushes.

Suddenly, I heard the swish of wings above me and glanced up to see several birds taking flight. What had spooked them, I wondered? Could it be the bear? Even though the buzzing of the insects still pulsed in the woods around me, I noticed all the twittering birds had gone silent.

Listening this intently made me think about the stories Jeb had told me about Native Americans and how they were so in tune with nature and the woods that they could hear things that other people couldn't hear and sense things that were so subtle as to be imperceptible to others. It was as if they could sense the very energy emanating from animals or people in the woods around them.

Is that what Lesley's psychic abilities were like, I wondered? Were people born with a special sensitivity to the unseen world or could it be learned? I wished I'd been born with it. How useful it would be! If I could lean back right now, close my eyes, and just think about Melanie and somehow tune into Melanie's energy, then I could lock on to it and follow it right to Melanie as if I were reading the headings on a compass. I closed my eyes and tried to focus on Melanie. In my mind, I could imagine her face, happy and lit up, just the way it had been when I had given her the Buffalo nickel.

"Where are you, Melanie?" I said aloud, but very softly. Immediately, a picture flashed in my mind of Melanie's little stuffed teddy bear. What did she call him? Brownie. He was tucked away in the little girl's backpack. Melanie's backpack. I could see it clearly in my mind the way it looked as it sat on the counter in the kitchen of the lodge. It was a bright pink, with a picture of a little pink princess bear imprinted on the back. The little princess bear was wearing a sparkly tiara of glitter.

I opened my eyes. What good was thinking about Melanie's teddy bear or her backpack? Of course, I hoped that Melanie had discovered the stuffed bear in the pack and that she found some comfort in his company. I sighed and stood up. I pulled my pack on again. It didn't look like I was going to sense where Melanie was, so I'd better stop wasting any more time. I looked back the way I had come, and it looked like a long dark tunnel of trees over the hiking trail. Branches of small trees, bushes and weedy grass nearly obscured the path. It wasn't a much-traveled trail – there were no trail markers or paint blazes slashed on the trees – but it was a discernible path just the same, perhaps used by hunters or by the hunted.

There was a snap of a breaking branch and a few more birds took wing in a poof-like fluttering as they careened away. Even the buzzing insects seemed to pause for a beat or two. I spun around and searched the dark woods for the source of the snapping sound.

I held my breath and listened intently. A moment or two passed and then the buzz of the insects returned, although the birds were still not chirping and tweeting to one another the way they had before. I waited another couple of seconds, breathing slowly and straining to hear something, but there was no sound. Finally, I took a deep breath and shook my head. It could've been a squirrel or chipmunk, perhaps. I didn't want to think about any of the possible larger animals that might be out in these woods today; besides bear, there were deer or moose, for instance. I sure didn't want to run into a moose out here. They may look dumb, but I knew they could be unpredictable and dangerous.

I turned and got my bearings, finding the continuation of the deer path once again at the other end of the small clearing. I felt better to be moving, that was for sure. I glanced further down the trail. There seemed to be a rise in the land, a hill or a cliff of some kind, up ahead. I could see that the path veered off to the right instead of climbing straight up or zigzagging with switchbacks as a hiking trail might.

I bent under a low hanging branch and when I straightened up on the other side, I noticed three huge glacial boulders to my left and behind them a cliff face jutting up higher than the surrounding trees. I started to follow the path to the right, but then I paused and looked speculatively at the boulders and cliffs above.

It might be worth climbing up to the top to get the lay of the land. Perhaps I could get a sense of where I was. I should be able to see Mount Tremont and Owl's Cliff from up there, or perhaps I was closer to Greens Cliff now? I turned off the path and picked my way among the rock field and around the first boulder.

On the other side, I found a small track that looked like it would take me up along the edge of the cliff face within the band of trees and shrubs where I could get good handholds to climb up the steep side of the ledge.

I began to climb. Even though it wasn't a particularly high cliff it was quite steep, and I was sweating and out of breath when I broke through the thick underbrush at the top. I stood up and drew in a deep breath. A breeze touched my face and it felt pleasantly cool where the sweat was drying along my hairline. Ah! I closed my eyes and enjoyed the sensation.

I looked out with a smile on my face. I could see several mountaintops from this knoll. I pulled my compass from my jeans' pocket and found north and then scrutinized the hills and surrounding woodland. If that tall cliff face over there was to my west, then it must be Greens Cliff. I should run into a small stream soon that I could follow out to Church Ponds; beyond that was a public campground and the Kancamagus Highway. I'd be back in civilization. Or I could continue to follow the deer path, which may or may not lead me further into the deeper wilderness between the Kancamagus Highway and Route 302.

As I thought about my choices, I pulled my water bottle out again and took a long sip. I would've loved to pour it over my head, but resisted the impulse, refusing to waste good drinking water. As I scanned the canopy of trees below, a movement caught my eye.

Although the light breeze was rustling leaves on the tree branches, this movement seemed out of place somehow.

Small trees were quivering one after the other in a line as if something large was touching the trunks below as it passed by. An animal? I watched in fascination, waiting for a break in the trees to get a glimpse of whatever was moving along beneath them.

It was a good distance away. I wished now that I'd brought the binoculars along. It hadn't occurred to me to add them to my pack before I left.

Suddenly, I saw a flash of color that was there and gone in the blink of an eye. But I had definitely seen it! Red? Yes, I decided that the flash of color had been red. But then, I reasoned, if it had been red, it probably wasn't an animal; it must be a person. My heartbeat sped up. Could it be Dad or Jeb? I didn't want them to find me before I located Melanie.

Instinctively, I crouched down as I remembered that if I could see the person, then it stood to reason that the person could see me, too. What to do? My mind raced but quickly settled on the one overriding goal: I was here to find Melanie. I would continue to follow the trail in the hope that it would lead me to her. But I'd have to go a bit quicker now that I knew someone was following me.

FIFTY-THREE

Looking for Angie

August 2006
Crawford Notch, NH

*** Alex ***

Jeb and Alex were far into the mountains by midday. They weren't certain they were on Angie's trail, or Keith's, for that matter. They had passed a number of indications that hikers had been on the trail recently, but nothing that definitively indicated it might be Angie or Keith. There had been a few indistinct boot heel prints. That was all. Jeb saw some bear paw prints, as well, but he was certain they were older than either of the other prints.

"What do you make of this Keith Jacobs thing?" Jeb asked Alex as they stopped for a drink of water and short rest.

"What d'ya mean?" Alex said, wiping his neck with a kerchief.

"Do you think he's gone nuts?"

Alex considered, "After what he's been through this week, I wouldn't be surprised if he has," Alex said.

Jeb nodded. "He's coming apart like a newspaper in the wind, isn't he?"

Alex grinned suddenly. "Nice simile," he said.

"Or is it a metaphor?" Jeb answered, scratching his chin in jest. They both chuckled. It was an old joke from their high school years in Montana when neither of them knew one literary device from another and had suffered through a senior English class with a teacher who was determined that they'd graduate fluent in every literary device known to man.

"Mrs. O'Grady!" Alex said, as her name suddenly popped into his mind.

"'Oh-Grade-yee', I believe we called her," Jeb responded with a wistful look on his face. He shook his head. "Could we ever have been that young and innocent?" He looked around the small clearing where they had stopped. Their backpacks were propped up against a paper birch, its peeling yellow-white bark looking ragged in the afternoon light.

"Did you think you were innocent back then?" Alex asked, looking up at his friend.

"Nah, I thought I was as worldly as they come. Heck, don't forget – I was the kid who'd been to Denver, remember?" Jeb hooted.

"What happened to those two young bucks? We had intended to end up as cowboys, didn't we?"

"With your dad teaching poly sci at the university, it wasn't bloody likely, though, was it?" Jeb said.

"True, but I sure was envious of your dad's ranch! Heck, I still am!"

They were quiet as both remembered the ranch and Jeb's father, who had died on his beloved ranch after Jeb came back from serving with the Marines in Beirut.

"Damn it, you know you're right! We should've become cowboys!" Jeb said. "What the hell were we thinking?"

Alex smiled and nodded wearily. "We'd have been happy cowboys, don't you think?"

Jeb grinned, "Poor cowboys, for sure, but yup, happy ones, too."

Alex chuckled. "So, it all comes down to money, after all, do you think?"

"Part of it, sure," Jeb said more seriously. "But I think we chose the lives we did for the traveling and seeing the world, too."

Alex nodded.

"The Europeans do it right, by my book," Jeb commented.

"Do what right?" Alex asked.

"Travel, see the world before they settle down to a job and wife and kids. Anywhere you go overseas you run into the Brits or Norwegians or Aussies or Kiwis with their hefty, little backpacks and wanderlust in their eyes. They get it right out of their systems in their early twenties and then go back to their homes and become adults with a sense of what the world is really all about. I admire them for being so smart about it."

"Why don't Americans go and see the world, do you think?"

"I've wondered about that. I think it's maybe because our country is so damn big, and the rest of the world seems so far away."

"Yeah, and most Americans can't speak any language except English. That's got to limit where they will comfortably go."

"Heck, Americans don't even speak English all that well!" Jeb said with a laugh.

"Damn those literary devices again, huh?"

"Yup. Sunk more than one boy, I can tell you," Jeb nodded in mock seriousness.

Alex stood up and stretched. "Well, we better get moving."

"Yup. But maybe we should call in before we move on," Jeb suggested.

"Good idea," Alex said, reaching into his pack and removing the walkie-talkie. He flipped it on and heard the static as he twirled the knob a bit until he found a clear line. He called in and was transferred over to Jerry Stockman. "Hey, Jerry, this is Alex," he said into the mouthpiece.

The muffled voice of Jerry Stockman came over the set. "Uh, Alex, glad you called in. I need to pass along some info to you. Can you hear me all right?"

"Loud and clear, Jerry. What's up?"

Jeb stepped over and bent in towards the small receiver.

"Uh, Nora Jacobs – Keith's wife – told us this morning that he's armed. Just wanted to let you guys know that."

"Armed?" Alex repeated incredulously into the walkie-talkie.

"Yeah. Turns out he has a small handgun for home protection. Nora says she's pretty sure he's carrying it with him."

Alex felt gooseflesh rise on his arms and along the back of his neck. "God! He has a gun? Are you kidding me?" Alex finally said.

"Sorry, no, I'm not kidding. Wish I was," Jerry responded. "Be careful, OK?"

"Yeah, will do. And thanks for letting us know, Jerry. We appreciate it."

"Better forewarned and all that," Jerry said dryly. "Have you seen any sign of him?"

"We've seen a few boot prints on the trail, but we can't be sure who they belong to."

"OK, then. Let us know when you have anything definite."

"Right. Talk to you later," Alex signed off.

"Jesus," Jeb said shaking his head. "We'd better find him before he finds Angie. That's all I can say. Who knows what he might do."

Alex felt his anger rise and his hand doubled into a fist. "He IS insane!"

"That's pretty much what I was saying earlier," Jeb said dryly. He shook his head again as they pulled on their packs in a troubled silence and headed out.

FIFTY-FOUR

Melanie Lost & Found

August 2006
Crawford Notch, NH

*** Angie ***

I picked up my pace after I got down from the cliff and returned to the deer trail. I felt a growing urge to get far ahead of the hiker that I knew was behind me somewhere, as well as to catch up with Melanie, if indeed she was up ahead.

After tromping along over rocks and small boulders and being careful of the tree roots that could trip me, it was with some surprise that an hour later I stepped into a clearing with long yellow-gold grass patted down and gently sloping to a small brook. I paused, looking around. I had the unsettling sense that I was being observed. It was such a strong sensation, in fact, that I felt the hair rise on the back of my neck. I turned around and looked up the path I had just been on, but there was nothing behind me except the occasional leaves fluttering in the breeze.

Then I heard a snuffling sound. It was the sort of sound you don't want to hear in the woods when you're alone. Immediately, I spun around but I didn't see anything in the clearing. The water burbled in the brook, the birds flitted from tree to tree in the branches around me, crickets hummed in the grass and low-lying bushes. It was eerie. Had I actually heard the snuffling sound or was my mind playing tricks on me? I held very still and waited. Better not to do anything than to do the wrong thing, I reminded myself severely. I let my eyes adjust to the tranquil scene in front of me. A cool breeze touched my face, and I felt a shiver run up my arms and around my back.

Although I didn't hear anything, I did sense something off to my right. It was a peculiar feeling; to be so certain of something that I couldn't see. Was that what Lesley meant when she said she could sense things?

I turned my head. I saw that the brook meandered into a stand of hemlock and white pine trees just beyond the clearing. There wasn't a path to follow, but if I kept the brook in sight, I'd be able to get back without losing my way, I reasoned. So, I kept the brook to my left and headed into the woods. Immediately I sank into the soft cushion of pine needles beneath my boots muffling my footfalls.

Pine forests are different from the usual temperate hardwood forests of maple, beech, and birches that I was used to. The needles that blanket the ground prevent thick underbrush from taking root, so the walking is actually easier. And the lovely smell of pine and balsams made me think happy thoughts of Christmas trees, snowfalls and sleeping forests. But it was deceptive.

I made sure the brook was still to my left as I continued on. A bit further I could make out some boulders up ahead with a rocky formation towering up just behind. I moved slowly towards it. Something was there. I knew it as well as I knew anything – I sensed it - but still I saw nothing.

"Melanie?" I called softly. I didn't know why, but the name came out of my mouth before I had a moment to think about it.

Then something did move, just under the huge hemlock tree to the right of the boulder. Pine needles and boughs rustled and fell away as Melanie sat up slowly rubbing her eyes. She looked groggily around.

I froze for one long moment unsure whether I had conjured up a hallucination of the child. Had the little girl really just risen up from the ground in front of me?

"Melanie?" I said again. And then all at once I knew that it was indeed really her. I broke into a huge grin and ran over and squatted next to her. "Are you all right, honey?" I asked gently, hearing the echo of my mother's intonation in my own. How odd to channel my mother, I thought.

Melanie nodded and smiled shyly. "I take a nap," she said, patting the boughs of hemlock covering her legs.

"What a good girl," I said approvingly. "Are you hungry or thirsty? Would you like me to make a sandwich for you?"

The little girl nodded. She pointed to the outcropping of rocks. "My pack-pack," she said.

I frowned and looked where the girl was pointing. "Your... Oh!" I laughed. "Your backpack, is that what you mean?"

Melanie nodded and stood up. She went over and slid easily between the boulders and when I followed, clambering less easily over them, I saw that there was a cave in the rocks. "Melanie," I said in warning. "I don't think we should go near the cave, honey."

Melanie looked up at me in surprise. "It's OK," she said reassuringly. "My bear is there."

I stopped. "Your bear?" I repeated. "Oh, you mean your teddy bear, Mr. Brownie?"

Melanie squinted at me. "Mr. Brownie is here," she said pulling the arm of the teddy bear from the backpack that I now saw was leaning against the rocks at the base of the cave opening. Melanie gave her teddy bear a big hug then tucked him under her arm. She squatted down and became engrossed in trying to zip the backpack closed.

There was the snap of twigs and footfalls behind us, and I crouched behind the boulder and looked out. It was an apparition. It had to be! Because I saw Mr. Jacobs weaving his way towards the boulders, his red hunting hat pulled down over his ears. He was holding a handgun in his right hand.

My heart squeezed in fear. What was he doing here? Then I remembered Melanie. Well, of course, everything would be fine

320 M.H. Sullivan - Trail Magic

once he saw his daughter was all right. I let my breath out and stood up.

Keith Jacobs jerked to a stop when he saw me standing between the boulders. He was obviously stunned to see me just standing there. But then, for some inexplicable reason he raised the gun and pointed it at me.

"Wait, Mr. Jacobs!" I said with wave. "Wait until you see!" I called excitedly to him.

Jacobs stared open-mouthed at me. Then without warning, he raised the handgun, took aim, and shot.

In the split second when I realized he was going to shoot at me, I instinctively dropped to my knees. Or perhaps my knees buckled in fright. I don't know. The bullet whistled by my ear, and I heard the explosion of gunshot and the ping of the bullet against the rock wall behind me. I froze in fear. There was a squeal behind me as Melanie cowered from the noise but then she caught sight of her father. She jumped up and started to clamber out from between the boulders. She got by me before I realized what she was doing and could reach out and grab her to pull her back to safety. But then, in a stroke of luck, the little girl tripped and went sprawling on the ground with a solid "Oomph".

The sudden appearance of Melanie and the sound of her high-pitched squeal seemed to stop Jacobs in his tracks. He lowered the gun and stared in confusion at Melanie lying on the ground and now rolling over to get up again. He paled and looked like he was seeing a ghost.

I felt relief that he had finally seen his daughter. Perhaps now he'd put the gun away. But, without warning I saw him raise the gun again and with an odd look of terror in his eyes he fired again. I felt the explosion and shards of rocks rain down on me from the spot above the cave that he had hit. I crouched down lower and reached out for Melanie who now sat in stunned amazement at the loud sound of the gunshot as well as the queer look on her father's face.

I was stunned into shocked confusion, too. Was he shooting at me? Or Melanie? Or at something else? I turned in time to see a very large, very angry black bear rear up and stand on its hind legs in front of the mouth of the cave just behind me. But before I could react, the bear charged past me over the boulder and raced towards Keith Jacobs. I didn't know a bear that size could move that fast.

Jacobs shot again as the bear closed in on him. The bear roared at the sound or perhaps from pain but didn't even pause as it rammed into Jacobs and flattened him on the ground. It cuffed him once, then again, with its clawed paw. Then it stopped and sat up alert and wary. Its head turned this way and that as it sniffed the air. After a moment, it looked towards Melanie and me, but strangely I didn't feel any fear. For a split second, I saw not a bear in the woods of New Hampshire looking at me, but the eyes of a hippo in a dark swamp along a lake in Africa. The look, if it was ever really there, was gone in a flash and then the bear lumbered away into the forest.

I sat in stunned silence for several long moments. Then I glanced at Melanie who was also staring after the bear.

"My bear," Melanie said, pointing to where the bear had been a moment before it disappeared.

I stared at the shrubs still swaying from the bear's passage. "Your bear?" I asked softly. "Melanie, was that your bear?"

Melanie smiled. "My bear," she said again with a nod. Then remembering her father, she turned back, and her bottom lip quivered. "Daddy?" she said, although I wasn't sure if she was talking to me or to her father, who lay on the ground not fifteen feet away.

I got up and walked slowly over to the body of Keith Jacobs. The handgun was lying in the pine needles not far from his outstretched hand. I leaned over and picked up the gun, flicked the safety back into place, then cradling it gently, I shimmied off my backpack, unzipped it and tucked the gun into zippered pocket inside. Then I turned back to look at Jacobs.

He hadn't moved and I thought, at first, that he must be dead. His left leg was bent at an unnatural angle and was surely broken. His left arm was bleeding where the bear had clawed him, and his face had nasty looking scratches across one cheek. I knelt down next to him and in a moment, I could feel Melanie's warm body leaning against me.

"Daddy?" Melanie said.

Jacobs moaned.

The sound took me by surprise. "Mr. Jacobs?" I said, touching his shoulder. "Mr. Jacobs?"

His eyelids fluttered and the fingers on his outstretched hand squeezed shut. He groaned.

"Mr. Jacobs, I think you're hurt pretty badly," I said as soothingly as I could. I didn't really know what else to say.

After a moment, he opened his eyes. They were unfocused and he squinted as if trying to read very small print. He groaned again. Then the fear came back into his eyes, and he looked at me, "The bear!" he said hoarsely.

"The bear's gone now," I said quietly, reassuringly. "Mr. Jacobs, I'm going to move your leg, so it's, uh, straight, OK?" I don't know if he understood me, but I didn't wait for a reply. I walked around him and gently picked up his left leg and placed it next to the right one.

Jacobs screamed out, and I instinctively took a step back. When he opened his eyes again, he must've seen the frightened look on his daughter's face because he tried to smile reassuringly. "It's OK, Mellie. Daddy's leg hurts but it'll be OK."

Melanie relaxed and curled up next to him laying her head on his chest. He put his arm over her, and gently patted her back. I could see tears, whether of joy or pain, drip down the side of his cheek. He glanced up at me and for a long minute we just looked at each other.

"I'm sorry," Keith Jacobs said finally, in a raspy voice. "I thought she was lost...forever." He closed his eyes for a second.

I nodded. Before I could say anything, I heard the thumping sounds of people running towards us. I spun around in time to see my father, his face streaked with sweat and his eyes full of anxious fear, barrel through the trees heading towards us. Jeb was right behind him. They slowed when they saw me. Then they saw Keith Jacobs lying on the ground at my feet. It was another second before they noticed that Melanie was there, too, curled up next to him.

"What...?" Dad started to say, looking from me to Jacobs and then to Melanie, "Angie, are you alright?" He was beside me in a moment and wrapped me in his arms. I breathed out, a long sigh of a breath, that I must've been holding for a while without realizing it. A hug never felt so good.

"We heard gunshots," Jeb said out of breath behind him. He reached out and touched my shoulder, as if by touching me he could reassure himself that I was safe.

"Yeah," I said, "the gunshots were Mr. Jacobs. He was...trying to scare away the bear, I think." I glanced down and saw Keith Jacobs had been looking at me. He closed his eyes.

Melanie lifted her head, "My bear," she said proudly.

I grinned at her. "Yeah, it was your bear, Melanie," I agreed.

"So, where's the bear now?" Jeb asked, scanning the wood around us.

"I think Mr. Jacobs nicked her – it was the mother bear, I think. Her ear was bleeding. She didn't seem badly hurt. She headed into the woods over that way," I said pointing to the woods where the bear had disappeared.

"No cub?" Jeb asked.

I looked up at him quizzically, "No. I thought there'd be one, too. From the paw prints?"

Jeb nodded and smiled.

I glanced down at Melanie and for the first time noticed her little pink sneakers, caked in mud but still very pink. "Hey," I said kneeling next to the little girl. "Let me see the bottom of your sneakers." Melanie lifted a foot, and I turned the sneaker over. I grinned and pointed to the sole. "Here's our bear cub paw prints."

Jeb shook his head in amazement, "Damn! Will you look at that!"

Dad knelt next to Keith Jacobs, checking him out. He quizzed me about what the bear had done to Mr. Jacobs and after asking Jacobs to describe how he was feeling and what hurt and so on, he finally looked up at Jeb. "We'll need help to get him out of here. His leg looks like it might be broken in a couple of places, and he may have some internal injuries. Maybe a concussion, too."

Jeb nodded. He took out the walkie-talkie and, in a few minutes, had reached Jerry Stockman. He relayed the good news about Melanie and me being found, and then he began describing Keith Jacobs' condition and our location as best he could. After a minute, he looked down at my dad, "Alex, they think they can send in a rescue helicopter. The clouds have broken up. What do you think? Is that clearing back there by the stream going to be big enough?"

I watched as the two men took over and I was happy they had shown up when they did. While they were putting together a makeshift litter to carry Keith Jacobs out to the clearing, I made a honey and peanut butter sandwich for Melanie and gave her some of the water I had saved for her.

Melanie seemed content, curled up next to her father, munching hungrily on the sandwich. When the sound of a helicopter's rotors could be heard she looked up. "Airplane," she said.

"That's right," I said. "You and your daddy get to go for a helicopter ride."

Melanie stood up and then an odd look crossed her features. She reached into her pocket and dug around in it for a second or two. When her hand came out, she had the buffalo nickel squeezed between her fingers. "I watched it for you," she said as she handed it to me.

I grinned. "Thanks, Melanie. Do you want to keep it?"

Melanie shook her head. "Yours," she said.

Soon the helicopter was hovering above us and it wasn't long before Keith Jacobs and Melanie were on board and airlifted away to the North Conway Memorial Hospital where Nora would be meeting them. For a second, I wished I could see the happy reunion, but then I turned and saw my dad and Jeb waiting for me and I knew that I'd rather be with them.

"Ready, honey?" Dad asked.

I nodded.

Jeb reached out and hugged my shoulders. "You did good, Angel. I'm really proud of you."

Dad nodded, "Except you should've let us know..."

"...And I shouldn't have gone alone. I know, Dad. I'm sorry."

He grinned, "You did good, though. I'm proud of you, too."

I grinned back at him and the three of us set out single file to hike back to the lodge.

We arrived just after sunset. The TV vans and reporters had all left by then, heading over to the hospital with Nora Jacobs to film the family's reunion for the six o'clock news. All was quiet at the campground as we came out of the woods. When we spotted the lodge from the other side of the stream, Dad held up his hand and Jeb and I stopped beside him.

He nodded towards the lodge with a smile and breathed out. "I just wanted for us to enjoy this for a moment before we go in."

I grinned as Jeb put his arm around me. "Home sweet home," Jeb said.

Dad looked down at me. "Angie, before we go in and see everyone, I wanted to ask you something."

I looked up at my father. "What?"

He cleared his throat and shifted from one foot to the other. "What I wanted to ask you, Angie, is what you'd think about going to the school in Bartlett this fall instead of being home schooled?"

I stared at him. Of all the things I thought he might say, that wasn't even remotely on the list! "Really?" I said.

He nodded. "We'll need to talk to Tessie, of course, but if you and Kay would like to try it out, we can go into town and look into it."

Jeb grinned at me, then he eyed Dad for a second before asking, "So, what changed your mind, Alex?"

Dad met his gaze. "Something Lesley said to me the other night about teenagers needing to learn to be a part of a community. I think it made a lot of sense."

Jeb nodded thoughtfully. "Yep, she's right. A person can't walk the trail alone forever. We all need help, huh? Especially when we get lost." He slapped Alex on the back and the three of us turned towards home.

FIFTY-FIVE

Kay & Angie Lost & Found

June 1998
Lake Langano, Rift Valley, Ethiopia

*** *Alex* ***

That night eight years before when they had been camping at Lake Langano and the girls had been lost in the swampy reeds on the lakeshore, it was all Alex could do to keep himself calm, much less keep Kathy from racing into the swamp after them.

"Honey, I want you to stay right here at the edge of the swamp until Stan and Joseph come back with more flashlights. When I call out, answer me, so I can gauge the direction. Once I get into the middle of this swamp, I may lose my bearing and I don't want to get lost." When she didn't respond, he touched her shoulder and bent close to her face. "Are you all right, Kathy?"

She nodded but must've realized that he couldn't see the movement, so she cleared her throat, "I'm OK. Oh, Alex, please find them!" Kathy said with a choke to her voice.

He took her hand in his and squeezed it. Her hand was icy. "They'll be all right."

"But what can I do?" Kathy asked, her anxiety barely under control.

"Answer me when I call out to you, so I don't get lost in there, too." Then he had turned and left her.

The beam of his flashlight bobbed along in front of him as it mapped his course through the swamp. He yelled out, "Kay! Angie!" over and over again and paused each time, listening for an answer. He knew that Kathy must have been straining to hear a responding voice, too.

Alex stepped carefully through the mud and could hear the sucking sound around the edges of his boots. As he scanned the ground with the flashlight his thoughts turned to snakes and rodents and other critters that liked this type of environment particularly at this time of night.

To heck with snakes and rats! He thought suddenly. What about crocs? Just after sunset was prime feeding time, wasn't it? He swallowed audibly. He could hear the whine of mosquitoes whirling around his head, as well, and as if he didn't have enough worries, he recalled another well-known African threat – malaria. Langano was several thousand feet lower in altitude than Addis Ababa and so the threat of contracting malaria from the mosquitoes down here in the Rift Valley was that much higher.

As an American he was used to feeling immune to the many diseases and health problems that plagued the local population. After all, good health and good hygiene, not to mention multiple inoculations, trumped most potential maladies. But that wasn't true for malaria. It wasn't unheard of for an American to contract malaria in this country, and even to die from it. The last malarial death of an American that was still talked about at the Embassy happened in 1972. The victim was a USAID employee who came down with blackwater fever, a particularly nasty strain of malaria, during a business trip to Dire Dawa, a town to the east of Addis Ababa. He returned home to Addis with his wife and children and was dead within a week.

"Damn!" Alex said under his breath. He knew better than to be stumbling along in the dark in a swampy area, didn't he? He swatted ineffectually at the high-pitched whine circling his left ear.

"Kay! Angie! Where are you?" he yelled again. He paused for a second, listening. He thought he heard a splash off to his left and he swung his flashlight towards the sound. His heart nearly stopped. He discovered he was just a step or two from walking right into the lake. And worse, at the upper edge of the halo of light from his flashlight was a pair of eyes gleaming back at him. He stared in horror at the half-submerged crocodile floating in the lapping lake water, its prehistoric eyes coldly studying him. The hair on his arms stood up and his skin seemed to ripple with some ancient cellular dread. His first instinct was to turn and run, to get as far away as fast as possible. He could feel his heart hammering in his chest.

Focus! He silently told himself. He took one very deep breath and let it out slowly. Then he turned and headed cautiously, but determinedly away from the edge of the lake. With each step, he felt slightly better, although if anything had touched him in those first few moments after he turned his back on the lake, he was sure he would've leapt right out of his skin with an undignified scream of terror.

When he'd put some distance between himself and the croc, he stopped and scanned what looked like a path through the tall grasses and shrubs. "Kay! Angie! Come to Daddy!" he called.

"Daddy?" It was Angie's voice. He swung the flashlight over to where he thought he'd heard the voice. And there in the circle of light he saw Angie leading her older sister, Kay, by the hand towards him.

"Oh, God!" he said, the relief in his voice was palpable. He squatted down and took both girls into a big hug, wrapping his arms around them and squeezing them tightly. He was glad they couldn't see the tears that silently streaked down his cheeks.

"Daddy!" Kay said squirming in his embrace. "You're hugging me too tight!"

Angie giggled and put her little arms around his neck. "I don't care! I like big hugs," she said. "But Daddy? Can we go back to the tent now? It's scary out here at nighttime."

He let his breath out and sighed. "You girls! Don't ever go off alone again, all right?"

"But we weren't alone, Daddy," Kay said logically. "We were together."

"And we were with the big hippos!" Angie said and giggled again. "I like hippos."

Alex stood up and scanned the trees and bushes around them. "Where are the hippos now, honey?" His voice sounded unnaturally calm, even to him.

Angie looked up at him. He could feel the warmth of her little hand holding onto his leg. "They're in the water back there somewhere."

"They went for a swim," Kay added.

Alex breathed a sigh of relief. "Good, let's get out of here!" He turned and then yelled to Kathy. "I've got them," he called out. "They're fine! Yell again so I can tell which way to go."

Kathy's voice was high-pitched with excitement, "Alex? You found them? Oh God, Alex!" Her voice seemed to be coming from a very long way away.

Alex leaned over and picked up Angie, hugging her against his body. He supported her small body with his wrist and forearm, so his hand was free to hold the flashlight. With his other hand he reached down and took Kay's hand firmly in his own. He wasn't going to lose either one of them on the walk back.

"Where are you, Kathy? Which way do we go?"

"I'm here, Alex. I'm here!"

He walked towards her voice.

Alex could hear her voice in his mind, even now, eight years later. He dreamt it often enough! In his dreams it was like a game of Marco Polo with her yelling out "Alex?" and him responding "Kathy?" That night at Langano, he was the one who had found the girls, but it was Kathy who had led them out of the swamp.

FIFTY-SIX

The Pamela Hollingworth Story

(Based on reports from the newspapers at the time)
Monday, Oct. 6, 1941.

Pammy was found on Monday, October 6, the eighth day of the search. In total, 500 people had been searching for her. She was found on the trail from Middle Sister, near Hobbs Brook, slightly northeast of White Ledge. 500 searchers moved into a new area nearer Chocorua Lake. Near dark, Forest Ranger Bill Matson of Troy brought his tired crew of CCC boys in. Talking loudly to each other to be heard over the noise of nearby Hobbs Brook, they were plodding along the trail from Middle Sister. Matson called a stop because he heard a faint noise. The men spread out along the brook and there was Pammy. She wasn't afraid and wasn't crying. She said she wasn't hungry. She just wanted to "see my Mummy." Forrest Oakes carried the note of her safety into the base camp, and they called her father by radio. He nearly got lost trying to get back to the camp as quickly as possible. She was taken to North Conway General Hospital and then transferred to Lowell General Hospital. Her feet were frostbitten and swollen, and she was slightly dehydrated and malnourished and had lost 8 pounds, but she was alert and oriented.

Apparently, she had kept warm by burrowing deep under the low-hanging boughs of spruce trees where the needles were thick. After the first frost, leaves fell off the trees and she covered herself with the leaves.

FIFTY-SEVEN

Return to the Lodge

August 2006
Wilderness Campground, Crawford Notch, NH

*** Angie ***

When we got back to the lodge it was pretty much as I thought it would be. Lots of hugging and kissing, pats on the back, and huge grins. Tessie made a celebratory dinner, and, for a change, it was a smallish affair, with us – Dad, Kay, me, Jeb, and Tessie - and of course, Lesley, Joe, Kevin and Jerry Stockman. Well, OK, that's nine people; maybe not quite as smallish as it seems in my memory. It did feel like it was just a lot of "us," though; with no outsiders, I mean.

We were talking about the bear and Melanie and soon the conversation veered back to the diary. While I was gone, Tessie had finished translating it and after much cajoling, she finally agreed to read the final entry to us.

Jean-Louis Duclos Diary, Sawyer River CCC Camp, Livermore NH,
October 1941
[The last entry in the journal]

vendredi, le 18 octobre 1941.

Friday, 17 October 1941. *I will bury this diary in a*
deep dark place and not speak or think of these
trying times again. But first, I must record the
final events, then I will close this chapter of my
life and not look back.

I returned to Sawyer River Camp on Monday after the little girl was found. The commander gave me the week off as a reward for helping with the search effort. I did not have to return until Sunday, but here I am back at camp, and it is only Friday.

On Tuesday, I rode the train to Portland and went straight to the hospital where Roland's sister had told me Lorraine was. When I got there, they would not let me see her. They had a rule about only letting family into her room. They asked if I was her husband. I laughed and said she did not have a husband. But they insisted that she did. I thought perhaps she had lied to them, because of the baby. But it was too late to change my story and they would not let me see her. Then, as I was leaving, a woman came to the desk and asked for Lorraine's room. I caught her arm and asked if she knew Lorraine. "Yes," the woman replied, "She is my sister. I am caring for her two small children." I was so taken aback! She has two small children! Mon Dieu! And she never spoke a word about them to me. The woman, seeing my shocked reaction, studied me for a long time and then inquired if I knew a man named Jean-Louis Duclos? I hesitated, but finally admitted that I was indeed him. She touched my hand. She said she had something to tell me.

We sat and she told me that indeed Lorraine had been married and had two small children from that marriage, but that her husband had died. Lorraine told her sister that she loved me! My Lorraine said that! But she was afraid that I could never accept another man's children, so she vowed to give away the baby she carried in her womb and would make a fresh start.

I was devastated. She has lied about everything! She was married. She has two children. And she would give up our love child.

I started to go away, numb and devastated, when the woman stopped me. "If you love her, you must go in and tell her so," her sister advised. "You must prevent her from giving away this child."

And that's how my Lorraine and I managed to save our child. I went in and confessed my love and my willingness to love the brother and sister of my unborn child as if they were my own. In tears she admitted that she never wanted to give away our child, but she didn't know how she could manage three children without a husband.

And so, she will be my wife.

Now I bury these thoughts and memories of our trials and tribulations as soon as I can find a safe place. I will place her picture and the trinkets of our past. By burying the past, we will be able to begin a new and better future.

(signed) Jean-Louis

"So, what do you think, Angie?" Tessie said looking up at me. "Does his story end the way you thought it would?"

"No," I said, shaking my head. "I thought Lorraine had already gotten rid of the baby. And I thought he'd lost her."

Joe reached out and took the small book from Tessie. "So, this is the diary that Angie has been translating?" he asked, flipping through the pages.

Tessie nodded.

Suddenly, Joe stopped thumbing through the pages. "Hey!" he said, sitting up straight. He flipped back to the beginning of the book then he looked up and shook his head with a big grin. "I don't believe it! I just don't believe it!"

"What, Joe?" Kay asked, leaning over to see what he was looking at in the book. "What don't you believe?"

"This guy!" Joe pointed at the diary and laughed again. "I think this guy, uh, Jean-Louis?" He shook his head. "I think that he's my grandfather – my mother's father – John Duclos – married to, I might hasten to add, my grandmother, Lorraine Duclos!"

Everyone around the table went silent.

"Oh my God! That makes such perfect sense!" I said, breaking the silence. "He's your grandfather, Joe, the one that you said worked at a CCC camp up here during the Depression, right?" I grinned. "So, of course, this would have to belong to your grandfather, because that's the way Trail Magic works!" I said with a laugh. Then I looked down the table and met Lesley's eyes.

She nodded and smiled at me and raised her glass of iced tea, "To Trail Magic!" she said.

Everyone raised their glasses and echoed her toast, "To Trail Magic!"

We were all just kidding, of course; well, all except me.

The End

FIFTY-EIGHT

Epilogue – Another Lost Child

The Sarah Whitcher Story

June 1783
Warren, NH

In June of 1783, Sarah Whitcher, age 3, wandered away from her family's home near Warren, New Hampshire. For four long days her family and neighbors searched for her. The story goes that just as they were going to call off the search, forsaking ever finding the little girl alive, a stranger showed up who said that he had had a dream about where to find her. He led them right to the little girl who was alive and well.

Everyone was amazed. How could a small child survive in the wilderness by herself? When asked, she said she was taken in and cared for by what she described as "a very big black dog." It was believed that what she was describing was a black bear, common then, as now, to New Hampshire's woods.

About the Author - M.H. Sullivan

Prior to moving to New Hampshire in 1977, the author spent most of the previous 20+ years living overseas. As the daughter of a U.S. State Department diplomat, she lived in Korea, Taiwan, the Philippines, Thailand, and Ethiopia.

After graduating from Boston University, Maureen worked in Washington, D.C. as a travel agent and then as a staff aide on Capitol Hill. After getting her Master's degree from Simmons College Graduate Program in Management, Maureen worked as a technical writer in the software industry and later in the medical devices industry. She moved to NH in 1977, married in 1978, and has lived in NH ever since. She has two daughters and two granddaughters.

Maureen was the publisher of the *Southern NH Children's Directory* and related publications from 1994 to 1999. In 2008, she published her first novel, *Travel Magic: Lost in Crawford Notch* (2nd edition released in 2026). In 2010, she published a memoir, *The Sullivan Saga: Memories of an Overseas Childhood.* A second novel, *Jet Trails: Looking for Blue Skies,* was published in 2015 (revised in 2026). Her third novel, *Goodbye Woodstock: The Last Reunion,* released in 2023 (revised in 2026).

Books by M.H. Sullivan:

Trail Magic: Lost in Crawford Notch

The Sullivan Saga: Memories of an Overseas Childhood

Jet Trails: Looking for Blue Skies

Goodbye Woodstock: The Last Reunion

For more information, go to www.romagnoli-publications.com.